ROBIN HOBB

City of Dragons

HARPER
Voyager

HarperCollins*Publishers*
77–85 Fulham Palace Road,
Hammersmith, London W6 8JB

www.harpercollins.co.uk

Published by Harper*Voyager*
An imprint of HarperCollins*Publishers* 2012
1

A catalogue record for this book
is available from the British Library

ISBN: 978 0 00 727380 5

Set in Sabon by Palimpsest Book Production Ltd,
Falkirk, Stirlingshire

Printed and bound in Great Britain by
Clays Ltd, St Ives plc

CITY OF DRAGONS

BY ROBIN HOBB

THE FARSEER TRILOGY

Assassin's Apprentice
Royal Assassin
Assassin's Quest

THE LIVESHIP TRADERS

Ship of Magic
The Mad Ship
Ship of Destiny

THE TAWNY MAN

Fool's Errand
The Golden Fool
Fool's Fate

THE SOLDIER SON

Shaman's Crossing
Forest Mage
Renegade's Magic

THE RAIN WILD CHRONICLES

The Dragon Keeper
Dragon Haven

The Inheritance

WRITING AS MEGAN LINDHOLM

The Reindeer People
Wolf's Brother

Harpy's Flight
The Windsingers
The Limbreth Gate
Luck of the Wheels

Cloven Hooves
Alien Earth

To the Little Red Hen

PROLOGUE

Tintaglia and IceFyre

She rode the air currents easily, her legs sleeked tight against her body, her wings spread wide. On the undulating desert sands below, her rippling shadow showed her as a serpentine creature with bat-like wings and a long, finned tail. Tintaglia thrummed deep in her throat, a purr of pleasure in the day. They had hunted at dawn and hunted well. They had made their separate kills, as they always did, and spent the morning in feasting and then sleep. Now, smeared still with the blood and offal of the hunt, the two dragons had another goal in mind.

Ahead and slightly below her, IceFyre was a gleaming black shape. His long body flexed as he shifted his weight to catch and ride the wind. His torso was thicker and heavier than hers, his body longer. Her feather-like scaling glittered a scintillating blue, but he was an even black all over. His long encasement in ice had taken a toll on his body, one that was taking years to heal. His larger wings still had rents in the heavy webbing between the finger ribs. The smaller injuries to his body were long gone, but the tears in his wings would knit more slowly, and the welted scars of their healing would always be visible. *Unlike my own azure perfection.* Out of the corner of her eyes, Tintaglia admired her glittering wings.

As if he sensed her lack of attention to him, IceFyre banked abruptly and began his circling descent. She knew their destination. Not too far away a rocky ridge erupted above the sand. Stunted trees and grey-green brush populated its jagged edges and rough gullies. Just before the brushy ridge was a hidden oasis, in a wide, sandy basin, surrounded by a scatter of trees. The water rose from the depths of the earth to form a wide, still pool. Even in winter, the depression cupped the day's warmth. They would spend their early afternoon soaking in the sun-warmed waters of the oasis to cleanse the blood from their hides and then rolling luxuriantly in the rough sand to polish their scales. They knew the spot well. They varied their hunting grounds over a wide range, but every ten days or so, IceFyre led them back here. He claimed it was a place he remembered from his distant youth.

Once, there had been a colony of Elderlings here that had tended the visiting dragons. Of their white stone buildings and carefully nurtured vineyards, nothing remained. The encroaching desert had devoured their settlement, but the oasis remained. Tintaglia would have preferred to fly much farther south, to the red sand deserts where winter never came, but IceFyre had refused. She suspected that he lacked the stamina for such a flight and had thought, more than once, of leaving him and going alone. But the terrible isolation of her long imprisonment in her cocoon had left its mark on her. Dragon companionship, even crotchety, critical companionship, was preferable to isolation.

IceFyre flew low now, nearly skimming the baked sand. His wings moved in sporadic, powerful beats that drove his glide and stirred the sand. Tintaglia followed, emulating him as she honed her own flying skills. There was much she did not care for in her mate, but he was truly a lord of the air.

They followed the contours of the land. She knew his plan. Their glide would carry them up to the lip of the basin, and then down in a wild slide that paralleled the slope of the dunes. It would end with both of them splashing, wings still spread, into the still, sun-warmed waters.

They were halfway down the slope when the sand around the upper edges of the basin erupted. Canvas coverings were flung aside and archers rose in ranks. A phalanx of arrows flew toward them. As the first wave of missiles rattled bruisingly off her wings and flanks, a second arced toward them. They were too close to the ground to batter their way to altitude again. IceFyre skimmed and then slewed round as he hit the shallow waters of the pool. Tintaglia was too close behind him to stop or change her path. She crashed into him and as their wings and legs tangled in the warm shallow water, spearmen rose from their camouflaged nests and came at them like an army of attacking ants. Behind them more ranks of men rose and surged forward with weighted nets of stout rope and chain.

Heedless of how he might injure her, IceFyre fought free of Tintaglia. He splashed from the shallow pool and charged into the men, trampling her into the water as he went. Some of the pike men ran; he crushed others under his powerful hind feet, then spun, and with a lash of his long tail, knocked down a score of others. Dazed, mired in the water, she saw him work his throat and then open wide his mouth. Behind his rows of gleaming white pointed teeth, she glimpsed the scarlet and orange of IceFyre's poison sacs. He spun toward his attackers and his hissing roar carried with it a scarlet mist of venom. As the cloud enveloped the men before him, their screams rose to the blue cup of sky.

The acid ate them. Armour of leather or metal slowed but did not stop it. The droplets fell from the air to the earth, incidentally passing through human bodies on the way. Skin, flesh, bone and gut were holed by the passing venom. It hissed as it struck the sand. Some men died quickly but most did not.

Tintaglia had stared too long. A net thudded over her. At every junction of knot, the ropes had been weighted with dangling lumps of lead. Chains, some fine, some heavy, and some fitted with barbed hooks, were woven throughout the net. It trapped and tangled her wings, and when she clawed at it with her front legs, it wrapped them as well. She roared her fury and felt her own poison sacs swell as spearmen waded out into the shallow waters of the pond. She caught a glimpse of archers beginning a stumbling charge down the sandy slopes, arrows nocked to their bows. She jerked as a spear found a vulnerable spot between the scales behind her front leg, in the tender place between leg and chest. It did not penetrate deeply, but Tintaglia had never been stabbed with anything before. She turned, roaring out her pain and anger and her venom misted out with her cry. The spearmen fell back in horror. As the venom settled on the net, the lines and chains weakened and then gave way to her struggles. Tangles of it still wrapped her, but she could move. Fury enveloped her. Humans dared to attack dragons?

Tintaglia waded out of the water and into the midst of them, slashing with her claws and lashing with her tail, and every scream of rage she emitted carried a wave of acid toxin with it. Soon the shrill shrieks of dying humans filled the air. She did not need to spare a glance for IceFyre: she could hear the carnage he was wreaking.

Arrows rattled off her body and thudded painfully against her entangled wings. She flapped them, tumbling a dozen men with them as she flung the last bits of netting free. But her opened wings had bared her vulnerability. She felt the hot bite of an arrow beneath her left wing. She clapped her wings closed, realizing too late that the humans had been trying to provoke her into opening them to expose the more tender flesh beneath. But closing her wing only pushed the arrow shaft in deeper. Tintaglia roared her pain and spun again, lashing with her tail. She caught a brief glimpse of IceFyre, a human clutched in his jaws and raised aloft. The dying man's shriek rose above the other battle sounds as the dragon severed his body into two pieces. Cries of horror from more distant ranks of humans were sweet to hear and she suddenly understood what her mate was doing.

His thought reached her. *Terror is as important as killing. They must be taught never even to think of attacking dragons. A few we must allow to escape, to carry the tale home.* Grim and terse, he added, *But only a few!*

A few, she agreed and waded out of the waters and in amongst the men who had gathered to slay her, batting them aside with her clawed front feet as easily as a cat would bat at a string. She snapped at them, clipping legs from bodies, arms from shoulders, maiming rather than killing quickly. She lifted her head high, and then flung it forward, hissing out a breath laden with a mist of acid venom. The human wall before her melted into bones and blood.

As afternoon was venturing toward evening, the two dragons flew a final circle around the basin of land. A straggle of warriors fled like disoriented ants toward the scrub-covered ridge. *Let them spread the word!* IceFyre suggested. *We should return to the oasis before their meat begins to spoil.* He banked his wings and turned away from their lazy pursuit and Tintaglia followed.

His suggestion was welcome. The spear had fallen out of the hole it had made in her hide, but the arrow on the other side had not. She had not meant to drive it deeper into herself.

In a quiet moment after the first slaughter was over and while the mobile survivors were fleeing, she had tried to pull it out. Instead, it had broken off and the remaining nub of wood that protruded was too short for her to grip with her teeth. Clawing at it had only pushed it deeper. She felt the unwelcome intrusion of the wooden shaft and metal head into her flesh with every beat of her wings.

How many humans fought against us? she wondered.

Hundreds. But what does it matter? They did not kill us, and those we allow to escape will carry the word to their kind that they were foolish to try.

Why did they attack us?

The attack did not fit with her experience with humans. The people she had encountered had always been in awe of her, more inclined to serve her than attack her. Some had squeaked defiance but she had found ways to bring them into line. She had fought humans before, but not because they had ambushed her. She had killed Chalcedeans only because she had chosen to ally herself with the Bingtown Traders, killing their enemies in return for their help for the serpents that would, after metamorphosis, become dragons. Could this attack be related to that? It seemed unlikely. Humans were so short-lived. Were they capable of such reasoned vengeance?

IceFyre's rationale was simpler. *They attack us because they are humans and we are dragons. Most humans hate us. Some pretend to awe and bring gifts, but behind their flattery and cowering, there is hatred for us. Never forget that. In this part of the world, humans have hated us for a very long time. Once, before I emerged as a dragon, the humans here sought to destroy all dragons. They fed slow poison to their own herds to try to kill us. They captured and tortured our Elderling servants in the hope of finding secrets they might use against us. They destroyed our strongholds and the stone pillars by which our servants travelled in an attempt to weaken us. Those few of us they managed to kill, they butchered like cattle, using the flesh and blood of our bodies as medicines and tonics for their feeble bodies.*

I do not recall any of this. Tintaglia searched her ancestral memories in vain.

There is much you do not seem to recall. I think you were encased too long. It damaged your mind and left you ignorant of many things.

She felt a spark of anger toward him. IceFyre often said such things to her. Usually after she had implied that his long entrapment in the ice had made him partially mad. She stifled her anger for now; she needed to know more. And the arrow in her side was pinching her.

What happened? Back then?

IceFyre turned his head on its long neck and gave her a baleful look. *What happened? We destroyed them, of course. Humans are nuisance enough without letting them think they can defy our wishes.*

They were nearing the spring at the heart of the oasis. Human carcasses littered the sand; swooping down into the basin was like descending into a pool of blood scent. In the late afternoon sun the corpses were starting to bake into carrion.

After we feed, we will leave here and find a cleaner place to sleep, the black dragon announced. *We will have to abandon this spot for a time, until jackals and ravens clean it for us. There is too much meat here for us to consume at one time, and humans spoil quickly.*

He skidded to a landing in the pool where a few human bodies still bobbed. Tintaglia followed him in. The waves of their impact were still brushing the shore when he picked a body out of the water. *Avoid the ones encased in metal*, he counselled her. *The archers will be your best choices. Usually they just wear leather.*

He sheared the body into two, and caught one of them before it could fall into the water. He tossed the half-carcass up into the air, then caught it in his jaws, tipping his head back to swallow it. The other half fell with a splash and sank in the pool. IceFyre selected another one, engulfing it head first, crushing the body with his powerful jaws before swallowing it whole.

Tintaglia waded out of the contaminated water and stood watching him.

They will spoil rapidly. You should eat now.

I've never eaten a human. She felt a mild revulsion. She'd killed many humans, but eaten none of them. That seemed odd, now.

She thought of the humans she had befriended: Reyn and Malta and her young singer Selden. She'd set them on the path to being Elderlings and not given much thought to them since then. *Selden.* She felt a spark of pleasure at her memory of him. Now there was a singer who knew how to praise a dragon. Those three humans she had chosen as her own, and made them her Elderlings. So they were different, perhaps. If she happened to be near one of them when they died, she'd eat the body, to preserve their memories.

But eating other humans? IceFyre was right. They were only meat. She moved along the shore of the pool and chose a body that was fresh enough to still be leaking blood. She sheared him in two, her tongue writhing at the feel of cloth and leather, and then chewed him a few times before consigning him to the powerful crushing muscles at the back of her throat.

The body went down. Meat was meat, she decided, and she was hungry after the battle.

IceFyre ate where he was, wading a few steps and then stretching his neck out to reach for more dead. There was no lack of them. Tintaglia was more selective. He was right about how quickly humans spoiled. Some already stank of decay. She looked for those who had died most recently, nosing aside the ones that were stiffening.

She was working her way through a pile of bodies when one gave a low cry and tried to crawl away from her. He was not large, and venom had eaten part of his legs away. He dragged himself along, whimpering, and when IceFyre, attracted by the sounds, approached, the boy found his tongue.

'Please!' he cried, his voice breaking back to a child's squeak on the word. 'Please, let me live! We did not wish to attack you, my father and me. They made us! The Duke's men took my father's heir-son and my mother and my two sisters. They said that if we did not join the hunt for you, they would burn them all. That my father's name would die with him, and our family line would be no more than dust. So we had to come. We didn't want to harm you, most beautiful ones. Most clever dragons.'

'It's a bit late to try to charm us with praise,' IceFyre observed with amusement.

'Who took your family?' Tintaglia was curious. The bone was showing in the boy's leg. He wouldn't survive.

'The Duke's men. The Duke of Chalced. They said we had to bring back dragon parts for the Duke. He needs medicine made from dragon parts to live. If we brought back blood or scales or liver or a dragon's eye, then the Duke would make us rich forever. But if we don't . . .' The boy looked down at his leg. He stared at it for a time and then something in his face changed. He looked up at Tintaglia. 'We're already dead. All of us.'

'Yes,' she said, but before the word settled in the boy's

mind, IceFyre had reached out and closed his jaws on the lad's torso. It happened as quickly as serpent strike.

Fresh meat. No sense letting him start to rot like the others.

The black dragon threw back his head, engulfed the rest of the boy's body, swallowed and moved away to the next pile of carcasses.

Day the 29th of the Still Moon
Year the 7th of the Independent Alliance of Traders

From Reyall, Acting Keeper of the Birds, Bingtown to Kim, Keeper of the Birds, Cassarick

Greetings, Kim.

I have been given the task of conveying to you a complaint that has been received from several of our clients. They allege that confidential messages received show signs of tampering, even though the wax plugs of the message cylinders appear intact. In two cases, a sealing wax stamp was cracked on a highly confidential scroll and in a third, the wax seal was found in pieces inside the message cylinder, and the message scroll appeared to have been spindled crookedly, as if someone had opened the cylinder, read the messages, and then replaced them, resealing the cylinders with Bird Keeper wax. These complaints come from three separate traders, and involve messages received from Trader Candral of Cassarick.

No official investigation has been requested yet. I have begged them to allow me to contact you and request that you speak with Trader Candral and ask for a demonstration of the sort of sealing wax and impression stamp that he is using for his messages. It is my hope and the hope of my masters here in Bingtown that this is merely a matter of inferior, old or brittle sealing wax being used rather than a case of a keeper tampering with messages. Nevertheless, we would request that you scrutinize any journeymen or apprentice keepers who have come into your employ in the last year.

It is with great regret that we ask this and hope that you will not take it amiss. My master directs me to say that we have the greatest confidence in the integrity of the Cassarick Bird Keepers and look forward to putting this allegation to rest.

The favour of a swift response is requested.

CHAPTER ONE

The Duke and The Captive

'There has been no word, Imperial One.' The messenger on his knees before the Duke fought to keep his voice steady.

The Duke, cushioned and propped on his throne, watched him, waiting for the moment he would break. The best a bearer of bad tidings could expect was a flogging. But delayed bad news merited death.

The man kept his eyes down, staring doggedly at the floor. So. This messenger had been flogged before. He knew he would survive it and he accepted it.

The Duke made a small gesture with his finger. Large movements took so much energy. But his chancellor had learned to watch for small motions and to respond quickly to them. He, in turn, made a more eloquent motion to the guard, and the messenger was removed. The boots of the guards thudded and the lighter sandals of the messenger pattered between them as they hurried him off. No one ventured a word. The Chancellor turned back to him and bowed low, his forehead touching his knees. Slowly he knelt, and then was bold enough to look at the Duke's sandals.

'I am grieved that you had to be subjected to such an unsatisfactory message.'

Silence held in the audience chamber. It was a large room with walls of rough stone that reminded all who entered that once it had been part of a fortress. The arched ceiling overhead had been painted a midnight blue with the stars of a midsummer night frozen forever there. Tall slits of windows looked out over a vista of sprawling city.

No point in this city was taller than the Duke's hilltop citadel. Once the fortress had stood upon this peak, and within its walls a circle of black standing stones under the open sky had been a place of great magic. Tales told of how those stones had been toppled, their evil magic vanquished. Those same stones, the ancient runes on them obscured and defaced, now lay splayed out in a circle around his throne, flush to the grey flagged floor that had been laid around them. The black stones pointed to the five corners of the known world. It was said that beneath each stone there was a square pit into which the sorcerous enemies of ancient Chalced had been confined to die. The throne in the centre reminded all that he sat where, of old, all had feared to tread.

The Duke moved his lips, and a page sprang to his feet and darted forward, a bowl of cool water in his hands. The boy knelt and offered it to the Chancellor. The Chancellor, in turn, advanced on his knees, to lift the bowl to the Duke's lips.

He tipped his head and drank. When he lifted his face another attendant had appeared, offering the Chancellor a soft cloth that he might dry the Duke's face and chin.

Afterwards, he allowed the Chancellor to retreat. Thirst sated, he spoke.

'There is no other word from our emissaries in the Rain Wilds?'

The Chancellor hunched lower. His robes of heavy maroon silk puddled around him. His scalp showed through his thinning hair. 'No, most illustrious one. I am shamed and saddened to tell you that they have not sent us any fresh tidings.'

'There is no shipment of dragon flesh on its way?' He knew the answer but forced Ellik to speak it aloud.

The Chancellor's face nearly touched the floor. 'Radiant lord, we have no word of any shipment, I am humiliated and abashed to tell you.'

The Duke considered the situation. It was too great an effort to open his eyes all the way. Hard to speak loud enough to make his voice carry. His rich rings of heavy gold set with massive jewels hung loose on his bony fingers and weighted down his hands. The lush robes of his majesty could not cloak his gauntness. He was wasting away, dying even as they stared at him, waiting. He must give a response. He must not be seen as weak.

He spoke softly. 'Motivate them. Send more emissaries, to every possible contact we have. Send them special gifts. Encourage them to be ruthless.' With an effort he lifted his head and his voice. 'Need I remind you, any of you, that if I die you will be buried with me?'

His words should have rung against the stones. Instead, he heard what his followers heard; the shrill outrage of a dying old man. Intolerable that one such as he might die without an heir-son! He should not have to speak for himself; his heir-son should be standing before him, shouting at the nobles and forcing them to swift obedience. Instead he had to whisper threats at them, hissing like a toothless old snake.

How had it come to this? He had always had sons, and to spare. Too many sons, but some had been too ambitious for his liking. Some he had sent to war, and some he had sent to the torture chamber for insolence. A few he had poisoned discreetly. If he had known that a disease would sweep away not only his chosen heir but his last three sons, he might have kept a few in reserve. But he had not. And now he was down to one useless daughter, a woman of near thirty with no children of her own and a mannish way of thinking and moving. A thrice-widowed woman with the ill luck never to have borne a child. A woman who read books and wrote poetry. Useless to him, if not dangerous as a witch. And he had no vigour left in his body to get a woman with child.

Intolerable. He could not die son-less, his name to become dust in the world's mouth. The dragon cure must be brought to him, the rich dragon blood that would restore his youth and manhood. Then he would get himself a dozen heirs and keep them safely locked away from all mishap.

Dragon's blood. So simple a cure, and yet none seemed able to supply it to him.

'Should my lord die, my sorrow would be so great that only interment with you would bring me any peace, most gracious one.' The Chancellor's ingratiating words suddenly seemed a cruel mockery.

'Oh, be silent. Your flattery annoys me. What good is your empty loyalty? Where are the dragon parts that would save me? Bring me those, and not your idle praise. Does no man here serve me willingly?" It demanded strength he could not spare, but this time his shout rang out. As his gaze swept them, not a one dared to meet his eyes. They cowered and for a time, he let them recall their hostage sons, not glimpsed by any of them for many months. He let them wonder for several long moments if their heirs survived before he asked in a conversational tone, "Is there any word from the other force we sent, to follow the rumours that dragons were seen in the desert?'

The Chancellor remained as he was, trapped in a frozen agony of conflicting orders.

Do you seethe within, Ellik? he wondered. *Do you remember that once you rode at my stirrup as we charged into battle? Look at what the warlord and his sword arm have become: the doddering old man and the cringing servant. If you would but bring me what I need, all would be as it once was. Why do you fail me? Do you have ambitions of your own? Must I kill you?*

He stared at his chancellor but Ellik's eyes remained cast down. When he judged that the man was close to breaking, he snapped at him, 'Answer!'

Ellik lifted his eyes and the Duke saw the fury contained behind his subservient grey gaze. They had ridden together too long, fought side by side too often for them to be completely successful at concealing their thoughts from one another. Ellik knew the Duke's every ploy. Once he had played to them. But now his sword hand was becoming weary of these games. The Chancellor took a deep breath. 'As of yet, there has been no word, my lord. But the visits of the dragons to the water have been irregular, and we have ordered our force to remain where they are until they are successful.'

'Well. At least we have not had word of their failure, yet.'

'No, glorious one. There is still hope.'

'Hope. You, perhaps, hope. I *demand*. Chancellor, do you *hope* that your name will survive you?'

A terrible stillness seized the man. His Duke knew his most vulnerable spot. 'Yes, Lord.' His words were a whisper.

'And you, you have not only an heir-son, but a second son as well?'

The Duke was gratified when the man's voice shook. 'I am so blessed, yes, gracious one.'

'Mmm.' The Duke of Chalced tried to clear his throat, but coughed instead, the sound triggering a scuttling of servants. A fresh bowl of chilled water was offered, as was a steaming cup of tea. A clean white cloth awaited in the hands of another knee-walking servant, while yet another offered a glass of wine.

A tiny flick of his hand dismissed them all. He drew a rasping breath.

'Two sons, Chancellor. And so you hope. But *I* have no son. And my health fails for lack of one small thing. A simple remedy of dragon's blood is all I have asked. Yet it has not been brought to me. I wonder: is it right that you have so much hope that your name will remain loud in the world's ear, while mine will be silenced for that lack? Surely not.'

Slowly the man grew smaller. Before his lord's stare, he collapsed in on himself, his head falling to his bent knees, and then his whole body sinking down, conveying physically his wish to be beneath his duke's notice.

The Duke of Chalced moved his mouth, a memory of a smile.

'For today, you may keep both your sons. Tomorrow? Tomorrow, we both hope for good news.'

'This way.'

Someone lifted the heavy flap of canvas that served as a door. A slice of light stabbed into the gloom, but as swiftly vanished, to be replaced by yellow lamplight. The two-headed dog in the stall next to his whined and shifted. Selden wondered when the poor beast had last seen daylight, real daylight. The crippled creature had already been in residence when Selden had been acquired. For him, it had been months, perhaps as long as a year, since he had felt the sun's touch. Daylight was the enemy of mystery. Daylight could reveal that half of the wonders and legends displayed in the tented bazaar's shoddy stalls were either freaks or fakes. And daylight could reveal that even those with some claim to being genuine were in poor health.

Like him.

The lantern light came closer, the yellow glare making his eyes water. He turned his face away from it and closed his eyes. He didn't get up. He knew the exact length of the chains attached to his ankles, and he had tried his strength against theirs when they had first brought him here. They had grown no weaker, but he had. He lay as he was and waited for the visitors to pass. But they halted in front of his stall.

'That's him? I thought he would be big! He's no bigger than an ordinary man.'

'He's tall. You don't notice it so much when he's curled up like that.'

'I can hardly see him, back in that corner. Can we go in?'

'You don't want to go inside the reach of his chain.'

Silence fell, and then the men spoke in low voices. Selden didn't move. That they were discussing him didn't interest him in the least. He'd lost the ability to feel embarrassed or even humiliated. He still missed clothing, badly, but mainly because he was cold. Sometimes, between shows, they would toss him a blanket, but as often as not they forgot. Few of those who tended him spoke his language, so begging for one did him no good. Slowly it came to his feverish brain that it was unusual that the two men discussing him were speaking a language he knew. Chalcedean. His father's tongue, learned in a failed effort to impress his father. He did not move or give them any sign that he was aware of them, but began to listen more closely.

'Hey! Hey, you. Dragon boy! Stand up. Give the man a look at you.'

He could ignore them. Then, like as not, they would throw something at him to make him move. Or they would begin to turn the winch that tightened the chain on his ankle. He'd either have to walk to the back wall or be dragged there. His captors feared him and ignored his claims to be human. They always tightened his chain when they came in to rake out the straw that covered the floor of his stall. He sighed and uncoiled his body and came slowly to his feet.

One of the men gasped. 'He *is* tall! Look at the length of his legs! Does he have a tail?'

'No. No tail. But he's scaled all over. Glitters like diamonds if you take him out in the daylight.'

'So, bring him out. Let me see him in the light.'

'No. He doesn't like it.'

'Liar.' Selden spoke clearly. The lantern was blinding him but he spoke to the second of the two shapes he could discern. 'He doesn't want you to see that I'm sick. He doesn't want you to see that I'm breaking out in sores, that my ankle is ulcerated from this chain. Most of all, he doesn't want you to see that I'm just as human as you are.'

'He talks!' The man sounded more impressed than dismayed.

'That he does. But you are wiser not to listen to anything he says. He is part dragon, and all know that a dragon can make a man believe anything.'

'I am *not* part dragon! I am a man, like you, changed by the favour of a dragon.' Selden tried to put force behind his shout, but he had no strength.

'You see how he lies. We do not answer him. To let him engage you in conversation is to fall to his wiles. Doubtless that was how his mother was seduced by a dragon.' The man cleared his throat. 'So. You have seen him. My master is reluctant to sell him, but says he will listen to your offer, since you have come so far.'

'My mother . . . ? That is preposterous! A wild tale not even a child would believe. And you can't sell me. You don't own me!' Selden lifted a hand and tried to shield his eyes to see the man. It didn't help. And his words didn't even provoke a response. Abruptly, he felt foolish. None of this had ever been about the language barrier. It had always been about their unwillingness to see him as anything other than a valuable freak.

They continued their conversation as if he had never spoken.

'Well, you know I'm only acting as a go-between. I'm not buying him for myself. Your master asks a very high price. The man I represent is wealthy, but the wealthy are stingier than the poor, as the saying goes. If I spend his coin and the dragon-man disappoints him, coin is not all he will demand of me.'

They were silhouettes before his watering eyes. Two men he didn't know at all, arguing over how much his life was worth. He took a step toward them, dragging his chain through the musty straw. 'I'm sick! Can't you see that? Haven't you got any decency at all? You keep me chained here, you feed me half-rotted meat and stale bread, I never see daylight . . . You're killing me. You're murdering me!'

'The man I'm representing needs proof before he will spend that much gold. Let me tell you plainly. For the price you are asking, you must let me send him something as a sign of good faith. If he is what you say he is, then your master will get the price he's asking. And both our masters will be well pleased with us.'

There was a long pause. 'I will take this matter to my master. Come. Share a drink with us. Bargaining is thirsty work.'

The men were turning. The lantern was swinging as they walked away. Selden took two more steps and found the end of his chain. 'I have a family!' he shouted at them. 'I have a mother! I have a sister and a brother. I want to go home! Please, let me go home before I die here!'

A brief flash of daylight was his only answer. They were gone.

He coughed, clutching at his ribs as he did so, trying to hold himself tight against the hurt. Phlegm came up and he spat it onto the dirty straw. He wondered if there was blood in it. Not enough light to tell. The cough was getting worse, he knew that.

He tottered unsteadily back to the heap of straw where he bedded. He knelt and then lay down on his side. Every joint in his body ached. He rubbed at his gummy eyes and closed them again. Why had he let them bait him into standing up? Why couldn't he just give up and be still until he died?

'Tintaglia,' he said softly. He reached for the dragon with his thoughts. There had been a time when she was aware of him when he sought for her, a time when she had let her thoughts touch his. Then she had found her mate, and since then, he had felt nothing from her. He had near-worshipped her, had basked in her dragon glory and reflected it back to her in his songs.

Songs. How long had it been since he had sung for her, since he had sung anything at all? He had loved her, and believed she had loved him. Everyone had warned him. They'd spoken of the glamour of dragons, of the spell of entrancement they used to ensnare humans but he hadn't believed them. He had lived to serve her. Worse was that, even as he lay on the dirty straw like a forgotten pet, he knew that if she ever found him again and so much as glanced at him, he'd once more serve her faithfully.

'It's what I am now. It's what she made me,' he said softly to the darkness.

In the next stall, the two-headed dog whined.

Day the 7th of the Hope Moon
Year the 7th of the Independent Alliance of Traders

From Kim, Keeper of the Birds, Cassarick to Reyall, Acting Keeper of the Birds, Bingtown

Please convey to your masters that I find it extremely distasteful that an underling such as yourself has been given the assignment of conveying these disgusting allegations against me. I believe that being allowed to act as Keeper of the Birds in Erek's absence has given you an inflated sense of importance that is entirely inappropriate for a journeyman to display to a Master. I suggest further that the Bird Masters of the Bingtown Bird Keepers' Guild look at your family connections and consider the jealousy your kin bear for me with regards to my promotion to Bird Keeper in Cassarick, for I think there they will find the heart of this vile accusation.

I decline to contact Trader Candral regarding this matter. He has lodged no grievance with our offices, and I am certain that if these complaints were genuine, he would have come to us in person to make his protest. I suspect the fault is not with his wax or seal, but with careless handling of the confidential message cylinders within the Bingtown aviary by those assigned to manage the birds from Trehaug and Cassarick. I believe that would be you, journeyman.

If the Bingtown Bird Keepers' Guild has a grievance with how official messages are handled in Cassarick, I suggest they send a formal complaint to the Cassarick Traders' Council and request an investigation. I believe you will find the Council has every confidence in the Cassarick Bird Keepers and that they will decline to pursue such a scurrilous charge against us.

Kim, Keeper of the Birds, Cassarick

CHAPTER TWO

Dragon Battle

The sun had broken through the clouds. The mist that cloaked the hillside meadow by the swift-flowing river was beginning to burn off. Sintara lifted her head to stare at the distant burning orb. Light fell on her scaled hide but little warmth came with it. As the mist rose in trailing tendrils and vanished at the sun's touch, the cruel wind was driving in thick grey clouds from the west. It would be another day of rain. In distant lands, the delightfully coarse sand would be baking under a hot sun. An ancestral memory of wallowing in that sand and scouring one's scales until they shone intruded into her mind. She and her fellow dragons should have migrated. They should have risen in a glittering storm of flashing wings and lashing tails and flown to the far southern deserts months ago. Hunting in the rocky uplands that walled the desert was always good. If they were there now it would be a time to hunt, to eat to satiation, to sleep long in the heat-soaked afternoon and then to rise into the bright blue sky, coasting on the hot air currents. Given the right winds, a dragon could hang effortlessly above the land. A queen might do that, might shift her wings and glide and watch the heavier males do battle in the air below her. She imagined herself there, looking down on them as they clashed and spat, as they soared and collided and gripped talons with one another.

At the end of such a battle, a single drake would prevail. His vanquished rivals would return to the sands to bask and sulk, or perhaps flee to the game-rich hills to take out their frustration in a wild killing spree. The lone drake would rise, beating his wings to achieve an altitude equal to the circling, watching females and single out the one he sought to court. Then a different sort of a battle would begin.

Sintara's gleaming copper eyes were half-lidded, her head lifted on her long and powerful neck, her face turned to the distant sun. A reflex opened her useless blue wings. There were stirrings of longing in her. She felt the mating flush warm the scales of her belly and throat and smelled the scent of her own desire wafting from the glands under her wings. She opened her eyes and lowered her head, feeling almost shame. A true queen worthy of mating would have powerful wings that could lift her above the clouds that now threatened to drench her. Her flight would spread the scent of her musk and inflame every drake for miles with lust. But a true dragon queen would not be marooned here on this sodden riverbank, companioned only by inept flightless males and even more useless human keepers.

She pushed dreams of glorious battles and mating flights away from her. A low rumble of displeasure vibrated her flanks. She was hungry. Where was her Thymara, her keeper? She was supposed to hunt for her, to bring her freshly-killed game. Where was the useless girl?

She felt a sudden violent stir of wind and caught a powerful whiff of drake. Just in time, she closed her half-opened wings.

His clawed feet met the earth and he slid wildly toward her, stopping just short of crashing into her. Sintara reared onto her hind legs and arched her glistening blue neck, straining to her full height. Even so, Kalo still towered over her. She saw his whirling eyes light with pleasure as he realized her disadvantage. The big male had grown and gained muscle and strength since they'd arrived at Kelsingra. 'My longest flight yet,' he told her as he shook his wide, dark-blue wings, freeing them of rain and spattering her in the process, then carefully folded and groomed them to his back. 'My wings grow longer and stronger every day. Soon I shall again be a lord of the skies. What of you, queen? When will you take to the air?'

'When I please,' she retorted and turned away. He reeked of lust; the wild freedom of flight was not his focus, but what might occur during a flight. She would not even consider it. 'And I do not call that flight. You ran down the hill and leaped into the air. Gliding is not flying.' Her criticism was not strictly fair. Kalo had been aloft for five wing beats before he had landed. Shame vied with fury as she recalled her first flight effort; the keepers had cheered as she leaped and glided. But her wings had lacked the strength to lift her; she had gone down, crashing into the river. She had been tumbled and battered in the current and emerged streaming muddy water and covered with bruises. *Don't recall that ignominy. But never let anyone see you fail again.*

A fresh gust of wind brought the rain down. She had come down to the river only to drink; she would return to the feeble shelter of the trees now.

But as she started away from him, Kalo's head shot out. He clamped his jaws firmly on her neck, just behind her head, where she could not turn to bite him or to spit acid at him. She lifted a front foot to claw at him, but his neck was longer and more powerful than hers. He held her away from his body; her claws slashed fruitlessly at empty air. She trumpeted her fury and he released her, springing back so that her second attack was as useless as her first.

Kalo lifted his wings and opened them wide, ready to bat her aside if she charged at him. His eyes, silver with tendrils of green, whirled with infuriating amusement.

'You should be trying to fly, Sintara! You need to become a true queen again, ruler of sea and land and sky. Leave these earthbound worms behind and soar with me. We will hunt and kill and fly far away from this cold rain and deep meadows, to the far deserts of the south. Touch your ancestral memories and remember what we are to become!'

Her neck stung where his teeth had scored her flesh, but her pride stung more sharply. Heedless of the danger, she charged at him again, mouth wide and poison sacs working, but with a roar of delight at her response, he leapt over her. As she spun to confront him, she became aware of scarlet Ranculos and azure Sestican lumbering toward them. Dragons were not meant for ground travel. They lollopped along like fat cattle. Sestican's orange-filigreed mane stood out on the back of his neck. As Ranculos raced toward them, gleaming wings half-spread, he bellowed aggressively. 'Leave her be, Kalo!'

'I don't need your help,' she trumpeted back as she turned and stalked away from the converging males. Satisfaction that they would fight over her warred with a sense of humiliation that she was not worth their battle. She could not take to the skies in a show of grace and speed; she could not challenge whoever won this foolish brawl with her own agility and fearlessness. A thousand ancestral memories of other courtship battles and mating flights hovered at the edge of her thoughts. She pushed them away. She did not look back at the roars and the sound of furiously slapping wings. 'I have no need to fly,' she called disdainfully over her shoulder. 'There is no drake here worth a mating flight.'

A roar of pain and fury from Ranculos was the only response. All around her, the rainy afternoon erupted into shouts of dismay and shrieked questions from running humans as the dragon keepers poured from their scattered cottages and converged on the battling males. Idiots. They'd be trampled, or worse, if they interfered. These were not matters for humans to intervene in. It galled her when the keepers treated them as if they were cattle to be managed rather than dragons to be served. Her own keeper, trying to hold a ragged cloak closed around her lumpy back and shoulders, ran toward her shouting, 'Sintara, are you all right? Are you hurt?'

She tossed her head high and half-opened her wings. 'Do you think I cannot defend myself?' she demanded of Thymara. 'Do you think that I am weak and—'

'Get clear!' A human shouted the warning and Thymara obeyed it, hunching down and covering the back of her head with her hands.

Sintara snorted in amusement as golden Mercor hurtled past them, wings spread wide, clawed feet throwing up tufts of muddy grass as he barely skimmed the earth. Thymara's fending hands could not have protected her if the dragon's barbed wing had so much as brushed her. The mere wind of his passage knocked Thymara to the ground and sent her rolling through the wet meadow grass.

Human shrieks and dragon roars culminated in a full-throated trumpeting from Mercor as he crashed into the knot of struggling males.

Sestican went down, bowled over by the impact. His spread wing bent dangerously as he rolled on it and she heard his huff of pain and dismay. Ranculos was trapped under the flailing Kalo. Kalo attempted to roll and meet Mercor with the longer claws of his powerful hind legs. But Mercor had reared onto his hind legs on top of the heap of struggling dragons. Suddenly he leapt forward and pinned Kalo's wide-spread wings to the ground with his hind legs. A wild slash from the trapped dragon's talons scored a gash down Mercor's ribs, but before he could add another stripe of injury, Mercor shifted his stance higher. Kalo's head and long neck lashed like a whip but Mercor clearly had the advantage. Trapped beneath the two larger dragons, Sestican roared in helpless fury. A thick stench of male dragon musk rose from the struggle.

A horde of frightened and angry keepers ringed the struggling dragons, shrieking and shouting the names of the combatants or attempting to keep other gawking dragons from joining the fray. The smaller females, Fente and Veras, had arrived and were craning their necks and ignoring their keepers as they ventured dangerously close. Baliper, scarlet tail lashing, prowled the outer edges of the conflict, sending keepers darting for safety, squeaking indignantly at the danger he presented.

The struggle ended almost as abruptly as it had begun. Mercor flung back his golden head and then snapped it forward, jaws wide. Screams from the keepers and startled roars from the watching dragons predicted Kalo's death by acid spray. Instead, at the last moment, Mercor snapped his jaws shut. He darted his head down and spat, not a mist or a stream, but only a single blot of acid onto Kalo's vulnerable throat. The blue-black dragon screamed in agony and fury. With three powerful beats of his wings, Mercor lifted off him and alighted a ship's length away. Blood was running freely from the long gash on his ribs, sheeting down his gold-scaled side. He was breathing heavily, his nostrils flared wide. Colour rippled through his scales and the protective crests around his eyes stood tall. He lashed his tail and the smell of his challenge filled the air.

The moment Mercor had lifted his weight off him, Kalo

had rolled to his feet. Snarling his frustration and humiliation, he headed immediately toward the river to wash the acid from his flesh before it could eat any deeper. Carson, Spit's keeper, ran beside him, shouting at him to stop and let him look at the injury. The black dragon ignored him. Bruised and shaken but not much injured, Ranculos scrambled to his feet and staggered upright. He shook his wings out and then folded them slowly as if they were painful. Then, with what dignity he could muster, he limped away from the trampled earth of the combat site.

Mercor roared after the retreating Kalo. 'Don't forget that I could have killed you! Don't ever forget it, Kalo!'

'Lizard spawn!' the dark dragon roared back at him but did not slow his retreat toward the icy waters of the river.

Sintara turned away from them. It was over. She was surprised it had lasted as long as it had. Battle, like mating, was something that dragons did on the wing. Had the males been able to take flight, the contest might have gone on for hours, perhaps the entire day, and left all of them acid-seared and bloodied. For a moment, her ancestral memories of such trials seized her mind and she felt her heart race with excitement. The males would have battled for her regard, and in the end, when only one was the victor, still he would have had to match her in flight and meet her challenge before he could claim the right to mate with her. They would have soared through air, going higher and higher as the drake sought to match her loops and dives and powerful climbs. And if he had succeeded, if he had managed to come close enough to match her flight, he would have locked his body to hers, and as their wings synchronized . . .

'SINTARA!'

Mercor's bellow startled her out of her reflection. She was not the only one who turned to see what the gold drake wanted of her. Every dragon and keeper on the meadow was staring at him. And at her.

The great golden dragon lifted his head and then snapped opened his wings with an audible crack. A fresh wave of his scent went out on the wind. 'You should not provoke what you cannot complete,' he rebuked her.

She stared at him, feeling anger flush her colours brighter. 'It had nothing to do with you, Mercor. Perhaps you should not intrude into things that do not concern you.'

He spread his wings wider still, and lifted his body tall on his powerful hind legs. 'I will fly.' He did not roar the words, but even so they still carried clearly through the wind and rain. 'As will you. And when the time comes for mating battles, I will win. And I will mate you.'

She stared at him, more shocked than she had thought she could be. Unthinkable for a male to make such a blatant claim. She tried not to be flattered that he had said she would fly. When the silence grew too long, when she became aware that everyone was watching her, expecting a response, she felt anger. 'So say you,' she retorted lamely. She did not need to hear Fente's snort of disdain to know that her feeble response had impressed no one.

Turning away from them all, she began stalking back to the forest and the thin shelter of the trees. She didn't care. She didn't care what Mercor had said nor that Fente had mocked her. There was none among them worth impressing. 'Scarcely a proper battle at all,' she sneered quietly.

'Was a "proper battle" what you were trying to provoke?' Her snippy little keeper Thymara was abruptly beside her, trotting to keep up. Her black hair hung in fuzzy, tattered braids, a few still adorned with wooden charms. Her roll down the hill had coated her ragged cloak with dead grass. Her feet were bound up in mismatched rags, the make-shift shoes soled with crudely-tanned deerskin. She had grown thinner of late, and taller. The bones of her face stood out more. The wings that Sintara had gifted her with bounced lightly beneath her cloak as she jogged. Despite the rudeness of her first query, Thymara sounded concerned as she added, 'Stop a moment. Crouch down. Let me see your neck where he bit you.'

'He didn't draw blood.' Sintara could scarcely believe she was answering such an impudent demand from a mere human.

'I want to look at it. It looks as if several scales are loosened.'

'I did nothing to provoke that silly squabble.' Sintara halted abruptly and lowered her head so that Thymara could inspect her neck. She resented doing it, feeling that she had somehow given way to the human's domineering manner. Anger simmered in her. Briefly she considered 'accidentally' knocking Thymara off her feet with a swipe of her head. But as she felt the girl's strong hands gently easing her misaligned neck scales back into smoothness, she relented. Her keeper and her clever hands had their uses.

'None of the scales are torn all the way free, though you may shed some of them sooner rather than later.'

Sintara sensed her keeper's annoyance as she set her scales to rights. Despite Thymara's frequent rudeness to Sintara, the dragon knew the girl took pride in her health and appearance. Any insult to Sintara rankled Thymara as well. And she would be aware of her dragon's mood, too.

As she focused more on the girl, she knew that they shared more than annoyance. The frustration was there as well. 'Males!' the girl exclaimed suddenly. 'I suppose it takes no more to provoke a male dragon to stupidity than it does a human male.'

Sintara's curiosity was stirred by the comment, though she

would not let Thymara know that. She reviewed what she knew of Thymara's most recent upsets and divined the source of her sour mood. 'The decision is yours, not theirs. How foolishly you are behaving! Just mate with both of them. Or neither. Show them that you are a queen, not a cow to be bred at the bull's rutting.'

'I chose neither,' Thymara told her, answering the question that the dragon hadn't asked.

Her scales smoothed, Sintara lifted her head and resumed her trek to the forest's edge. Thymara hurried to stay beside her, musing as she jogged. 'I just want to let it alone, to leave things as they've always been. But neither of them seems willing to let that happen.' She shook her head, her braids flying with the motion. 'Tats is my oldest friend. I knew him back in Trehaug, before we became dragon keepers. He's part of my past, part of home. But when he pushes me to bed with him, I don't know if it's because he loves me, or simply because I've refused him. I worry that if we become lovers and it doesn't work out, I'll lose him completely.'

'Then bed Rapskal and be done with it,' the dragon suggested. Thymara was boring her. How could humans seriously believe that a dragon could be interested in the details of their lives? As well worry about a moth or a fish.

The keeper took the dragon's comment as an excuse to keep talking. 'Rapskal? I can't. If I take him as a mate, I know that would ruin my friendship with Tats. Rapskal is handsome, and funny . . . and a bit strange. But it's a sort of strange that I like. And I think he truly cares about me, that when he pushes me to sleep with him, it's not just for the pleasure.' She shook her head. 'But I don't want it, with either of them. Well, I do. If I could just have the physical part of it, and not have it make everything else complicated. But I don't want to take the chance of catching a child, and I don't really want to have to make some momentous decision. If I choose one, have I lost the other? I don't know what—'

'You're boring me,' Sintara warned her. 'And there are more important things you should be doing right now. Have you hunted for me today? Do you have meat to bring me?'

Thymara bridled at the sudden change of topic. She replied grudgingly, 'Not yet. When the rain lets up, I'll go. There's no game moving right now.' A pause, and then she broached another dangerous subject. 'Mercor said you would fly. Were you trying? Have you exercised your wings today, Sintara? Working on the muscles is the only way that you will ever—'

'I have no desire to flap around on the beach like a gull with a broken wing. No desire to make myself an object of mockery.' Even less desire to fail and fall into the icy, swift-flowing river and drown. Or over-estimate her skills and plummet into the trees as Baliper had done. His wings were so swollen that he could not close them, and he'd torn a claw from his left front foot.

'No one mocks you! Exercising your wings is a necessity, Sintara. You must learn to fly; all of the dragons must. You all have grown since we left Cassarick, and it is becoming impossible for me to kill enough game to keep you well fed, even with the larger game that we've found here. You will have to hunt for your own food, and to do that, you must be able to fly. Would not you rather be one of the first dragons to leave the ground than one of the last ones?'

That thought stung. The idea that the smaller females such as Veras or Fente might gain the air before she did was intolerable. It might actually be easier for such stunted and scrawny creatures to fly. Anger warmed her blood and she knew the liquid copper of her eyes would be swirling with emotion. She'd have to kill them, that was all. Kill them before either one could humiliate her.

'Or you could take flight before they did,' Thymara suggested steadily.

Sintara snapped her head around to stare at the girl. Sometimes she was able to overhear the dragon's thoughts. Sometimes she was even impudent enough to answer them.

'I'm tired of the rain. I want to go back under the trees.'

Thymara nodded and as Sintara stalked off, she followed docilely. The dragon looked back only once.

Down by the river, other keepers were stridently discussing which dragon had started the melee. Carson the hunter had his arms crossed and stood in stubborn confrontation with Kalo. The black dragon was dripping; he'd rinsed Mercor's acid from this throat, then. Carson's small silver dragon, Spit, was watching them sullenly from a distance. The man was stupid, Sintara thought. The big blue-black male was not fond of humans to start with: provoked, Kalo might simply snap Carson in two.

Tats was helping Sylve examine the long injury down Mercor's ribs while his own dragon, Fente, jealously clawed at the mud and muttered vague threats. Ranculos was holding one wing half-opened for his keeper's inspection. It was likely badly bruised at the very least. Sestican, covered in mud, was dispiritedly bellowing for his keeper but Lecter was nowhere in sight. The squabble was over. For one moment, they had been dragons, vying for the attention of a female. Now they were back to behaving like large cattle. She despised them, and she loathed herself. They weren't worth her time to provoke. They only made her think of all they were not. All she was not.

If only, she thought, and traced her misfortune back, happenstance after happenstance. If only the dragons had emerged from the metamorphosis fully-formed and healthy. If only they had been in better condition when they cocooned to make the transition from sea serpent to dragon. If only they had migrated home decades ago. If only the Elderlings had not died off, if only the mountain had never erupted and put an end to the world they had once known. She should have been so much more than she was. Dragons were supposed to emerge from their cocoons capable of flight, and take wing to make that first rejuvenating kill. But none of them had. She was like a bright chip of glass, fallen from a gorgeous mosaic of Elderlings and turreted cities and dragons on the wing, to lie in the dirt, broken away from all she that had once been her destiny. She was meaningless without that world.

She had tried to fly, more than once. Thymara need never know of her many private and humiliating failures. It was infuriating that dim-witted Heeby was able to take flight and hunt for herself. Every day, the red female grew larger and stronger, and her keeper Rapskal never tired of singing the praises of his 'great, glorious girl' of a dragon. He'd made up a stupid song, more doggerel than poetry, and loudly sang it to her every morning as he groomed her. It made Sintara want to bite his head off. Heeby could preen all she liked when her keeper sang to her. She was still dumber than a cow.

'The best vengeance might be to learn to fly,' Thymara suggested again, privy to the feeling rather than the thought.

'Why don't you try that yourself?' Sintara retorted bitterly.

Thymara was silent, a silence that simmered.

The idea came to Sintara slowly. She was startled. 'What? You have, haven't you? You've tried to fly?'

Thymara kept her face turned away from the dragon as they trudged through the wild meadow and up toward the tree line. Scattered throughout the meadow were small stone cottages, some little more than broken walls and collapsed roofs while others had been restored by the dragon keepers. Once there had been a village here, a place for human artisans to live. They'd plied their trades here, the servant and merchant classes of the Elderlings who had lived in the gleaming city on the far side of the swift-flowing river. She wondered if Thymara knew that. Probably not.

'You made these wings grow on me,' Thymara finally replied. 'If I have to have them, if I have to put up with something that makes it impossible to wear an ordinary shirt, something that lifts my cloak up off my back so that every breeze chills me, then I might as well make them useful. Yes, I've tried to fly. Rapskal was helping me. He insists I'll be able to, one day. But so far all I've done is skin my knees and scrape the palms of my hands when I fall. I've had no success. Does that please you?'

'It doesn't surprise me.' It did please her. No human should fly when dragons could not! Let her skin her knees and bruise herself a thousand times. If Thymara took flight before she did, the dragon would eat her! Her hunger stirred at the thought and she became sensible. There was no sense in making the girl aware of that, at least not until she'd done her day's hunting.

'I'm going to keep trying,' Thymara said in a low voice. 'And so should you.'

'Do as you please and I'll do the same,' the dragon replied. 'And what should please you right now is that you go hunting. I'm hungry.' She gave the girl a mental push.

Thymara narrowed her eyes, aware that the dragon had used her glamour on her. It didn't matter. She would still be nagged with an urgent desire to go hunting. Being aware of the source of that suggestion would not make her immune to it.

The winter rains had prompted an explosion of greenery. The tall wet grasses slapped against her legs as they waded through it. They had climbed the slope of the meadow and now the open forest of the hillside beckoned. Beneath the trees, there would be some shelter from the rain, although many of the trees here had lost their foliage. The forest seemed both peculiar and familiar to Sintara. Her own life's experience had been limited to the dense and impenetrable forest that bordered the Rain Wilds River. Yet her ancestral memories echoed the familiarity of woods such as this. The names of the trees – oak and hickam and birch, alder and ash and goldleaf – came to her mind. Dragons had known these trees, this sort of forest and even this particular place. But they had seldom lingered here in the chill rains of winter. No. For this miserable season, dragons would have flown off to bask in the heat of the deserts. Or they would have taken shelter in the places that the Elderlings created for them, crystal domes with heated floors and pools of steaming water. She turned and looked across the river to fabled Kelsingra. They had come so far, and yet asylum remained out of reach. The swift-flowing river was deep and treacherous. No dragon could swim it. True flight was the only way home.

The ancient Elderling city stood, mostly intact, just as her ancestral memories had recalled it. Even under the overcast, even through the grey onslaught of rain, the towering buildings of black and silver stone gleamed and beckoned. Once, lovely scaled Elderlings had resided there. Friends and servants of dragons, they had dressed in bright robes and adorned themselves with gold and silver and gleaming copper. The wide avenues of Kelsingra and the gracious buildings had all been constructed to welcome dragons as well as Elderlings. There had been a statuary plaza, where the flagstones radiated heat in the winter, though that area of the city appeared to have vanished into the giant chasm that now cleft its ancient roads and towers. There had been baths, steaming vats of hot water where Elderlings and dragons alike had taken refuge from foul weather. Her ancestors had soaked there, not just in hot water, but in copper vats of simmering oils that had sheened their scales and hardened their claws.

And there had been . . . something else. Something she could not quite recall clearly. Water, she thought, but not water. Something delightful, something that even now sparkled and gleamed and called to her through her dim recollection of it.

'What are you looking at?' Thymara asked her.

Sintara hadn't realized that she had halted to stare across the river. 'Nothing. The city,' she said and resumed her walk.

'If you could fly, you could get across the river to Kelsingra.'

'If you could think, you would know when to be quiet,' the dragon retorted. Did the stupid girl not realize how often she thought of that? Daily. Hourly. The Elderling magic of heated tiles might still work. Even if it did not, the standing buildings would provide shelter from the incessant rain. Perhaps in Kelsingra she would feel like a real dragon again rather than a footed serpent.

They reached the edge of the trees. A gust of wind rattled them, sending water spattering down through the sheltering branches. Sintara rumbled her displeasure. 'Go hunt,' she told the girl, and strengthened her mental push.

Offended, her keeper turned away and trudged back down the hill. Sintara didn't bother to watch her go. Thymara would obey. It was what keepers did. It was really all they were good for.

'Carson!'

The hunter held up a cautioning hand, palm open, toward Sedric. Carson stood his ground, staring up at the blue-black dragon. He was not speaking but had locked gazes with the creature. Carson was not a small man, but Kalo dwarfed him to the size of a toy. A toy the infuriated dragon could trample into the earth, or melt to hollowed bones with a single blast of acid-laced venom. And Sedric would be able to do nothing about it. His heart hammered in his chest and he felt he could not get his breath. He hugged himself, shivering with the chill day and with his fear. Why did Carson have to take such risks with himself?

I will protect you. Sedric's own dragon, Relpda, nudged him with her blunt nose and her thoughts.

He turned quickly to put a restraining hand on her neck as he tried to force calm on his own thoughts. The little copper female would not stand a chance if she challenged Kalo on Sedric's behalf. And any challenge to Kalo right now would probably provoke an irrational and violent response. Sedric was not Kalo's keeper, but he felt the dragon's emotions. The waves of anger and frustration that radiated from the black dragon would have affected anyone.

'Let's step back a bit,' he suggested to the copper, and pushed on her. She didn't budge. When he looked at her, her eyes seemed to spin, dark blue with an occasional thread of silver in them. She had decided Kalo was a danger to him. *Oh, dear.*

Carson was speaking now, firmly, without anger. His muscled arms were crossed on his chest, offering no threat. His dark eyes under his heavy brows were almost kind. The wet wind tugged at his hair and left drops clinging to his trimmed ginger beard. The hunter ignored the wind and rain as he ignored the dragon's superior strength. He seemed to have no fear of Kalo or the dragon's suppressed fury. Carson's voice was deep and calm, his words slow. 'You need to calm down, Kalo. I've sent one of the others to find Davvie. Your own keeper will be here soon, to tend your hurts. If you wish,

I will look at them now. But you have to stop threatening everyone.'

The blue-black dragon shifted and scintillations of silver glittered over his scaling in the rain. The colours in his eyes melted and swirled to the green of copper ore; it looked as if his eyes were spinning. Sedric stared at them with fascination tinged with horror. Carson was too close. The creature looked no calmer to him, and if he chose to snap at Carson or spit acid at him, even the hunter's agility would not be enough to save him from death. Sedric drew breath to plead with him to step back, and then gritted his teeth together. No. Carson knew what he was doing and the last thing he needed now as a distraction from his lover.

Sedric heard running feet behind him and turned to see Davvie pelting toward them as fast as he could. The young keeper's cheeks were bright red with effort and his hair bounced around his face and shoulders. Lecter trundled along in his wake though the soaked meadow grass, looking rather like a damp hedgehog. The spines on the back of his neck were becoming a mane down his back, twin to the ones on his dragon, Sestican. Lecter could no longer contain them in a shirt. They were blue, tipped with orange, and they bobbed as he tried to keep up with Davvie, panting loudly. Davvie dragged in a breath and shouted, 'Kalo! Kalo, what's wrong? I'm here, are you hurt? What happened?'

Lecter veered off, headed toward Sestican. 'Where were you?' his dragon trumpeted, angry and querulous. 'Look, I am filthy and bruised. And you did not attend me.'

Davvie raced right up to his huge dragon with a fine disregard for how angry the beast was. From the moment the boy had appeared, Kalo's attention had been fixed only on him. 'Why weren't you here to attend me?' the dragon bellowed accusingly. 'See how I am burned! Your carelessness could have cost me my life!' The dragon flung up his head to expose the raw circle on this throat where Mercor's acid had scored him. It was the size of a saucer.

Sedric flinched at sight of the wound, but Davvie went pale as death.

'Oh, Kalo, are you going to be all right? I'm so sorry! I was around the river bend, checking the fish trap, to see if we'd caught anything!'

Sedric knew about the fish trap. He'd watched Davvie and Carson install it yesterday. The two baskets were fixed on the ends of arms that rotated like a wheel propelled by the current. The baskets were designed to scoop fish from the water and drop them down a chute into a woven holding pen. It had taken Davvie and Carson several days to build it. If it worked, they were going to build more to try to lessen the burden of constantly hunting for food for the dragons.

'He wasn't checking the fish trap,' Carson said in a low voice as he joined Sedric. Kalo had hunkered down and Davvie was making worried sounds as he examined the dragon's spread wings for any other injury. Lecter, looking guilty, was leading Sestican down to the river to wash him.

Sedric watched the lad surreptitiously adjust his belt buckle. Carson was shaking his head in displeasure but Sedric had to grin. 'No. They weren't,' he concluded.

Carson shot him a look that faded the smile from his face.

'What?' Sedric asked, confused by the severity of his expression.

Carson spoke in a low voice. 'We can't condone it, Sedric. Both boys have to be more responsible.'

'We can't condone that they're together? How can we condemn it without being hypocrites?' Sedric felt cut by Carson's words. Did he expect the boys to conceal that they were infatuated with one another? Did he condemn their openness?

'That's not what I mean.' The larger man put a hand on Sedric's shoulder and turned him away from Kalo. He spoke quietly. 'They're just boys. They like each other, but it's about physical discovery, not each other. Not like us. Their sort of games can wait until after their chores are done.' The two men began to trudge up the hill through the soaking grass. Relpda followed them for a few steps and then abruptly turned and headed toward the riverbank.

'Not like us.' Sedric repeated the words softly. Carson looked sideways at him and nodded, a small smile curling the corners of his mouth and igniting flames in Sedric's belly. Sedric hoped that Carson's direction meant they were bound for their cottage. The small chill structure of bare stone with the flagged floor was little better than a cave, but at least the roof shed rain and the chimney drew well. If they built up a blazing fire in the hearth, it was almost comfortably warm. Almost. He thought of other ways to stay warm there.

As if he could read Sedric's mind, Carson said, 'Some chores won't wait. We should go up to the forest and see if we can find more dry deadfalls. That green wood you were trying to burn last night was all smoke and no heat.' He glanced back at Davvie and Lecter. Kalo had crouched low and stretched out his neck so the boy could examine the acid scald on his neck. Under the boy's touch, the great beast had calmed and seemed almost placid.

'He's a much better match for Kalo than Greft was,' Sedric observed.

'He could be, if he tried a bit harder.' It was always hard for Carson to praise the lad. He loved Davvie like a son and made a father's effort to hold him to the highest standards. He looked away, shaking his head. 'I understand he and Lecter are infatuated with each other but that still doesn't excuse either of them neglecting their duties. A man tends to his responsibilities first and his pleasures later. And Davvie is old enough now that I expect him to act like a man. The survival of this expedition is going to depend on each of us pulling his fair weight. When spring comes, or when we get fresh supplies, then Davvie can relax a bit and indulge himself. But not until then. Both of them have dragons to see to every day, before they think of anything else.'

Carson intended no rebuke for him with the words, Sedric knew. Nonetheless, there were times when he felt more keenly his own lack of useful skills. As useless as teats on a bull, his father used to say of people like him. *It's not my fault* he assured himself. *I'm just a fish out of water here. Were I to abruptly transport Carson to the sort of society I was accustomed to in Bingtown, he would be the one to feel useless and ill at ease.* Was it truly a fault that Sedric would have been more competent at choosing a series of wines to complement a banquet, or giving a tailor instructions on how a jacket was to be altered rather than swinging an axe to render a dead log into firewood or cutting an animal up into pieces that would fit in a pot? He didn't think so. He was not a useless or incompetent person. He was simply out of his area of expertise. He looked around himself at the rainy hillside and the looming forest. Far out of his area of expertise.

And weary of it. He thought of Bingtown with longing. The clatter and chatter of the market place, the city's wide, flagged streets and well-kept manor houses, its friendly taverns and teashops! The open circuit of the market, and the cool shade of the public gardens! What would Jefdin the tailor think to see his best customer in rags? He suddenly longed for mulled wine and spices in a nice warm mug. Oh, what wouldn't he give for one meal that wasn't cooked over a hearth fire? One glass of good wine, one piece of bread? Even a bowl of simple hot porridge with currants and honey. Anything that wasn't game meat or fish or gathered greens. Anything that was the slightest bit sweet! He'd sacrifice anything for one well prepared meal served on a plate at a table with a cloth!

He glanced at Carson walking beside him. His cheeks were ruddy above his carefully trimmed beard, his dark eyes brimming with his concerns. A recent memory intruded. Carson sitting on a low stool, his eyes closed, his expression that of a stroked cat as Sedric used a small comb and tiny scissors to shape his beard to his face. He had been still and obedient, turning his head only as Sedric bade him, rapt as he basked in his attention. To see the powerful man quiescent under his touch had filled Sedric with a sense of mastery. He had trimmed Carson's wild mane as well, but not too much. Strange to admit that part of the hunter's attraction for him was his untamed aspect. He smiled to himself, a small shiver of recalled pleasure standing up the hair on his neck and arms. Well, perhaps there was one thing Sedric would not be willing to sacrifice to return to Bingtown!

He contrived to brush shoulders with Carson as they walked. The hunter grinned and immediately threw his arm around Sedric. No hesitation. Sedric's heart gave a bump. Hest would never have shown him such casual affection in public. Nor in private, if he was truthful. Carson tightened his hug and Sedric leaned into his embrace as they walked. The hunter was solid and muscular; it was like leaning on an oak. Sedric smiled to realize that he thought of his lover in such terms. Maybe he was becoming accustomed to living here in the wilds. Carson's coarse cloak and his bound hair smelled of woodsmoke and man. Silvery glints of scaling were starting to show at the corner of his eyes. His dragon was changing him. Sedric liked the way it looked.

Carson rubbed his upper arm. 'You're cold. Why don't you have your cloak on?'

Sedric's original cloak was long gone, eaten by the acid waters of the Rain Wild River. The garment Carson was referring to was a roughly tanned deer hide with the hair still on it. Carson himself had skinned it off the animal, tanned it and cut it to shape. It tied around Sedric's neck with leather thongs he had sewn onto it. Sedric was accustomed to furs that were soft and lined with fabric. This cloak was slightly stiff, the skin side of it a creamy colour. It crackled when he walked. Deer hair was not fur: it was stiff and bristly. 'It's so heavy,' Sedric replied guiltily. He would not mention that it smelled like, well, like a deer hide.

'Indeed it is. But it would shed the rain and keep you warmer.'

'It's too far to go back for it now.'

'Yes. But gathering firewood will warm both of us.'

Sedric didn't reply that he could think of better ways to warm them both. He was not a lazy man, but he had an aversion to the hard physical labour that Carson routinely accepted as his life. Before Alise had kidnapped him on her crazed adventure up the Rain Wild River, Sedric had always lived as befitted a young Bingtown Trader, even if his family had not been all that well-to-do. He'd worked hard, but with his mind, not his back! He'd kept accounts, both for the household and for the many business contracts that Hest negotiated for his family. He had minded Hest's wardrobe and overseen his social appointments. He had passed Hest's instructions on to the household staff, and dealt with their complaints and questions. He'd kept track of the arrival and departure dates of the ships in the harbour, making sure that Hest had the pick of incoming cargos and that he was the first to contact new merchants. He had been essential to the smooth running of Hest's household and business. Essential. Valued.

Then a memory of Hest's mocking smile confronted and scattered his warm memories of that time. Had any of his life truly been the way he thought it was? he wondered bitterly. Had Hest valued him for his social and organizational skills? Or had he simply enjoyed the use of Sedric's body, and how well he endured the humiliations that Hest heaped on him? He narrowed his eyes against the sting of the lancing rain. Had his father been right about him? Was he a useless fop, fit only to fill the fine clothes that his employer paid for?

'Hey. Come back.' Carson shook his shoulder gently. 'When you get that look on your face, it bodes no good for either of us. It's done, Sedric. A long time over and gone. Whatever it was. Let it go and stop tormenting yourself.'

'I was such a fool.' Sedric shook his head. 'I deserve to be tormented.'

Carson shook his head and a touch of impatience came into his voice. 'Well, then stop tormenting me. When I see that look on your face, I know you're thinking about Hest.' He paused suddenly, as if he'd been on the verge of saying something and then changed his mind. After a moment, he said with forced cheer, 'So. What brought him to mind this time?'

'I'm not missing him, Carson, if that's what you think. I've no desire to return to him. I'm more than content with you. I'm happy.'

Carson squeezed his shoulder again. 'But not so happy that you can stop thinking of Hest.' He tipped his head and looked at him quizzically. 'I don't think he treated you well. I don't understand his hold on you.'

Sedric shook his head as if he could shake all memories of Hest out of his mind. 'It's hard to explain him. He's very charismatic. He gets what he wants because he truly believes he deserves it. When something goes wrong, he never takes the blame as his own. He puts it on someone else, and then just steps away from whatever the disaster was. It always seemed to me that Hest could just step away from anything terrible that happened, even if he caused it. Whenever it seemed that he would finally have to face the consequences of what he did, some other passage would suddenly open for him.' His voice ran down. Carson's dark eyes were on him, trying to understand.

'And that fascinates you still?'

'No! At the time, it always seemed as if he had extraordinary luck. Now, when I look back, I see him as being very good at shifting the blame. And I let him. Often. So I'm not really thinking of Hest. I'm thinking about my life back in Bingtown, about who he made me . . . or rather who I let myself become.' Sedric shrugged. 'I'm not proud of who I became when I was with Hest. Not proud of things I planned to do, or the ones I did. But in some ways, I'm still that person. And I don't know how to change.'

Carson gave him a sideways glance, his smile broad. 'Oh, you've changed. Trust me on that, laddie. You've changed quite a bit.'

They'd reached the eaves of the forest. The bare-leaved trees at the outer edges did little to break the incessant rain. There were evergreens a bit higher up the hill, offering more shelter, but there were more dead and fallen branches for firewood here.

Carson halted near a grove of ash trees. He produced two long leather straps, each with a loop at the end. Sedric took his, muffling a sigh. He reminded himself of two things: when he worked, he did stay warmer, and when he kept pace with Carson, he gained more respect for himself. *Be a man*, he told himself, and shook the strap out into a loop on the ground as Carson had taught him. Carson had already begun to gather faggots and place them on the strap. The big man sometimes cracked a branch over his thigh to break it down to a manageable size. Sedric had tried that; it left remarkable bruises on him, ones that made Carson wince just to look at. He hadn't attempted it since then.

'I need to come back with the axe and take down a couple of those fir trees. Big ones. We can fell them and let them dry for a season, and next year we'll chop them up and have some good long-burning logs. Something more substantial than these, something that will burn all night.'

'That would be good,' Sedric agreed without enthusiasm. More back-breaking work. And thinking about firewood for next year made him realize that next year he'd probably still be here. Still living in a cottage, eating meat cooked over a fire, and wearing Sa knew what for clothes. And the year after. And the year after. Would he spend his life here, grow old here? Some of the other keepers had said that the changes the dragons were putting them through would make them into Elderlings, with vastly extended life spans. He glanced at the fish-fine scaling on the back of his wrists. One hundred years here? Living in a little cottage and caring for his eccentric dragon. Would that be his life? Once Elderlings had been legendary creatures to him, elegant and lovely beings that lived in wondrous cities full of magic. The Elderling artefacts that the Rain Wilders had discovered as they dug up the buried cities had been mystical: jewels that gleamed with their own light, and perfume gems each with their own sweet scent. Carafes that chilled whatever was put into them. Jidzin, the magical metal that woke to light at a touch. Wonderful wind chimes that played endlessly varying harmonies and tunes. Stone that held memories that one could share by touching . . .

so many amazing things had belonged to the Elderlings. But they were long gone from the world. And if Sedric and the other keepers were to be their heirs, they would indeed be the poor branch of the family, allied with dragons that could scarcely fly and bereft of Elderling magic. Like the crippled dragons of this generation, the Elderlings they created would be poor and stunted things, eking out an existence in primitive surroundings.

A gust of wind shook down a shower of drops from the naked tree branches above him. He brushed them off his trousers with a sigh. The cloth had worn thin and the cuffs were frayed to dangling threads. 'I need new trousers.'

Carson reached out a callused hand to rumple his wet hair. 'You need a hat, too,' he observed casually.

'And what shall we make that out of? Leaves?' Sedric tried to sound amused rather than bitter. Carson. He did have Carson. And would not he rather live in a primitive world with Carson than in a Bingtown mansion without him?

'No. Bark.' Carson sounded pragmatic. 'If we can find the right sort of tree. There was one merchant in Trehaug that used to beat tree bark into fibres and then weave them. She treated some of them with pitch to make them waterproof. She made hats and I think cloaks. I never bought one, but given our circumstances now, I'm ready to try anything. I don't think I've a whole shirt or pair of trousers left to my name.'

'Bark,' Sedric echoed gloomily. He tried to imagine what such a hat would look like and decided he'd rather go bareheaded. 'Maybe Captain Leftrin can bring fabric back from Cassarick. I think I can manage with what I've got until then.'

'Well, we'll have to, so it's good that you think we can.' Such a remark from Hest would have been scathing sarcasm. From Carson, it was shared amusement at the hardships they would endure together.

For a moment they both fell silent, musing. Carson had amassed a substantial bundle of wood. He pulled the strap tight around the sticks and hefted it experimentally. Sedric added a few more sticks to his, and regarded the pile with dread. The bundle was going to be heavy and the sticks would poke him and his back would ache tonight. Again. And here came Carson with *more* sticks, helpfully increasing the size of his pile. Sedric tried to think of something positive. 'But when Leftrin returns from Cassarick, won't he be bringing us more clothing in his supplies?'

Carson added the sticks he'd brought to the stack and wrapped the strap around it experimentally. He spoke as he tightened it. 'A lot will depend on if the Council gives him all the money they owe him. I expect they'll drag their feet. Even if they pay him, what he can bring back is going to be limited to what he can buy in Cassarick and maybe in Trehaug. Food will come first, I think. Then supplies like tar and lamp oil and candles and knives and hunting arrows. All the things that help us survive on our own. Blankets and fabric and suchlike will come last. Woven goods are always dear in Cassarick. No grazing lands in the swamps, so no sheep for wool. These meadows are one reason Leftrin was so excited about putting in an order for livestock from Bingtown. But we can expect livestock to take months to arrive and Tarman will have to make a return trip for them.'

Captain Leftrin had gathered them for a meeting on the *Tarman* a few nights previously. He'd announced that he'd be making a run back down the river to Cassarick and Trehaug to buy as many supplies as they could afford. He'd report to the Rain Wild Council that they had accomplished their undertaking and he'd collect the monies owed them. If keepers wanted anything special from Cassarick, they could let him know and he'd try to get it for them. Two of the keepers had promptly said that their earnings should be sent to their families. Others wanted to send messages to kin. Rapskal had announced that he wished to spend all his money on sweets, sweets of any kind.

The laughter hadn't died down until Leftrin had asked if anyone wanted to be taken back to Trehaug. There had been a brief silence then as the dragon keepers had exchanged puzzled glances. Go back to Trehaug? Abandon the dragons they had bonded with, and return to their lives as outcasts among their own people? If they had been shunned for their appearances when they left Trehaug, what would the other Rain Wilders think of them now? Their time among the dragons had not lessened their strangeness. Quite the opposite: they had grown more scales, more spines, and in the case of young Thymara, a set of gauzy wings. The dragons seemed to be guiding their changes now, so that they were more aesthetically pleasing. Even so, most of the keepers had clearly left humanity behind. None of them could return to the lives they had known.

Alise had not bonded to a dragon, and remained very human in appearance, but Sedric knew she would not return. There was nothing for her in Bingtown but disgrace. Even if Hest were willing to take her back, she would not return to that loveless sham of a marriage. Ever since he had confessed his own relationship with Hest to her, she had regarded her marriage contract with the wealthy Trader as void. She'd stay here in Kelsingra and wait for her grubby river captain to return. And even if Sedric could not understand what attracted her to the man, he was willing to admit that she seemed happier living in a stone hut with Leftrin than she had ever been in Hest's mansion.

And for himself?

He glanced over at Carson and for a moment just looked

at him. The hunter was a big, bluff man, well-kept in his own rough way. Stronger than Hest could ever be. Gentler than Hest would ever be.

When he thought about it, he was happier living in a stone hut with Carson than he had ever been in Hest's mansion. No deceit left in his life. No pretence. And a little copper dragon who loved him. His longing for Bingtown faded.

'What are you smiling about?'

Sedric shook his head. Then he answered truthfully. 'Carson, I'm happy with you.'

The smile that lit the hunter's face at the simple words was honest joy. 'And I'm happy with you, Bingtown boy. And we'll both be happier tonight if we have this firewood stacked and ready.' Carson stooped, seized the strap of his bundle, and heaved it up onto his shoulder. He came back to his feet easily and waited for Sedric to do the same.

Sedric copied him, grunting as he hefted his own bundle onto his shoulder. He managed to remain upright only after taking two staggering steps to catch his balance. 'Sa's breath, it's heavy!'

'Yes it is.' Carson grinned at him. 'It's twice what you could carry a month ago. Proud of you. Let's go.'

Proud of him.

'I'm proud of myself,' Sedric muttered, and fell into step behind him.

Day the 7th of the Hope Moon
Year the 7th of the Independent Alliance of Traders

From Detozi, Keeper of the Birds, Trehaug to Reyall, Acting Keeper of the Birds, Bingtown

Dear nephew, greetings and good wishes to you.

Erek and I both counsel you to keep your temper in this matter. Do not let Kim provoke you to anger or to accusations we cannot prove. This is not the first time we have had unpleasant correspondence with him. I still believe that he rose to his post by bribery but as that would indicate he has friends on the Cassarick Council who confirmed his promotion, taking a complaint there may get us no results.

I still know a number of his journeymen, for they began their apprenticeships here with me in Trehaug. I will make a few quiet enquiries among them. In the meantime, you have been wise to pass the message on to your masters and defer the handling of it to them. Until your Master status is confirmed, it is difficult for you to speak to Kim as an equal. Both Erek and I question the wisdom that assigned this difficult question to you.

For now, you have done all that can be expected of you in your position. Erek and I continue to have the highest confidence in your bird-handling abilities.

In kinder news, the two speckled swift birds that you sent to us as a wedding gift have selected mates here and begun to breed. I look forward to shipping some of their youngsters to you soon, so that we may time their return flights. I have great enthusiasm for this project.

Erek and I are still discussing which of us will relocate permanently; it is a difficult question for us. At our ages, we desire to be wed quickly and quietly, but neither of our families seemed so inclined. Pity us!

With affection and respect,
Aunt Detozi

CHAPTER THREE

Pathways

Thymara had lived all her life in the Rain Wilds, but she had never experienced rain like this. In her childhood in Trehaug and Cassarick, the immense trees that populated the banks of the Rain Wild River had spread their many layers of canopy and shade over those tree-house cities. The driving rains of winter had been thwarted and diverted by the infinitude of leaves between her and the sky. Of course, they had blocked the direct sunlight as well, but Thymara had felt differently about that. If she wanted sunlight, she could climb for it. She could not recall that she had ever wished to feel the full onslaught of a rain storm.

Here, she had no choice. The meadow that edged the river was not like the shadowy undergrowth of the Rain Wilds. Thick grasses grew hip- to shoulder-deep. Rather than being swampy, the earth was firm under her feet, and salted with rocks, a bewildering array of hard chunks of different textures and colours. She often wondered where they all came from and how they had come to be here. Today the wind swept across the naked lands and slapped the unimpeded rain into her face and down her collar. Her worn clothes, weakened by too-frequent contact with the acidic waters of the Rain Wild River, were no protection. Limp and soaked, they clung to her skin. And she could look forward to being cold and wet all day. She rubbed her red, chilled hands together. It was hard enough to hunt well with the battered assortment of gear she had left. Numbed hands only made it harder.

She heard Tats coming before he called to her: the wet grass slapping against his legs and his hard breathing as he ran up behind her. She did not turn to him until he breathlessly called to her, 'Going hunting? Want some help?'

'Why not? I could use someone to carry my kill back to the dragons.' She didn't mention what they both knew: that Carson didn't like any of them hunting alone. He claimed to have seen signs of big predators, ones that might be large enough to attack a human. 'Large game usually attracts large predators,' he had said. 'When you hunt, take a partner.' It was not so much that Carson had authority over them as that he had experience.

Tats grinned at her, his teeth white in his finely-scaled face. 'Oh. So you don't think I'm capable of bringing down meat that you'd have to help me drag back?'

She grinned back. 'You're a good enough hunter, Tats. But we both know I'm better.'

'You were born to it. Your father taught you from the time you could teeter along a tree branch. I think I'm pretty good, for someone who came to it later.' He fell into step beside her. It was a bit awkward on the narrow trail. He bumped elbows with her as they walked, but he neither moved ahead of her nor fell back. As they entered the eaves of the forest, the meadow grasses grew shallower and then gave way to a layer of leaf mould and low-growing bushes. The trees cut the wind, for which Thymara was grateful. She bobbed her head in acceptance of Tats's compliment.

'You're a lot better than when we left Trehaug. And I think you may adapt to this ground hunting faster than I will. This place is so different from home.'

'Home,' he said, and she could not tell if the word was bitter or sweet to him. 'I think this is home now,' he added, startling her.

She gave him a sideways glance as they continued to push forward through the brush. 'Home? Forever?'

He thrust out his arm toward her and pushed up his sleeve, baring his scaled flesh. 'I can't imagine going back to Trehaug. Not like this. You?'

She didn't need to flex her wings, nor look at the thick black claws she'd had since birth. 'If acceptance means home, then Trehaug was never home for me.'

She pushed regrets and thoughts of Trehaug aside. It was time to hunt. Sintara was hungry. Today Thymara wanted to find a game trail, a fresh one they hadn't hunted before. Until they struck one, it would be hard going. They were both breathing hard, but Tats was less winded than he would have been when they first left Trehaug. Life on the Tarman expedition had muscled and hardened all of them, she thought approvingly. And all of the keepers had grown, the boys achieving growth spurts that were almost alarming. Tats was taller now and his shoulders broader. His dragon was changing him, too. He alone of the keepers had been fully human in appearance when they had left Trehaug. Offspring of the freed slave population that had immigrated to Trehaug during the war with Chalced, his slavery as an infant had been clearly marked on his face with his former owner's tattoo. A spider web had been flung across his left cheek, while a small running horse had been inked beside his nose. Those had changed as his dragon had begun to scale him. The tattoos were stylized designs now, scales rather than ink under skin. His dark hair and dark eyes remained the same as they had always been, but she suspected that some of his height was due to his transformation to Elderling rather than being natural growth. His fingernails gleamed as green as Fente, his ill-tempered little queen dragon. When the light struck his skin, it woke green highlights on his scaling. He was leaf shadow and pine needle, the greens of her fores . . . She reined in her thoughts.

'So. You think you'll live out your life here?' It was a strange concept to her. She'd been at a bit of a loss since they'd achieved their goal of finding the city. When they all left Trehaug, they had signed contracts, acknowledging that their goal was to settle the dragons upriver. Finding the legendary city of Kelsingra had scarcely been mentioned. She'd taken the job to escape her old life. She'd thought no further in her plans than that. Now she ventured to picture herself living here forever. Never facing again the people who had made her an outcast.

The other half of that image was never going home again. She hadn't liked her mother; and it had been mutual. But she had been very close to her father. Would she never see him again? Would he never know she'd achieved her goal? No, that was a ridiculous thought. Captain Leftrin was going to make a supply run back to Cassarick. Once he arrived there, the news of their find would swarm out like gnats to every ear in the Rain Wilds. Her father would soon hear of it. Would he come here to see for himself? Would she, perhaps, go home to visit him? A night ago, at the meeting, Leftrin had asked if anyone wanted to go back to the city. A silence had fallen after his query. The keepers had looked at one another. Leave their dragons? Go back to Trehaug, to return to their lives as pariahs there? No. For the others, the answer had been easy.

It had been less easy for her. There were times when she

wanted to leave her dragon. Sintara was not the most endearing creature in the world. She ordered Thymara about, exposed her to danger for her own amusement, and once had nearly drowned her in the river in her haste to get a fish. Sintara had never apologized for that. The dragon was as sarcastic and cynical as she was magnificent. But even if Thymara was considering abandoning her dragon, she did not want to get back on the *Tarman* and go downriver. She was still sick of being on the barge and of the endless journeying in close quarters. Going back to Trehaug with Leftrin would mean leaving all her friends, and never knowing what they discovered in the Elderling city. So for now she'd stay here, to be with her friends and continue her tasks as a hunter for the dragons until Leftrin returned with fresh supplies. And after that? 'Do you plan to live here forever?' she asked Tats again when she realized he hadn't answered her first question.

He replied quietly, in keeping with their soft tread through the forest. 'Where else could we go?' He made a small gesture at her and then at his own face. 'Our dragons have marked us as theirs. And while Fente is making more progress toward flying than Sintara is, I don't think either queen will be self-sufficient soon. Even if they could hunt to feed themselves, they'd still want us here with them, for grooming and companionship. We're Elderlings now, Thymara. Elderlings have always lived alongside dragons. And this is where the dragons are staying. So, yes, I suppose I'm here for the rest of my life. Or for as long as Fente is.'

He lifted a hand and pointed silently in what he thought was a better direction. She decided to agree with him and took the lead. He spoke from behind her as they slipped single-file through the forest. 'Are you saying what I think you're saying? Are you truly considering going back to Trehaug? Do you think that's even possible for ones like us?

I know that Sintara doesn't always treat you well. But where else can you live now? You have wings now, Thymara. I can't see you climbing and running through the tree tops like you used to. Anywhere you go, people are going to stare at you. Or worse.'

Thymara folded her wings more tightly to her body. Then she frowned. She hadn't been aware she was going to do that. The foreign appendages were becoming more and more a part of her. They still made her back ache and annoyed her daily when she tried to make her worn clothing fit around them. But she moved them now without focusing on the task.

'They're beautiful,' Tats said as if he could hear her thoughts. 'They're worth anything you have to endure for them.'

'They're useless,' Thymara retorted, trying not to let his compliment please her. 'I'll never fly. They're like a mockery.'

'No. You'll never fly, but I still think they're beautiful.'

Now his agreement that she could never fly stung more sharply than his compliment could soothe. 'Rapskal thinks I'll fly,' she retorted.

Tats sighed. 'Rapskal thinks that he and Heeby will visit the moon some day. Thymara, I think your wings would have to grow much bigger before you could fly. So big that perhaps you'd be bent over by the weight of them when you walked. Rapskal doesn't stop to think how things really work. He is full of his wishes and dreams, now more than ever. And we both know he wants you and will say anything to you that will win your favour.'

She glanced back at him, a sour smile twisting her lips. 'Unlike you,' she observed.

He grinned at her, his dark eyes alight with challenge. 'You know I want you. I'm honest about that. I'm always honest with you, Thymara. I think you should appreciate the truth from a man who respects your intelligence rather than preferring a crazy man full of wild compliments.'

'I value your honesty,' she said and then bit her tongue before she could remind him that he hadn't always been so honest with her. He hadn't told her that he was mating with Jerd. But neither had Rapskal admitted it to her. Of course, in Rapskal's case, he hadn't really concealed it from her. He simply hadn't thought it all that important.

After all, most of the male keepers seemed to have enjoyed Jerd's favours. And probably continued to, for all Thymara knew. The question came back to her. Why was it so important to her? Tats wasn't with Jerd any more. He didn't seem to attach any real importance to what he had done. So why did it matter so much to her?

Thymara slowed her pace. They were approaching an opening in the forest and where the trees thinned there was more light ahead. She made a motion to Tats to be quiet and slow his pace, took the best of her unsatisfactory arrows and set it to the bow. Time to move her eyes more than her body. She set her shoulder to a tree to steady her stance and began a slow survey of the forest meadow before them.

She could focus her eyes but not her unruly thoughts. Jerd had been very quick to cast off the rules of their Rain Wilds upbringing. Girls such as she and Jerd and Sylve were not allowed to take husbands. All knew that Rain Wild children who were scaled or clawed at birth would likely not grow to adulthood. They were not worth the resources it would take to raise them, for even if they lived, they seldom bore viable children. Those who tried usually died in labour, leaving the monsters that survived the births to be exposed. Husbands were forbidden to those strongly Touched by the Rain Wilds, as deeply forbidden as mating outside the marriage bed was forbidden to all Rain Wilders. But Jerd had chosen to ignore both those rules. Jerd was lovely, with her fair hair and piercing eyes and lithe body. She had chosen which keepers she wished to bed, and then picked them off one at a time like a cat at a mouse nest, and with as little compunction about the outcome of her appetite. Even when some of the youths came to blows over her, she seemed to accept it as her due. Thymara had been torn between envy for the freedom Jerd had claimed and fury at the swathe of emotional discord she cut through the company.

Eventually, she'd paid the price, one that Thymara did not like to remember. When her unlikely pregnancy ended in a premature birth, Thymara had been one of the women to attend her. She had seen the tiny body of the fish-girl before they delivered the corpse to Veras, Jerd's dragon. It was strange to think that Thymara had taken a lesson from that, but Jerd had seemed unaffected by it. Thymara had refrained from sharing her body with any of the keepers, while Jerd continued to take her pleasure where ever she pleased. It made no sense. Some days she resented Jerd's stupidity that could bring trouble for all of them; but more often she envied how the other girl had seized her freedom and her choices and seemed not to care what anyone else thought of her.

Freedom and choices. She could seize the one and make the other. 'I'm staying,' she said quietly. 'Not for my dragon. Not even for my friends. I'm staying here for me. To make a place where I do belong.'

Tats looked over at her. 'Not for me?' he asked without guile.

She shook her head. 'Honesty,' she reminded him quietly.

He glanced away from her. 'Well, at least you didn't say you were staying for Rapskal.' Then, quite suddenly, Tats made a sound, a hoarse intake of breath. A moment later Thymara whispered on a sigh, 'I see him.'

The animal that was moving cautiously from the perimeter of the forest and into the open meadow was magnificent. Thymara was slowly becoming accustomed to the great size that the hoofed creatures of this dry forest could attain. Even so, this was the largest she had seen yet. She could have slung a sleeping net between the reaches of his two flat-pronged antlers. They were not the tree-branch-like horns she had seen on the other deer of this area. These reminded her of hands with wide-spread fingers. The creature that bore them was worthy of such a massive crown. His shoulders were massive, and a large hummock of meaty flesh rode them. He paced like a rich man strolling through a market, setting one careful foot down at a time. His large, dark eyes swept the clearing once, and then he dismissed his caution. Thymara was not surprised. What sort of predator could menace a beast of that size? She drew the bowstring taut and held her breath, but her hope was small. At best, she could probably deliver a flesh wound through that thick hide. If she injured him sufficiently or made him bleed enough, she and Tats could track him to his death place. But this would not be a clean kill for any of them.

She gritted her teeth. This could very well take all day, but the amount of meat would be well worth it. One more pace and she would have a clear shot at him.

A scarlet lightning bolt fell from the sky. The impact of the red dragon hitting the immense deer shook the earth. Thymara's startled response was to release her arrow: it shot off in wobbly flight and struck nothing. In the same instant, there was a loud snap as the deer's spine broke. It bellowed in agony, a sound cut short as the dragon's jaws closed on the deer's throat. Heeby jerked her prey off the ground and half-sheared the deer's head from his neck. Then she dropped it before lunging in to rip an immense mouthful of skin and gut from the deer's soft belly. She threw her head back and gulped the meat down. Dangling tendrils of gut stretched between her jaws and her prey.

'Sweet Sa have mercy!' Tats sighed. At his words, the dragon turned sharply toward them. Her eyes glittered with anger and spun scarlet. Blood dripped from her bared teeth.

'Your kill,' Tats assured her. 'We're leaving now.' He seized Thymara by the upper arm and pulled her back into the shelter of the forest.

She still gripped her bow. 'My arrow! That was the best one I had. Did you see where it went?'

'No.' There was a world of denial in Tats' single word. He hadn't seen it fly and he wasn't interested in finding it. He pulled her deeper into the forest and then started to circle the meadow. 'Damn her!' he said quietly. 'That was a lot of meat.'

'Can't blame her,' Thymara pointed out. 'She's just doing what a dragon does.'

'I know. She's just doing what a dragon does, and how I wish Fente would do it also.' He shook his head guiltily at his own words, as if shamed to find fault with his dragon. 'But until she and Sintara get off the ground, we're stuck with providing meat for them. So we'd best get hunting again. Ah. Here we are.'

He'd struck the game trail that had brought the big buck to the forest meadow. Reflexively, Thymara cast her gaze upward. But the trees here were not the immense giants that she was accustomed to. At home, she would have scaled a tree and then moved silently from limb to reaching limb, travelling unseen from tree to tree as she stalked the game trail. She would have hunted her prey from above. But half these trees were bare of leaves in the winter, offering no cover. Nor did the branches reach and intermingle with their neighbours as they did in her Rain Wild home. 'We'll have to hunt on foot, and quietly,' Tats answered her thoughts. 'But first, we'll have to get away from Heeby's kill site. Even I can smell death.'

'Not to mention hear her,' Thymara answered. The dragon fed noisily, crunching bones and making sounds of pleasure with each tearing bite. As they both paused, she gave a sudden snarl, like a cat playing with dead prey; a large cracking sound followed it.

'Probably the antlers,' Thymara said.

Tats nodded. 'I've never seen a deer that big.'

'I've never seen any animal that big, except dragons.'

'Dragons aren't animals,' he corrected her. He was leading and she was following. They trod lightly and spoke softly.

She chuckled quietly. 'Then what are they?'

'Dragons. The same way that we aren't animals. They think, they talk. If that's what makes us not animals, then dragons are not animals, too.'

She was quiet for a time, mulling it over. She wasn't sure she agreed. 'Sounds like you've given this some thought.'

'I have.' He ducked low to go under an overhanging branch and she copied him. 'Ever since Fente and I bonded. By the third night, I was wondering, what was she? She wasn't my pet, and she wasn't like a wild monkey or a bird. Not like the tame monkeys that a few of the pickers used to go after high fruit. And I wasn't her pet or her servant, even if I was doing a lot of things for her. Finding her food, picking vermin away from her eyes, cleaning her wings.'

'Are you sure you're not her servant?' Thymara asked with a sour smile. 'Or her slave?'

He winced at the word and she reminded herself whom she was talking to. He'd been born a slave. His mother had been enslaved as punishment for her crimes, so when he was born, he was born a slave. He might have no memory of that servitude, for he had been a very small child when they escaped it. But he'd grown up with the marks on his face, and the knowledge that many people thought differently of him as a result.

They had come to a low stone wall, grown over with vines. Beyond it, several small huts had collapsed on their own foundations. Trees grew in and around them. Thymara eyed them thoughtfully but Tats pressed on. Ruins in the forest were too common even to comment on. If Sintara were not so hungry, Thymara would have poked around in the shells looking for anything useful. A few of the keepers had found tool parts, hammer heads, axe bits and even a knife blade in the debris of some of the collapsed huts. Some of the tools had been of Elderling make, still holding an edge after all the years. One collapsed table had held cups and the remains of broken plates. Whatever had ended Kelsingra had ended it swiftly. The inhabitants had not carried their tools and other possessions away. Who knew what she might find buried in the rubble? But her dragon's hunger pressed on her mind like a knife at her back. She'd have to come back later when she had more time. If Sintara ever let her have time to herself.

Tats's next words answered her question and her thoughts.

'I'm not her slave because I don't do those things the way a slave would do them. At first it seemed almost like she was my child or something. I took pride in making her happy and seeing how pretty I could make her. It was really satisfying to put meat or a big fish in front of her and feel how good it made her feel to eat.'

'Glamour,' Thymara said bitterly. 'We all know about dragon glamour. Sintara has used it on me more than once. I find myself doing something because I think I really want to do it. Then, when I've finished, I realize that it wasn't my desire at all. It was just Sintara pushing me, making me want to do whatever she wants me to do.' Just the thought of how the big blue queen could manipulate her made her want to grind her teeth.

'I know Sintara does that to you. I've seen it happen a few times. We'll be in the middle of talking about something, something important, and suddenly you stop even looking at me and say that you have to go hunting right away.'

Thymara kept a guilty silence. She didn't want to tell him he was mistaken, that going hunting was her best excuse for avoiding him whenever their conversations became too intense.

Tats seemed unaware of her lack of assent. 'But Fente doesn't do that to me. Well, hardly ever. I think she loves me, Thymara. The way she's changing me, being so careful about it. And after I've fed her and groomed her, sometimes she just wants me to stay right there with her and keep her company. Because she enjoys my company. That's something I've never had before. My mom was always asking the neighbours to watch me when I was little. And when she killed that man, she just took off. I still think it was an accident, that she only meant to rob him. Maybe she thought she'd just have to hide for a short time. Maybe she meant to come back for me. She never did. When she knew she was in trouble, she just ran away and left me to whatever might happen to me. But Fente wants me to be with her. Maybe she doesn't really "love" me, but she sure wants me around.' He gave a half shrug as he walked, as if she would think him sentimental. 'The only other one who ever seemed to like me was your father, and even he always kept a little distance between us. I know he didn't like me spending so much time with you.'

'He was afraid of what our neighbours might think. Or my mother. The rules were strict, Tats. I wasn't supposed to let anyone court me. Because it was forbidden for me to get married. Or to have any child. Or to even take a lover.'

Tats gestured in wonder at the antler scores on a tree they passed. The deer that had done it must have been just as immense as the one Heeby had just killed. She touched them with a finger. Antler scores? Or claw marks? No, she couldn't even imagine a tree cat that large.

'I knew his rules for you. And for a long time, I didn't even think of you that way. I wasn't that interested in girls then. I just envied what you had, a home and parents and a regular job and regular meals. I wished I could have it, too.'

He paused at a split in the game trail and raised an eyebrow at her.

'Go left. It looks more travelled. Tats, my home was not as wonderful as you thought it was. My mother hated me. I shamed her.'

'I think . . . well, I'm not sure she hated you. I think maybe the neighbours made her ashamed of wanting to love you. But even if she did hate you, she never left you. Or threw you out.' He sounded almost stubborn in his insistence.

'Except that first time when she gave me to the midwife to expose,' Thymara pointed out bitterly. 'My father was the one that brought me back and said he was going to give me a chance. He forced me on her.'

Tats was unconvinced. 'And I think that's what really shamed her. Not what you were, but that she hadn't stood up to the midwife and said she was keeping you, claws and all.'

'Maybe,' Thymara replied. She didn't want to think about it. Useless to think about it now, so far away from it in both time and place. It wasn't as if she could go and ask her mother what she had felt. She knew her father had loved her, and she'd always hold that knowledge close. But she also knew he had agreed with the rules that said she must never have a lover or a husband, never produce a child. Every time she thought of crossing that boundary, she felt she was betraying him and what he had taught her. He had loved her. He'd given her rules to keep her safe. Could she be wiser than he was in this matter?

It seemed as if it should be her decision. Actually, yes, it was her decision. But if she decided her father was wrong, if she decided she was free to take a mate, did that somehow damage her love for him? His love for her? She knew, without doubt, that he would disapprove of her even considering such a thing.

And even at this distance, his disapproval stung. Perhaps more so because she was so far from home and alone. What would he expect of her? Would he be disappointed if he knew how much kissing and touching she'd indulged in with Tats?

He would. She shook her head and Tats glanced back at her. 'What is it?'

'Nothing. Just thinking.'

But as she said it, she became aware of a rhythmic pounding. Something was running, with no effort at stealth, coming up the trail behind them.

'What is that?' Tats asked and then glanced at the trees nearby. She knew what he was thinking. If they had to take refuge, climbing a tree might be their best hope.

'Two legs,' she said abruptly, surprising even herself that she had deduced that from the sounds.

An instant later, Rapskal came into view. 'There you are!' he shouted merrily. 'Heeby said you were nearby.'

He was grinning, full of joy at finding them. Full of pleasure in life itself, as he always was. Thymara could seldom look at Rapskal without returning that smile. He'd changed a great deal since they had left Trehaug. The boyishness of his face had been planed away by hardship and the approach of manhood. He'd shot up, taller than anyone should grow in a matter of months. Like her, he had been born marked by the Rain Wilds. But since their expedition had begun, he'd grown lean and lithe. His scaling was unmistakably scarlet now, to complement Heeby's hide. His eyes had always been unusual, a very pale blue. But now the lambent blue glow that some Rain Wilders acquired with age gleamed constantly in them, and the soft blue sometimes had the hard silver bite of steel. Instead of becoming more dragonlike, the features of his face were chiselled to classical humanity: he had a straight nose, flat cheeks and his jaw had asserted itself in the last couple of months.

He met her gaze, pleased at her stare. She dropped her eyes. When had his face become so compelling?

'We were trying to hunt,' Tats responded irritably to Rapskal's greeting. 'But between you and your dragon, I suspect anything edible will have been scared out of the area.'

The smile faded slightly from Rapskal's face. 'I'm sorry,' he responded sincerely. 'I just wasn't thinking. Heeby was so glad to find so much food and it feels so good when she's happy and has a full belly. It made me want to be with my friends.'

'Yes, well, Fente isn't so fortunate. Nor Sintara. We've got to hunt to feed our dragons. And if Thymara had brought down that deer, instead of Heeby crashing on it, we would have had enough to give both of them a decent meal.'

Rapskal set his jaw and sounded defensive as he insisted, 'Heeby didn't know you were nearby until after she'd killed her meat. She wasn't trying to take it from you.'

'I know,' Tats replied grumpily. 'But all the same, between the two of you we've wasted half the day.'

'I'm sorry.' Rapskal's voice had gone stiff. 'I said that already.'

'It's all right,' Thymara said hastily. It was unlike Rapskal to become prickly. 'I know that you and Heeby didn't mean to spoil our hunt.' She gave Tats a rebuking look. Fente was just as wilful as Sintara. He should know that there would not have been anything Rapskal could have done to stop Heeby from taking the deer, even if he'd known they were stalking the same prey. The lost meat was not the main source of Tats's irritation.

'Well, there's a way that you can make it up,' Tats declared. 'When Heeby's finished, maybe she can make a second kill. One for our dragons.'

Rapskal stared at him. 'When Heeby has eaten, she'll need to sleep. And then finish off whatever is left of the meat. And, well, dragons don't hunt or make kills for other dragons. It's just not . . . just not something she'd ever do.' At the stern look on Tats's face, he added, 'You know, the real problem is that your dragons don't fly. If they would fly, they could make their own kills and I'm sure they'd love it as much as Heeby does. You need to teach them to fly.'

Tats stared at him. Sparks of anger lit his eyes. 'Thanks for telling me the obvious, Rapskal. My dragon can't fly.' He rolled his eyes in exasperation. 'That's a real insight into the problem. So useful to know. Now, I need to go hunting.' He turned abruptly and stalked off.

Thymara watched him go, open-mouthed. 'Tats!' she called. 'Wait! You know we aren't supposed to hunt alone!' Then she turned back to Rapskal. 'I'm sorry. I don't know what made him so angry.'

'Yes, you do,' he cheerily called her on her lie. He caught up her hand and held it as he spoke on. 'And so do I. But it doesn't matter. You were the one I wanted to talk to anyway. Thymara, when Heeby wakes up from her gorge, do you want to go to Kelsingra? There's something there I want to show you. Something amazing.'

'What?'

He shook his head, his face full of mischief. 'It's us. That's all I'm going to tell you. It's us. You and me. And I can't explain it; I just have to take you there. Please?' He was bouncing on his toes as he spoke, incredibly pleased with himself. His grin was wide and she had to return his smile even as she reluctantly shook her head.

Kelsingra. Temptation burned hot. He would have to ask Heeby to fly her over. Riding on a dragon! Up in the air over the river. It was a terrifying yet fascinating thought.

But Kelsingra? She was not as certain about that part.

She'd been to the Elderling city exactly once and only for a few hours. The problem had been the river crossing. The river was rain-full now, swift and deep. It wandered in its wide riverbed during the summer, but now it filled it from bank to bank. A wide curve in the river meant that the current swept most swiftly and deeply right past the broken docks of ancient Kelsingra. Since they'd arrived, the Tarman had made two forays for the far shore. Each time, the current had swept the barge swiftly past the city and downriver. Each time, the liveship and his crew had battled their way back to the other side of the river and then back to the village. It had been horribly frustrating for all of them, to have come so far seeking the legendary city, and then not be able to dock there. Captain Leftrin had promised that when he returned from Cassarick he'd bring sturdy line and spikes and all else needed to create a temporary dock at Kelsingra.

But the young keepers had been unable to wait that long. Thymara and a handful of the other keepers had made the crossing once in two of the ship's boats. It had demanded a full morning of strenuous rowing to cross the river. Even so, they had been pushed far downstream of the city's broken stone docks and had to make their tedious way back. They'd arrived in late afternoon with only a few hours of rainy daylight left in which to explore the massive city of wide streets and tall buildings.

Thymara had always lived in a forest. That had been a strange thing to realize. She'd always thought of Trehaug as a city, a grand city at that, the largest in the Rain Wilds. But it wasn't.

Kelsingra was a real city. The hike from the outskirts to the old city dock, portaging their boats, had proved that to her. They had left their small boats stacked there and ventured into the city. The streets were paved with stone and incredibly wide and empty of life. The buildings were made of immense blocks of black stone, much of it veined with silver. The blocks were huge and she could not imagine how they had been cut, let alone transported and lifted into place. The buildings had towered tall, not as tall as the trees of the Rain Wilds but taller than any human-created thing had a right to be. The structures were straight-sided, uncompromisingly man-made. Windows gaped above them, dark and empty. And it had been silent. The wind had whispered as it crept through the city as if fearful of waking it to life. The keepers who had made the crossing had kept to their huddle as they trudged through the streets and their voices had been muted and swallowed by that silence. Even Tats had been subdued. Davvie and Lecter had gripped hands as they walked. Harrikin had peered about as if trying to wake from a peculiar dream.

Sylve had slipped close to Thymara. 'Do you hear that?'

'What?'

'Whispering. People talking.'

Thymara had listened. 'It's just the wind,' she had said, and Tats had nodded. But Harrikin had stepped back and taken Sylve's hand. 'It's not just the wind,' he had asserted, and then they hadn't spoken of it again.

They'd explored the portion of the city closest to the old docks and ventured into a few of the buildings. The structures were on a scale more suited to dragons than humans. Thymara, who had grown up in the tiny chambers of a tree-house home, had felt like an insect. The ceilings had been dim and distant in the fading afternoon light, the windows set high in the walls. Inside, there lingered the remnants of furnishings. In some, that had been no more than heaps of long-rotted wood on the floor, or a tapestry that crumbled into dangling, dusty threads at a touch. Light shone in colours through the streaked stained-glass windows, casting faded images of dragons and Elderlings on the stone floors.

In a few places, the magic of the Elderlings lingered. In one building, an interior room sprang to light when a keeper ventured into the chamber. Music, faint and uncertain, began to play, and a dusty perfume ventured out into the still air. A sound like distant laughter had twittered and then abruptly faded with the music. The group of keepers had fled back to the open air.

Tats had taken Thymara's hand and she had been glad of that warm clasp. He had asked her quietly, 'Do you think there's even a chance that some Elderlings survived here? That we might meet them, or that they might be hiding and watching us?'

She'd given him a shaky smile. 'You're teasing me, aren't you? To try to frighten me.'

His dark eyes had been solemn, even apprehensive. 'No. I'm not.' Looking around them, he had added, 'I'm already uneasy and I've been trying not to think about it. I'm asking you because I'm genuinely wondering.'

She replied quickly to his unlucky words, 'I don't think they're here still. At least, not in the flesh.'

His laugh had been brief. 'And that is supposed to reassure me?'

'No. It's not.' She felt decidedly nervous. 'Where's Rapskal?' she had asked suddenly.

Tats had halted and looked around. The others had ranged ahead of them.

Thymara had raised her voice. 'Where's Rapskal?'

'I think he went ahead,' Alum called back to them.

Tats kept hold of her hand. 'He'll be fine. Come on. Let's look around a bit more.'

They had wandered on. The emptiness of the broad plazas had been uncanny. It had seemed to her that after years of abandonment, life should have ventured back into this place. Grasses should have grown in the cracks in the paving stones. There should have been frogs in the green-slimed fountains, bird nests on building ledges and vines twining through windows. But there weren't. Oh, there had been tiny footholds of vegetation here and there, yellow lichen caught between the fingers of a statue, moss in the cracked base of a fountain but not what there should have been. The city was too aggressively a city still, still a place for Elderlings, dragons and humans, even after all these years. The wilderness, the trees and vines and tangled vegetation that had formed the backdrop of Thymara's life had been able to gain no foothold there. That made her feel an outsider as well.

Statues in dry fountains had stared down at them, and Thymara had felt no sense of welcome. More than once as she stared up at the carved images of Elderling women, she had wondered how her own appearance might change. They were tall and graceful creatures, with eyes of silver and copper and purple, their faces smoothly scaled. Some of their heads were crested with fleshy crowns. Elegant enamel gowns draped them, and their long slender fingers were adorned with jewelled rings. Would it be so terrible, she wondered, to become one of them? She considered Tats: his changes were not unattractive.

In one building, rows of tiered stone benches looked down at a dais. Bas reliefs of dragons and Elderlings, their mosaic colours still bright after all the years, cavorted on the walls. In that room, she had finally heard what the others were whispering about. Low, conversational voices, rising and falling. The cadence of the language was unfamiliar, and yet the meaning of the words had pushed at the edges of her mind.

'Tats,' she had said, more to hear her own voice than to call his name.

He had nodded abruptly. 'Let's go back outside.'

She had been glad to keep pace with his brisk stride as they hurried out into the fading daylight.

Some of the others had soon joined them and made a silent but mutual decision to return to the river's edge and spend the night in a small stone hut there. It was made of ordinary river stone, and the hard-packed silt in the corners spoke of ancient floods that had inundated it. Doors and windows had long ago crumbled into dust. They had built a smouldering fire of wet driftwood in the ancient hearth, and huddled close to its warmth. It was only when the rest of their party joined them that Rapskal's absence had become obvious.

'We need to go back and look for him,' she had insisted, and they had been splitting into search parties of three when he came in from the rising storm. Rain had plastered his hair to his skull and his clothing was soaked. He was shaking with cold but grinning insanely.

'I love this city!' he had exclaimed. 'There's so much to see and do here. This is where we belong. It's where we've always belonged!' He had wanted them all to go with him, back into the night to explore more. He had been baffled by their refusal, but had finally settled down next to Thymara.

The voices of wind, rain and the river's constant roar had

filled the night. From the distant hills had come wailing howls. 'Wolves!' Nortel had whispered and they had all shivered. Wolves were creatures of legend for them. Those sounds had almost drowned out the muttering voices. Almost. She had not slept well.

They had left Kelsingra in the next dawn. The rain had been pouring down, wind sweeping hard down the river. They had known they would battle most of the day to regain the other side. In the distance, Thymara could hear the roaring of hungry dragons. Sintara's displeasure thundered in Thymara's mind, and by the uneasy expression on the faces of the other keepers, she knew they were suffering similarly. They could stay in Kelsingra no longer that day. As they pulled away from the shore, Rapskal had gazed back regretfully. 'I'll be back,' he said, as if he were promising the city itself. 'I'll be back every chance I get!'

Thanks to Heeby's powers of flight, he had kept that promise. But Thymara hadn't been back since that first visit. Curiosity and wariness battled in her whenever she thought of returning to the city.

'Please. I have to show you something there!'

Rapskal's words dragged her back to the present. 'I can't. I have to get meat for Sintara.'

'Please!' Rapskal cocked his head. His loose dark hair fell half across his eyes and he stared at her appealingly.

'Rapskal, I can't. She's hungry.' Why were the words so hard to say?

'Well . . . she should be flying and hunting. Maybe she'd try harder if you let her be hungry for a day or—'

'Rapskal! Would you let Heeby just be hungry?'

He kicked, half angrily, half shamed, at the thick layer of forest detritus. 'No,' he admitted. 'No, I couldn't. Not my Heeby. But she's sweet. Not like Sintara.'

That stung. 'Sintara's not so bad!' She was, really. But that was between her and her dragon. 'I can't go with you, Rapskal. I have to go hunting now.'

Rapskal flung up his hands, surrendering. 'Oh, very well.' He favoured her with a smile. 'Tomorrow then. Maybe it will be less rainy. We could go early, and spend the whole day in the city.'

'Rapskal, I can't!' She longed to soar through the morning sky on a dragon's back. Longed to feel what it was to fly, study just how the dragon did it. 'I can't be gone a whole day. I need to hunt for Sintara, every day. Until she's fed, I can't do anything else. Can't patch the roof of our hut, can't mend my trousers, can't do anything. She nags me in her thoughts; I feel her hunger. Don't you remember what that was like?'

She studied his face as he knit his finely-scaled brows. 'I do,' he admitted at last. 'Yes. Well.' He sighed abruptly. 'I'll help you hunt today,' he offered.

'And I would thank you for that, and it would help today.' She well knew that Tats had stalked off without her. There'd be no catching up with him. 'But it won't do a thing about Sintara being hungry tomorrow.'

He bit his upper lip and wriggled thoughtfully as if he were a child. 'I see. Very well. I'll help you hunt today to feed your lazy dragon. And tomorrow, I'll think of something so that she can be fed without you spending the whole day on it. Then would you come with me to Kelsingra?'

'I would. With my most hearty thanks!'

'Oh, you will be more than thankful at what I wish to show you! And now, let's hunt!'

'Get up!'

Selden came awake shaking and disoriented. Usually they let him sleep at this time of day, didn't they? What time of day was it? The light from a lantern blinded him. He sat up slowly, his arm across his eyes to shelter them. 'What do you want of me?' he asked. He knew they wouldn't answer him. He spoke the words to remind himself that he was a man, not a dumb animal.

But this man did speak to him. 'Stand up. Turn around and let me take a look at you.'

Selden's eyes had adjusted a bit. The tent was not completely dark. Daylight leaked in through the patches and seams, but the brightness of the lantern still made his eyes stream tears. Now he knew the man. Not one of those who tended him, who gave him stale bread and scummy water and half-rotted vegetables, nor the one who liked to poke him with a long stick for the amusement of the spectators. No. This was the man who believed he owned Selden. He was a small man with a large, bulbous nose, and he always carried his purse with him, a large bag that he carried over one shoulder as if he could never bear to be parted from his coin for long.

Selden stood up slowly. He had not become any more naked than he had been, but the man's appraising scrutiny made it feel as if he had. His visitors from earlier in the day were there also. Big Nose turned to a man dressed in the Chalcedean style. 'There he is. That's what you'd be buying. Seen enough?'

'He looks thin.' The man spoke hesitantly, as if he were trying to bargain but feared to anger the seller. 'Sickly.'

Big Nose gave a harsh bark of laughter. 'Well, this is the one I've got. If you can find a dragon-man in better condition, you'd best go buy him instead.'

There was a moment of silence. The Chalcedean merchant tried again. 'The man I represent will want proof that he is what you say he is. Give me something to send him, and I'll advise him to meet your price.'

Big Nose mulled this over for a short time. 'Like what?' he asked sullenly.

'A finger. Or a toe.' At the outrage on Big Nose's face, the merchant amended, 'Or just a joint off one of his fingers. A token. Of good faith in the bargaining. Your price is high.'

'Yes. It is. And I'm not cutting anything off him that won't grow back! I cut him, he takes an infection and dies, I've lost my investment. And how do I know that one finger isn't all you really need? No. You want a piece of him, you pay me for it, up front.'

Selden listened and as the full implication of their words sunk into him, he reeled in sick horror. 'You're going to sell one of my fingers? This is madness! Look at me! Look me in the face! I'm a human!'

Big Nose turned and glared at him. Their eyes met. 'You don't shut up, you're going to be a bloody human. And you heard me tell him, I'm not cutting anything off you that won't grow back. So you got nothing to complain about.'

Selden thought he had already experienced the depths of cruelty that these men were capable of. Two cities ago, one of his tenders had rented him for the evening to a curious customer. His mind veered from recalling that and as Big Nose's grinning assistant held up a black-handled knife, Selden heard a roaring in his ears.

'It has to be something that proves he is what you say he is,' the buyer insisted. He crossed his arms on his chest. 'I'll pay you ten silvers for it. But then if my master is satisfied and wants to buy him, you have to take ten silvers off your price.'

Big Nose considered it. His assistant cleaned his nails with the tip of the knife.

'Twenty silvers,' he countered. 'Before we cut him.'

The Chalcedean chewed his lower lip. 'For a piece of flesh, with scales on it, as big as the palm of my hand.'

'Stop!' Selden bellowed, but it came out as a shriek. 'You can't do this. You can't!'

'As big as my two fingers,' Big Nose stipulated. 'And the money here in my hand before we begin.'

'Done,' said the buyer quickly.

Big Nose spat into the straw and held out his hand. The coins chinked, one after another, into his palm.

Selden backed away as far as his chains would allow him. 'I'll fight you!' he cried. 'I'm not going to stand here and let you cut me.'

'As you wish,' Big Nose replied. He opened his purse and dropped the money in. 'Give me the knife, Reever. You two get to sit on him while I take a piece off his shoulder.'

Day the 14th of the Hope Moon
Year the 7th of the Independent Alliance of Traders

From Kim, Keeper of the Birds, Cassarick to Trader Finbok, Bingtown

Sent in a doubly sealed messenger tube, with plugs of green and then blue wax. If either seal is missing or damaged, notify me immediately!

Greetings to Trader Finbok.

As you requested, I have continued to inspect shipments from my station. You know the hazards this presents for me, and I think you ought to be more generous in rewarding my efforts. My gleanings have been a bit confusing, but we both know that where there is secrecy, there is profit to be made. While there is no direct word of your son's wife or on the success or failure of the Tarman *expedition, I think that tidings I have sent you may be valuable in ways we cannot yet evaluate. And I remind you that our agreement was that you would pay me for the risks I took as much as the information I gleaned. To put it plainly and at great risk to myself if this message should fall into other hands, if my spying is discovered, I will lose my position as Bird Keeper. If that befalls me, all will want to know for whom I was spying. I think that my promise to keep that information private no matter what befalls me should be worth something to you. Think carefully before you rebuke me again for how paltry my tidings are. A man cannot catch fish when the river is empty.*

For this reason, you must speak to a certain bird seller in the city, a man called Sheerup on the street of the meat vendors. He can arrange for me to receive a shipment of birds that will return to him rather than to the Guild cages, ensuring the privacy of our communication. He will then pass on my messages to you. This will not be cheap, but opportunities always go to the man who makes them his.

Convey my greetings to your wife, Sealia. I am sure her continued comfort and well-being as the wife of a wealthy Trader are important to both of you.

Kim

CHAPTER FOUR

Kelsingra

She walked the deserted streets alone. A gleaming Elderling robe of coppery fabric sheathed her body. In strange contrast, her boots were worn, and her flapping cloak was mottled with long use. Her bare head was bent to the wind that tugged her hair free of its pinned braids. Alise squinted her eyes against the tearing chill of the moving air and trudged doggedly on. Her hands were nearly numb but she clutched a floppy roll of bleached fabric in her hands. The doorway of a nearby house gaped open and empty, its wooden shutter long rotted away.

When she stepped inside, she gave a shuddering sigh of gratitude. It was no warmer, but at least the wind no longer tore away her body's heat. The Elderling robe that Leftrin had given her kept her body warm, but it could not protect her head and neck, nor her hands and feet. The susurrus that filled the moving air and tugged at her attention died away. She hugged herself, warming her hands under her arms as she gazed around the abandoned dwelling. There was little to be seen. Outlines on the tiled floor told of wooden furniture long rotted away to crumbly splinters. She scuffed a boot across the floor. The tiles beneath the dust were a rich dark red.

A rectangular hole in the ceiling and a heap of ancient debris beneath it spoke of a stairway decayed to dust. The ceiling itself was sound. Long 'beams' of cut stone supported a structure of interlocked blocks. Before she came to Kelsingra she'd never seen the like, but fitted stonework seemed to predominate here, even in the smallest homes.

A hearth in the corner of the room had survived. It jutted out into the room, and was adorned with tiles. Alise gathered the tail of her cloak and rubbed it across the smoothly tiled mantel and then exclaimed in delight. What she had thought was smeared dirt on the red tiles were actually black etchings. As she studied them, she recognized that they had a theme. Cooking and foods. Here was a fat fish on a platter, and next to it a bowl full of round roots with the leaves still attached. On another tile, she found a steaming pot of something, and a third showed a pig roasting on a spit. 'So. Elderlings appear to have enjoyed the same foods we do.'

She spoke softly almost as if she feared to wake someone. It was a feeling that had possessed her ever since Rapskal's dragon had first brought her to visit the ruined city. It seemed empty, abandoned and dead. And yet she could not shake the feeling that around any corner, she might encounter the inhabitants in the midst of their lives. In the grander buildings built of black stones veined with silver she had been sure she had heard whisperings and once, singing. But calling and searching had revealed no one; only deserted rooms and the remains of furniture and other possessions turning to dust. Her shouts did not send squirrels scurrying or set invasion of pigeons to flight. Nothing prospered here, not a mouse, not an ant, and the scattered plant life she encountered looked unhealthy. Sometimes she felt as if she were the first visitor here in years.

A silly thought. Doubtless the winter winds had swept away all signs of previous passage, for wildlife was abundant, not only here but on the other side of the river. The rolling hills that surrounded the city were thickly forested and Heeby's easy success in hunting attested to the thriving animal population. Only yesterday, Heeby had found and routed a whole herd of some heavy-bodied hoofed creatures that she had no name for. The red dragon had terrorized them from above, stampeding them down the hill, willy-nilly through the forest and to the riverside, where all the dragons had fallen on them and feasted to temporary satiation. So, the land on both sides of the river teemed with wildlife. But none of it ventured into the city.

It was but one of the mysteries of Kelsingra. So much of it stood, perfectly intact, as if every inhabitant had simply vanished. The few instances of damage seemed random, with one exception. A huge cleft, as if someone had taken a titanic axe and chopped a wedge into the city, interrupted the streets. The river had flowed in to fill it. She'd stood on the edge of that deep blue gash and stared down into what appeared to be endless depths. Was this what had killed the city? Or had it happened years later? And why did buildings stand independently of one another in this Elderling settlement, while the buried structures of Trehaug and Cassarick had all been constructed as one continuous warren of city? There were no answers for her questions.

She finished cleaning the hearth. One row of tiles was loose, sliding free in her hand. She caught one and gently set it on the floor. How many years had this homely hearth remained whole, to be undone by just her dusting? Well, she had seen it intact, and the image of what it had been would be recorded. It would not be completely lost as so much of Trehaug had been and Cassarick would be. There would at least be a record of *this* Elderling city.

Alise knelt before the hearth and unrolled her fabric. Once

it had been part of a white shirt. Washing it in river water had yellowed the fabric and the seams of the garment had given way to the river's acidity. So, the remaining rag was serving as parchment. It wasn't very satisfactory. The ink she possessed had already been diluted more than once and when she tried to write on the fabric, the lines spread and blurred. But it was better than nothing, and when she had proper paper and ink again, she could transcribe all her notes. For now, she would not risk losing her first impressions of the place. She would record all she saw, to confirm it properly later. Her survey of the untouched Elderling city would survive anything that might happen to her.

Or to the city itself.

Anxiety made her grit her teeth. Leftrin planned to leave tomorrow morning to make the long run back to Cassarick and possibly Trehaug. In the treetop Rain Wild city, he'd collect the pay owed to all of them from the Rain Wild Council, and then he would buy supplies. Warm clothes and flour and sugar. Oil and coffee and tea. But in the course of it, he'd have to reveal that they'd rediscovered Kelsingra. She'd already discussed with him what that might mean. The Traders would be eager to explore yet another Elderling domain. They'd come, not to learn but to plunder, to find and take whatever remained of the magical Elderling artefacts and art. Looters and treasure hunters would arrive in droves. Nothing was sacred to them. All they thought of was profit. The hearth in this humble dwelling would be robbed of its tiles. The immense bas-reliefs on Kelsingra's central tower would be cut free, crated and shipped off. The treasure hunters would take the statuary from the fountains, the scraps of documents from what appeared to be a records hall, the decorative stone lintels, the mysterious tools, the stained glass windows . . . and all of it would be jumbled together and carried off as mere merchandise.

She thought of a place that she and Leftrin had discovered. Boards of ivory and ebony, dusty playing pieces still in place, had rested undisturbed on low marble tables. She had not recognized any of the games, nor the runes on the jade and amber chips that were scattered in the wide bowl of a scooped-out granite stand. 'They gambled here,' she suggested to Leftrin.

'Or prayed, perhaps. I've heard of priests in the Spice Isles that use rune stones to see if a man's prayers will be answered.'

'That could be it, too,' she'd replied. So many riddles. The walkways between the tables were wide, and on the floor of the room, large rectangles in a different stone gleamed black. 'Are those warming places for dragons? Did they come in here to watch the gambling, or the praying?'

Leftrin's reply had been a helpless shrug. She feared she would never know the answer to that question. The clues that could tell what Kelsingra had been would be torn away and sold, except for what she could document before the scavengers arrived.

The plundering of Kelsingra was inevitable. Ever since she'd realized that, Alise had begged passage to the city every day on which it was clear enough for Heeby to fly. She had spent every daylight hour visiting and recording her impression of every structure, rather than rushing from building to building. Better to have a detailed and accurate recording of part of the ancient city than a haphazard sampling of all of it, she'd decided.

Now, she heard footsteps on the pavement outside and went to the door. Leftrin was striding through the empty streets, his hands stuffed under his crossed arms for warmth and his chin tucked into his chest. His grey eyes were narrowed against the sharp breeze. The cold had reddened his cheeks above his dark beard and the wind had mussed his always-unruly hair. Even so, her heart warmed at the sight of him. The blocky ship's captain in his worn jacket and trousers would not have merited a second glance from her during her days as a respectable Bingtown Trader's daughter. But in the months of their companionship on board the Tarman, she'd discovered his true worth. She loved him. Loved him far more than she'd ever loved her cruel husband Hest, even in the first heady days of her infatuation with the handsome fellow. Leftrin was rough-spoken and scarcely educated in any of the finer things of life. But he was honest and capable and strong. And he loved her, openly and whole-heartedly.

'I'm here!' she called to him, and he turned his steps her way and hurried to join her.

'It's getting colder out there,' he greeted her as he stepped into the small shelter of the house. 'The wind is kicking up and promising rain. Or maybe sleet.'

She stepped into his embrace. His outer clothes were chill against her but as they held one another, they warmed. She stepped back slightly to capture his rough hands and hold them between her own, chafing them. 'You need gloves,' she told him, uselessly.

'We all need gloves. And every other kind of warm clothing. And replacements for all the gear, tools and food supplies we lost in that flood-wave. I fear Cassarick is our only source.'

'Carson said he could—'

Leftrin shook his head. 'Carson's bringing down lots of meat, and the keepers are getting better at hunting in this new kind of terrain. We're all staying fed, but it's only meat and the dragons are never full. And Carson's tanning the skin off every creature, but it takes time, and we don't have the proper tools. He can make stiff hides that work as floor coverings or to cover windows. But to make serviceable bed furs or leather to wear requires time and equipment we don't have. I have to go to Cassarick, my dear. I can't put it off any longer. And I want you to go with me.'

She leaned her forehead on his shoulder and shook her head. 'I can't.' Her words were muffled in his embrace. 'I have to stay here. There is so much to document, and I have to get it done before it's spoiled.' She lifted her face and spoke before he could launch into the familiar reassurances. Useless to talk about it. 'How did your work go?' she asked, changing the subject.

'Slowly.' He shook his head. He had taken on the task of designing a new landing for the city. 'Really, all I can do is plan and make a list of what I need to buy. The river sweeps past the front of the city; the drop-off is immediate, the water is deep and the current swift. There's no place to put Tarman aground, and nothing I trust to tie up to. Even with every sweep manned, we were carried right past the city and downriver. I don't know if it has always been that way, but I think not. I suspect the depth of the water varies quite a bit and that when summer comes the water will recede a bit. If so, summer will be our time to build.

'I've tested the old pilings that are left. The wooden ones are only shells, but the stone ones seem sturdy. We can go upriver on the other side, cut timber there, and then raft it downriver to the city. Landing the logs here will be the challenge. But it would be a waste of time to attempt it right now. We don't have tools and fasteners to build the sort of dock we'd need before a large ship could safely tie up here. And the only place to get those is—'

'Trehaug,' she finished for him.

'Trehaug. Possibly Cassarick. A long journey either way. I stocked the ship for an expedition, not to found a settlement. And the keepers lost so much of their basic equipment and extra clothes and blankets in that flash flood that, well, there just isn't enough to go round. It's going to be a hard winter here until I return with fresh supplies.'

'I don't want to be separated from you, Leftrin. But I'm going to stay here and keep working. I want to learn as much about the city as I can before the Traders descend on it and tear it apart.'

Leftrin sighed and pulled her in close. 'My dear, I have told you a hundred times. We'll protect this place. No one else knows the way here and I don't plan to pass my charts around. If they try to follow us back here, well, they'll discover that Tarman can move by night as well as by day. Even if they manage to follow us this far, they'll have the same problem docking a ship here that we do. I'll hold them off as long as I can, Alise.'

'I know.'

'So. Can we talk about the real reason you don't want to go back to Trehaug?'

She shook her head, her face against his shoulder, but then admitted, 'I don't want to go anywhere that I have to remember that I was Alise Finbok. I don't want to touch any part of that old life. I just want my life to be here and now, with you.'

'And it is, my lady, my darling. I'm not going to let anyone steal you from me.'

She pulled back and looked up into his eyes. 'I had an idea today, while I was working. What if you reported my death when you went back? You could send a bird to Hest and one to my parents, saying I'd fallen overboard and drowned. As clumsy and foolish as they think me, they'd surely believe it.'

'Alise!' He was horrified. 'I never want to speak such words aloud, not even as a lie! And your poor family! You couldn't do that to them!'

'I think they'd be relieved,' she muttered, but knew that they still would weep for her.

'And there is your work to think of. You can't be dead and do your work!'

'What?'

He let go of her and stepped back. 'Your work. Your studies of the dragons and the Elderlings. You've worked too long on all of that just to let it go. You need to finish it, if it's a thing that can be finished. Keep your logs, make your drawings. Meet with Malta and Reyn the Elderlings and tell them what you've found. Share your findings with the world. If you claim to be dead, you can't very well take credit for what you've discovered. Let alone protect it.'

She had no name for the emotion that flooded her. It was hard to believe that anyone would say such words to her. 'You . . . you understand what that means to me?' She looked away, suddenly embarrassed. 'My writings and my silly little sketches, my attempts at translations, my—'

'Enough!' There was shocked rebuke in his voice. 'Alise, there is nothing "silly" about what you are doing, any more than my charting the Rain Wild River is "silly". Don't you belittle our work! And don't ever speak poorly of yourself, especially to me! I fell in love with that earnest woman with her sketchbooks and journals. I felt flattered that such an educated lady would even spend time explaining it all to me. What you are doing is important! For Rain Wilders, for dragons, for history! We are here, seeing something happen with these dragons and their keepers. Those youngsters are changing into Elderlings. First dragons and now Elderlings are coming back into our world. For now, it's just here. But can you look at the dragons and the keepers and doubt what must follow? Heeby gets stronger every day. Most of the other dragons have managed short flights, even if some ended by crashing into the river or the trees. By winter's end, I think most of them will be able to hunt and fly at least a little. And none of the keepers have spoken about returning to Trehaug or Cassarick. They're staying here and some of them are pairing up. Sa help us all! This is the start of something, Alise, and you're already a part of it. Too late to back out now. Too late to hide.'

'I don't really want to hide.' She walked slowly to the hearth and knelt down. Reluctantly, she picked up one of the decorated tiles from the floor. 'I made a promise to Malta. I intend to keep that.' She studied the tile. Delicate brushstrokes had delineated a bubbling kettle of soup. A wreath of herbs framed it. 'I'll send this with you for her, when you go. With a message from me, to let her know that we really have found Kelsingra. That there is still a place for dragons and Elderlings in this world.'

'You could go with me. Tell her yourself.'

Alise shook her head, almost vehemently. 'No, Leftrin. I'm not ready to face that world yet. I'll give you messages to send to my family, to let them know I'm alive and fine. But no more than that. Not yet.'

When she glanced over her shoulder at him, he was looking at the floor. His mouth was flat with disappointment. She rose and went to him.

'Don't think that I'm not going to confront what I must do. I'm going to cut myself free of Hest. I want to stand freely by your side, not as his runaway wife, but as a woman free to choose her own life. Hest broke our marriage contract. I know I'm no longer bound to him.'

'Then send word of that to the Bingtown Council. Renounce him. He broke his promises to you. The contract is void.'

She sighed. This was another conversation they'd had before. 'You just chided me for wanting to pretend I was dead, saying it would hurt my family. Well, I don't see a way to force Hest to release me without hurting an even wider circle of people. I can say he was unfaithful but I don't have witnesses who will stand up and confirm that. I can't ask Sedric to come forward, not with the shame it would bring on his family! He is building something new here, just as I am. I don't want to drag him away from Carson and back to Bingtown, to make him a source of scandal and cruel jokes. Hest would simply call him a liar, and I know that he could find plenty of his friends who would swear he spoke truth, no matter what he said.'

She took a breath and added, 'It would ruin my family socially. Not that we have much stature in Bingtown. And, and I would have to stand before the Bingtown Council and admit that I had been a fool, not just in marrying Hest, but in staying with him all those wasted years . . .'

Her voice trailed away. Sick shame rose up and engulfed her. Every time she thought she had set it all behind her, the issue of how Hest still bound her would bring this back. For years she had wondered why he treated her so poorly. She had humiliated herself trying to gain his attention. All she had won was his contempt for her efforts. It was only when she had left Bingtown to pursue a brief interlude of study of her beloved dragons in the Rain Wilds that she had discovered the truth about her husband. He had never cared for her at all. The marriage had been a ruse to mask his true preferences. Sedric, her childhood friend and her husband's assistant had been far more than a secretary and valet to him.

And all Hest's friends had known.

Her guts tightened and her throat closed up. How could she have been so blind, so stupid? So ignorant, so blissfully naïve? How could she have gone for years without questioning his odd behaviour in the marital bed, lived with his sharp little jibes and social neglect? She had no answers for those questions except that she had been stupid. Stupid, stupid, stu—

'Stop that!' Leftrin took her arm and gently shook it. He shook his head at her as well. 'I hate to see you go off like that. Your eyes narrow and you grit your teeth, and I know just what is running through that head of yours. Stop blaming yourself. Someone deceived you and hurt you. You don't need to take on the burden of that. That man who committed the offence is at fault, not the person he wronged.'

She sighed but the weight inside her remained. 'You know what they say, Leftrin. Fool me once, shame on you. Fool me twice, shame on me. Well, he fooled me a thousand times, and I don't doubt that many in his audience enjoyed it. I don't ever want to go back to Bingtown. Never. I never want to look at anyone I knew there and wonder who knew I was a fool and didn't tell me.'

'Enough,' Leftrin said abruptly, but his voice was gentle. 'The light is going out of the day. And I feel a more serious storm rising. It's time we went back to our side of the river.'

Alise glanced outside. 'I don't want to be caught on this side after dark,' she agreed. She looked at him directly and waited for him to add something, but he was silent. She said no more. There were times when she realized that as close as they were, he was still a Rain Wilder while she had grown up in Bingtown. There were some things he didn't talk about. But this was something, she abruptly decided, that could not remain undiscussed. She cleared her throat, and said, 'The voices seem to get louder as we get closer to night.'

Leftrin met her gaze. 'They do.' He went to the door and looked out as if scouting for danger. That simple measure sent a chill up her back. Had he expected to see something? Someone? He spoke quietly. 'It's the same in some parts of Trehaug and Cassarick. The buried ruins, I mean, not the treetop cities. But it's not the dark that brings them out. I think it's when you're alone, or feel alone. One becomes more susceptible. It's stronger in Kelsingra than I've ever before sensed it. But it's not as bad in this part of town where simple folk lived. In the parts of the city where the buildings are grand and the streets so wide, I hear the whispers almost all the time. Not loud, but constant. The best thing to do is ignore them. Don't let your mind focus on them.'

He looked back over his shoulder at her, and she had the feeling she had learned as much as she wanted to know, for now. There was more he could tell her; she sensed that, but she would save her questions for when they were warming themselves by a cosy fire in a well-lit room. Not here, in a cold city with the shadows gathering.

She gathered her things, including the loose tile from the hearth. She studied the picture again, and then handed it to Leftrin. He took a well-worn kerchief from his pocket and wrapped the precious thing. 'I'll take good care of it,' he promised before she could ask. Arm in arm, they left the cottage.

Outside, the overcast day had darkened as the clouds thickened and the sun sank behind the gentle hills and the steeper cliffs that backed them. The shadows of the houses loomed over the winding streets. Alise and Leftrin hurried, the chill wind pushing them along. As they left behind the modest houses Alise had been investigating and entered the main part of the city, the whispers grew stronger. She didn't hear them with her ears and she could not pick out any individual voice or stream of words: rather, it was a press of thoughts against her mind. She shook her head, refusing them, and hurried on.

She'd never been in a city like this one. Bingtown was a large and grand city, a city built for show, but Kelsingra had been built to a scale that dwarfed humans. The passageways in this part of Kelsingra were wide, wide enough for dragons to pass one another in the streets. The gleaming black buildings, too, were sized to admit dragons. The roofs were higher, and the doorways both wide and tall. Whenever they came to steps, the central sections were always wide and shallow, not sized for a human's stride at all. Two steps to cross each step and then the hop down. At the edges, flights scaled for humans paralleled the course.

She passed a dry fountain. In the middle, a life-sized dragon reared on his hind legs, clasping a struggling stag in his jaws and forepaws. Around the next corner, she encountered a memorial to an Elderling statesman carrying a scroll in one long slender hand while he pointed aloft with his other. It had been crafted from the same black stone threaded with fine silver lines. It was plain that Elderlings and dragons had both dwelt here, side by side and possibly sharing abodes. She thought of the keepers, and how their dragons were changing them, and wondered if some day this city would shelter such a population again.

They turned onto a wide boulevard and the wind roared with renewed strength. Alise clutched her poor cloak closer about her and bent her head to the wind's buffeting. This street led straight down to the river port and the remains of the docks that had once awaited ships there. A few remnant stone pilings jutted from the water. She lifted her gaze and through streaming eyes beheld the gleaming black surface of the river. On the horizon; the sun was foundering behind the wooded hills. 'Where is Rapskal?' She half-shouted the words to push them through the wind. 'He said he'd bring Heeby to the water's edge at sunset.'

'He'll be there. The lad may be a bit strange, but in some ways he's the most responsible keeper when it comes to keeping his word. Over there. There they are.'

She followed Leftrin's pointing hand and saw them. The dragon lingered at the edge of an elevated stone dais that overlooked the water. The dais adjoined a crumbled ramp. Alise knew from the bas reliefs that decorated it that once it would have led to a launching platform for dragons. She surmised that perhaps older and heavier dragons needed a height advantage to get their bulk off the ground. Before the blocks of the ramp had given way to decades of winter river floods, it had probably been very high. Now it terminated just beyond the statue's dais.

Heeby's keeper had clambered up onto the dais and stood at the base of a many-times-larger-than-life statue of an Elderling couple. The man gestured wide with an out flung arm, while the woman's pointing finger and gracefully tilted head indicated that her gaze followed something, possibly a dragon in flight. Rapskal's head was tipped back and he had stretched up one hand to touch the hip of one Elderling. He stood, staring up at the tall, handsome creature as if entranced.

Heeby, his dragon, shifted restlessly as she waited for him. She was probably hungry again already. All she did of late was hunt and feed and hunt again. The red dragon was twice the size she had been when Alise had first met her. She was no longer the stumpy, blocky creature she had been: her body and tail had lengthened, and her hide and half-folded wings gleamed crimson, catching the red rays of the setting sun and throwing them back. Muscle rippled in her sinuous neck as she turned to watch their approach. She lowered her head suddenly and hissed low, a warning. Alise halted in her tracks. 'Is something wrong?' she called.

The wind swept away her words and Rapskal made no reply. The dragon shifted again and half-reared on her hind legs. She sniffed at Rapskal and then nudged him. The boy's body gave to her push but he made no indication that he was aware of her.

'Oh, no,' Leftrin groaned. 'Please, Sa, no. Give the boy

another chance.' The captain released her arm and lurched into a run.

The dragon threw back her head and whistled loudly. For a tense moment, Alise expected the creature to charge or spit acid at Leftrin. Instead, she nuzzled Rapskal again, with as little response. Then she dropped onto all fours again and stood staring at them. Her eyes whirled. She was plainly distressed about something, which did nothing to reassure Alise. A distressed dragon was a dangerous dragon.

'Rapskal! Stop day-dreaming and tend to Heeby! Rapskal!' Her shout fought the wind.

The young keeper stood as still as the statue he touched, and the dwindling daylight glittered on the scarlet scaling on his bared hands and face. Heeby moved to block Leftrin but the sailor dodged adroitly around her. 'I'm going to help him, dragon. Stay out of my way.'

'Heeby, Heeby, it will be all right. Let him pass, let him pass!' Heedless of her own danger, Alise did her best to distract the anxious dragon as Leftrin set his palms to the chest-high pedestal and then vaulted up onto it. He seized Rapskal around the chest and then spun away from the statue, tearing the boy's grip from the stone. As he did so, the keeper cried out wordlessly and suddenly went limp in the man's arms. Leftrin staggered with his sudden weight and both of them sank down to sit at the statue's feet.

Heeby shifted restlessly, swinging her head back and forth in agitation. She was the only dragon that had never spoken to Alise. Despite being the only dragon that could both fly and hunt capably now, she had never seemed especially bright, although she had always seemed to share her keeper's sunny temperament. Now as Leftrin held the youngster in his arms and spoke worriedly to him, the dragon seemed more like an anxious dog than a powerful predator.

Even so, Alise gave her a wide berth as she made her way to the dais. It took her considerably more effort to gain the top of it than it had Leftrin, but she managed. The captain knelt on the cold stone cradling Rapskal. 'What's wrong with him? What's happened?'

'He was drowning,' Leftrin said in a low voice full of dread.

But as Rapskal's face lolled toward her, she saw only his idiotically bemused grin and barely open eyes. She frowned. 'Drowning? He looks more drunk than drowned! But where did he get spirits?'

'He didn't.' Leftrin gave him another shake. 'He's not drunk.' But his next actions seemed to belie his statement as he gave Rapskal another shake. 'Come out of it, lad. Come back to your own life. There's a dragon here that needs you, and night is coming on. Storm's coming in, too. If we're to get to the other side before it's dark, we need you to wake up.'

He glanced at Alise and became Captain Leftrin dealing with an emergency.

'Jump down and take his legs when I pass him down,' he commanded, and she obeyed. *When had the lad got so tall?* she wondered, as Leftrin eased the limp Rapskal down into her arms. When she'd first met him, he'd seemed just past boyhood, made younger than his peers by his simplicity. Then he and his dragon had vanished and all had believed them both dead. Since their return, the dragon had proved her competence as a predator and Rapskal had seemed both older and more ethereal, sometimes a mystical Elderling and sometimes a wondering boy. Like all the keepers, his close contact with his dragon was changing him. His ragged trousers exposed the heavy red scaling on his feet and calves. It reminded Alise of the tough orange skin on a chicken's legs. And like a bird, he weighed less than she had expected as

Leftrin let go of Rapskal and she took his full weight to keep him upright. His eyes were wide open.

'Rapskal?' she said, but he folded laxly over her shoulder.

With a thump and a grunt, Leftrin landed beside her. 'Give him to me,' he said gruffly as Heeby pressed her nose against Rapskal's back, sending Alise staggering back against the statue's pedestal. 'Dragon, stop that!' he commanded Heeby, but as the dragon's eyes spun swiftly, he added more gently, 'I'm trying to help him, Heeby. Give me some space.'

It wasn't clear she understood him, but she did step back as Leftrin stretched Rapskal out on the cold stone. 'Wake up, lad. Come back to us.' He tapped his face with light slaps, then took him by the shoulders, sat him up and shook him. Rapskal's head snapped back on his neck, eyes wide, and then, as his head came forward again, life came back to his face. His affable smile, never long absent, blossomed as he looked up at them beatifically. 'Dressed for the festival,' he said cheerily. 'In a gown made of eel skin dyed pink to match her brow scaling. More delicate than a tiny lizard on an air-blossom, she was, and her lips softer than a rose's petals.'

'Rapskal!' Leftrin rebuked him severely. 'Come back to us now. Here. We are cold and night is coming on and this city has been dead for Sa knows how long. There is no festival, and no woman wearing a gown such as you describe. Come back now!' He seized the youth's face between his hands and forced the boy to meet his glowering stare.

After a long moment, Rapskal abruptly pulled his knees up to his chest and began to shiver violently. 'I'm so cold!' he complained. 'We need to get back to the other side and warm ourselves at a fire. Heeby! Heeby, where are you? It's getting dark! You need to carry us across to the other side!'

At the sound of his voice, the dragon thrust her head into the midst of the huddled group, sending both Leftrin and

Alise staggering back. She opened her mouth wide, tasting the air all around Rapskal as he exclaimed, 'Of course I'm all right! I'm just cold. Why did we stay here so long? It's nearly dark.'

'It is dark,' Leftrin retorted gruffly. 'And we stayed here so long because you were careless. I can't believe that you didn't know better! But for now, we won't talk about it. We just need to get back to our side of the river.'

The keeper was rapidly coming to his senses. Alise watched him sit up straight and then stagger to his feet, lurching toward his dragon. As soon as he could touch Heeby, they both seemed to calm. The dragon ceased her restless shifting. Rapskal drew a deeper breath and turned toward them. His face had relaxed into its handsome lines. He pushed his dark hair back and spoke almost accusingly. 'Poor Heeby will be flying in the dark by the time she makes her third trip. We need to start now.'

Leftrin spoke. 'Alise first. Then you. Then me. I want someone on the opposite shore waiting for you. And I don't want you here alone in the dark, with no one watching you.'

'Watching me?'

'You know what I'm talking about. We'll discuss it when we're safe on the other side by a fire.'

Rapskal shot him a wounded look but said only, 'Alise goes first, then.'

It was not her first time to ride the dragon, but she thought she would never become accustomed to it. Alise knew that the other dragons did not approve of Heeby allowing mere humans to mount her back and ride her as if she were a beast of burden and dreaded that they might decide to confront her about it. Sintara, the largest female dragon, had been particularly outspoken in that regard. But that concern was the smallest part of the emotions that sent her heart hammering. There was no harness to cling to, not even a piece of twine. 'What would you need it for?' Rapskal had asked her incredulously the first time he had asked Heeby to carry her across the river and she had enquired about something to hold onto. 'She knows where she's going. Just sit tight and she'll get you there.'

Leftrin boosted her up and the dragon crouched considerately, but even so it was a scrabble up the smoothly-scaled shoulder. Alise straddled Heeby just in front of where her wings attached to her body. It was not dignified. She had to lean forward and place her hands flat on the sides of the dragon's neck, since there was nothing to grip. Heeby had learned to fly by running and leaping into the air. It was how Rapskal had thought a dragon would launch, but the other dragons found fault with it, saying that she should simply leap clear of the ground and beat her way into the sky. Nonetheless, every flight began with Heeby's lolloping run down the hill toward the river. Then came the lurch of the wild leap, the snap as she opened her wings and then the heavy and uneven beating of her wide leathery wings. Alise was never absolutely certain that Heeby would gain the air, let alone remain there.

But once aloft, the rhythm of her wings steadied. They ventured higher. The cold wind sliced past Alise, burning her cheeks and penetrating her tattered clothing. She leaned close, clasping sleek, scaled, muscular flesh. If she slipped, she would fall into the frigid river and die. No one could save her. Heeby had had a terror of the water since she had been swept helplessly away in the flood. She would never plunge into the icy water after a fallen rider. Alise pushed the disheartening thoughts from her mind. She wouldn't fall. That was all.

Through squinted eyes she stared at the small lights on the

far side of the river and willed herself to be there soon. There were not many lights. The keepers and the ship's crew had claimed the few cottages and dwellings that could be made habitable and done their best to make them warm and weatherproof. Even so, there were not enough souls there to form even a village. But more would come, Alise thought sadly, when the news of their discovery leaked out. More would come. And with them, perhaps, the end of Kelsingra.

Leftrin watched the scarlet dragon dwindle in darkness and distance. 'Sa watch over her,' he prayed under his breath and then twisted his mouth in wry wonder at himself. He'd never been a praying man before Alise came into his life. Now he caught himself at it every time she insisted on taking chances. Exploring abandoned cities, attempting to hunt, riding on flying dragons . . . He shook his head as he watched Alise vanish into the darkness. As much as he feared for her, it was her adventurous nature that had first attracted him. That first time she'd appeared on the docks, in her hat and veil and flouncy skirts, he'd been dumbstruck. Such a fine lady to be chancing herself on the dangerous Rain Wild River and his barge.

Now her hands were roughened and her hair bundled back, and the veils and ribbons long gone. But she was still the fine lady, as elegant as ever, in the same way a fine tool, no matter how battered, retained its integrity. She was one of a kind, his Alise. Tough as wizardwood and fine as lace.

Now he could no longer see her or the dragon. The darkness had swallowed them. He stared anyway, willing that Heeby would make the flight safely, willing that Alise be safe on the other side.

'They're on the ground,' Rapskal said quietly.

Leftrin turned to him in surprise. 'You can see that far?'

Rapskal grinned merrily. His eyes gleamed blue in the dimness. 'My dragon told me. She's on her way back to us already.'

'Of course,' Leftrin replied. He sighed to himself. Sometimes it was easy to forget his bond with the dragon. Easy to forget the boyish side of the young Elderling. Like all growing boys, Rapskal toyed with danger. He had been reckless tonight. Even his dragon had sensed that. He couldn't be permitted to risk himself like that again.

Leftrin cleared his throat. 'What you were doing when we found you? There's no excuse for that. You're Rain Wild bred. Don't tell me you didn't know the danger. What were you thinking? Do you want to drown yourself in memories? To be lost to us forever?'

Rapskal met his gaze squarely. His eyes gleamed blue in the darkness, as brightly as if he were an old man with years of Change on him. His smile grew wider as he admitted cheerfully, 'Yes, actually, I do.'

Leftrin stared at him. His words were shocking. But he did not speak them cheekily but with sincerity. 'What are you saying? That you want to become a drooling idiot? Wander forever in Elderling memories while your body loses control of itself? Become a senile burden to everyone who loves you, or starve to death in your own filth when everyone abandons you to your selfishness? It will happen, you know.'

He painted the death of a man who drowned in memories as harshly as he could. The boy had to be dissuaded from engulfing his mind in the pleasure of a past that was not his. 'Drowning in memories' was the Rain Wild euphemism for it. It was not as common a fate as it had been when the Elderling cities had first been discovered, but it still happened and most often to youngsters like Rapskal. The temptation to linger in contact with certain stone walls and statues was great. Life in the Rain Wilds was not as harsh as it once had been, but no Rain Wilder enjoyed the life of opulence and luxury that was recorded in the stones of the city. Once a lad had explored one of those memories, the temptation to return over and over to a dream of remembered feasts and music and romance and indulgences would prove too great for some to resist. Left to themselves, they literally drowned in the memories, forgetting their own lives and the needs of their real bodies to indulge in the pleasures of a city and a civilization that no longer existed.

Leftrin understood the pull of it. Almost every adventurous Rain Wild lad had sampled memory diving at least once. The secrets of where the best and most intense memories were stored were passed on privately by generation after generation. His mind darted back to certain stone carvings in a little-used hallway of the Elderling city buried under Trehaug. With a touch of the hand, one could experience a lavish banquet followed by a lovely concert of Elderling music. There were rumours of another carving that had held records of one powerful Elderling's sexual conquests. Years ago, the Rain Wild Council had ordered it destroyed, saying that enough young men had perished due to its attraction. Yet the tales of it persisted.

Looking at Rapskal now, Leftrin wondered what he had discovered when he had touched the statue. What sort of memories did it hold and how strong would its attraction be once the word spread to the other keepers? He imagined having to tell Alise it must be destroyed, and then considered the intense physical labour of breaking it to pieces. The Elderlings had built for the ages. Nothing they had created gave way easily to nature or man. Destroying the statue would take days, possibly weeks. And it would be hazardous work. To those who were vulnerable to it, memory stone was dangerous even to casual touch. Even breathing the dust could have serious consequences.

'What did you find in the statue, boy? Is it worth giving up your true life for it?'

Rapskal's grin flashed. 'Captain, you needn't worry so much. I know what I'm doing. And it's what I'm supposed to do. What Elderlings have always done. It's why the memories were stored. They won't hurt me. They will make me what I'm supposed to be.'

Leftrin's heart sank deeper with each of the boy's confident assertions. Already, he sounded like a stranger, not like impetuous, random Rapskal at all. How could he have fallen so far so fast? Leftrin spoke sternly. 'So it may seem to you now, keeper. So it has seemed to many others, and when they plunged deep and lost the way, it was too late for them to think again about it. I know the attraction, Rapskal. I was a lad, once. I've set my hand to a memory stone and been swept up in it.'

'Have you?' Rapskal tilted his head as he regarded Leftrin. In the tattering sunset, he could not read the look in the boy's steady gaze. Was it scepticism? Even, perhaps, condescension? 'Perhaps you have,' Rapskal went on in a gentler voice. 'But it would not have meant the same thing to you at all. It would be like reading someone else's diary.' He lifted his eyes suddenly and smiled his generous smile. 'And here she comes, my beauty, my darling, my scarlet wonder!'

The red dragon, wings wide and flapping as she slowed herself, skittered to a halt a score of paces from them as she landed. Her gleaming eyes whirled with pleasure at the boy's praise.

'Your turn,' he said to Leftrin, smiling.

Leftrin didn't return the smile. 'No. You go. Send your dragon back for me. I don't want to leave you here alone with the statue.'

Rapskal gazed at him for a long time and then shrugged one narrow shoulder. 'As you wish, Captain. But, you know, I am less alone in this city than anywhere else I have ever been in my life.' Arms wide as if to embrace her, he strode toward his dragon. The little scarlet queen reared up on her hind legs and then came down. She snaked her head toward him, and made a sound between a snarl and a purr as he reached her and clambered up onto her shoulder.

'I'll send her back for you!' he promised, and then the dragon spun about on her hind legs and began her race down the hill.

Day the 5th of the Change Moon
Year the 7th of the Independent Alliance of Traders

From Reyall, Acting Keeper of the Birds, Bingtown to Detozi, Keeper of the Birds, Trehaug

Contents: a notice from Trader family Meldar and Trader family Kincarron, renewing the offer of a substantial reward for any information about the location and well being of Sedric Meldar and Alise Kincarron Finbok, with the request that all posted notices be renewed in both Trehaug and Cassarick, and an announcement of the rewards be made at any convening of the Traders at either Trader concourse, all fees having been paid in advance for these services.

Detozi, a small note appended here. Thank you for your advice and please thank Erek as well. With difficulty, I have held my tongue and made no complaint about Kim's message to me. Now several complaints have been lodged about the condition of messages received from Cassarick. I will stand quietly, as befits my youth, and let others consider if the mails are being tampered with at that location.

CHAPTER FIVE

A Bingtown Trader

The door swung open into dimness. Hest advanced into the room cautiously, wrinkling his nose at the smell of faded perfume and disuse. Whoever had tidied the room last had done a poor job. The cinders of a long-dead fire lay in the small hearth, contributing a stink of old ashes. Several strides of his long legs carried him to the window. He pushed the curtains back, letting thin grey winter light into the room. Unlatching the window, he let it swing wide to the wintry day.

This small chamber had been intended to be Alise's sewing room. His mother had taken a great deal of pleasure in arranging it for his bride-to-be; she had selected the chairs by the hearth, the little tables, the deep blue draperies and the rug with the floral pattern. But his inconvenient wife had no interest in sewing or embroidery. Not Alise, oh no. While other men's wives were happily occupied with decorating new hats for themselves or stitching mottos, his woman was out wandering the markets, finding old scrolls at exorbitant prices to buy and drag home. The shelves of the room, painted gilt and white and intended for trinkets, sagged under their burdens of scrolls and books and stacks of notes. The top of the large wooden desk that had replaced the dainty sewing table was bare; he'd give Alise that: at least she'd tidied away her mess before she went.

Then he realized that her desk was *completely* bare. NO! She couldn't have taken it with her! Not even Alise was so obsessed as to risk the Elderling scroll he'd given her as an engagement gift. It had been ridiculously expensive. Knowing its value and fragility, she'd put the damned thing in a special case to preserve it from dust and curious touches. Alise would not take such a rare, such an irreplaceable, such an exceedingly valuable item on a boat ride up the Rain Wilds River. Would she?

Sedric had been the one to track the scroll down for him, back in the days when Hest had been courting Alise. It was one of only a handful of intact Elderling documents recovered from Cassarick. Sedric had assured him that it was priceless and that even the exorbitant sum he was paying for it was a bargain. Not only would he acquire a unique Elderling artefact, but in the process, he'd win Alise's marriage consent. It was a Trader's dream, a consummate bargain in which he gave something away, only to immediately regain it and the woman as well. They had laughed about it the evening before he had gone to present it to the dowdy little creature.

Hest scowled disdainfully as he recalled that night. Well, he had laughed about the bargain. Sedric had sat quiet, biting his lip and then dared to ask him, 'Are you sure you want to go through with this? It's the perfect gift. I'm sure that this, if nothing else, will win Alise's regard for you. It will open the door for you to court her and make her your wife. But are you sure, really sure, that's what you want?'

'Well, of course it isn't!' They'd been drinking in Hest's study, comfortably watching a gnarled apple wood log burn down to ash. The house had been quiet and calm, the curtains drawn to close out the night. The war with Chalced was over, trade was resuming, and the world was coming back to normality. Good wine and fine brandy, song and entertainment had returned to Bingtown. Inns and taverns and playhouses were being rebuilt, rising from the ashes to even greater splendour than old Bingtown had possessed before it was burnt and pillaged. There were fortunes to be made. It was a wonderful time to be young and unattached and wealthy.

Then Hest's misguided father had to ruin it all by insisting that Hest must get a wife and make an heir for the family or forfeit his right to be the sole inheritor of the Finbok family fortune. 'It it were left to me, I'd live my life exactly as I am. I have my friends and my occupations, my business affairs prosper, and I have you in my bed when I want you. The last thing I need is a busy little woman cluttering up my house and demanding my time and attention. Even less do I desire squalling babies and messy little children.'

'But while your father lives and wears the Trader robe and controls not only the vote but the purse strings of the estates, you'll have to do what pleases him.'

Sedric's words had made him scowl, then and now. 'Wrong. I'll have to *appear* to do what pleases him. I have no intention of ceasing my ongoing efforts to please myself.'

'Well, then.' Sedric had pointed, a bit drunkenly, at the scroll in its ancient decorated case. 'Then that's exactly the item you want, Hest. I've known Alise for years. Her fascination with the ancient Elderlings and dragons consumes her. A gift such as that will win her to your side.'

And it had. At the time, the ridiculous price that he'd paid for the damn thing had seemed worth it. She'd agreed to marry him. After that, his courtship of her had simply followed the customs of Bingtown, as easily as following a road on a map. They'd married, his family had provided a comfortable new home and a larger allowance to him, and they'd settled in. Oh, from time to time, his father or mother would moan or complain that her belly didn't swell with a child, but that was scarcely Hest's fault. Even if women had appealed to him, he doubted he would have chosen one that looked like Alise. Unruly red hair, freckles thick as pox marks on her face and forearms and shoulders. She was a sturdy little woman who should have conceived easily and given him a brat right away. But she hadn't even done that right.

And then, years after he thought she'd settled in her place, she'd had the wild impulse to take herself off to the Rain Wilds to study dragons. And damned if Sedric hadn't supported her in the idea. They'd both had the gall to remind him that he'd agreed to such a journey as one of the terms of the marriage contract. Perhaps he had, but no proper wife would ever have insisted on such a ridiculous thing. Thoroughly incensed with both of them, he'd sent them off together. Let Sedric see just how much he'd enjoy his 'old friend's' endless whining and wearisome ways. Let Sedric remember what it was like to live peasant-poor on a smelly ship on a reeking river. The ungrateful wretch. Both of them were ungrateful, stupid, selfish, common idiots. And now to find that they'd stolen from him, that they'd taken the most valuable scroll in the whole expensive collection that the stupid red cow had assembled was more than any man could tolerate.

He strode back to the door of the chamber and thrust his head out. 'Ched! Ched, attend me this moment.'

'Coming, sir!' The voice of his steward was distant; perhaps from the wine cellar. Lazy bastard. He was never to hand with Hest wanted him.

Hest paced impatiently round the room, seeking but not finding the scroll. The bitch had stolen it! He clenched his fists. Well, she'd find out soon enough that he'd cut her off without a copper shard. And faithless Sedric as well! When he had returned from his own trading voyage to discover that neither his wife nor his secretary had returned from their ill-advised trip to the Rain Wilds, he'd been furious. Even so, he'd held back his hand until the ugly rumours that they had run off together had begun to poison his social standing. The inner circle of his friends knew that it couldn't be true, since Sedric would no more run off with a woman than he'd develop a spine and assert himself. But there had been others in Bingtown society who had believed it and had dared to pity Hest, dared to see him as the cuckolded husband. They sympathized with him, and believing his heart was broken, had dared to advise him on how best to win her back if she did return. Worse had been the ambitious matrons who had privately encouraged him to evoke the dissolution clause in his marriage contract and find a 'more suitable, fertile wife'; inevitably, they had a daughter, niece or grand-daughter who would fill the bill admirably. One widow had even dared to offer herself. Such importunings were humiliating, but the pity others offered was the worst. They seemed to think his lack of reaction to Alise's absence indicated that he was pining mournfully for his red cow!

That was when he had sent the notices to be published in every significant town on the Rain Wild River. He'd made it known clear and plain that anyone so foolish as to extend credit to the runaways had best not expect to be paid back out of Hest's pockets. Alise and Sedric wanted to be away from him? Fine! Let them see how well they could manage when cut off from his fortune. And it was a plain signal to all of just how little he cared what became of either of them.

Where was his damn steward? He leaned out of the door again. 'Ched!' he bellowed, furious this time, and his anger was not soothed when the man startled him by saying, 'I'm here, sir,' from the corridor behind him.

'Where were you? When I call you, it means I need you immediately.'

'Sir, I'm sorry, but I was admitting a guest and settling him in your visiting room. He came very finely dressed, sir, with a hired carriage and team of the finest quality. He says he has come all the way from Chalced on a ship that arrived just this morning and that you were expecting him.'

'What's his name?' Hest demanded. He wracked his brain but could recall no scheduled meetings

'He was most adamant, sir, that he would not share his name. He said it was a matter of great delicacy and that he bore gifts and messages not only for you but for someone named Begasti Cored. And he spoke of Sedric Meldar as having arranged all this months ago, and how expected shipments had not arrived and someone must pay for the delay . . .'

'Enough!' Damned Sedric again! He was tired of thinking of the man. Had Sedric run off and left the threads of a business agreement to unravel? That was unlike him. He was keener on details and arrangements than anyone Hest had ever known. But then it was also unlike the sucking little tick to stay away so long from comfort and wealth. Unless this was part of some other, unknown plot against Hest. That was a very disturbing thought. Sedric and Alise had been friends since childhood. Had the two of them collaborated in some plot to steal trade business from Hest? Was that why they had vanished and not returned? What could the two trade in? Abruptly he recalled why he had summoned Ched. 'Turn your mind to this. There was a scroll on that table, a very valuable one, in a wooden case with a glass lid. It was there, and now it's gone. I want it found.'

'I don't know . . .' the incompetent fool began.

'Find it!' Hest snapped at him. 'Find it now, or face charges of theft!'

'Sir!' the steward objected, aghast. 'I know nothing about the contents of this room. When I first arrived, you said it was the province of the lady's maids. Then, after you ordered the lady's maids let go, I did not take up its care as you didn't tell me that—'

'Find the scroll!' Hest bellowed the words. He turned his back on the man and strode off toward the visiting room. 'And have refreshments sent to me while I find out what other arrangements you have bungled.'

There was satisfaction in shouting, a small relief in his tension that he could leave the steward pale and shaken, in fear for his livelihood. It would have been much better if the man had immediately produced the missing scroll, but he would eventually.

Unless Alise and Sedric had stolen it. And what of the other extremely expensive scrolls that the graceless little woman and his lackey had been acquiring for years? He halted mid-stride, thinking back to how assiduously Sedric had searched out costly and ancient writings for her, and how relentlessly he had encouraged Hest to purchase them, saying that it was only to keep Alise occupied. Toward the end of their time together, Sedric had even dared to assert that she 'deserved' such gifts, as recompense for a marriage of convenience! Hest had countered that she had known what she was getting into when she signed their marriage contract. He'd made it plain to her from the beginning that it was about appearances, convenience and an heir. Now he wondered starkly just how much of his fortune she'd spent on her tattered bits of cowhide and musty books. There would be an accounting somewhere, some sort of an inventory of them. Sedric was fastidious in his record keeping. But where? Or had they taken that along with the precious artefacts with them when they'd run off together?

Damn them! Of course they had. It all made sense now. Sedric's insistence that Alise be allowed to make her useless journey to the Rain Wilds. His foolish quarrelling with Hest that had led to Hest ordering him to go with her. Of course. He ground his teeth in fury. They'd collaborated against him, made him a fool in his own home, with his own money. Well, they'd see that he was not to be trifled with. He'd track them down and get his own back, leave them penniless and shamed!

His breath was coming fast, his heart hammering high in his chest. He forced himself to stand still, took deep calming breaths, and then paused a few moments to tug his jacket straight and arrange his collar and cuffs. He didn't know who the Chalcedean in his visiting chamber might be, but it was possible he was a loose end in Sedric's plot against him. And if so, Hest intended to get every bit of information out of the man that he could. Then he'd have Ched throw him out of the house.

Calm and composed, at least on the surface, he entered the chamber, a blandly polite smile on his face. The Chalcedean man who awaited him was young and muscular. He wore a brocaded vest over a loose white shirt. His flowing trousers were quilted silk, his short boots of gleaming black leather. The blade that rode at his hip was neither sword nor knife but something curved and nasty between the two. The hilt was black, wrapped in leather. Not decorative but very functional. On the floor beside him was a satchel bearing the device of the Duke of Chalced. The man looked up from ransacking the drawers of Hest's desk. His close-cropped dark hair and trimmed beard did nothing to hide the scarlet scar that ran from the corner of his left eye down across his cheek and over his mouth and chin. It appeared to be a recent injury and his lips had not healed well. The edges of the scar were rubbery and bulging and when he spoke, caused his words to be badly formed.

'Where is the promised merchandise? You will not get another chance simply to deliver it. Every day that it is delayed will cost you.'

Hest's outrage at finding someone pawing through his desk abruptly shifted to fear as the man's hand settled on the hilt of his weapon. Neither he nor Hest spoke for a long moment. When Hest found his voice, the words had no force behind them. 'I don't know what you are talking about. Get out of my house or I'll summon the City Guard.'

The man looked at him, his grey eyes flat and considering. No fear, no anger. Only evaluation. It was chilling.

'Get out!'

The Chalcedean wheeled away from the desk and its disarrayed contents. As the man started past him, Hest pointed a disdainful hand at the door that still stood ajar. In one fluid and continuous motion, the man seized Hest's wrist with his left hand as his right drew his blade and cut the captive hand, a long shallow slice from Hest's palm to the tip of his index finger. Then the stranger released his wrist and sprang back.

Blood sheeted from the long gash and the pain was exquisite. Hest bent over his hand, roaring with pain as the Chalcedean walked over to the window and casually wiped his blade on the curtain. He spoke over his shoulder, unconcerned how Hest might be reacting. 'A little reminder not to lie. The reminder not to be late on promised merchandise would be much more severe. More on the scale of the reminder that the Duke's swordsman gave to me when I was forced to report that I had not received any recent word from either Begasti Cored or Sedric of Bingtown.'

Hest had a tight grip on his wrist, trying to throttle the searing pain that was shooting up into his arm. Blood was pouring from his hand, dribbling off his fingers onto the expensive carpets in the study. He took a breath. 'Ched!' he shouted. 'Ched! I need help! Ched!'

The door began to swing open but with a catlike spring the Chalcedean was there, stopping the door before it could open fully. He wedged his body into the opening. 'Tea and biscuits! How thoughtful. I'll take them and please see we are not disturbed. This is an extremely confidential matter that your master and I are discussing.'

'Sir?' Ched's querulous tone aggravated Hest.

'Save me!' he shouted as the Chalcedean whirled, his hands full with a tea tray. Without spilling a drop, the man set the tray at his feet and then spun back to shut and bolt the door.

'Sir? Are you all right?' Ched's confused voice barely reached through the heavy doors.

'No! He's mad, get help!'

'Sir?'

Before Hest could draw breath, the Chalcedean was standing before him. This time the drawn knife was at his throat. The Chalcedean smiled, stretching his scars. Blood broke out on his lower lip, the injuries were so recent. He spoke in a soft, rational voice. 'Tell your slave that you are fine, that we must have quiet and he is to go away. Tell him *now*.' The knife flicked and Hest's collar was suddenly loose. The sting of sliced skin and flow of warm blood followed a heartbeat later.

Hest gasped and drew breath to scream. The man slapped him abruptly, an open-handed blow to his cheek.

The door-knob rattled uselessly. 'Sir? Should I fetch help, sir?'

The Chalcedean was smiling and the knife was back,

weaving a pattern before Hest's eyes. The man was damnably fast. 'No!' Hest shouted as the knife dabbed at the end of his nose, and then, as it went back to the hollow of his throat, 'NO, Ched, no! You misunderstood me! Leave us! No disturbance. Leave us!'

The door handle stopped its jiggling dance. 'Sir? Are you certain, sir?'

'Leave us!' Hest bellowed as the knife blade traced a line up his throat. 'Go away!'

'As you wish, sir.'

And then silence. But still the knife tip rested under Hest's chin, lifting him up onto his toes, and still his hand burned and throbbed and the blood dripped from his fingers. An eternity passed in that motionless torment, before the Chalcedean abruptly swept his knife to one side. In two swift strides, he was at the door again and hope leapt in Hest that he was going to leave, his mad rampage over. Instead the man stooped and lifted the tea tray. He brought it to Hest's desk, stepping over his satchel and carelessly sweeping papers from the desk top to set it down. He watched Hest with his cold grey eyes as he flicked up a clean white napkin and wiped his knife on it. It left a scarlet stripe on the linen. He snapped it toward Hest. 'Bind your hand. And then it will be time for you to deliver the promised merchandise.'

Awkwardly, Hest wrapped his injured hand. It was agony to put the cloth against the cut. Blood blossomed through the napkin. He drew a ragged breath and swiped his sleeve across his face, feigning that he wiped sweat, not tears, from his eyes. He could not show weakness. The foreigner was mad and capable of anything. His sleeve came away bloody and Hest suddenly realized, 'You cut my nose! You cut my face.'

'A tiny jab, the smallest prick of the knife's tip. Pay no mind to it.' The Chalcedean poured steaming tea into a cup for himself, sniffed it thoughtfully, and then took a sip. 'Boiled leaves. I do not understand it, but it does not taste so bad on a chilly day like this one. So. The merchandise. Now.'

Hest retreated on shaking legs. 'Truly, sir, I've no idea what you are talking about.'

The Chalcedean followed him, teacup in one hand and knife in the other. He herded Hest away from the heavily-draped windows and backed him into the corner. Hest's heart-beat thundered in his ears. The man took a sip of tea and smiled.

'I will listen,' he said conversationally. 'For the time it takes me to drink this cup. Then, you and my blade will tread the dance of truth.'

'I cannot tell you anything. I don't know anything.' Hest heard his own shaking voice and did not recognize it.

'Then let us summon your slave Sedric. He was the one, was he not, who struck this bargain with Begasti Cored?'

Hest's mind raced. Begasti. A balding man with extremely bad breath. 'I've had dealings with Begasti Cored, but those were in the past. And Sedric is not my slave, he's my . . . assis-tant. And . . .' The connection between the names formed in his mind and suddenly he knew what it was all about. He spoke quickly, his eyes on the hovering knife. 'And he betrayed me and ran off with some very valuable scrolls. To the Rain Wilds. He may have struck a bargain of his own with Begasti Cored. The little traitor probably did. I suspect he did a lot of business behind my back and without my knowledge. Sedric is the man you should be speaking to about this . . . merchandise.' Dragon parts. That was what the man expected him to hand over. Dragon liver and dragon blood, bone and teeth and scales. Dragon parts to make medicines to cure the ancient, ailing and quite probably mad Duke of Chalced. Impossible to obtain, highly illegal dragon parts. What had Sedric dragged him into?

The man drank the last of his tea. He held the empty cup for a moment, and then casually tossed it over his shoulder. It fell on the rug and rolled in a half circle without breaking. Hest's ears rang and the room seemed to grow dim. When the man gestured with the razor-sharp knife, Hest could not contain the small sound in his throat. The Chalcedean appeared not to notice. He cocked his head at Hest and smiled like a flirtatious snake. 'You will sit now, there, at your desk, and we will tease out a bit more of the truth here. I see it hiding in your eyes.'

'I don't know the truth. I have suspicions, nothing more.' But the suspicions were rapidly weaving themselves into a logical pattern. Alise and her obsessive study of the dragons. Sedric's sudden support for her ridiculous Rain Wild expedition to see the creatures. He'd even mentioned Begasti's name, hadn't he, in the midst of their last quarrel? Or the one before? Some foolishness about a fortune to be made . . . Hest made a disgusted noise in the back of his throat. For the past few years, Sedric had watched him manoeuvre his way through the trading world. He'd run Hest's errands, fetched his tea, brushed his jackets and yes, warmed his bed. But obviously he'd thought himself better and more deserving than that. He'd thought he was clever enough to cut this little side trade on his own. If he'd only put himself and Alise at risk, Hest might have found it amusing. But as he crossed the room on rubbery legs and took a seat at his desk, blood dripping from his slashed face and his mutilated hand, all he could feel was fury at Sedric's incompetence and betrayal.

The Chalcedean took a perch on the corner of the desk and sat looking down on Hest. He smiled. 'I see a bit of anger there, now. You are thinking, "his blood should be soaking this napkin, not mine". I am right, am I not? So. Summon your slave and let us apply this pain where it belongs.'

Hest fought to keep his voice steady. 'I told you. He ran off. He stole from me and he ran off. I have nothing to do with him now. Whatever bargain he struck with Begasti Cored, he negotiated on his own. It's nothing to do with me.' Sudden outrage that Sedric could have precipitated this disaster gave him courage. He leaned forward in his chair and shouted, 'You, sir, have made a serious mistake!'

The Chalcedean was unimpressed. He cocked his head and leaned closer, smiling a thin-lipped smile. But his amusement did not seem to reach his eyes. 'Have I? But not as grave as yours. You are responsible and you will be held responsible. What a man's slave does or does not do reflects on his master. You have let one of yours run off and make bargains and steal from you, and done nothing to correct him. So you must pay, just as if your horse had run wild in a market or your dog bitten a child's face. Do not you know the saying, "When a slave lies with your tongue, it is still your mouth it is cut from"? What your man did in your name, you must answer for. Perhaps with a finger, perhaps with your hand . . . perhaps with your life. It is not up to me to decide how heavily you must pay, but answer you will.'

'If he signed a contract with Begasti Cored, I have no knowledge of it. I am not legally bound by it.' Hest fought to keep his voice steady.

'In Chalced, we care very little for what is legal in Bingtown. Here is what we do care about. The Duke, a wise and august personage, suffers from ill health. We know that the proper ministration of medicines made from dragon parts would restore him to health. Begasti Cored is one of our foremost merchants in exotic wares, and he was one of those honoured with the mission of obtaining the necessary parts. To see that his mind was free of all cares while he undertook this errand, the Duke took Cored's entire family under his protection. It is, as you can imagine, a large honour as well as a responsibility to be entrusted with such an undertaking. Nonetheless, for some time, little progress was made, despite great encouragement from the Duke and his nobles. So, it was with satisfaction that we received the news that Begasti Cored had finally recruited a Bingtown Trader who had such a solid reputation to aid him in obtaining the required merchandise.' The Chalcedean and his knife came even closer as he added, 'It was not just this Sedric who was mentioned to us, but you: Trader Hest Finbok. You are well known to so many of our merchants. You are, they all said, a versatile and resourceful merchant, one who drives a shrewd bargain but is able to obtain the finest quality merchandise. So. Where is our merchandise?'

I don't know. Hest bit down on the words before he could say them, suspecting the Chalcedean would react strongly to hearing them again. He closed his eyes for a moment and tried to find a tactic that would extricate him from this situation. He fell back on an old Trader technique. Pretend to be able to meet the customer's expectations. Later, one could make excuses. Or call the City Guard.

'This is what I do know,' he said carefully. He lifted his bandaged hand to dab at the blood at the end of his nose. A mistake. The clot came away on the napkin and it began to drip blood again. Firmly he set his hands on the desktop and tried to ignore it. 'Sedric went to the Rain Wilds. He took with him a woman with great knowledge of dragons. I suspect he hopes to use her knowledge to win him close contact with the dragons. I had to leave on my own trading journey. When I returned, I found no messages from him. The news from the Rain Wilds is that he was part of a party that accompanied the dragons on an expedition up the Rain Wild River. No word has been received from the expedition. They and the dragons may have perished.'

'Pah! Old news is what you offer. When Begasti Cored sent him on his way, your Sedric was not our only emissary for this task. Our other spies have been more prompt in their reporting. We have bent ourselves to this task with every resource at our disposal. Your Sedric was but one of many possible connections we cultivated. So put aside your lies. We already know many things. Do you think you can tell me old news and I will be content with it? Do you think to distract me from my task? Do you think that I do not have concerns of my own bound up with this undertaking? You are a fool, then. And you will find there is a high cost for thinking us fools as well.'

'Truly, I know no more than what I have told you!' Desperation broke through in his voice. To so betray himself ran counter to every rule of wise bargaining, to all he had ever been taught about dealing with Chalcedeans. Show no fear, no doubt, and no weakness. But the burning pain from his hand, the smell of his own dripping blood and the complete foreignness of the experience had him literally trembling.

'I believe you,' the Chalcedean said suddenly. He hopped off the corner of the desk and sauntered back to the window. He tested his blade on the drapery, shredding them in the process. He was staring out the window as he spoke. 'I believe you because we have a similar problem. We are not certain where Begasti Cored is; we believe that he, too, has gone to the Rain Wilds. Perhaps that means he is close to obtaining the required merchandise.'

Hest eased himself silently out of the chair. The door was not so far away. The rugs were thick. Could he move slowly and quietly toward the door, unlatch it and flee to safety before the man was aware he was escaping? He suspected that if he failed to get through the door, he might pay with his life. And if he got through the door, where would he flee?

The Chalcedean would give chase, he was sure. His terror sickened him, dizzied him with weakness.

'You know, of course, how difficult it is for a Chalcedean to obtain passage up the Rain Wild River. That Begasti managed such a feat speaks well of his resourcefulness. We suspect that he was aided by Sinad Arich. Perhaps they are both working toward fulfilling their tasks. But it does put them out of our reach. And that will not do. It will not do at all.'

Hest made one step toward the door. The man had his back to him. Another step. The Chalcedean drew the blade up and down the expensive draperies, almost as if he were whetting it on the fine fabric. Hest didn't care. Whatever kept him busy was fine. He slid another step closer to the door. One more silent step and then he would spring for it, fling the latch back, open the door and run like a scalded cat.

'So we do what we must. We bring our messages to the one we can reach. And he, in turn, relays the message where we cannot go ourselves. Very swiftly he does this.'

The man turned. There was a sudden thud, as if someone had knocked once, heavily, upon the door. Hest turned, hoping Ched had returned. Instead, a short knife with a very gaudy handle quivered stiffly in the hard wood. For a moment, he made no sense of what he saw. The Chalcedean cleared his throat and Hest looked at him. Another little knife, its hilt a gay pattern of red and blue and green, sat balanced in the man's hand.

'Can you run as fast as a knife can fly? Shall we find out?'

'No. Please, no. What do you want of me? Say it clearly and if I can give it to you, I will. Do you want money? Do you want—?'

'Hush.' A gentle word spoken harshly. Hest fell silent.

'It is so simple. We want the merchandise that was

promised. Dragon parts. Scales. Blood. Teeth. Liver. We do not care now who delivers it, as long as it arrives swiftly. When it does, you will see what a generous man the Duke of Chalced is. He who brings what is required will be richly rewarded with honours as well as coin! For generations, your house will be praised and respected by all who serve his lordship.

'So. You will begin by finding Sinad Arich and Begasti Cored. There is a small box for each of them, there beside your fine desk. Each contains a gift that they will value above their lives from the Duke. Don't lose either of them. They are irreplaceable. If they are lost, you will pay for them with your life. When you deliver them, you should remind each of them that their eldest sons send greetings to them and assure them that their heir sons are prospering in the Duke's care. This is not something that every member of their families can say, but for their eldest sons, it is still true. For it to remain true, all they must do is complete their missions. Suitably motivated, we are certain that these two will be eager to help you locate your runaway slave. And the merchandise that we have been promised.'

His heart had sunk deeper into despair with every word the man uttered. He made a final effort. 'It may not be possible to obtain dragon parts. The dragons have left Cassarick. They and their keepers are gone. All of them may be dead for all I know.'

'Well. You should hope that at least one of them is still alive. And that your slave is in a position to keep the bargain he made on your behalf. It if is otherwise . . . Well. I am sure neither of us desires to think of how *that* ends. And now, I must be going.'

Abruptly, the man sheathed his gleaming blade. The tiny throwing knife vanished back to wherever it had come from.

The relief Hest felt weakened his knees almost more than his terror had.

'I will do what I can.'

It was easy to say the words, to make any promise as the Chalcedean moved toward the door. 'I know you will,' the man replied. He paused, his fingers closing on the hilt of the knife he had thrown and with a sudden jerk freed it from the dark panelling. He examined it for a moment. 'Your parents have a lovely home,' he observed. 'And for her years, your mother is still quite an attractive woman. Plump and pretty. Unscarred.' He smiled as he said the word, and made the knife disappear.

Then he worked the latch on the door, stepped through it and was gone. Hest reached it in two bounds, slammed it shut and latched it firmly. His legs gave out under him and he sank to the floor. He took deep ragged breaths in an attempt to calm himself. 'I'm safe now,' he said aloud. 'I'm safe.' But the words were hollow. The man's threat to his family had been clear. If he thought Hest wasn't obeying him, he'd kill Hest's mother and probably his father. And then he'd come after Hest himself again.

With difficulty he got to his feet and staggered to his chair, not yet daring to open the door and shout for Ched. The Chalcedean might still be lurking outside it. He poured himself a cup of the tea. It still steamed as it came out of the pot. Had it been such a short time ago that that idiot Ched had left the tea and abandoned Hest to a sadistic assassin? Was it possible it was still morning? It felt as if days had passed.

He gripped the cup with two shaking hands and sipped the tea, letting the hot liquid steady him. His glance fell on the satchel the man had left beside his desk. It was in the Chalcedean style, an open-topped loosely woven bag. Inside it there were two boxes of wood with enamel insets. The sigil worked in gleaming scarlet and black was the

Duke's symbol, the grasping claw of a raptor. The edges of the box were studded with alternating pearls and small rubies. The boxes alone were worth a small fortune. What did they hold? Something irreplaceable. He turned one over and over in his hands, looking for a hidden catch. His napkin-wrapped hand leaked blood onto the pearls, making them rosy.

Whatever was in them would be small recompense for what he had gone through this morning. It was no more than any of them owed him. Anger was beginning to assert itself. He would go to the City Guard. The Bingtown Traders had small tolerance for Chalcedeans at the best of times. When they heard that an insane assassin was loose in the city, they'd hunt him down like a dog. And, Hest reflected, if word got out that it was the treachery of Sedric Meldar that had lured such a villain to Bingtown, well, Sedric and his family's reputation were not Hest's concern. He should have thought of those things before he stole from him.

A sharp rap at the door jerked him from the chair. He stood trembling, the box forgotten in his hands. Then, another sharp knock, and Ched's voice.

'Sir? Your guest is gone. I thought you'd like to know I found the scroll you wanted. The one in the glass-topped rosewood box? It had been stored in one of the cabinets, along with several others. Sir?'

Hest staggered to the door. With his good hand, he lifted the latch. 'Call a healer, you fool! You left me at the mercy of a madman! And fetch the City Guard, right away!'

The man stood gaping at him, the precious scroll in its decorative box in his hands. The box that Hest held made a sudden small click; his unwary touch had released a hidden catch. The twin halves of the lid rose of their own accord. There was a smell, of spices and dirty salt. Hest looked inside.

The hand inside the box was small but well preserved. A child's hand, palm up, the fingers open as if pleading. The silver bracelet that bound the ragged stump of the wrist did not conceal the two arm bones that protruded. They were uneven, crushed as much as cut.

'Sweet Sa, have mercy,' Ched breathed. He looked as if he might faint.

Hest found breath to speak. 'Just a healer, Ched. A discreet one.'

'Not the City Guard, sir?' The servant looked baffled.

'No. And not a word of this to anyone.'

Day the 12th of the Change Moon
Year the 7th of the Independent Alliance of Traders

From Detozi, Keeper of the Birds, Trehaug to Reyall, Acting Keeper of the Birds, Bingtown

Reyall, I regret to inform you that we have now received a complaint of tampering. Malta Vestrit Khuprus entered a notice with the Trehaug Bird Keepers that her last two messages from her mother, Keffria Vestrit Haven of Bingtown, appear to have been opened, read, and resealed with inferior wax. While she reports that neither message contained any sensitive material, being only family news and a discussion of the disappearance of Selden Vestrit, both women are concerned that a pattern of damaged wax or oddly spindled messages is developing for all their correspondence by bird. The integrity of the Bird Keepers is at stake here. I do not need to remind you that keeping Trader business private and protecting confidential communication is the only foundation that protects our guild from private competition. If the Traders lose faith in our integrity, all our livelihoods will be at risk. Although I am sure there will be formal discussions at all level of the Guild, I beg you to keep all communication with Erek and me at a professional level, and to keep your eyes open for any discrepancies. Log anything you notice faithfully, and please keep Erek and me informed of anything you notice about birds, message tubes, wax and lead seals, and conditions of messages received. We are gravely concerned.

Detozi and Erek

CHAPTER SIX

Marked by the Rain Wilds

'You're packing.'

Malta could tell that Jani was trying not to sound accusing. She set down her powder brush and replied easily, 'Yes. I'm going to Cassarick with Reyn.' She regarded Jani in the mirror before her. Only a soft tap at the door had warned her of her mother-in-law's entrance. Malta tried not to frown. She'd been toying with her cosmetics, trying to disguise the deepening darkness under her eyes. The fine scaling on her face made the masquerade of powder and paint much more difficult than it had been when she was a smooth-faced young woman.

'You don't think he could attend to this on his own? It's only a problem with the diggers, and Reyn knows more about excavation issues than any of us.'

'Of course he does.' Malta had always taken pride in her husband's competence in that difficult area. 'But I want to go. There may be news of the *Tarman* expedition. Even if it's only rumour. And Cassarick is only a day's journey up the river. I don't think we'll stay more than two weeks.'

She took up the powder brush and gave one final quick

swipe to the back of her neck. Her upswept hair bared the silvery-gray mark there, the peculiar scar a legacy of a very strange encounter years ago. It had left her flesh unnaturally sensitive. A kiss from Reyn there was almost as sensual as a touch to the Elderling crown that had developed on her brow. As Malta rose to return to her wardrobe and packing, Jani ventured into her chamber. She closed the door behind her, shutting out the rising wind of yet another winter storm.

It was not unusual for her husband's mother to drop in for a visit, unannounced. Over the years of her marriage, Malta had become accustomed to it. Her room might be a completely separate structure but it was still part of Reyn's ancestral home. All of the various rooms and chambers in this tree were all a part of Jani Khuprus's 'house', just as Malta's bedchamber in her Bingtown family home was still a part of her mother's house. To Jani, it was not a visit, but just a stroll down a corridor, even if that corridor was an airy pathway that followed the sweep of a vast tree limb.

Generations ago, when the Satrap of Jamaillia had first exiled 'criminals' to the Rain Wilds, Reyn's ancestors had chosen this tree. The sturdy lower branches that had once held their first dwellings now supported their counting houses and places of commerce, the shops where Elderling artefacts were cleaned and examined for magical properties, the work areas where sawyers had once sliced sections of wizardwood logs into planks and the warehouses where, to this day, merchandise was stored and displayed until buyers could be found for it. The next layer of branches supported the dwelling chambers of the family. There was a large formal dining hall, built of solid wood and surrounding the entire trunk of the tree. It was as sturdy as any Bingtown mansion. Beyond, in chambers radiating out from the central trunk, were studies and morning rooms, bedchambers and sewing rooms, rooms for guests and bathing chambers and gaming rooms. Each structure stood apart from the others. Some sat solidly upon a fan of adjacent branches; others swung like bird-houses, suspended where they might capture sunlight and gentle winds. They were connected by pathways that followed the supporting limbs of the trees or man-made bridges and trolleys.

As the years had passed and both family and tree put out branches and new limbs, the Khuprus family had added more and more chambers that ventured higher and higher into the family tree. Malta and Reyn lived in a fine set of sturdy rooms built close to the trunk and only one level above Jani's own rooms. Even by Bingtown standards, the rooms were large and well appointed. The corridors between the different chambers of their dwelling might be the paths and bridges that followed the branches or stretched from limb to limb, but Malta had grown accustomed to that. It was home now, and even the casual visiting habits of Reyn's relatives seemed normal now.

Jani had raised an eyebrow at the overflowing travel trunk. 'For a few days' visit?'

Malta laughed self-consciously. 'I've never learned to travel light. I know it drives Reyn mad. But you just never know what sort of clothes you'll need. Especially since we'll be dealing with the Cassarick Traders' Council. I may go to some of the meetings he must attend, and I must be whatever he needs me to be. I don't know if I'll need to look regal and daunting, or simple and unassuming.'

'Regal and daunting,' Jani decided for her. 'There isn't a one of them on that council who isn't a self-important upstart. The Rain Wild Council was foolish to allow Cassarick to start a council of their own. It gave them a false sense of importance. If you accompany Reyn to any of the meetings, don't let them cow you. Squash them from the beginning, and don't let them dare to attempt to dictate to you. Take the power and keep it, from start to finish.'

'I fear you are right. They are so intent on making a profit they've forgotten that the Trader traditions value honesty and fairness.'

'Wear your flame gems. Flaunt them. And your Elderling cloak. Remind them that you come from one of the original Trader families of the Rain Wilds. Demand that they treat you both with respect. When it comes to digging, let them recall that we were among the first to risk our lives in the early excavation of Trehaug. We have paid our dues and have a right to what we claim. And if there is news of the *Tarman* expedition, demand all of it. Remind them of their original agreement with Tintaglia. And that some day the dragon queen may demand an accounting of all they did for her fellow dragons.'

'Or didn't do. It worries me that we've had no news of the *Tarman* at all. I sent a message asking if they would not send another ship to find what had become of them. The response was that "at present, there is no suitable vessel to send".' Malta sighed heavily and subsided onto the bed. Reyn had raised the bed platform so that she was able to sit and stand from it more easily. She sat for a moment, catching her breath, while Jani watched her quietly. Malta smiled. 'Aren't you going to remind me that I'm pregnant and ask me why on earth I'd choose to travel at such a time?'

Jani returned the smile, her finely-scaled face rippling as she did so. 'I know your answers almost as well as you know what my questions are likely to be. The closer it comes to your time, the more you wish to be near Reyn. That you feel that way brings me only satisfaction. Yet we both know you are taking a risk. We both know what it is to miscarry; and more than once. We both know that miscarriages either happen or don't. We've seen the women who take to their beds the very first month and keep as still as a cocoon, hoping to save what grows inside them.' Jani sighed suddenly. 'And we've seen them lose the child despite that. Or give birth to a child so weak or so Changed by the Rain Wilds that it cannot be allowed to survive. You have choices as I did, to continue to lead a hearty life, to walk and work with no guarantees that your child will be robust. But I know from my own child-bearing years that it is better to do that than to wait in still-ness in a dim room and fill the long months with hoping and worrying.'

Jani stopped speaking, as if suddenly realizing that neither she nor Malta wanted to consider yet again the darker aspects of her pregnancy. She changed the topic abruptly. 'So. You will go to Cassarick with Reyn. He told me that he wishes to speak with the Vargus family about how they are excavating our site. Reyn told me that he has heard rumours they move too fast and do not reinforce the tunnels as they should. He fears that they are placing quick profit above human lives. That was not our agreement when we entered into the part-nership with them.'

'It's worse,' Malta confirmed, grateful for the change in conversation. 'Reyn says they are using Tattooed to dig. They pay them poorly and do not care as much for their safety as if they were Rain Wild bred. They receive no share of what they find, no matter how valuable it is, and no extra pay for the dangers they enter. They do not understand that an Elderling city has stranger and greater threats than cave-ins and flooding. The Vargus Traders are sending them where only experienced diggers should go, ones wise both in excava-tion and in the other dangers of the city.'

'I've heard the rumours,' Jani conceded uneasily. 'They lead to theft and carelessness by the workers. When there is no personal reward for a chamber well excavated but only a day's pay, why should they go cautiously and keep meticulous records? When the Vargus traders treat them as little better than slaves, why should they behave any better?

'But I've also heard what the Tattooed say. We promised them that we would welcome them and make them part of us. That they could work and have homes and vote on their fates. That they would not be lesser citizens here but could live among us, marry among us, and we hoped, have healthy children to repopulate our cities. *I* made those promises to them.' She shook her head bitterly. 'Well, we've seen where that has taken us. Traders such as the Vargus family treat them poorly and disdain them for anything but physical labour. In retaliation, many of the Tattooed hold themselves apart. They keep to their own sections of the city and do not share in the upkeep of the public ways and bridges. They marry only their own kind, and produce lots of children while our population continues to dwindle. They outlive us by decades. And they do not respect our ways. And that leads only to more resentment, as the established Rain Wild families fear they will be displaced by them.' She sighed again, more heavily and said, 'It was my idea to bring them here. In the dark days of the war with Chalced, it seemed a brilliant idea, one that would benefit all of us. When I told them they could live among us where their tattooed faces would not be a badge of shame, but only markings on their skin, I thought they would accept the changes that the Rain Wild causes in us. I thought they would know that those things were likewise skin deep.'

'But it did not work that way, not entirely,' Malta agreed. She heard guilt in Jani's voice. It was a familiar conversation as the older woman went over what she had negotiated and wondered how it had gone wrong. Malta reached over and picked up a pair of stockings. Slowly she rolled them into a ball. 'Jani, it is not your fault. At the time, it seemed a brilliant solution, for them and for us. You bargained in good faith, and no one can fault you if it did not turn out as you planned. We cannot force them to join us. But we all know that eventually, they will. Already the Rain Wilds have touched some of them, though not as heavily as it did the early settlers. Some of the Tattooed who came here as adults have begun to scale as they age, and their youngsters more so. Their children are being born with copper glints in their eyes and that sheen to the skin that speaks of pebbling later in life. Their children will be Rain Wilders whether they like it or not.' Malta set her feet firmly on the floor and stood up. Her lower back protested and without thinking, she set her hands to her belly, supporting her growing child.

Jani smiled. 'As will your child, Malta Vestrit Khuprus.'

Malta's smile was more tenuous. She turned away hastily to drop the balled-up stockings in her case, then turned back to her wardrobe to look for a winter cloak to add to what she had packed. Tears stung her eyes, and she did not want Reyn's mother to see them.

Jani spoke quietly. 'Sometimes, sharing a fear or sorrow can lessen it.'

'Oh,' Malta said, striving for a casual note in her voice and failing as her throat closed on the words. 'It was just something the midwife said yesterday when I went to see her.'

'Koli is one of our best midwives. She has been helping with births for years.'

'I know. She is just so blunt sometimes. About our chances. About what she thinks of us for even trying for a child.' Malta searched through the wardrobe and found the cloak she wanted. It was scarlet and lined with velvet, so soft against her skin. She held a fold of it to her cheek. 'She said we can hope for the best but we must plan for the worst. That we must choose now what we will do if the child is born breathing but so Changed that survival is unlikely.' She tried to steady her voice. 'If I wish, she can smother or drown our baby in warm water before she is exposed for the animals to devour. She can let us see it dead and say farewell. Or we can leave it to the midwife to whisk it away, to make her decision, and never speak of it again. If I choose that, we don't have to know if the baby ever drew a breath or was stillborn.' Despite her resolution, her voice was trembling. 'She said that only the mother has the right to make those choices. But I cannot, Jani. I cannot. Yet each time I see her, she presses me for answers.' Malta clutched the cloak to her as if it were a child about to be torn from her arms. 'But I cannot.'

'It's her job,' Jani said softly. 'Years of doing it have hardened her in some ways. Ignore her words. It's her hands and her skills that we'll be paying Koli for, not her opinions.'

'I know.' Malta barely breathed the word. She didn't want to think about what else the pessimistic old woman had said. She might be a skilled midwife, but she was also a mean and bitter old woman with no living offspring of her own. There were words so harsh she would not inflict them on her husband or his mother. 'No right to try for a baby; his brother Bendir already has an heir. What need do you have of a child? You know the baby will be a monster. All your miscarriages and stillbirths have been monsters.' Such words were hard to ignore when the accusations were so true.

Malta held back a sob. Stop being silly. Everyone said that being pregnant made a woman prey to her emotions. Focus on the task at hand. Packing. She forced herself to fold the cloak and set it in the trunk. She was going to go to Cassarick with her husband. And his sister Tillamon was coming along, to visit one of her girlhood friends who had moved. It would be a pleasant afternoon boat ride up the river. A nice day to enjoy getting out of the house for a time, and having Reyn's company for a full day. Choose a warm cloak; it would be windy and rainy on the river.

Next to the red winter cloak's hook hung another favourite, one that was black and embroidered with green and blue and red dragons in flight. It had been a gift from a weaver in Jamaillia in the days when she and Reyn had been guests of the Satrap of Jamaillia and honoured by him as the 'king' and 'queen' of the Elderlings. Elderlings they might truly be; so Tintaglia the dragon had named them. But dragons were no more honest than humans and would say whatever pleased them at the moment. There were days when she doubted her Elderling status. Perhaps both she and Reyn and even Selden were simply Changed by the Rain Wilds and merely more fortunate that in their cases the changes had imbued them with an exotic beauty. So, Elderlings, perhaps. But never had they been king and queen of anything, save in the boyish Satrap's fancy.

After their 'great adventure' in the Pirate Isles, after she had saved Satrap Cosgo's sorry life more times than she could count, it had pleased him to present Reyn and her to his court as Elderling royalty. At the time, she had relished the attention and luxury he bestowed on them. Several harsh years of hardship had left her starved for pretty trinkets and lovely clothes and extravagant parties. But his honouring of them had gone far beyond that. The Jamaillian nobility had showered them with gifts and praise. Songs had been composed in their honour, tapestries and stained glass windows created to commemorate their visit and exotic dishes of supposed Elderling delicacies were contrived. It had been a soap bubble illusion, a few months of everything she had ever imagined her life could ever be. Balls and dinners, jewellery and feasts, perfumes and performances . . . it still startled her that she and Reyn had both eventually tired of it and longed to go home to be wed and begin their life together. She drew the cloak out and folded it softly over her arm. The faded perfume of a long-ago ball rose from its soft folds, sweeping her back into a memory of a wild whirling dance, of looking up into the handsome face of the young man who would become her husband.

The tears that had threatened her a moment ago were suddenly gone.

'There's that smile, the one that made my boy fall in love with you,' Jani said fondly.

'Oh, I feel so foolish. One moment, my eyes are full of tears and the next I am floating with joy.'

Jani laughed out loud. 'You're pregnant, my dear. That's all.'

'That's all?' Reyn's voice was full of mock outrage as he swept into the room, pushed along by a gust of wind. He slammed the door against winter's chill thrust. 'That's all, Mother? How can you say that when for years, all we've heard is "that is everything! Make another little Khuprus, Malta dear! Replenish the family coffers with an heir or two!"'

'Oh, I am not that bad!' Jani Khuprus exclaimed.

'You make me sound like a brood cow!' Malta exclaimed.

'Ah, but such a pretty little cow! One that will make us all late if she doesn't finish her packing right away and waddle down to the boat with me.'

'You, sir, are a beast!' Malta attempted outrage but spoiled it by laughing.

'Mannerless boy,' his mother rebuked him with a fond push. 'Don't you tease her! She has a fine baby belly, something to be proud of!'

'And proud I am,' Reyn said, setting his hands gently to

either side of the mound of her belly. His eyes gleamed with such tenderness that Malta felt a blush rise to her cheeks and his mother turned discreetly away as if what passed between them were too personal a thing for her to witness.

'I'll find a man to take the trunks down. You watch over her, son, and not just on the way down to the boat.'

'I will. I always do,' he replied, and neither seemed to take much notice of the door closing behind her. Nonetheless, as soon as he heard the latch set, Reyn leaned in over her belly to set his mouth softly on his wife's. He held the kiss, as tender and passionate as if they were still newlywed, until she broke away and leaned her head on his chest. He stroked her gleaming golden hair, and then let his hand wander to her brow where his fingers caressed the scarlet crest that marked her as an Elderling. She trembled at his touch and, murmuring a soft rebuke, moved her head away from his hand.

'I know,' he sighed. 'Not while we might hurt the baby or bring it too soon. I will wait. But I don't want you to think I'm waiting too patiently!'

She laughed quietly and stepped free of his embrace. 'Then be patient now and let me finish choosing what I must take.'

'No time,' he told her. Stepping to the wardrobe, he considered its contents for a moment. Then he darted swiftly in, seized a fat armful of clothes, turned and deposited them in the travelling trunk. As Malta voiced a hopeless protest, he tucked them ruthlessly down and shut the lid on them. 'There! All done! And now I will whisk you away. We will be taking the lifts down rather than the trunk stairs, and you know how slow they can be.'

'I could still manage the stairs,' Malta insisted indignantly, but secretly she was glad of his thoughtfulness. She did not feel as agile as she usually did, and her feet were often swollen and tender.

'Off we go, then. I'm sure I've put enough of everything in that trunk, and if not, there is the first one that was taken down to the boat this morning.'

'That was just the baby's things. Just in case he surprises us in Cassarick. And Tillamon? Is she packed yet?'

'My sister is waiting for us at the lift.'

Malta cast a longing eye at the other wardrobe, but Reyn seized her hand, tucked it firmly into his arm and opened the door. From the set of his mouth, Malta decided it was time to pretend to be meek and wifely. She caught up only one extra cloak and swirled it around her shoulders as he led her out into the day.

Not much sunlight reached the household level of the family tree even on a bright day. On grey winter days like this one, forest twilight was the rule. In the high treetops, a wind was battering the forest. She knew it only by the occasional flurries of leaves and needles that drifted down. Most of the trees that would shed their leaves for this season were already bared, but there were enough evergreen trees in this section of the Rain Wilds to shelter them from all but torrential rains.

The lifts were a series of platforms with basket-weave sides that travelled vertically from canopy to earth, operated by stoutly muscled men working a system of lines and pulleys and counterweights. Malta did not enjoy using the lifts but she no longer feared them as she once had. In truth, she had dreaded taking the long spiralling staircases that wound around the tree trunks and were the only alternate routes to the forest floor.

Tillamon, cloaked and heavily veiled, awaited them. Malta wondered why, but said nothing. Reyn, in his typically brotherly fashion, was not so discreet. 'Why are you veiled as if for a trip to Bingtown?'

Tillamon stared at him through a mask of lace. 'To visit

the lower levels now is almost like going to Bingtown. There are so many staring outsiders in the city now. And not all of us, little brother, are so fortunate as to have had our changes make us lovelier.'

Malta knew the rebuke was for Reyn, not her. Even so, she repressed a squirm. Of late she had become more aware that she possessed everything that Tillamon had ever longed for. She had a husband and a child on the way. And she was undeniably beautiful. The changes the Rain Wilds had wrought on her had all been kindly ones. The fine scaling on her face was supple, the colours flattering. She had grown taller than she had expected, and her long hands and fingers were graceful. When she contrasted that to Tillamon's pebbly face and the multiple dangling growths that fringed her jaw and ears, it was hard not to feel guilty at her good fortune, though none of Reyn's sisters had ever seemed to resent her for it.

She followed Tillamon into the lift and waited for Reyn to join them. Reyn tugged the cord. High above them, a lift-tender rang a bell in response and from below she heard his partner's answering whistle. For a brief time they dangled, waiting. Then, with a small hitch and a lurch of Malta's heart, they were descending.

The lift dropped more swiftly than she liked and she found herself clutching Reyn's arm. She was grateful when they reached the bottom of the first lift's run and stepped out and then into the next lift. 'Slower, please,' Reyn warned the tender sternly, and the man bobbed his head in response. He was Tattooed, she noted, and watched how his eyes lingered curiously on Tillamon's veil. Tillamon noticed also, for she turned away from him to gaze out into the forest. She spoke only after the lift was in motion. 'Sometimes I feel that I am the stranger here, when they stare at me like that.'

'He is ignorant. He will learn better,' Reyn said.

'When?' Tillamon replied acerbically.

'Perhaps when he has a child and it is born Changed by the Rain Wilds,' Malta said quietly.

Reyn turned startled eyes on her but Tillamon gave a bitter laugh. 'What will he learn then? To kill the children that can never be pretty? But I was *born* pretty. My changes came on me early, and now I walk in death. There will never be a marriage for me, never a child. He stares at me rudely but my own people look away. Perhaps I should be grateful that at least someone sees me.'

'Tillamon! I see you. I love you.' Reyn was aghast. He set a hand on her shoulder, but she did not turn into his embrace. Her voice was muffled by her veil.

'You love me, little brother, but do you really see me? Do you see who I am becoming?'

'I don't know—' Reyn began, but the lift had arrived at its next stop, and Tillamon lifted a lace-gloved hand to silence him.

Malta felt a wave of despair rise in her. She could think of nothing to say to Tillamon, but as they moved to the next lift, she quietly took her hand.

As the lift lurched into motion, Reyn began, 'Tillamon, I—' but his sister quickly said, 'You know, we should not speak of troubling things now. While Malta is with child, she should think only calm and pleasant thoughts.' Tillamon gave Malta's hand a brief squeeze before releasing it.

It was clear that Tillamon wished to change the direction of the conversation and Malta was happy to help her. 'Look. Down there, through the trees. Is that our boat?' It was a long, narrow craft manned by many rowers, designed to defeat the river's current as it moved upstream. Aft, there was a small cabin for passengers. A long deck for freight ran down the middle of the ship. At the very back of the vessel, a brawny man leaned idly on the sweep that was also the tiller for the ship. He looked bored.

'That's the *River Snake*. And yes, she's waiting for us.' There was relief in Reyn's voice. He, too, preferred to think of pleasant things. Perhaps, for a short time, she could allow him that.

Tillamon asked, 'Is that one of the new boats I've been hearing about? The Bingtown ones that can withstand the river water as well as a liveship?'

'No, she's Rain Wild made and crewed. But you may get a glimpse of one of the Bingtown ships before we return. I'd heard one was making a tour of the Rain Wild settlements, to show how impervious it is to the acid and also how swiftly it can move, even in shallower channels. That's what the Jamaillian boat builder is calling them: impervious boats. That one is supposed to make a stop in Trehaug, and then go up to Cassarick. You know that's been a choke point in the movement of goods: the locks we built for helping the serpents reach Cassarick are mostly destroyed now; the winter floods took them out. And the deep draught liveships can't navigate past that stretch of the river. A freight vessel that can run the shallows and doesn't melt after half a dozen trips would revolutionize how we trade up and down the river.'

'And they are made in Bingtown?'

'Yes. That one, at any rate. A Pirate Isles fellow came up with the formula for the hull coating, so it will be a joint venture. Some Jamaillian boat builder is financing the undertaking, I'm told.'

'Oh.' Tillamon's voice went flat suddenly. 'So once the ships start plying our waters, there will be more Bingtowners and Tattooed and Jamaillians than ever in the Rain Wilds.'

Reyn looked startled. 'I . . . suppose there will.'

'Not an improvement,' Tillamon said decisively, and stepped off the lift briskly as it halted on the landing platform.

A final lift carried them all the way down to the ground and released them onto the wooden walkway. Walking on solid ground felt strange now, even if Malta was glad to be off the lift. Reyn took her arm and Tillamon followed as they hurried toward the waiting boat. Malta heard a thud behind her and turned to see a faster freight lift arrive with her trunk on board. The servant who had brought it hefted it to his shoulder and followed them. 'I hope they have saved room on the freight deck,' she said and Reyn replied, 'We are the only passengers today, and they didn't have much of a load. There will be plenty of room.'

Stepping out of the forest's eternal shadows and into full sunlight was almost as much of a shock as setting foot on earth had been. *I'm truly becoming a Rain Wilder in all things*, Malta thought to herself. She glanced down at the finely-scaled skin on the back of her hand. *All things*. The wind off the river struck her and she wrapped her cloak more tightly.

The captain of the *River Snake* had freight to deliver and was eager to be on his way. Malta, Reyn and Tillamon were scarcely in the passenger cabin before he was having his crew untie from the docks. In a matter of moments, the rowers had the long ship free and headed out into the river. Malta sat down gratefully on one of the padded benches that lined the walls of the cabin but Tillamon stood at the aft window, looking out longingly. 'It has been so long since I've been away from home to go anywhere. Ages since I felt full sunlight on my face.'

'You don't need my permission,' Reyn commented.

'No, and I never did. I just need to find my courage. That's all.'

Malta followed her gaze. There was a small square of deck

outside the cabin and then the tillerman's area. The man was working the long sweep in a series of steady arcs, holding only when the captain called a course correction to him. There was a strange beauty in the man's strength and sureness as he either guided or pushed the ship along. Somehow he became aware of their scrutiny and glanced back at the cabin. His face was pebbled so that his brow overhung his eyes; a string of growths that reminded Malta of a fish's barbels lined his jaw. 'I think I'll go out,' Tillamon declared abruptly. She lifted her veil and discarded it with the hat that had secured it, then peeled off the long lacy gloves that had covered her hands and arms. Without another word, she set the garments on the bench beside Malta and opened the small aft door to step out on the deck. Chill wind gusted in; it didn't deter her. She went immediately to lean on the railing, turning her face up to the sun that was peeping through a break in the overcast sky.

Reyn moved aside his sister's hat, veil and gloves and sat down beside Malta. She leaned her head on his shoulder and for a moment was happy. Sunlight made a bright square on the floor of the cabin. The only sounds were that of the ship, of the creaking oars as they moved in rhythm and occasionally the captain's shout back to the tillerman. She yawned, suddenly sleepy.

'What is it that I don't see about my sister?' Reyn asked her plaintively. He lifted up the hat and the attached veil. 'Is this so terrible? When I came to Bingtown to court you, I was as heavily veiled. It was tradition.'

'Tradition born out of discomfort,' Malta observed. 'Rain Wilders were thought grotesque. They still are. I have lived among you and become one of you. But I know what Tillamon knows. If she were to go to Bingtown and walked unveiled, people would stare. Some, even some born in Bingtown, would say unkind things, mock her or turn aside in horror. People want the treasures of the Rain Wilds but don't want to see the price it exacts from those who provide them.'

'Did you think I was grotesque? When you first met me and I went veiled?'

She laughed softly. 'I was a silly little girl then, full of odd tales of the Rain Wilds. I was sure that my cruel mother had sold me off to some frightful creature. Then I discovered the frightful creature was incredibly wealthy, burdened with hundreds of little presents for me, and full of compliments that I could not wait to hear. So then you became mysterious. Unknowable. And dangerously desirable.'

She smiled and gave a little shiver as a thrill ran up her back.

'What was that?' Reyn demanded. He set aside his sister's hat and took her hand.

Malta laughed aloud, mildly embarrassed. 'I was thinking of the first time you kissed me. My mother had left the room and the only servants there were yours, all veiled and suitably busying themselves with tasks. You leaned in close to me and I thought you would tell me a secret. But then you kissed me. I felt your lips through the lace of the veil. And the tip of your tongue, I thought. It was . . .' She paused and was surprised to realize she was blushing.

'Very erotic,' Reyn finished quietly for her. A slow smile spread over his face and his eyes gleamed with remembered pleasure. 'I had only thought to steal a kiss while your mother was not looking. I had not realized that the barrier to our touch would only enhance the moment.'

'You were a wicked boy. You had no right to kiss me.' Malta tried to sound affronted but failed. She shared his smile, with a touch of sadness for the foolish girl she had been.

He held up his sister's veil before his face. She could scarcely see his features through the multiple layers of dark lace. 'And now I do. Should we try that again?'

'Reyn!' she rebuked him, but he did not pause. He draped the veiling over his face and leaned in to kiss her.

'It's Tillamon's best veil!' she objected. But then the lace brushed her face and she closed her eyes as he kissed her, a very chaste kiss that nonetheless swept her back into memories of their first passion.

When he drew back from her, he wondered in a husky voice, 'Why does the forbidden always add that edge of sweetness?'

'It's true. But I don't know why.' She leaned her head on his chest and asked mischievously, 'Does it mean that now that you have a right to me, I am less sweet?'

He laughed. 'No.'

For a time they were silent together and content. The boat rocked as the rowers battled the current. Malta gazed out the small window. Behind them, the river stretched gleaming, its grey turned to silver in the lingering sunlight. Tillamon leaned on the railing, lost in thought. The wind stirred her hair. From behind she could have been any young woman, lost in her dreams. But what did she dream of? What did the future offer her? What would it offer Malta's child, if she or he were similarly Changed?

'You sigh. Again. Are you uncomfortable?' Reyn set a gentle hand on her belly. She put both her hands over his. This was the time, much as she dreaded it.

'We have some hard questions to discuss, my love. Things I did not and do not want to talk about. But we must.' She took a deep breath and then quickly, like tearing a bandage from a wound, told him of the midwife's demands that they make decisions.

He recoiled from her, his face full of horror. Anger swiftly replaced the horror. 'How can she speak of such things to you? How dare she?'

'Reyn!' The anger in his eyes was both reassuring and

frightening. 'She has to ask these questions. With my other pregnancies, well, they did not last long, did they? I think she knew they would come to nothing. But now we have felt the child move and with each passing day we are closer to a birth. And these are the decisions that all parents in the Rain Wilds or Bingtown must face. Harsh as they seem, they are decisions that have been faced by generations of Rain Wild folk. So.' Malta took a steady breath. 'What should I tell her?'

Reyn was breathing as hard as if he faced a fight. 'Tell her? Tell her that I care nothing for custom or decorum! Tell her that I will be by your bedside for every moment, and that the instant our child is born, he will be safe in my arms. Should Sa take his life from us, then I will mourn. But if anyone else threatens him, in any way, I will kill them. That is what you can tell her. No. That is what *I* will tell the meddling old hag!'

He stood up abruptly and paced a quick turn around the small cabin before coming to a standstill, staring bleakly out of the window at the passing trees. 'Did you doubt that I would protect our child?' he asked her quietly. There was hurt in his eyes when he turned to her. 'Or is this . . .' he hesitated. 'Is this not what you want? If our child is born Changed, do you wish to, to set him aside? To . . .' His words tapered away to silence.

Malta was shocked. The silence grew longer and the hurt on Reyn's face grew deeper. 'I did not think I had a choice,' she said at last. Tears filled her eyes but did not spill. 'It is done, even in Bingtown. Seldom does anyone speak of it. When I was little, I would see a pregnant woman, and then she would be apart from us for a time, and sometimes she came back with a child and sometimes not. I don't even remember when I first understood that some babies were not kept. It was just something all girls knew, growing up. When women do talk about it, most say it is for the best, that it happens quickly, before the mother can come to know the child and love it. But—' She set both hands to her belly and felt the child turn restlessly inside her, as if he knew they were deciding his fate. 'But I already *know* this child. I already love him. Or her. I do not think I will care if he has a scaled brow when he is born, or if his nails are black. Or hers.' She tried for a smile and failed as the tears suddenly spilled down her face. 'Reyn, I have been so frightened. One night, I dreamed that when the pains came, I ran off into the forest alone to have our baby, to keep her safe. And when I woke, I wondered if I might not do just that. And I had to wonder what you would think of me if I did, if I brought back a Changed child and refused to give it up. Or what your mother would think.'

She sniffed and Reyn was at her side. She found a handkerchief and wiped at her wet eyes. 'I saw some of the dragon keepers. They were just children. And almost every one of them was marked so heavily that I knew they must have been born Changed. Their parents kept them. They grew, they lived. Perhaps they could not marry or have children of their own, but I looked at them and thought, "Their lives are not useless. Their parents were right to keep them, no matter what their neighbours may have said." But now I look at how unhappy Tillamon is. I see how she is stared at, and I know that sometimes ignorant people say things aloud to her. She stays at home almost always now, not even venturing down to the markets. She seldom visits her friends. She was not born Changed. And she has never done anything to deserve a punishment. But punished she is.'

A silence fell. Both of them looked out at Reyn's sister. The clouds were closing over the sun and the day abruptly went from sunny to dim but Tillamon pulled her cloak more closely around her and turned her face to the wind as if drinking it in.

'Perhaps our child will be born untouched. Or perhaps, as

we are Elderling now, so the child will be, with Changes that are . . .'

'Beautiful,' Malta filled in when he hesitated. 'Beautiful and exotic, as we are. By our good fortune, we are changed in a way that makes people smile when they see us. Or used to. Now, as often, I see something else in their faces. Resentment. I hear rumours that they say we give ourselves airs, pretend to be better than our fellows, simply because a dragon chose to gift us with good looks. It isn't the Trader way, Reyn, for any person to be set above another. Oh, Traders will always think themselves better than the Tattooed or the Three Ships folk in Bingtown, far better than any brutish Chalcedean or barbarian Six Duchies man. But there were many who were angered that the Satrap chose to call us "king" and "queen". They were angry then, saying that we made decisions for the Traders that we had no right to make, even if the Council later ratified those decisions. There are some who are offended by us, Reyn. And others who would use us. You know that.'

'I do.' He put his arm around her and pulled her close again. 'I suppose I have not thought about how it would affect our child. If he is born Changed and we insist on keeping him it may cause ill feeling for the Khuprus family. And he may find few playmates. But I cannot imagine letting anyone take him from us. Or drowning him ourselves.'

At those words, Malta choked back a sob.

Reyn leaned his head over hers. 'Don't be afraid, my dear. Whatever comes, we will face it together. I will not give up this child to tradition. If Sa grants that he draws breath on his own, then breathe he shall, and no one shall stop that breath save Sa alone. This I promise you.'

Malta swallowed back her tears. 'And this I promise you, as well,' she told him. And closed her eyes in a silent prayer that she would be able to keep that promise.

Day the 20th of the Change Moon
Year the 7th of the Independent Alliance of Traders

From Detozi, Keeper of the Birds, Trehaug to Reyall, Acting Keeper of the Birds, Bingtown

Red quarantine capsule

I am sending this bird as a solo, to minimize the risk. The cold rainy weather has been harsher than usual, and birds here are sickening at an alarming rate. Please enact quarantine measures immediately for all birds arriving at your cotes, as we have already done so here. I have selected an apparently healthy bird to carry this message. Some of the sickened birds appear to be afflicted with an unusual form of red lice. Please watch for them on any of your birds and isolate immediately.

Will this foul weather never end?

Erek is in an agony of frustration that this is happening while he is here in Trehaug and trapped here for our wedding preparations. I am completely in sympathy with him. Please do all you can to keep his cotes and birds in good condition until he returns. For that is our thought now, that we will settle in Bingtown, though I have many misgivings as to how I will be accepted there. Erek sees none of my flaws nor how heavily Touched I am by the Rain Wilds. Such a man!

CHAPTER SEVEN

Dragon Dreams

Flight was effortless. Sintara's scarlet wings caught the rising heat from the wide grain fields below her and lifted her. She lofted through the skies. Below her, fat white sheep cropped the grass in a green pasture. As her shadow passed over the grass, they scattered in fright. Foolish creatures. She wanted nothing of their sticky wool in her mouth. Few of the dragons enjoyed eating them except when hunting did not appeal to them. Privately, she suspected that was why the humans kept so many of them. Cattle were far more appetizing to dragons. But to a true hunter such as herself, diving on a penned beast offered little satisfaction. She would far rather hunt for her meal, seek out some large, horned creature that offered a bit of a challenge and perhaps even a battle before she won its meat.

But not today. She had fed heavily yesterday, and slept long, an afternoon and a night, after her gorging. Now it was thirst she sought to slake, and not a thirst for blood or for thin river water. She banked her wings and drifted back over Kelsingra. The Silver Plaza was empty at last of other dragons. She would alight there and not have to wait a turn for the

Elderlings to . . . To do what? Something she wanted. Something she wanted very badly that eluded her memory. Something that was secret. She stirred restlessly.

She was not Sintara. Deep in her sleep, she hid from her growling hunger and chilled flesh in a memory of another time and place. Some scarlet ancestor of hers had flown over Kelsingra in that abundant time, on that sunny day. She had known not only the freedom of flight, but the pleasure of the friendship of Elderlings in a time when they had lived in symbiosis with the dragons. It had been a good time for both races. She did not know with certainty what had ended it. In her dreams, she both escaped an unsatisfactory present and explored the past for hints as to what she might do to restore the future to what it should have been.

A sudden gust of wind-driven rain spattered against her face and scattered her dream memories. Sintara opened her eyes to night and storm. The shelter Thymara had built for her was a flimsy thing, a lean-to of logs thatched with branches. Her bed was a thick layer of pine boughs that kept her from the ground, but not by much. She had grown since Thymara had built it, and now she was cramped when she curled herself within its confines. The girl should have built it larger, with thicker walls, perhaps covered in mud, and thatched it more tightly. Sintara had told her so. And her keeper had responded irritably, asking her how long she wished to go without food while Thymara spent her time building her a shelter. The thought of the girl's answer renewed her annoyance with her. She did nothing well. The dragon must shiver in a poorly built shelter even as her hunger clawed at her guts. She had no satisfaction anywhere in her life. Only hunger, discomfort and frustrating dreams.

Sintara slithered from the low-roofed shelter on her belly. It was raining. It seemed always to be raining. The clouds covered the moon and the stars but she widened her eyes and saw without effort. Here in the open forest of scattered trees and brush, the keepers had built a village of shelters for the dragons. As if they were humans who always had to cluster close to one another! None of the sheds were sturdy or intended to be permanent. Hers was no worse than any of the others and better than most. It still stirred vague ancestral memories of stables and kennels. They were shelters for animals, not housing fit for the Lords of the Three Realms.

True, the keepers had little better for themselves. They had moved into the remnants of the shepherds' and farmers' homes that had been built on this side of the river in ancient times. Some were little more than standing walls, but they had made them somewhat habitable. She'd heard their talk and thoughts. They believed that they would be far more comfortable if only they could get across the river to where grand Kelsingra had withstood the depredations of time and weather. They could have gone, one at a time, ferried across by foolish Heeby who seemed to think herself more carthorse than dragon. But they would have had to abandon the dragons to do so.

And they had not.

She resented the tiny trickle of gratitude she felt for that. Gratitude as an emotion was both unfamiliar and uncomfortable, something inappropriate for a dragon to feel, especially toward a human. Gratitude implied a debt: but how could a dragon be indebted to a human? As well be indebted to a pigeon. Or to a piece of meat.

Sintara sheathed her eyes against the falling rain and shook the thought from her mind with the raindrops that she shivered from her wings. It was time. The wind had died down, it was dark, and everyone else slept. She moved quietly over the carpet of wet leaves and forest debris as she left the shelters behind and ventured down the hillside toward an open meadow that faced the river.

She halted when she reached the meadow, staring about her with eyes that opened the night to her vision. No one and nothing stirred. Game of any useful size had fled this area weeks ago, when they had first arrived here. Creatures that had looked at dragons in wonder when they first arrived had quickly learned that fear was the proper response. She had the meadow to herself. Far below, the river flowed swiftly, rich from all the rain, and even here, the sound of it filled the night. It was wide and dark and cold and deep, and strong enough to pull a dragon under and hold her there until she drowned. She had ancient memories of actually landing in this river, when the shock of the cold water on her sun warmed body had been almost welcoming. Memories of letting the water cushion her impact, of letting her body sink down, her wings clasped tight, until she felt sand and gravel beneath her claws, and then, nostrils shut tight against the water, fighting the current to wade up and out of the shallows and onto the riverbank with water streaming from every glistening scale.

But those memories were old ones. Now, from what the keepers told her, there was no sandy sloping riverbank, only a hungry drop-off to deep water at the edge of the city. If she attempted flight and accidentally landed in the river, chances were that it would tumble her in its rough current and she would never emerge again. She looked all around herself again. Only the river, the wind and the rain spoke. She was alone. No witnesses to mock a failure.

She opened her wings wide and shook them; they made a sound like wet canvas sails slapping in a breeze. She paused only for an instant to wonder how she knew that, and then dismissed it as a useless titbit of information. Not all memories were worth saving, and yet she had them. She moved her wings slowly, stretching them out, trying each claw-tipped vane, then lifting them to feel the wind against them. The right wing was still smaller than the left. Weaker, too. How could a dragon fly when one wing was less able than the other?

Compensate. Build the muscle. Pretend that it was an injury taken in battle or the hunt rather than a flaw since her emergence from her cocoon.

She opened and shut her wings a dozen times, and then, wings wide, beat them as strongly as she could without battering them against the ground. She wished there were a cliff to launch from, or at least an open hilltop. This sloping meadow with its tall wet grass would have to do. She opened her wings wide, discerned the direction of the wind and then began a clumsy downhill gallop.

This was no way for a dragon to learn to fly! If she had hatched healthy and whole, her first flight would have been made then, while her body was light and lean and her wings outsized for her. Instead, she lumbered like a run-away cow, her body heavy and muscled for walking, not flight, her wings scarcely developed to lift her bulk. When the wind gusted, she sprang into the air and beat her wings hard. She did not have enough altitude. The tip of her left wing caught in the tall wet grass and spun her to one side. Frantically, she tried to correct and instead slammed to the earth. She landed on her feet, jolted and frustrated.

And angry.

She turned and trudged up the hillside again. She would try again. And again. Until dawn greyed the sky and it was time to slink back to her stable. She had no choice.

Somewhere, Alise thought, there is blue sky. And a warm breeze. She pulled her worn cloak more snugly around her as she watched Heeby turn away from her and charge down the wide street before leaping into the air. Her wide scarlet wings seemed to battle the morning rain as they lifted her. The dragon was becoming more graceful, Alise decided. More competent at getting into the air. And she seemed to grow every day, and with that growth, become more difficult to bestride. She was going to have to convince Rapskal that his dragon needed a harness of some sort. Or she would soon have to give up riding on Heeby to reach Kelsingra.

A sweep of wind pushed her, bringing a stronger shower of rain with it. Rain, rain, rain. Sometimes summer and dry warm days seemed like something she had imagined. Well, standing here and staring after the dwindling dragon would neither warm her nor get her day's work accomplished. She turned her back on the river and looked up at her city.

She had expected to feel the lift of heart that the sight of it usually brought her. Most days when Heeby brought her here and she looked up at Kelsingra spread out before her, she felt a surge of anticipation for the day's work. Today, she always told herself. Today might be the day that she made some key discovery, unearthed some find that gave her fresh perspective on the ancient Elderlings. But today, anticipation failed her. She looked up the wide avenue before her, and then lifted her eyes higher, to see the full panorama of the city. Today, instead of lingering on the standing buildings her eyes seemed to snag on the cracked domes and fallen walls. It was vast, this ancient place. And the task she had taken on and pursued in such an orderly fashion was a hopeless one. She could not complete it even in a dozen years. And she did not have a dozen years.

Even now, Tarman and Captain Leftrin were drawing closer to Cassarick. Once he reported there, once word of their discovery was noised from the Rain Wilds to Bingtown, the stampede would begin. Treasure hunters and younger sons, the rich seeking to get richer and the poor hoping for a chance at fortune would all follow him back. There would be no stopping that flood, and from the moment they set foot on the shore, the city would begin to disappear. A wave of despair swept over her as she imagined them, picks and crowbars on their shoulders, barrels and crates to hold their troves stacked on the shores. When they came, the old city would come to life again. The push to plunder would bring the money to rebuild the docks and bring ships and trade. A mockery of life would precede its destruction.

She took a deep breath and sighed it out. She couldn't save the city. All she could do was try to document it as it had been when they discovered it.

Suddenly she missed Leftrin with a terrible hollowness that was emptier than hunger. He had been gone for over a month and there was no knowing when he would return. It was not that he could change the outcome of what must happen but that he had been here with her for a time, witnessed the amazing stillness of the place, walked with her where no other feet had trod since the time of the Elderlings. His presence had made it all more real; since he had left the things she had seen and found and documented felt less substantial. Unconfirmed by his interest.

Alise started to turn left, to follow a narrower road that would let her resume her careful mapping and exploration in her usual rote way. Then she halted. No. If she kept on the way she was going, she'd never even get to enter the grander buildings before they were plundered. So, a change of plan today. It would not be a day of documenting and drawing and note taking. Today she would simply explore, walking wherever she felt drawn.

She turned back to the broad avenue that led straight up

from the river toward the distant mountains. The wind was at her back and her eyes squinted against the falling rain. She looked from side to side as she walked, pausing at each divergence of the road. There was so much here to explore and catalogue and record. She reached the top of a gentle hill and after a moment of consideration turned right.

Along this wide street the buildings were grander by far than the humble homes and small stores she had been visiting closer to the waterfront. The black stone that made up so much of these buildings shone with the wet of the rain and glittered where threads of silver ran through it. Many of the lintels and columns of the structures were decorated. Here were pillars carved with twining vines and animals peering from behind them. There, an entry was shielded with stone that had been artfully carved into the shape of a trellis and vine.

On the next structure, there was a portico under which she took refuge from the increasing violence of the downpour. The columns were carved in the shape of acrobats supporting one another, feet on shoulders and then hands upholding the ceiling. Tall doors of silvery and splintering wood barred her from entering. She pushed gently at one, wondering if some ancient latch still held it closed. Her hand sank through the disintegrating wood. Startled, she pulled her hand back and then stooped to peer through the fist-sized hole. She could see an antechamber, and then another set of doors. She took hold of the door handle and tugged on it, only to have it pull partially free. Appalled at the damage she was doing, she let go, only to have the heavy brass knob tear free and fall at her feet with a clang. *Oh, well done, Alise*, she scolded herself sourly.

And then, with the wind and rain howling past, she stooped down to pull handful after handful of wood away until she had an opening big enough to wriggle through. On the other side, she stood up and looked all around. She could no longer hear the patter of the rain and the wind was hushed and distant. Light fell in soft-edged rectangles on the floor from the high windows. A carpet disintegrated under her feet as she walked into the middle of the room. She looked up: the ceiling was painted with a swarm of dragons. Some carried beribboned baskets in their claws, and in the baskets and dangling from them were brightly-garbed figures.

A second set of tall wooden doors beckoned her. She crossed the room to them and found them much better preserved than the exterior doors. She clasped a gleaming brass handle and turned it, pushing against the door. It swung almost easily, with only a tiny squeal of disuse.

The revealed chamber had a sloping floor that descended gently to a grand stage in the centre of a theatre. It was an island surrounded by a space of empty floor, then by tiered benches and finally chairs bearing the dusty ghosts of cushions. When she lifted her eyes she saw that curtained boxes looked grandly down upon the stage. Light came from an overhead dome of thick glass. Decades of dust dimmed the light that shone in from the overcast day. It could not disperse the lurking shadows that stood frozen at the outermost edges of the room. The waiting figures, half glimpsed, seemed to have frozen at her sudden intrusion.

Alise took a careful breath and lifted her hand to wipe raindrops from her lashes. She knew they would vanish. It was a trick of the black stone, she was coming to understand. Sometimes it whispered, sometimes it sang loudly, and sometimes, when she came around a corner quickly or happened to brush her hand against a wall, she would have a glimpse of people and horses and carts, of all the life that the city still remembered. She rubbed her eyes thoroughly, dropped her hands and looked around again.

They still stared at her from the shadows, every head turned toward her. The bright motley they wore proclaimed their profession: they were tumblers and acrobats, rope-climbers and jugglers, performers such as she might have seen in a troop at a Summer Fest or performing solo for tossed coins at the edge of the Great Market in Bingtown. They were impossibly still and even after she had fully realized that they were statues, she still ventured a wavering, 'Hello?'

Her voice carried through the hall and bounced back to her. On the far side of the room, the curtains that draped a theatre box suddenly gave way and fell with a *whoosh* to the floor in a cascade of thread, fluff and dust. She jumped, startled, and then stood, clutching her own hands and watching the myriad motes of dust stir and dance in the thin sunlight. 'Just statues,' she insisted aloud. 'That's all.'

She forced herself to turn and walk the aisle that circled the seating to reach the first of the figures.

She had thought that up close they would be less unsettling. They weren't. Each was exquisitely carved and painted. A juggler clad in blue and green had paused, two balls cupped in one hand and three in another, his head cocked quizzically, his copper-green eyes squinting in the beginning of a smile. Two steps beyond him, a tumbler had halted, one hand held out to his partner, chin tucked in to his chest as he stared curiously out at the empty seats. His partner was dressed in yellow-and-white stripes to match his motley, and her hair was an untidy tumble of black curls. Her lips were curved in a mischievous smile. Beyond the couple, a stilt-walker had dismounted from his sticks and leaned them against his shoulder to regard the empty hall. He wore a bird-beak mask and an elegant headdress mimicked a bird's top-knot of feathers.

On and on she walked, but no two figures were alike. Here

was a slender boy stepping up on an offered knee preparatory to mounting his partner's shoulders. Here was a man with a flute set to his lips and three small carved black dogs at his feet, all on their hind legs and ready to dance to his tune. The next was a girl with her face and arms painted white, in a gown decorated with gilt to mimic golden thread. Gilded, too, was her crown of feathers and rooster heads, and in her hands a sceptre that looked more like a feather duster. Beyond her were twin girls, as lithely muscled as ferrets and clad only in brief bright skirts and a twist of cloth that scarcely covered their breasts. The skin of their arms and bellies and legs was painted with extravagant curlicues of blue and red and gold. Alise paused before them, wondering if the designs had been tattooed on or if they had been painted afresh for each performance. She had no doubt that each carving represented a very real and individual member of an entertainment troupe that had once performed in this very theatre.

Completing her slow circuit of the theatre, she stood once more looking down on the stage. How did one document this? How explain it? Why bother? A year from now, or two, every one of them would be gone, separated from their company and carted off to Bingtown to be sold to the highest bidder. She shook her head but could not clear it of the dismal thought. 'I'm sorry,' she told them softly. 'I'm so sorry.'

As she turned to leave she noticed a gleam of something on the floor. She scuffed her rag-wrapped boot across it, baring a silver strip as wide as her hand. She knelt down, pulling off her worn glove, and brushed her hand to clear the dust from it. But at the touch of her hand, the silvery strip sprang to life. Light raced away from her touch in all directions, ribbons of it emanating from where she stood, outlining the aisles and racing up the walls to frame the distant overhead window in a complicated knot of silvery gleaming light.

'Jidzin,' she said quietly, almost calmly. 'I've seen this before, the metal that lights at a touch. There was a lot of it in Trehaug, once.' But she doubted it had been like this. This was completely intact and functional. She remained stooped, touching the strip and looking up in wonder at how the silver light woke the ancient hall to gaiety. Almost she expected the music that would announce the pause before the beginning of a performance.

Every hair stood up on her body as a ghostly music began to play. It was thin and distant but unmistakably cheery. A horn tootled merrily and some string instrument pursued it, note for note. And then the statues began to move. Heads nodded in time to the music, the feather duster became a baton, the twin girls moved in unison, a step forward, a step back. Alise gave a sob of terror as they came to life. She tried to get to her feet and instead sat down flat. 'No,' she whispered in an agony of fear.

But the statues came no closer. The music played and they moved, nodding time, waving hands gently, lips smiling but eyes unseeing. As she watched, the music faltered, the statues' gestures became more hesitant and sporadic and then, as the music broke and wavered unevenly, the statues shuddered to a halt. The music ceased and the silvery shining of the jidzin slowly failed. In moments, the only light in the great hall came once more from the distant overhead glass dome and the statues fell to stillness.

Alise sat on the floor, rocking herself gently. 'I saw it. It was real,' she assured herself. And knew as she spoke the words that she was the last person who would ever see this particular Elderling magic.

Outside, the rain had ceased. The wind was cold but it was pushing the clouds clear of the sun, and the additional light was very welcome. Alise pulled her damp cloak closer but the wind found every tear in it and fingered its way in to touch her with chill hands. She hurried along, then turned down a side street to escape the direct push of the wind. She startled when a raven gave a sudden disapproving caw and lifted from the eaves of a building to sweep away in flight. Here, if she walked close to the front of the buildings, she was sheltered and the weak sunlight even held a trace of warmth. She pulled her gloves back on as she walked. When was the last time she had felt warm all the way through? The answer came quickly: the night before Leftrin had left to return to Cassarick. She wondered where he was on the river, and how the storms were affecting his passage. He had assured her that the trip downriver would be much swifter than the one upriver had been, and that the shallows that had slowed their passage and confounded them for days would no longer exist.

'All we'll have to do is follow the strongest current downstream; there's no trick to it. And if we have doubts, well, I just let Tarman have his head, and he'll find the way for us. Trust me. And if you cannot trust me, trust my ship! He has protected generation after generation of my family from this river.'

And she did trust, both her captain and his liveship. But she wished Leftrin was here. She longed for his return as much as she dreaded it, for when he came back, the days of this untouched city would be numbered. A pang of guilt struck her. There was work to be done, a vast amount of work. The short winter day was passing swiftly, and she had to be back and waiting for the dragon before the sunset.

She walked quickly past two buildings that had fallen prey to time or earthquake or perhaps both. The façade of one had collapsed, leaving a heap of rubble that spilled out into the street, revealing its deserted interior. As she clambered over it, she marked how the building next to it leaned on the first. Cracks ran up through the black stone foundation. She hastened past them on the far side of the street.

Shivering now, and hungry Alise decided to find shelter in which to eat her noon meal. She had strips of dried smoked meat in a packet and a small bottle of water. Simple food, but her hunger made her mouth water at the thought of it. What wouldn't she give, though, for a cup of steaming tea, spiced with cinnamon and sweetened with honey? And a few of those greasy sausage rolls that the street vendors sold in Bingtown! Tubes of flaky pastry, oily and brown-edged, stuffed full of spiced sausage and onion and sage.

Don't think about such things. Don't think about hot rich food, or new warm woollen stockings or her heavy winter cloak with the fox fur collar and hood, folded uselessly on a shelf in Hest's house. How she longed to feel its welcome weight on her shoulders.

At the end of the street an immense plaza, paved all in white stone, glittered in the sun dazzling her eyes. It seemed to have been created for giants. A huge dry fountain held a statue of a green dragon clawing his way into the sky, his gleaming wings half-opened. Was it over-sized, or could the creatures truly attain that size? She gaped at it, imagining a horse sliding down that throat in one gulp.

Beyond the fountain a wide set of steps led up to an immense building. Gigantic white figures in bas-relief graced the outside of the black walls. A woman was ploughing a field behind a team of oxen. She wore a crown of flowers and her skilfully portrayed diaphanous robes appeared to billow behind her in the wind. Her slender feet were bare. The image made Alise smile as she imagined what the woman would look like at the end of a single furrow, let alone a whole ploughed field.

Someone had indulged a very artistic imagination in that image!

She lifted her eyes to consider the tower that reared up from the massive building. At the very top was a dome made with curved glass panels. A glance around her assured her that she had come to the tallest structure on this hilltop, and perhaps the tallest in the city. As she dropped her eyes again, her gaze fell on the inscription chiselled above the entry way. The Elderling characters writhed and danced, enticingly familiar in their evasion of her understanding. Lions of stone guarded the entryway.

Very well. She would go inside, eat her meal, and then see if the steps to the tower were still intact. If they were, she would take advantage of that viewpoint to create a grand sketch of the entire city, something she should probably have done when she first came here! She began the long climb to the entrance. The steps were broad and shallow. 'What an annoying design,' she muttered, and then gave a snort of laughter. They were annoying to a human's legs and strides. For a dragon, they would be perfect. She looked up to the looming black gap of the entrance. The great wooden doors to this chamber had long since collapsed. Bits of them littered the steps. She reached the doorway and stepped over the rubble of fallen wood and brass fasteners and into the interior.

A surprising amount of light entered the interior chamber. Its vast marble floor was littered with the scattered remnants of furnishings. Desks or tables? Had this been a bench? Tapestries that had once graced the walls between the windows now hung as tattered remnants. She advanced into the room, fragments of desiccated wood from the door crunching under her feet.

There were stone benches in the window alcoves, and Alise chose a likely one for her luncheon. She sat on the cold bench, pulled her knees up to her chest and carefully tucked her damp cloak in close all around her, hoarding the warmth of her body. She thought of the Elderling robe that Leftrin had given her; if she had been wearing it now, she would have been warm. But despite the apparent sturdiness of the ancient fabric, she preferred not to wear it outdoors. It was as irreplaceable as any artefact from this city, and something to preserve and study rather than use as a common garment.

She took her packet of smoked meat out of her bag and unslung the leather water-bottle from her shoulder. Stripping her gloves from her hands, she unwrapped her meal. The twisted sticks of reddish meat were tough, but the alder smoke had made it flavourful. She chewed doggedly and followed each bite with a sip of water. The water was water. A simple meal and not a large one, it was soon over, but she reminded herself to be grateful for what she had. As she ate, she watched the fading day through the broken door. Winter days were so brief. She would climb as high as she could, look out on the city and sketch what she could before returning to the old docks to wait for Heeby.

Across the room from the fallen doors, wide stairs ascended into shadows. She stood up, slung her water bottle on her shoulder again, and crossed to them. A fair-sized orchard could have grown on the amount of ground she covered. As she left the doors behind, the very vastness of the room made her feel smaller and more vulnerable. The distant whispering of the shadow denizens of the city grew louder. The deeper she went into the building, the more pervasive the lingering presence of ancient Elderlings became. She thought she caught a whisk of movement from the corner of her eye, but when she looked, no one was there. She steeled herself and went on.

It was useless to be afraid, she told herself. Afraid of what?

Afraid of memories stored in stone? They couldn't hurt her, not unless she allowed them to dominate her and draw her under their spell. And she wouldn't. She simply wouldn't. She had work to do. She increased the length of the stride and refused to look behind her as the whispers grew louder. The stairs were steeper than the outside steps; these, at least, had been structured for the convenience of humans. She set her hand to the banister as she ascended.

And then a hubbub broke out all around her. Three young pages rushed past her, their youthful voices accusing one another of some fault that doubtless all had committed. Coming down the stairs, scowling at the wayward pages, were at least a dozen tall folk clad in yellow robes. Their eyes gleamed, copper and silver and gold, and when one woman gestured with a long-fingered hand, Alise flinched back from a ghostly touch that never reached her. She snatched her hand from the banister, and the room quieted. But once wakened to her senses, the ghosts seemed to have gained power. The murmur of their business ebbed around her ears. She might not see them as clearly as she ascended, her hands clasped together in front of her, but she could still sense them.

Reaching a landing, Alise glanced out across a wide room. Ghosts of benches and desks stood above their own crumbled remains. She heard a bell rung impatiently and turned her head to almost see a page in a short pale yellow tunic and blue leggings dash to answer the summons. She turned back. Government business, she judged. Perhaps a hall of records, or a chamber for the establishing of laws.

Up she went. The stairs were lit only by the wide windows at each landing. The panes were clouded with thick rain streaks. The first one had shown only the neighbouring buildings. From the second, she glimpsed roofs. That was as far as the grand staircase went. She crossed a spacious room to find a smaller staircase for the next ascent. But at the next landing, her hopes of viewing the city were frustrated by an opulent stained glass window. The daylight was too dim to do it justice, but she could make out an Elderling woman with black hair and dark eyes in intense conversation with a coppery dragon. The landing opened into a sort of gallery room, tall windows admitting more light than had been present on the lower floors. The walls between the windows were decorated with friezes of Elderlings ploughing fields, reaping crops . . . and preparing for war?

She stepped into the room to study them more closely. Yes. In one of the friezes, a powerfully muscled Elderling hammered sparks from a glowing blade. In another, a lithe green dragon reared on her hind legs beside a slender Elderling woman with red hair. The woman's fists were set on her hips above her sword belt. Her rounded arms were muscled, her legs armoured with what looked like flexible silver scaling. A blue dragon wore spiked harness and glowered at the Alise with scarlet eyes.

She walked the room slowly, trying to commit each picture to memory. The Elderlings and dragons were individuals, she was sure. She could almost read the inscriptions that gleamed beneath each image. She paused long before a scene of a red-and-silver dragon. The Elderling beside him was red and silver as well, and their matching armour was studded with black spikes. The man clutched a peculiar bow, short and fitted with a pulley. The dragon's harness bristled with spikes and quivers of additional arrows. A sort of throne with a tall back and dangling straps was fixed to the dragon's back. There the warrior had ridden into battle with his dragon. So, despite how Sintara decried Heeby allowing Rapskal to ride her, ancient Elderlings *had* ridden on dragons. She wondered who their enemy had been. Men? Other Elderlings? Other dragons?

Her long held perceptions of that ancient time wavered and reformed. She had thought the Elderlings peaceful and wise, too wise for warfare. She sighed.

She lingered too long. The dimming images told her that the brief winter day was giving way to evening. Time to move on if she was to finish her tour of the building. The next stairway was a spiralling one and she suspected she had finally come to the base of the tower she had glimpsed from outside. Her path followed the outside wall and her way was lit by deep narrow windows that showed only tiny slices of view. She came to a door, but it was locked, as was the next, and the one after that. Surely no one would lock a door on an empty chamber? Whatever had called away the populace of this city, they must have left something behind these locked doors that had merited protection. She imagined racks of scrolls or shelves laden with books. Perhaps this was the treasure house of the city, and the doors concealed struck coins and other wealth.

As Alise continued to climb the winding stair she encountered more locked doors, one at each brief landing. She tried each one, bracing herself each time she touched the metal handles with the small insets of black stone. Each time, it was like a strike of lightning that briefly burned an image of activity and life into her eyes before she snatched her hand back and restored the tower to silence and gloom. At each landing, the stairs grew narrower and steeper.

Then abruptly she climbed up and into a much larger chamber than she had expected. The top of the tower was like the cap of a mushroom on a stem, and domed with a thick glass ceiling. It had begun to rain again, and the rain ran down the grimy glass in tiny rivulets as if she looked up at the bellies of snakes. The walls of this domed chamber were made of alternating panels of glass and stone. One, she saw to her shock, was broken. She walked hesitantly around a collapsed table in the middle of the room. As she drew closer, she scowled. Someone had started a fire in the room! And the window had been broken deliberately: the glass shards were both on the floor and also on the parapet that ran round the outer edges of the tower. There was a clear handprint in the soot on the wall beside the window.

Outrage flooded her. What had Rapskal been thinking? For he was the most likely culprit. He had spent more time in the city than anyone, had been the most curious to explore it, and was the only keeper she could think of who would be so impulsive as to do such a thing simply so he could lean out and have an unimpeded view of the city.

It was the same temptation that called her now. She leaned out briefly to confirm what she already knew. The sun was going down and the rain had returned. Then, her heart in her mouth, she ventured out past the jagged shards that still clung in the framework and onto the parapet. A chill wind tugged at her and broken glass gritted under her feet. The walkway that encircled the tower was narrow and the railing that edged it was ridiculously low.

She kept close to the wall as she circled the tower cautiously, peering through the rain at the city and its surroundings. Mist and oncoming darkness frustrated her. The outflung city was a huddle of buildings against the dim land. Across the shining black river, she could see sparks of light from the keepers' settlement, but grand Kelsingra slept in darkness. She had almost completed her circuit when she saw the narrow gate set in the railing. Heart in her mouth, she forced herself to step to the edge and look down. Yes. The gate gave onto a ladder that descended to another encircling balcony. She divined their purpose at once. Access for cleaning the windows. She gripped the railing in both hands and leaned out. The ladder went down several stories; the locked chambers that she had passed on her climb had windows. If it had been a dry bright day she would have risked going down to see if she could enter the locked rooms that way. But alone and in the wet wind and with the light fleeing was not the time for her to risk a fall. She squeezed back into the tower room and stood blinking raindrops off her lashes.

The pile of rubble in the middle of the room claimed her attention. She crouched down to peer at it. There had been a large round table, and it had collapsed. But there had been something on the table. She stared at it for a time before she made out what it was. It was a model of a city, of *this* city! Here was the river harbour and here the docks, a bit degraded where the rain had driven in through the broken pane. But the rest of the model was remarkably intact. The tower she was in seemed to also be in the centre of the city as it was portrayed, making the panels of glass the corresponding viewpoints to the map itself.

If only she had a torch! The light was going too quickly. She would have to come back here first thing tomorrow, and bring something to draw on. And this wondrous map of the city had to be preserved somehow! Rapskal's careless vandalism had put this precious artefact in danger. She'd have to speak to him tonight, to be sure he understood the damage he had done. She only hoped he hadn't been so destructive elsewhere. Whatever had he been thinking?

She rose with a heartfelt sigh, reluctant to leave the wondrous map but equally reluctant to face finding her way back down the stairs in the gathering darkness. A final glance at the map as she left the room made her halt. Her breath caught in her throat. A bridge? There was a bridge over the river? But there couldn't be! No one could construct a bridge that long over such a raging torrent. Yet there it was, a tiny model of a black bridge spanning the wide river. She oriented herself and once more ventured out onto the rain-slippery parapet. She peered through mist and rain and saw nothing. Likely it had perished long ago.

She returned to the tower room and began her long descent of the steps. Going down the stairs now was like descending into a well. She managed the first flight before the darkness defeated her and she was forced to let her hand trail the black wall beside her. To her astonishment, instead of the mere support she had sought, her touch woke the tower to light, for her fingers had found a jidzin strip set into the wall just above the banister. The light raced ahead of her, not bright but certainly preferable to the darkness and enough to guide her feet. There were fewer Elderling memory-ghosts on the stairs, and those she saw carried brooms and dusters. Once, she saw a yellow-robed official with some sort of shoulder decorations to indicate his importance emerge from one of the locked doors. He carried an armful of scrolls and moved ponderously as he trudged down the stairs. It took her two flights of steps before she had the courage to push through the insubstantial vision and hurry past him. She glanced back up at him and his preoccupied scowl ignored her as if she were the ghost.

Crossing the darkened rooms was a challenge. When finally she reached the ground floor and saw grey evening through the fallen doors, she burst into a run to be out of the building. Her footsteps echoed on the floor and the terror she had not allowed herself to feel till now suddenly gained control of her and she fled as fast as she could from the Elderling tower, out into the streets and down to where Heeby would be waiting for her.

Day the 25th of the Change Moon
Year the 7th of the Independent Alliance of Traders

From Kim, Keeper of the Birds, Cassarick to Detozi, Keeper of the Birds, Trehaug

How dare you imply that I am the source of the lice problem! It is just as likely the birds could have picked up these pests when they overnighted in the forest during one of their flights. You may hide yourself behind the Guild inspectors, but I know who lodged this complaint and provoked these unjustified and inconvenient inspections of my lofts and cotes! You and your family have never forgiven the fact that a Tattooed came among you and rose by diligence and hard work to be a Bird Keeper. This is how you people welcome us to the Rain Wilds and 'equality', with lies and sneaking accusations! You scale-faced, boy-chested lizard-bitch! I will be bringing grievances of my own to the Council, beginning with how you and Erek and your nephew have conspired against me and slandered me ever since I assumed this post! You may think you can end this vendetta now, but I will not be finished with you until your cotes are emptied and your Bird Keeper papers retracted!

CHAPTER EIGHT

Other Lives

It was their second day without rain. Sedric would have felt more blessed if the day had warmed a bit, too. Cold rain chilled them almost every day now. He had wondered aloud once, 'Why on earth did Elderlings settle here? Why build a city in such a rainy place instead of choosing a beach by a warm sea? Dragons love sun. Why did the Elderlings settle here?'

Carson had given him a piercing look. 'A very good question. Sometimes, when Spit is dreaming and his thoughts push into my mind, I feel like I'm on the edge of knowing why. There was definitely a reason and an important one for Kelsingra to be built where it is. I feel it in his memories. Dragons coming to this city were filled with fierce anticipation. I share it in his dreams and almost I know why. Then the knowledge flits away from me. But I've wondered the same thing myself.'

Small comfort. Well, at least today there was no rain. Sedric reminded himself of that and tried to find some gratitude in his heart. It was hard. On days when it didn't rain, Carson rose even earlier to take advantage of the better weather.

Sedric had awakened that morning to the sounds of a hammer tapping gently on the outside of the cottage, right by the bed. He glanced up at the framed opening in the wall above their bed. The sound came from there.

At one time there had been glass in the windows of the cottage, and perhaps even shutters. The stone walls were well made, as was the stone hearth. The roof had been long gone when they'd chosen the cottage. Carson had rebuilt it, with rough-hewn timbers to support it, and branches and grass bundles from the meadow as thatch. When they had first moved in to the cottage, they had curtained the empty window frames with extra ship's blankets. But as the days and nights grew colder, they had reclaimed the blankets for their bed and Carson had pegged hides up instead which had blocked not only the rain and wind but also kept out daylight. The crudely tanned leather had contributed to the endless smell of dead animal that permeated Sedric's life. Carson had promised, several times, to try to find a better solution. The stiff hide was now moving in gusts to the rhythm of the tapping hammer. Why Carson had to do this at the crack of dawn, Sedric didn't know.

He rolled from the crude pallet they shared and wandered over to the hearth. The fire had burned low. He added a couple of logs even though he knew it meant that he'd have the task of hauling more firewood in. Then he felt the garments they had washed out and hung up not last night, but the night before. The shirts were dried, but the seams and waistband of the trousers were still damp. It was almost impossible to get anything completely dry during the days of constant rain. With a sigh, he pulled on the driest clothes he could find and then rearranged the rest of the laundry in the hope that it would dry by nightfall. He longed to be able to fold it and put it away. Living in a small cottage that smelled like hides and required him to dodge dangling socks at every step was severely affecting his spirits. He longed for cleanliness and tidiness: it was hard to find peace in the middle of disorder. He had always felt this way. He'd always had to tidy his workroom before he could settle to his tasks. The tapping outside the window had continued and was becoming more urgent.

Hungry. His dragon pushed her complaint into his mind, driving away every other thought.

I know you are, my beauty. I'll remedy that as soon as I can. Let me wake up a bit first.

Hungry all night. Hungry today. You sleep too much.

You are right, little queen. I will do better. Sometimes it was just easier to agree with Relpda than to argue with her. The little copper dragon was demanding, imperious, and as thoughtless as a child of anyone else's needs.

She also worshipped him and depended on him as no creature ever had before. And he had fallen in love with the jealous, selfish and spiteful little creature. 'Little,' he said aloud as he buttoned his shirt and laughed at himself. Little only in comparison to the other dragons. Feeding her was becoming next to impossible. He was fortunate that Carson's fish trap continued to supply a steady stream of fish. Without a daily morning ration of that, he knew that Relpda would have made his life miserable. As it was, he was feeling not just his own hunger pangs but hers too.

He looked at the hearth. Hanging in the chimney, above the flames and in the smoke, were several sides of bright-red fish. The smoke both cooked and preserved the meat. It also added its own aromatic note to the various smells in the cottage. He was so tired of smelling things. He took his worn cloak from the hook by the door and gave it a shake before swinging it around his shoulders. Time to get the day started.

Things to do. Haul water for washing and cooking. Feed his dragon, feed himself. But first he'd find out what it was that Carson was attempting to do. The tapping had become an uneven pounding.

He walked around the corner of the house to find Carson wrestling with a rough wooden frame. He had stretched a piece of leather over it, hooking it over pegs tapped into the sides. This 'window' was what he was trying to force into the opening. As Sedric approached, the brittle leather split. 'Damn the luck!' Carson cursed, and threw frame and leather to one side.

Sedric stared at his partner as he directed a kick at the unsatisfactory construction. 'Carson?' he asked hesitantly.

The word jerked the hunter's attention to Sedric. A sudden flush suffused his face. 'Not now, Sedric! Not now.' He turned and stalked off, leaving Sedric staring after him in astonishment. He'd never seen Carson so out of temper, let alone expressing it in such a childish way. It summoned unwanted memories of Hest. *Except that Hest would have turned his anger on me, not stalked off to brood*, he thought to himself. *Hest would have made it all my fault, for speaking to him.*

He walked over to Carson's abandoned project, picked up the frame, which was not much damaged by the kick, and regarded the stretched leather thoughtfully. He felt a pang of guilt as he recognized what it was. Leather scraped so thin that it still allowed light in but kept out wind and rain. Leather scraped of all hair and dried hard, so it would not smell as strongly. This was Carson's response to Sedric's complaint about the window coverings. Sedric scratched his stubbled chin, considering. He'd complained, with no thought that Carson would take the complaint as a criticism, or put so much thought and effort into trying to remedy things.

He was still holding the frame when he heard footsteps

behind him. Carson took the window out of Sedric's hands, saying gruffly, 'It was supposed to just slide into place, so you'd wake up to light. But the opening is too far out of square. I wanted it to be a surprise for you, but it's not going to work. I know how to do it, but I don't have the right tools. I'm sorry.'

'No. I'm sorry. I don't mean to complain so much.'

'You're used to better. A lot better than this.'

There was no arguing with that statement. 'But that's not your fault, Carson. And when I complain, well, I'm just complaining. I don't mean that it's up to you to make things better. It's just . . .'

'You're not comfortable here. I know that. You're used to better, Sedric. You deserve better, but I don't know what I can do about that.'

Sedric choked back a laugh. 'Carson, it's not as if anyone else has an easier life than we do. When the boat comes in, things will be better.'

'Only a little bit. Sedric, I watch you. I see how tired you are of all this. And it worries me.'

'Why?'

Carson gave him an odd look. 'Perhaps because I was there when you made a very sincere effort to take your own life. Perhaps because I worry that the next time you try it, I might not be there. And you might succeed.'

Sedric was shocked. 'I'm a different person now! I'm stronger than that,' he objected. Carson's words had stung him yet he could not have said why. An instant later, he knew. 'You think I'm weak,' he accused the hunter before he had known he would say the words.

Carson lowered his eyes and shook his shaggy head. His response was reluctant. 'Not weak, Sedric. Just . . . not tough. Not in the way that deals with hardship that just goes on and on and on. It doesn't make you a bad person, just—'

'Weak.' Sedric chose the word for him. He hated that Carson's comments hurt so badly, hated worse the sting of tears in his eyes. No. He wasn't going to weep over this. That would only prove him right. He cleared his throat. 'I have to go to the fish trap and get something for Relpda. She's hungry.'

'I know. So is Spit.' Carson shook his head as if tormented by gnats. 'I think that's part of why I'm out of temper today. It's not you, Sedric. You know that.' He spoke the words almost pleadingly. He shook his head again. 'That damn Spit. He knows he can make me feel his hunger. He pushes it at me. It puts me on edge all the time. It makes it hard to think, and even harder to be patient even with a simple task.' Carson jerked his head up and met Sedric's stare. There was determination in his eyes. 'But I'm not going to bring him food. Not yet. I've got to let him be hungry, hungry enough to try to do something about it. He's a lazy little bastard. He should be trying harder to learn how to fly. But as long as I'm around to feed him every time he gets a hunger pang, he isn't going to put any real effort into it. I've got to let him suffer a bit or he'll never learn to take care of himself.'

Sedric pondered his words. 'Do you think I should do the same with Relpda? Let her be hungry?' Even as he spoke the words aloud, he felt his dragon become aware of the thought.

No! I don't like to be hungry. Don't be mean to me!

'I know it seems harsh,' Carson said, almost as if he, too, had shared Relpda's thought. 'But we have to do something, Sedric. It can't go on this way. Even if I hunted morning until night every day and was successful in every hunt, it wouldn't be enough to feed them all. All of them are hungry, all the time, some more than others. But there's a limit to what we keepers can do. The dragons need to make the effort to fly, and to feed themselves. And they need to do it now, before it's too late.'

'Too late?'

Carson looked grim. 'Look at them, Sedric. They should be creatures of the air, but they are living like ground animals. They aren't growing properly. Their wings are weak and on some they're simply too small. Rapskal had the right of it. From the time he first took charge of Heeby, he made her try to fly, every day. Look at her, some time, and compare the lines of her body to those of the other dragons. Look where the muscle is developed, and where it's not.' He shook his head. 'Trying to get Spit to exercise his wings is difficult. He's wilful, and he knows full well that he's bigger and stronger than I am. My only handle on him is food. He knows my rule. He tries to fly. And then I feed him. He has to try every day. And that's what the other dragons have to do. But I don't think they will until they're forced to it.'

Not liking Carson.

But we know it's true, Relpda. You're too big for me to keep you fed. I know how hungry you get. I bring you food, but it's never enough. It's never going to be enough until you can fly and make your own kills. We both know that.

Falling hurts.

Being hungry hurts, too. All the time. Being hurt from falling will stop once you learn to fly. But if you don't learn to fly, the hurt of being hungry will go on always. You have to try. Carson is right. You have to try harder, and you have to try every day.

Not liking YOU, now.

Sedric tried to mask how much that hurt his feelings. *I'm not trying to hurt you, Relpda. I'm trying to get you to do what you have to do in order to, well, to be a full dragon.*

I AM a dragon! The force of her incensed thought nearly

drove him to his knees. *I am a dragon, and you are my keeper. Bring me food!*

In a while. He hoped she could not sense that he was deliberately making her wait. His own stomach rumbled in protest.

Carson gave him a sideways glance. 'You should eat something.'

'I'd feel guilty to eat while she goes hungry.'

Carson sighed. 'It's not going to be easy. But I've been thinking about it for some days now. Left to themselves, the dragons are just not trying that hard to learn for themselves. Right now, we can get enough fish in our traps to keep them from starving. And we've had a few windfalls, such as Heeby being willing to drive game for them. But we can't count on things like that. The fish run could dwindle or end any day. And the more we hunt locally and Heeby hunts close to our camp, the less game there will be. These are big predators with large appetites. They need to expand their hunting territory and they need to be able to feed themselves. Otherwise, this area will simply turn into a second Cassarick for them. We didn't come all this way to allow that to happen.'

Sedric listened in chilled dismay. Now that Carson laid it out so clearly, he wondered how he could not have seen it for himself. *Because I've been like the dragons,* he thought to himself. *I thought it would just go on as it had before, with the keepers finding meat for them all, no matter what.*

His stomach growled again and Carson laughed, sounding almost like himself. 'Go eat something. The smoked fish should be done enough. And take something to Relpda.'

'Are you going to take something to Spit?'

Carson shook his head, not in denial, but at himself. 'Yes. Eventually. But not until I've shown him that he can't push me around. He has a different temperament from Relpda.

That little silver has a streak of mean and resentment that your copper doesn't have. It's not just toward the other dragons. It's for all the keepers, too. It's for anyone who is whole and functioning when he isn't.'

'I thought she could only carry one rider at a time.' Thymara was still uncertain about this whole venture.

Rapskal looked down at her from Heeby's shoulders. 'She has been growing. Bigger and stronger. And her wings keep growing most of all. She says she can do this. Come on up.' He bent at the waist and leaned down to stretch his hand out toward her. He was grinning at her in a way that was obviously a challenge. She couldn't back down now. She reached up to grip his wrist as he seized hers. There was nothing else to hold onto. All of Heeby was gleaming and overlapping crimson scales, smoother then polished stone. She scrabbled up the dragon's shoulder, worried that she was offending her with such an ungainly climb onto her back. Once she was behind Rapskal, sitting spraddle-legged behind him on the dragon's wide back, she asked, 'What do I hold onto?'

He looked back over his shoulder at her. 'Me!' he replied, and then, leaning forward, he said quietly to his dragon, 'We're ready.'

'No, I'm not!' Thymara protested, but it was too late. Too late to decide she didn't want to risk her life riding a dragon across a river, too late even to find time to tuck her cloak more tightly around her or be sure of her seat. The dragon lurched into motion, running down the grassy hillside. Thymara was uncomfortably aware for a moment that the other keepers were watching them take flight together. But in the next instant, as Heeby made a wild leap, landed hard, and then leapt again, abruptly snapping her wings wide open, she could think only of holding tight to Rapskal's tattered coat. She tried not to worry about what he was holding onto. She hugged herself to his back, turning her head sideways and closing her eyes as the flapping of the dragon's wings drove the cold air against her face. She was too aware of the dragon's muscles moving beneath her, straining mightily and then suddenly the lurching stride was gone and they were rising, the rhythm of Heeby's wings gone from the frantic fluttering of a sparrow to the steady strokes of a big bird of prey.

Thymara risked a peek. At first all she saw was Rapskal's neck. Then, as she dared to turn her head, she saw the panorama of the river spread out below her. She tipped her head slightly and tried to look down, but she was too cautious to lean out. All she could see was the side of her own body and then the side of the dragon's wide chest.

'Loosen your arms. I can barely breathe!' Rapskal complained, shouting the words at her through the flow of air.

Thymara tried to obey him and found she couldn't. She might will her grip to loosen but her arms were reluctant to obey her. She compromised by shifting her grip slightly. Her hands still clutched his shirt tightly. Now she really regretted agreeing to this. What had she been thinking? One slip from Heeby's back meant certain death in the swift cold water below. Why had it seemed like an invitation to an exciting and daring adventure rather than an irrational opportunity to risk her life? Surely they must nearly be to the other side by now! Then, as she realized that landing there meant that she would have to brave another flight back, her courage departed completely and she was gripped by sheer fear. This wasn't fun, or adventure. It was a stupid jaunt into danger.

She tried to get her panic under control. What was wrong with her? She wasn't a person who got scared easily. She was competent and strong. She could take care of herself.

But not in a situation like this, a situation in which her skills meant nothing and she had no control over the risks involved. That, she realized abruptly, was what she disliked. The risks were wildly out of her control. She was in a situation where she depended entirely on Rapskal's good sense and Heeby's flight skills to keep her safe. And she was not truly confident of either of those things. She leaned forward to speak right by his ear.

'Rapskal! I want to go back. Right now!'

'But we haven't reached Kelsingra. I haven't shown you the city.' He was clearly startled by the request.

'I'll wait. I'll see it when the others do, when we get the docks repaired so that Tarman can tie up to them.'

'No. There's no reason to wait. This is too important! There's something I have to show to you now, today. You're the only one that will understand it right away. I know that Alise Finbok doesn't. She thinks the city is some big dead thing that we have to keep just the way it is. But it's not. And Kelsingra is not for her, anyway. It's for us. It's waiting for us.'

Rapskal's words distracted her from her terror. 'The city isn't for Alise? That's crazy. She came so far just to help find it, and she already knows so much about it. She loves Kelsingra. And she wants to protect it. That's why she was angry at you for breaking a window. She said that you must have more respect for the ruins, that we have to keep everything safe and exactly as it is until we've learned everything we can from them.'

'The city isn't meant to be kept safe. It's meant to be used.'

A new uneasiness stirred in Thymara. 'Is that what this trip is about? Using the city?'

'Yes. But it doesn't hurt it. And I didn't break any window! I told her that. Yes, I went up in that tower; I've been into just about all the big buildings. But I didn't break anything. That panel was broken when I got there. If you want, I'll take you there and show you what she was so upset about. It's pretty amazing up there; you can see almost as much from that tower as you can see from Heeby's back. And there's this sort of map thing that shows what the city used to look like. But that's not the most important thing. It isn't what I want to show you first.'

'I can see it all later. Please, Rapskal. I don't like this.' She forced the words past her teeth. 'Look. I'm scared. I want to go back.'

'We're more than halfway. Look around, Thymara. You're flying! When your own wings get big and strong enough, you'll be able to do this on your own. You can't be afraid of it now!'

She had never, she suddenly knew, believed that she was going to be able to fly. She'd never truly realized what flying would be, how high above everything she would be. How swiftly the wind would pass her. Tears flowed from the corner of her slitted eyes as she tried to take his advice and look around. Open air around them and the mountains in the distance. She tipped her head slightly so she could look down. There was the city, spread wide before them. She had not realized it was so big! It sprawled on a flat stretch of land between the riverbank and the mountains. From here, the damage to Kelsingra was far more evident. Trees and brush cloaked an ancient landslide that had buried part of the city. And a great cleft reached into the city from the river, damaging the buildings there. She blinked, turned her head and looked far upriver. Her breath caught as she glimpsed the beginning of a bridge's arch. It ended abruptly and the river rippled over the fallen remnants of stone at the water's edge. It was hard for her to conceive that anyone had ever thought they could span such a river with a bridge, let alone that once the bridge had existed.

'Hold tight to me. Sometimes she stumbles a bit when she lands, still.'

He didn't need to repeat the advice. Thymara clung to him like a limpet on a rock as the dragon dipped down toward the city. Lower and lower Heeby went, and the chill and deadly river grew larger and wider beneath them. She slowed the beat of her wings and Thymara felt as if they were dropping far too fast. She clenched her teeth, willing herself not to scream. Then the wide streets of the city were right in front of them, rushing up at them as Heeby suddenly beat her wings frantically. The wind of that motion plucked at Thymara, trying to tear her free of her frantic grip on Rapskal. Then the dragon landed, feet braced and claws skittering on the pavement stones. Thymara slewed wildly on the creature's back, gripping Rapskal's shirt for dear life. Her head snapped forward, her forehead banging into his back, and then whipped back. It was too much. Before Rapskal could utter a syllable, she let go of his shirt, slid sideways off Heeby's back and landed sprawling on hard, solid stone. For a moment she didn't move, only savoured the sensation of stillness. Safe. Safe on the ground again.

Rapskal tugged at her. 'Hey? Are you all right? Get up, Thymara. Are you hurt?'

She took another deep breath and wiped her face against her shoulder. Those tears were from the wind in her eyes, not from terror, nor gratitude to be on the ground again! She pushed Rapskal's hands away and got to her feet. The knee of her trousers had torn a bit more and she'd skinned both her knees from her abrupt dismount. 'I'm fine, Rapskal. I just landed wrong.' She lifted her head to look around and stopped breathing as she took in her first view of Kelsingra in full daylight.

City. So this was what that word really meant. It wasn't

like the tree city of Trehaug where she had been born. This was a city built on solid earth. As far as she could see, in all directions, there were no trees. No open meadows; virtually no plant life at all. Here, all was worked stone. Straight lines, and hard surfaces, broken by the occasional arch or dome, but even those were precisely-shaped geometric figures. All around her loomed the work of human hands.

'Go hunt, Heeby. That's my pretty girl. Go kill something big and have a nice meal. But don't sleep too long afterwards! Come back for us, my lovely red darling! We'll be waiting for you down by the river like always.'

Dimly she was aware of the scarlet dragon lurching into a run down the street toward the river. In moments, she heard the slapping of her wings and then the sound faded. She didn't turn to watch the dragon go. The city held her enthralled. All of this was made. None of it had grown. The huge buildings. The immense blocks that fit so squarely, one atop another, without a gap or a variation from perfectly straight lines. The interlocking stones that paved the street. All created by hands, all flawlessly shaped. But who could ever cut such large stones, let alone lift them into place?

She turned her head slowly, trying to take it all in. Statues in fountains. Carved stone decorating building fronts. All precise. Even the statues were perfect images of perfect creatures, caught and frozen in the stone. *I don't belong here*, she thought to herself. She was not perfect like these carvings, not precisely formed like the fitted paving stones and squared doors. She was lesser, deformed, unfit. As she had always been.

'Don't be stupid. Of course you belong here!' Rapskal sounded impatient.

Had she spoken the words out loud?

'This is an Elderling city, built by Elderlings, especially for Elderlings. Just as Trehaug and Cassarick were . . . Well, the true Elderling parts, the buried parts, were. That's what I've discovered in my time here. And I want to show it to you because I think you can explain it to Alise. And make the others understand it, too. We, all of us, dragons and keepers, need to get across to this side of the river. That side over there, all those huts and things, those were built for the humans. The ones that didn't want to change or couldn't change. This side, all of this, this is for us. It's what we need. And so we all need to get over here and make the city work. Because once we get the city working, then the dragons will be better, too.'

She stared at him, and then back to the city again. Dead and lifeless. Nothing to eat, no game, no growing food. 'I don't understand, Rapskal. Why would we want to be *here*? We'd have to go so far to get firewood or meat that we'd be exhausted just by those tasks. And the dragons? What is here for the dragons?'

'Everything!' he said urgently. 'It's all here, everything we need to know about being Elderlings. Because being an Elderling is a lot like being a dragon. And once we know more about being Elderlings, I think we can help the dragons. There was some special . . .' He knit his brow as if trying to recall something. 'Maybe. Well, I haven't found anything yet that would help with dragons that can't fly, but there might be something here, and it would be a lot easier to find if I weren't the only one looking for it, and if Alise wasn't telling us all that we shouldn't bother the city, we should just let it sleep. We only just started being Elderlings, so we don't have the memories we need to make all the magic work. But the memories are here, stored in the city, waiting for us. We just need to come here and get them and start being Elderlings. Then we can make the city work again. Then everything will get better. Once we have the magic, I mean.'

The cold wind swept through the silent city and she stared at him for a long time.

'Thymara!' he exclaimed at last in annoyance. 'Stop making that face at me. You said we didn't have much time, that you'd have to get back before dark to feed Sintara again. So we can't just stand around like this.'

She gave her head a quick shake. Tried to find sense in his words, tried to make them apply to her. Elderlings. Yes, she had known that's what their changes meant. The dragons had said so, and there was no reason to assume they would lie. Well, Sintara might lie to her, but she doubted that all the dragons would lie to their keepers. Not about something like that. And she knew that some of them had begun to resemble the images of Elderlings that she had seen in Trehaug. Not that she had seen many of them. Most of the tapestries and scrolls that had survived were things of great value, sold off through Bingtown generations before she had been born. But she knew what people said, that Elderlings were tall and slender, and that their eyes were unusual colours and that the portrayals of them seemed to indicate their skins had been different also. So, she had known, yes, that she was becoming an Elderling.

But a real Elderling, with magic? The magic they had used to build these magnificent cities and to create their wondrous artefacts? That was to be given to the keepers also?

To her?

'Come on!' Rapskal commanded her imperiously. He took her arm and she let him guide her and tried to listen to his rambling comments about the city. It was hard to keep her mind on his words. He had become inured to what surrounded them, or perhaps it had never stunned him with its strangeness and beauty as it did her. Rapskal tended simply to accept things as they came. Dragons. Becoming an Elderling. An ancient city that offered its magic to him.

'And I think that one was just for taking baths. Can you imagine that? A whole building, just for getting clean? And that one? A place for growing things. You go inside and there's this big room with all these pots of earth. And pictures made out of little bits of rock, um, mosaics, that was what Alise called them. Pictures of water and flowers and dragons in water and people in water and fish. Then, you go into another room, and there are these really, really big tanks that used to have water in them. But they don't now. But I learned from the stones that they used to have water in them and one was really hot and one was only warm and another was cool and then one was cold as river water. But here's the thing. There are tanks for humans, and then, on the other side of this building, there's an entrance for dragons, and there are tanks in there with sloping bottoms that dragons would wade right into to soak in hot water. And the roof on the other side is sloped and it's all glass. Can you believe it, that much glass? Do you want to come inside with me and look? We could look, just for a minute, if you want.'

'I believe you,' she said faintly. And she did. It was easier to believe that a building that size had a sloping roof made of glass than it was for her to believe that Elderling magic could be hers. Or anyone's. Could any of the keepers gain it? She thought of Jerd possessing Elderling magic and repressed a shudder. She halted suddenly and Rapskal stopped too with an exasperated sigh.

'Tell me about the magic, Rapskal. Will we really learn it? Is it written down, like spells we could memorize, like in the old magic tales from Jamaillia? Is it in a book or a scroll? Do we have to gather magic things, the liver of a toad and . . . Rapskal, this isn't about using dragon parts, is it? Eating part of a dragon's tongue to be able to speak to animals and things like that?'

'No! Thymara, that stuff isn't real. Those are just stories for children.' He was incredulous that she would even ask such a thing.

'I knew that,' she said stiffly. 'But you were the one who said we would have Elderling magic.'

'Yes. But I mean the *real* magic.' He spoke as if he had just explained everything. He tried to take her hand again, and when she allowed him to do so, he tugged on it, trying to get her moving. She didn't budge.

'What is the real magic, then? If it's not spells and potions?'

He shook his head helplessly. 'It's just the magic we'll be able to do because we're Elderlings. Once we remember how. I don't know that part yet. I think it's one of the things we have to remember. I'm trying to take you to what I want you to try, but you keep stopping. Thymara, if I could just tell you about it and you'd understand, don't you think I'd have done that? You have to come with me. That's why I brought you here.'

She looked into his eyes. He met her gaze squarely. There were times when Rapskal still seemed to be the slightly daft boy she had met on the day that she left Trehaug. Times when he rattled on endlessly, chattering about nothing, seemingly fascinated by the most trivial of oddities. Then there were times when she looked at him and saw how much he had grown and changed, not just as a youth who had suddenly attained the beginnings of manhood, but as a human who had crossed a line and was now an Elderling. He was red now, as scarlet as his dragon. His eyes had a gleam in them, a lambent light that was visible almost all the time now. She looked down at the hand she clasped, and saw how her blue-scaled hand fit into his scarlet one. 'Show me, then,' she said quietly, and this time, when he broke into a jog and pulled her along, she ran to keep pace with him.

He spoke as he trotted, his words broken with breathlessness. 'There are a lot of memory places. Some, like some of the statues, they have just memories from one Elderling. And it's like being that one Elderling for the time that you touch. Those are the best kind, I think. There are other places that are all about everything. And some that are just telling the laws or who lives in a house or who a business belongs to. There are some that are poems and music. And then there are some on the avenues that are, well, everything that has ever happened there. I think you could just stand there, day after day, and see everyone who ever passed by and hear what they said and smell what they ate and everything. I didn't see much use in that, myself.'

He turned from the main avenue, away from the towering buildings, down a more modest street. These structures were homes, she found she knew. She tried to imagine a family requiring more than one door, and sometimes a second or even third storey. There were balconies on some of them, and some had flat roofs with railings around the edges. Thymara had grown up in tiny structures built high in trees. If she stood and stretched out her arms in her bedchamber in her father's house in Trehaug, she could touch both walls. And the ceiling. How could people need or use so much space?

Rapskal turned a corner and she hastened beside him as he followed an uphill boulevard. The paved road was wide; she had never seen such a wide path. The houses here were staggered, looking out over one another toward the river. Gigantic pots held the skeletons of long-dead trees. Troughs of earth by doorways had once been small gardens. Dry bowls had cupped fountains.

She knew these things. Knew them as if someone had whispered them into her ear the moment she wondered. The gleaming stone, black with sparkling veins or sometimes gleaming white threaded with silver, spoke to her. They tugged at her with memories. She shook her head and focused herself on what Rapskal was saying to her.

'But when I found these two and I listened to him for a while and I thought, yes, that's what I want to know and who I want to be. And she was right there next to him, and he told me all about her and I thought, "Well, that's almost like Thymara, and she could be her."'And once we both take all that, then we'll know more, to make the city work and maybe help the dragons.'

She was losing her breath as she trotted alongside him. 'I still don't understand, Rapskal.'

'We're here. They can explain a lot better than I can. See? What do you think?'

She stared where he pointed and saw nothing unusual. The street ended in a cul-de-sac on the top of the hill. The entrance to the house at the top was framed by a series of open arches supported by stone pillars that glistened black and silver in the winter sunlight, marching in pairs toward the entry. To the left, they were marked with smiling suns. Those on the right each bore a gleaming silver medallion of a full moon smiling with a woman's features.

'Let me show you. It's so much easier than talking about it.' Rapskal pulled her forward. When they reached the first arch, he halted.

Thymara looked around. There were urns full of earth by each arch. 'Vines,' she said, and abruptly she remembered them, the glossy dark leaves and the multitudes of tiny white flowers in clusters. They had bloomed in the heat of summer every year and their sweet fragrance had scented every room in the house. There had been a fruit that followed, tiny clusters of bright orange berries that had no name in her language but were 'gillary' and every autumn, they had made a wine from them, one that kept the orange hue of the berries. It had been potent and sweet.

She swayed a little on her feet as she blinked her way back into her own life. She tried to take a few steps backwards but Rapskal tightened his grip on her hand. 'Not like that,' he told her. 'Well, you can, but then it's all in pieces. Like coming up to a storyteller at a trunk market when he's in the middle of telling the tale, and only getting a part of the story. That's not how they saved it for us. It's all here, in order, in the pillars. We should start with the first ones. The moon ones are for you.'

'How do you know?' She still felt disoriented. For a time, long or short, she could not tell, she had been in another time. More than that, she realized. She had been another person. She pulled her hand free of his and took two steps back. 'Drowning in memories! That's what they meant. Rapskal, this is dangerous. My father warned me about stones like this! They pull you in and fill your mind with stories and you forget how to come back and be yourself. After a while, you're just lost, not in that life and not in this one. How can you even think of doing this? You're a Rain Wilder! You know better than this. What is the matter with you?'

She was horrified. It was bad enough that he would indulge in such a dangerous pastime. And monstrous that he had tried to drag her into it.

'No,' he said. 'It's not like that.'

She turned away from him.

'Thymara, please, just listen to me. Everything you know about memory stone and drowning in it is wrong. Because the people you learned it from, well, this wasn't for them. It's for us, for Elderlings. Look around the city and see how much there is of it. You've heard the whispers; I know you have. Would they have put this stone everywhere if it was so dangerous? No. They put it here because, to Elderlings, it's not dangerous. It's important. We need these stones. We need to use them to become who we are meant to be.'

'I don't need them. I have my own life, and I won't lose it to something stored in stone.'

'Exactly!' He looked delighted at her assertion. 'You don't lose it. You find it. Think about the dragons, Thymara. They have memories that go way back, to their mothers and great great-grand fathers. But they don't lose their lives. They just have what they need to know how to be dragons. Elderlings needed the same thing, but they weren't born with it like dragons. To be companions to dragons, they needed to remember a lot more than just one human lifetime. So, this is how they did it. They stored it. They stored their lives, so that other Elderlings could have their memories.' He shook his head, his eyes wide and his thoughts far away. 'The special stone can hold so much, do so much. I don't understand it all, yet. But I'm learning a lot, every time I come here. And one thing I do know is that because I'm an Elderling, I'll likely live a long time, so I have time to learn things. The stone tells you things fast, like a minstrel singing the whole song of a hero's life in just a few hours.' He shifted his pale gaze back to her and his whole face was lit with excitement.

'Here's the thing, Thymara. I've done things in these stones that I've never done in this life. I've been places, far away places where their sailing ships used to go. I've hunted for big deer, and killed one all by myself. I've been over those mountains, trading with the people that used to live on the far side of them. I've been a warrior, and a leader of other warriors. I live in their memories and they live in me.'

She had been caught up in his words, tempted wildly right up until he said that. 'They live in you,' she said slowly.

'A little bit,' he dismissed it. 'Sometimes, in the middle of something else, one of their memories will pop up in my mind. It doesn't hurt anything; it's just something extra for me to know. Or maybe I want to sing a song he knew, or cook some meat a certain way. Thymara,' he cut in hastily as she tried to ask more questions, 'We don't have that much time here. Just try it with me. Just one try and if you don't like it, I'll never ask you to do it again. You can't drown in memories if you only do it once. Everyone knows that! And because you're an Elderling, I don't think you can drown at all, even if you do it a thousand times. Because we're supposed to. That's what the memory stone in the city is all about. Just try it.' He looked deep into her eyes. 'Please.'

His gaze trapped her. It was so earnest. So loving. She felt her breath catch. 'What do we do?' She could scarcely believe she was asking the questions.

'Only what you've already done. Only with purpose. Here. Give me your hand,' and he took her black-clawed hand into his narrow, sleekly scarlet fingers. His scaling whispered against her skin. 'I'm going with you. I'll be right here beside you. You hold my hand, and you set your hand to that pillar, because it was hers. And I'll put my hand on this one, because it was his. These first pillars, this is where they begin.'

His scaled hand was warm and dry in hers. The stone pillar was smooth and chill under her touch.

Sintara was hungry. It was Thymara's fault. The stupid girl had brought her only a couple of fish in the very early morning. She had promised her more food later. Promised that she would be back before evening and that before dark she would bring her meat. Promised her.

The dragon lashed her tail angrily. The promise of a human. What was that worth? She shifted unhappily, feeling as if emptiness had filled her belly and was now climbing up her throat. She was hungry, not again, but *still.* She tried to remember the last time she had felt full. Days ago; when Heeby had driven the hoofed herd over the cliffs to their deaths. All the dragons had descended on the riverbank for that glorious feed. Hot meat, running blood . . . The memory was a torment to her now. That was what she needed. Not a couple of cold fish that did not even fill her mouth, let alone her belly.

Sintara lifted her head and then reared onto her back legs, sniffing the air. Her tongue forked out, tasting for scents. All she scented were the other dragons and their keepers. The riverbank and the open meadow and the deciduous forest that backed it were not as confining as the hatching beach at Cassarick, but it was rapidly becoming as trodden and smelly. Dragons were not creatures to be corralled like cattle, doomed to wander through their own droppings and trampled paths. Yet even without fences or thick rainforest, they were confined here.

Only Heeby was truly free. She flew and hunted and fed. She came back to this place only out of affection for her half-wit keeper. Sintara dropped back onto all fours. And Thymara had gone off with Heeby and Rapskal that morning. Was that what her keeper expected of her? That she should learn to fly so that she could be a mount for Thymara and her friends?

She'd sooner eat them.

Her stomach clenched again. Where was the girl?

Reluctantly, because it was not fitting that a dragon seek for a human, let alone admit that she needed her aid, she reached out to touch minds with Thymara.

And could not find her. She was gone.

What shocked her was not just that the girl was gone, but the depth of her own dismay. *Gone*. Thymara was gone. Gone most likely meant dead, because it was unlikely that her keeper could have moved so far physically as to make contact difficult, or so quickly learned sufficient control of her thoughts that she could block the dragon from touching her. So, her keeper was dead. Her supplier of easy meat and fish was gone. Sintara's mind leapt to the next step. She'd have to have another keeper. But all of them were taken, unless she focused on Alise again, and Alise was hopeless as a hunter. Amusing to taunt, and excellent at flattery, but useless when one was hungry.

Taking another dragon's keeper would likely mean a fight. She was not the only dragon that was still painfully dependent on her keeper. And the sad truth was that Thymara had been the best of the lot. Not only could she hunt, she had a mind and some spirit that added spice to their frequent clashes. Her only real alternatives to Thymara were Carson and Tats. The hunter belonged to Spit and she had no wish to do battle with the nasty little silver. He was potently venomous now and malevolently clever. Besides, Carson was not someone she could bully. Spit had been loud all day long in his complaints that his keeper was starving him in an attempt to force him to fly. She had no desire to accept such an iron-willed keeper.

Tats belonged to Fente, and for a moment, Sintara relished the idea of ripping apart the nasty little green queen. Except that if she struck out at any female, all of the males would intervene, especially Mercor. Outnumbered as the males were, they viewed a threat to any of the females as a danger to the possibility that they might some day mate. Not that any of them had much chance of that.

Sintara huffed in anger and felt the poison sacs swell in her throat. The entire situation was completely unacceptable. How had her foolish keeper managed to kill herself in such a way that Sintara had not even noticed? The previous times that Thymara had encountered danger, Sintara's head had been full of her shrill squeaking and squealing. So what had happened to her?

The answer came to her instantly. Heeby. It was the red dragon's fault. She'd probably dropped her in the river, to sink like a stone. Or in her dimness, she'd forgotten the girl was Sintara's keeper and had eaten her. The mere thought that the half-wit red dragon had dared to eat her keeper filled Sintara with fury. She reared onto her hind legs and then came down with a crash, whipping her head on her serpentine neck, stimulating her poison glands to full action. Where was the damned little red newt? She flung her consciousness wide and touched her and her fury roared to fresh flames. Heeby was *asleep*! Fat and full-bellied, she sprawled asleep beside her third kill of the day. She hadn't even eaten it all: Sintara could sense how Heeby smelled the pleasing odour of bloody flesh as she slept.

It was too much, insult upon injury. The little scarlet queen would pay, and Sintara did not care how much Mercor or anyone else objected.

Tail lashing, she strode through the scattered trees and out onto the open hillside that fronted the riverbank. She would find Heeby and she would kill her. She could feel her eyes growing scarlet with blood, feel how their colours spun and how her blue wings flushed with blood and colour as she unfolded them and shook them out. They were strong, stronger than they had been when she'd hatched, stronger than they had been the time she'd managed that first long glide that had ended so ignominiously in the river. She could fly. The only thing that had been holding her back was foolish caution, her unwillingness to fail before the others or to risk it all in a long glide out over the river. But those fears and cautions were gone, burned away by her fury. Heeby had killed her keeper and Sintara would not tolerate that insult. The red queen would pay!

She looked at the wide open hillside before her and at the swift cold river at the bottom of it. So be it. She opened her wings and sprang into the air. Beat, beat, touch the ground, beat, beat, beat, touch the ground but more lightly, beat, beat, beat, beat . . .

And suddenly there was a gust of wind off the water and she caught it under her wings and lifted on it. She stroked her wings more strongly, tucking her forelegs to her chest and stretching her back legs into alignment with her tail, until she offered only smoothness and no resistance to the air. Her wings propelled her forward as her head cleaved the wind. *Flying*. Her body reached for memories of how to do this and she let it, refusing to let her mind interfere. Flying was like breathing, not a thing to ponder but a thing to do.

She caught another updraft and rose on it, and caught, too, the trumpeting of dragons from far below. She beat her wings more strongly. Let them look at her, let them see that she, the blue queen Sintara, had achieved full flight before any of them! She tipped her wings to circle wide over them, filled her lungs and trumpeted her triumph to the skies. *Flying!* A dragon was flying! Let all look up in awe!

She glanced down. And saw nothing but moving water below her and felt a lurch of terror. Memories of being trapped and tumbled in the icy flow for a moment overwhelmed her unthinking flight. For a terrifying instant, she forgot how to fly, forgot everything except the danger of the river. Her forelegs twitched reflexively in a swimming motion and she lashed her tail. *Falling*. She was falling, not flying and then as full panic set in and she beat her wings frantically, she rose again. But the smooth effortlessness of flight was broken. She felt too clearly the uneven musculature of her wings; sudden weariness made her wings feel heavy. Flight was work, hard work and she had had almost nothing to eat today, and not much more the day before.

All thoughts of vengeance on Heeby, all fear of the river was suddenly cast out by her overwhelming hunger. She needed food, needed fresh bloody meat now, at any cost. The urgency of her hunger steadied her. Hunt and feed or die, her body told her. It had no patience with her vanity or fear. Hunt and feed. She poured all her effort into the beating of her wings and circled wider, taking her flight over the keepers' pathetic settlement and beyond, back into the hills and valleys. She opened all her senses to the need for sustenance.

And then she glimpsed them, a small group of horned creatures making their way along a stony ridge. They were in clear view, but soon they would vanish into the trees . . .

They became aware of her almost as soon as she spotted them. Two broke from the group, galloping wildly toward the trees, but the other four craned their necks and stared stupidly up as she dived on them.

Sintara's weaker wing buckled just before she hit them, sending her slewing to one side. But her wide reaching claws still laid one open, shoulder to woolly hip, and she landed on top of another. It bleated once as they tumbled together, a most ungainly and bruising landing for a dragon. Then Sintara clutched it to her breast, snaked her head down and seized it in her jaws. Her mouth enveloped its bony head as her forelegs squeezed its ribs. It was dead before she and the creature skidded to a halt on the steep and rocky hillside. Dead but only just, as she tore at it frantically, heedless of bone and horn and hoof as she ripped it into chunks she could gulp down whole.

Feeding in such a way was painful. She swallowed

convulsively, not pausing to enjoy any part of it. When it was gone, she hunched, head down, simply breathing past the burden of the food moving through her gullet. There was no sense of satiation, only discomfort.

There was a bleat and Sintara lifted her head. Another creature! The one she had scored in passing! It was down, kicking all four legs in a way that said it would soon be dead. Sintara clawed her way up the steep hillside, feeling rocks displaced by her feet tear free and bound down the hill behind her. She didn't care. She gained ground and then literally fell upon her prey. She clutched it to her, feeling the precious warmth of fresh blood, and almost tenderly closed her jaws on it, squeezing the breath out of it. Moments later, it shuddered and was still. Only then did she drop it.

This animal she ate in a more leisurely fashion, clawing its belly open and eating the tender, steaming entrails before shearing off satisfyingly large pieces of meat with her ranks of sharp teeth. When she had swallowed the last bite, she sank down slowly on the bloody site of her kill, sighed out a deep breath and sank into a stupefied sleep.

She was in love with him as she had never loved any of the other men in her life. Their courtship had been slow and delicious, a delicate dance of shyness and uncertainty, followed by the warlike strategies that her jealous nature and his charming ways were bound to provoke. All of their friends had cautioned both of them against taking the relationship too seriously. She knew how his friends had warned him of her, knew that they thought her jealous and possessive. Well, she was. And she was determined to have him, for herself alone, forever. Never had she felt that way about any other men she had taken to her bed.

Her own companions had warned her she could not hold

him. Tellator was too handsome for her, too clever and charming. 'Be content with Ramose,' they had urged her. 'Go back to him; he'll take you back and with him you will always be comfortable and safe. Tellator is a warrior, always going into danger, called away at a moment's notice. He will always put his duty ahead of whatever he feels for you. Ramose is an artist, like you. He will understand your moods. He will grow old with you. Tellator may be handsome and strong, but can you ever be sure he will come home at night?'

But she had lived too long in comfort and safety; that was no longer what she wanted. And she could not ignore Ramose's infidelities. If all of her was not enough for him, then let him have none of her and seek what he needed elsewhere. As she, Amarinda, had sought and found Tellator.

She awaited Tellator in the garden court outside a little gaming parlour, a venue so discreet and select that it did not even hang a blue lantern by its door to attract its clientele. She had left Tellator throwing the bones of chance with a tubby little merchant newly come to Kelsingra, and walked through the open doors and out into the summer evening. The music of trickling water in one fountain vied with the leaping flames of a dragon-fount in the centre of the garden. Evening-blooming jasmine trailed from hanging pots, scenting the air. She found a bench in a very private corner of the grounds and took a seat there. A serving girl, a pretty barefoot child clothed in the shimmering colours of the gaming parlour followed her, and asked if she wished refreshments. After a short time, the girl returned with apricot biscuits and a gentle spring wine. She dismissed the girl, assuring her that she need not return.

Amarinda sipped her wine. And waited.

She knew the risk she took. She was making him choose. He had lifted his eyes briefly as she departed. He could remain where he was, in the light and glitter and sparkle of the gaming parlour with his friends. There was music there, and sweet smoke and rare cinnamon wine from the South Islands. And one of the players at the gaming table was a slender Elderling minstrel, newly arrived in Kelsingra from a city in the north, her scaling gold and cobalt around her eyes, and the rumours of her amorous skills as exotic and varied as the notes she plucked from her harp. Tellator had looked at her and smiled. Amarinda had smiled, too, as she departed the gathering and left him there to choose, knowing that it was really to herself that she was giving the ultimatum. If she did not win him this night, if he did not forsake all other pleasures to come to her, then she would never give him another chance.

Because the risk to her own heart was too great. She had come to care for him too deeply. If he did not reciprocate fully, then her only choice was to turn aside. She had loved like that once before, and vowed never to do so again.

The chained moments of the evening slipped by. The night grew cooler, and so did her heart. The dark jewels set in the walls of the garden awoke and their soft glow gave back to the night the light they had stolen from the day. There were caged crickets in the garden. They sang for a time, and then stopped as the night deepened. Her heart grew emptier by the moment. Finally, she rose to go. Leaning forward over the small table, she pinched out the flame of the rose-scented candle as if she were pinching a dead blossom from a flowering plant.

She straightened, sighed and as she turned, she walked straight into his arms. In the dimness of the garden, he dared to enclose her in his embrace. 'Here you are!' He spoke softly, his voice muffled by her hair. 'Someone said you had left. I've been all the way to your home, where I made a complete fool of myself with your servants before I came back here. I even sought you at your shop, but the door was locked and windows dark. Coming back here was my final resort. They didn't want to let me back into the parlour; they are trying to close for the night.'

In her surprise at the encounter, she had raised both her hands. They rested now, flat against the starched lace of his shirt front. The solid muscles of his chest were warm beneath her hands. She should just push him away. Or should she? Were his words true, or an excuse for coming to her only after he had dallied at his game and flirtation? Indecision held her motionless in his arms. She breathed in his smells as if he, too, were a night-blooming plant. The cinnamon wine spiced his breath. His skin smelled of sandalwood.

And nothing else, she realized. Her rival had reeked of patchouli, as if she had bathed in it, drunk it and then drenched her clothes in it. But Tellator did not. She let her hands slip around him, finding no words to say. A seed of doubt had been planted in her heart, and nourished by the delay, a delay created by her own foolish plan to test him. Had he mastered her challenge?

'Amarinda,' he said, his voice gone suddenly husky. He pulled her firmly to him, pressed the length of his body against hers so that she could feel how much he desired her. She lifted her face to counsel him to restraint, but his head darted down and his mouth seized hers in a kiss. She tried to turn her head aside, but he would not let her. Instead he held the kiss and deepened it, pushing her back and then astonishing her when he lifted her onto the table. 'Here,' he said, and, 'Now,' he demanded. He pushed the panels of her skirts aside and set his warm hands on her knees to open her legs.

'We cannot! Tellator, not here, not like this!' She was horrified, not only by his assumption that she would agree but her body's hungry response to him.

'Oh, but we can. And I must. I cannot wait, not another moment. Not another breath.'

Something. Distress. Danger.

Thymara pried her eyes open. She was sitting, not on a table in a garden on a warm summer evening, but on the hard stone steps with a chill winter day dying around her. Yet she was not cold. She was panting still with the passion she had shared, and Amarinda's heat and desire still warmed her. She cleared her throat, coughed and then was suddenly aware that she held his hand. Tellator looked at her from Rapskal's eyes. 'Here,' he said quietly. 'And now. There is no better time than this.'

He set his long, scaled hand to the line of her jaw and lowered his face to hers. Rapskal kissed her knowingly, his mouth moving gently on hers. She was paralysed with desire and wonder. Where did they stop, where did they begin? It was all one. The man who knelt suddenly on the steps before her, opening her worn blouse to his greedy kisses was not a clumsy boy but a skilled lover. Her own skilled lover, long schooled to what would most stir her. There was nothing new in how he touched her or what she longed to do with him. She gasped at the touch of his teeth and put her hand on the back of his head. Her fingers tangled in his dark hair, and she guided his mouth against her. She sighed his name and he laughed softly, his mouth still against her skin. 'Rapskal,' he corrected her. 'But you can call me Tellator. Just as I can call you Amarinda.' He lifted his face to smile deep into her eyes. 'Do you see now, Thymara? Do you understand? Everything we need to know about being Elderlings, we can learn here. Even this. And you won't fear it any more, because you've already done it. And you know how good it will be between us.'

She didn't want him to talk. She didn't want him to pause, didn't want to think about what she was going to do. He was right. She didn't need to. Others had made all the decisions for them, all those years ago. She leaned back, letting him do as he knew she wished.

'I didn't fear this,' she told him breathlessly. 'It was just . . .' She lost her words and her thought in his touch. Why had she been so reluctant?

'I didn't think you did, really.' His voice was deep with pleasure as he fumbled at his clothing. 'I knew Jerd was wrong when she said that you were afraid, that watching was as much as you'd ever want to do.'

Jerd? The name was like a bucket of cold water dashed against her. Thymara jerked back from Rapskal, and then hitched away from him, pulling her shirt closed over her breasts. 'Jerd?' she demanded of him, incensed. 'Jerd! You discussed my doing this with Jerd? You took her advice on how best to accomplish what you wanted?' Fury washed through her, drowning desire. *Jerd.* She could just imagine her laughing, mocking, making lewd suggestions to Rapskal as to just how he could persuade her to mate with him. *Jerd!*

She shot to her feet, her arousal vanished. Her fingers flew as she refastened her clothing. She sought for furious words and couldn't find any sharp enough to fling at him. Turning away from him, she stared at the wall feeling dizzied, almost ill. It had all changed too swiftly. She had been Amarinda and so infatuated with Tellator. Then she had entered that odd middle ground in which she had felt as if she possessed two lives, and had absolutely no qualms about sharing herself with him. Now she didn't even want to look at him.

I'll have to hold onto him when I fly back on Heeby. That intrusive thought only intensified her anger. Right now, all she wanted was to walk away from him and never speak to him again. Jerd. He'd gossiped about her with Jerd! Believed that Jerd knew what she was talking about.

'Thymara! It wasn't like that!' Rapskal stumbled to his feet, stuffing himself back inside his trousers and tying up the ragged drawstring. 'I was just there, and Jerd was talking to some of the others. It wasn't that I asked her advice. Some of us were just sitting around a fire a few nights ago, talking, and someone said something about Greft and missing him despite all he had done. And she agreed, and talked about him a bit, and then she told how sometimes you'd follow them and watch them when they were mating. And she was the one making mock and saying it was probably as much as you'd ever do. Saying you were pretending that you were saving your virginity or didn't want to get pregnant, but actually you were just afraid of doing it.'

Thymara spun back to stare at him in horror. 'She talked like that about me in front of everyone? In front of who? Who was she talking to? Who heard all this?'

'I don't know . . . some of us, we just get together in the evenings, to sit around a fire like we used to. Um, I was there, but Jerd wasn't really talking to me. She was talking to Harrikin. Kase and Boxter were there, I think. And maybe Lecter. And I just, I just listened. That was all. I didn't say anything.'

'So no one defended me? Everyone just sat there and let her talk about me like that?'

Rapskal cocked his head at her. 'Then it's not true that you used to watch them?'

'Yes. No! I watched them once. By accident. Sintara said they were hunting and that I should go join them. So I went to where they were and I saw what they were doing. That was all.' Well, not quite all, but as much as she would admit to. She'd been trapped in horrified fascination and she had neither left nor taken pains to let them know she was there. It was only fair, she told herself. If Jerd could wildly exaggerate what she had done, then she could cut it back in her own telling.

'Then it's not because you're afraid? I mean, that you're still a virgin.'

She knew what he meant. 'No. I'm not afraid. Not afraid of mating, but yes, I'm afraid of getting pregnant. Look what happened to Jerd. She had a miscarriage. But what if she'd carried the baby to term and then it needed all sorts of things we didn't have? Or if she had the baby, and then she died and we all had to take care of it? No. Now is not the time for me to be taking that kind of a chance. Or for Jerd to be doing it with everyone. She's just selfish, Rapskal. Look how she behaved when she was pregnant, expecting everyone to care for her dragon and to do her share of the chores and give her more than her share of the food. She liked everyone scrambling around to make her life easy.' Thymara pulled her cloak closer around her. She was cold now, she realized. How long had they been here in the city, standing still in the chill winter day? All the warmth she had recalled had fled. The tips of her ears and the tops of her cheeks burned with chill. 'I want to go back now.' She spoke the words sullenly.

Rapskal's response came slowly. 'Not quite yet, we can't. Heeby made a kill and ate a lot. She's still sleeping.'

She folded her arms tightly around her. 'I'm going inside somewhere. Out of the wind. Call me when we can leave.'

'Thymara, please. Wait. There's something important you should know.'

She ignored him, walking away. She didn't want to go into Amarinda's house. She knew what she would see there. Oh, doubtless the rich wooden furniture and the embroidered tapestries and thick woollen carpets were gone. But the frescoed walls of her Bird Room and the deep marble tubs of her bath would still be there. And she didn't want to see them and remember more things. Didn't want to recall making love with Tellator in the deep warm waters of that bath, his muscled soldier's body filling her arms.

The thought tugged at her and she nearly turned around. She did want more of it, did want to experience all of their amorous adventures together. She was tired of being cold and now that she was all the way back in her own body, she was hungry, too. It would be so easy to go back into that house and become Amarinda again.

Being Thymara had never been all that much fun. And it did not seem as if it was going to become more enjoyable any time soon.

Abruptly, she felt icy cold all over and she strangled as if she could not take a breath of air. The cold was so sharp it was like being stabbed by knives. It tumbled her and she felt disoriented. She coughed and drew in a breath.

'Thymara?' There was alarm in Rapskal's voice. 'Are you all right?'

'Sintara!' She shrieked her dragon's name as she jerked her head up straight and stared all around, as if to see what she was feeling so palpably. 'She's drowning! She's fallen in the river and she's drowning!'

Day the 25th of the Change Moon
Year the 7th of the Independent Alliance of Traders

From Detozi, Keeper of the Birds, Trehaug to Kim, Keeper of the Birds, Cassarick

Kim, you are a fool. All cotes and lofts, public and private, are being inspected. No one has reported you or singled you out. As you yourself noted, most likely this plague of deadly lice began in the wilds and is afflicting us all.

My first temptation was to turn your most recent note over to the Guild, as it contains not only an insult but a threat. You may thank Erek that I have restrained myself, for he pointed out that at this time the Guild must focus itself on saving our remaining birds. Bear in mind that I shall save your correspondence, and if any mishaps befall my cotes, lofts or birds, I will not hesitate to present it to the Guild.

I suggest you look to the health of your birds, including this bluewing I'm sending back to you. I have cleaned him of all lice, but have noted how poorly nourished he was in my log books. His cross beak is an indication of inbreeding; are you not minding your breeding records? I suggest you be sure that the peas and grain the Guild supplies for your birds is going into their mouths and not your own.

CHAPTER NINE

Return to Cassarick

Word of their return had preceded him. As the barge approached the city dock, he saw the waiting runner push his wet hair back from his eyes and give a quick nod to himself before darting off among the trees. Captain Leftrin had expected something of the sort. Tarman had encountered some little fishing boats upriver of Cassarick, and two had immediately shot downstream to the treetop city to spread the news: the liveship *Tarman* was returning from its expedition upriver. The big news would be that no dragons accompanied it.

Leftrin had not given any details of the expedition to the fishermen. To their shouted queries, he'd responded only that he'd tie up in Cassarick soon enough and he'd report everything to the Cassarick Traders' Council then. Knowledge was power, and he had no intent of sharing that power until he'd used it to his utmost. Let them wait a bit and wonder what had become of the malformed dragons and their keepers. Suspense was an excellent tool for keeping powerful people off balance. It gave one bargaining power. Bargaining power he suspected he was going to need.

A winter rain was falling, shushing the river with a million tiny splashes. Water ran off the decks and back into the grey waters of the wide Rain Wild River. To either side of the river, tall dense forest loomed. The rain pattered on an infinity of leaves there, working its way down from the canopy of the trees through the layers of life and greenery, past all the strata of cottages and mansions built in the mighty tree limbs until at last it fell to the permanently sodden forest floor. It was both very familiar and suddenly strange to come back to the towering trees that lined the river. Kelsingra had shown him a terrain far out of his experience. Dry firm land and rolling hills were nice, but Leftrin suspected this would always be home for him.

He squinted through the rain as they approached the docks. There was a strange vessel tied up there and he scowled at the look of it. It was long and narrow, of shallow draught, fitted for both sails and oars. Bright blue paint and gold trim on the deckhouse gleamed even through the misty rain. Competition for Tarman? Perhaps the owners might think so, but he doubted it. No other vessel had ever excelled his in navigating the shallower waters of the Rain Wild River. *Impervious One* he read on her bow. Well, time would tell if that were true. Over his years on the river, he'd seen all sorts of boats that were supposed to be immune to the acid waters of the river. And he'd seen them all sink, eventually. Wizardwood was the only stuff that lasted.

The driving rain made miserable work for Swarge on the barge's tiller, and was scarcely better for the rest of the crew as they maintained their façade of manning their poles and guiding the barge into the dock. They nudged past the *Impervious One* and found a place to tie up. Leftrin gripped the bow rail, squinting through the downpour. Through the wizardwood railing under his hands, he was aware of his ship. Tarman was grateful for the crew's show; the rains had swelled the Rain Wild River to near flood stage; it was difficult for the liveship to keep his grip on the bottom. His hidden feet, the secret of his ability to manoeuvre rapidly through areas where other ships went aground, clawed at the mud, caught, lost touch, and then scrabbled again. With a lurch, Tarman brought himself alongside the docks and Skelly leapt over the side, clutching the thick mooring line and scampering toward a heavy cleat. She secured it there and then raced aft, to catch the second line that Hennesey tossed to her. In a trice, they were safely fastened to the dock. Tarman and his captain relaxed as the crew moved through the routines of adjusting the moorage lines.

Captain Leftrin had thought the driving rain might keep the Council members safe and dry indoors today. It had. But as the crew brought Tarman in to Cassarick's floating dock, the drenched young runner had pelted off through the rain to the nearest stair and scampered up the steps like a tree monkey scaling a trunk. Leftrin smiled to see him go. 'Well. Soon enough they'll get word that we've docked. And then we'll see how well we can play the cards we've been dealt. Skelly!'

At his bark, his niece jumped nimbly from the dock to the barge and then hurried up to stand at his elbow. 'Sir?'

'You'll stay aboard. I know your folks will be wanting to see you, and we both have some serious news to share with them. I'd like it if we were together when we let them know that your fortune has changed. That all right with you?'

She blinked rain from her lashes and grinned. Her family had expected that Skelly would be his heir. On the strength of that expectation, they had negotiated a profitable betrothal for her, one that she was most anxious to break now that she had met Alum and become infatuated with the quiet dragon keeper. Leftrin did not know if he and Alise would ever have a child to take over ownership of Tarman, but even if they did not, the possibility of an heir displacing her changed Skelly's fortune completely. She was hoping the boy's family would decline the betrothal now that her future was uncertain. Leftrin doubted that her parents would be as pleased at the prospect as she was. He didn't want her to break the news to them alone. That he would speak for her obviously pleased her as she asked, 'Is my uncle offering that service or my captain?'

'Don't get sassy with me, sailor!'

'Sir, yes, regardless of who's asking.' She grinned insouciantly at him. 'I'd like that best myself, if we did it together. And they'd expect me to stay aboard until you reported to the Council. If any of them drop by to visit me here before you get back, I'll say nothing and tell them the story has to come from you.'

'Good lass! Now, I want no one else to come aboard Tarman while I'm gone. Crew family, that's okay. Tell them little, and bid them keep what they do hear to themselves. They'll understand. But no merchants, no Council members and I'll tell Hennesey no whores. He can leave the ship for that if he must, but he can't bring any guests back with him. Not right now.' Leftrin scratched at his wet cheek. His scaling had increased lately, and it itched constantly. Damn dragons. Probably their fault. 'I'll be giving the rest of the crew shore time, but either Swarge or Hennesey must be on board at all times. Bellin, I'll take your list to the ship's chandlery and have it filled and sent down. As soon as I've wrung our wages out of the Council, I'll pay off the merchants and send the rest of the money here. Big Eider will go see his mother, as he always does. And you'll stay aboard and wait until I have time to take you to visit your parents.'

'Yes, sir.'

The rest of his crew, their docking tasks completed, had drifted closer to them. They were weary and haggard, rain-drenched and triumphant. He raised his voice to be heard over the rattling of the rain on Tarman's decks. 'I'm counting on all of you to trust me to strike our best deal. Mum's the word on where we've been and what we've seen until after I finish our negotiation. Got that?'

Swarge ran a big hand through his hair, pushing the lank strands back from his face. 'It's all agreed to, Cap. You told us before and we haven't forgotten. Nothing for you to worry about here. Good luck.'

'Squeeze those bastards dry,' Hennesey suggested, and Big Eider's broad face cracked wide in a grin of agreement.

The others were nodding. Leftrin nodded back, and felt their confidence in him as both armour and liability. There was a lot depending on him this time, much more than merely getting their pay for a journey accomplished. The councils were notoriously tight-fisted, he thought as he returned to his stateroom. He grinned like a snarl; he'd always wrung his contract money out of them before and he'd do it this time, too. The signed document that had sent him and his ship on the expedition up the river was already snugly stowed in a waterproofed tube. He hefted it approvingly. They'd live up to their terms of the bargain; they wouldn't like it, but he'd hold them to their written words, and they'd pay out the coin they'd never expected to spend.

Malta Khuprus sat before her mirror, drawing her comb through the gleaming gold streaks in her softly curling hair. Then she twisted it and slowly began to pin it into place. As her hands worked, almost by themselves, she stared at her reflection in the glass. When would the changes stop? Ever since she'd first come to the Rain Wilds, her body had been changing. Now the gold in her hair was literally gold, not the glossy blonde that some folks called gold. The nails of her fingers were crimson. The rosy skin of her face was as finely scaled as a little tree lizard's belly and as soft. The scarlet 'crown' above her brow gleamed.

Her scaling was edged in red; the creamy skin of her childhood still shone through the nearly translucent scales on her cheeks, but her brows were layered rows of ruby scales now. She turned her head, watching the light move over her face and then sighed.

'Are you well?' Reyn crossed the small room they had rented, covering the distance between them in two strides. He set his hands to her shoulders and stooped to look at her.

'I'm fine. A bit tired, that's all.' She set her hands to the small of her back and pressed on her spine. Her back ached abominably, as it had all day. The pull of the weight in her belly could no longer be eased, not by sitting or standing. Yesterday at the negotiation table with the Tattooed diggers had been a day of torment. She'd come back to their rented room hoping to sleep.

A wasted hope. Reclining was the most uncomfortable position of all. She'd let Reyn have the bed and slept propped up with cushions. Now she gave a small grunt of pain as she pressed on her back, and a frown of concern rippled Reyn's brow. She pushed a smile onto her face and looked up at him in her mirror. 'I'm fine,' she repeated, and then took a moment to gaze at her husband. His changes were as marked as her own. His eyes gleamed a warm copper. His skin beneath the bronze highlights of his scaling was blue, as blue as the dragon Tintaglia. He smiled at her with sapphire lips. His dark curling hair had taken on steel-blue glints. Her husband. The man who had risked so much to find and claim her. 'You are so beautiful,' she said, the compliment escaping her lips easily.

Reyn's deep eyes danced. 'What prompts such wild flattery?' He cocked his head at her, his expression becoming mischievous. 'Now what trinket does my lady desire? A necklace of sapphires? Or is it yet another food craving? Do you desire a platter of steamed humming-bird tongues?'

'Ew!' Malta turned, laughing, to put an arm around her husband's narrow hips and drew him close to her. Reyn bent to kiss lightly her scarlet crown. She shivered at the touch and tilted her head to look up at him. 'Can't I simply say something nice to you without you reminding me of what a spoiled child I was when we first met?'

'Of course not. I'll never miss a chance to remind you of what a brat you were. A gloriously beautiful and very spoiled brat. I was utterly charmed by your complete self-absorption. It was rather like courting a cat.'

'You!' she rebuked him fondly and turned back to her mirror. She set a hand on the marked swell of her belly. 'And now that you've made me fat as a pig with your baby, I suppose I'm not as "gloriously beautiful" to you.'

'And now she fishes for compliments! And comes up with a net full. My darling, it only makes you the more lovely to me. You glow, you gleam, you scintillate with your pregnancy.'

She could not control the smile that wreathed her face. 'Oh, and *you* accuse *me* of flattery! Here I waddle about like a fat old duck and you try to tell me I'm lovely.'

'I am not the only one who says so. My mother, my sisters, even my cousins stare at you!'

'That's the envy that every Rain Wild woman has for a pregnant woman. It doesn't mean they think I'm beautiful.' She put her hands on the vanity table and pushed herself to her feet. As always, the sight of her belly in a mirror startled her. She set her narrow, long fingered hands on the bulge and stared. Becoming an Elderling had elongated so many of her body parts; her hands, her fingers, the long bones of her arms and legs – now this round bump in the middle of her frame seemed startling. 'I look as if I swallowed a melon,' she said to herself.

Reyn looked over her shoulder into the mirror. 'No. You look as if you carry our child within you.' He slid his hands down to just beneath the curve of their child and cradled it. The nails of his hands were a midnight blue, contrasting sharply with the soft white tunic she wore. He kissed the side of her face. 'There are times when I still cannot believe in my good fortune. All we went through, all the times we nearly lost one another, and now, soon, we will have—'

'Hush!' she cautioned him. 'Don't speak it aloud. Not yet. We have been disappointed too many times.'

'But this time, I'm sure, all will be well. Never before have you managed to carry a child this long. You've felt him move, I've seen him move! He's alive. And soon he will be where we can see him.'

'And if "he" is a girl?'

'I promise you, I will be just as content.'

They felt the branch that supported the small house give to someone's tread. There came a tap at the door. They moved apart reluctantly, Malta resuming her seat before her mirror and Reyn moving swiftly to the door. 'Yes?'

'Please, sir, I've news!' a breathless and boyish voice responded.

'News of what?' Reyn opened the door wider. The lad on the doorstep was no runner. His clothes were ragged and he was thin. He looked up at Reyn hopefully. Tattoos marred both his cheeks.

'Please, sir, I heard at the trunk market that someone named Malta Elderling would want to know about the ship what's come in. That she might pay a penny for such news.'

'What news? What ship?'

The boy hesitated until Reyn groped in his belt purse and held up a coin.

'*Tarman*, sir. That boat what went out with the dragons. It's back.'

Malta lurched to her feet as Reyn slid the flimsy door open.

Rain from high above pattered down in stray droplets but the runner who still stood outside was soaked with it. 'Come in,' Reyn invited him, and he stepped gratefully into the chamber and over to the firepot on its baked-clay hearth. He warmed his hands, his clothes dripping water onto the rough plank floor.

'What of the dragons?' Malta demanded.

The lad lifted gleaming blue eyes to meet her gaze. 'I saw no dragons when I went down to look. I didn't wait to ask, lady, but only came to tell you the barge has docked. I was not the first to know, but I wished to be the first to give my news. To earn a penny, as I understood it.' The lad looked worried.

But Reyn was now offering him a handful of coins and Malta nodded. 'You've done well. Only tell me what you saw. There were no dragons with the vessel? Did you see any of the young keepers? Did the barge look battered, or in good condition?'

The runner wiped a hand over his wet face. 'There weren't any dragons. I saw only the barge, and the crew working it. It didn't look battered but the crew looked tired. Tired and skinny and more on the ragged side than you'd expect.'

'You did well. Thank you. Reyn, where is my cloak?'

Her husband saw the boy to the door before turning to look at her. 'Your cloak is on the back of your chair, where you last left it. But you cannot be thinking of going out in this downpour?'

'I must. You know I must, and you must come with me.' She glanced around the room, but saw nothing more she needed. 'Fortune has favoured us to be here in Cassarick! I will not lose this chance. I need to be there when Captain Leftrin reports to the Council. All *they* will care about is that they are rid of the dragons. I need to know how they fared, how many survived, where he left them, if he found Kelsingra at all . . . oh.' She stopped abruptly and caught her breath.

'Malta? Are you all right?'

'I'm fine. He just kicked me, hard, right in my lungs. Took my breath away for a moment.' She grinned. 'You win, Reyn. He must be a boy. It seems that whenever I get excited about something, he must dance a jig inside me. No well-mannered little girl would do that to her mother.'

Reyn snorted. 'As if I would expect any daughter of yours to be a "well mannered little girl". Darling. Why don't you stay here and let me go in your place? I promise I would come back immediately and give you word of all I heard and saw.'

'No. No, dear.' Malta had found her cloak and was putting it on. 'I have to be there. If you went for me, I'd only ask you a hundred questions you hadn't thought to ask and then be frustrated when you did not know the answers. We'll leave a note for Tillamon so that she doesn't worry about me if she comes by this evening.'

'Very well.' Reyn agreed reluctantly. He found his own cloak, still wet from an earlier outing, shook it out and slung it around his shoulders. 'I wish Selden were here. He is the one who should be handling this.'

'I just wish I knew where he was. It has been months now since we've heard from him. That last letter he sent didn't sound like him, and it didn't look like his hand to me. I fear something has befallen him. Yet even if my brother were here, I'd still have to go, Reyn.'

'I know that, my dear. We were raised in the old ways of the Traders, you and I. But even I wonder if we keep faith with a dead dragon. No one has seen her or heard rumour of her for years, now. Is she dead and our agreements dead with her?'

Malta shook her head stubbornly as she lifted the large hood of her cloak and set it carefully on her pinned hair. 'Contracts are written on paper, not air, and signed with ink, not breath. It does not matter to me if she is dead. Regardless of what others may do, we remain bound by our signed words.'

Reyn sighed. 'Actually, we said only that we would help the serpents and protect the serpents' cases until the dragons hatched from them. In which case, our part of the bargain is done.' He grimaced as he pulled up the wet hood of his cloak.

'I was raised to keep the spirit of an agreement, not just the letter of it,' Malta responded tartly. Then, as she realized it was her aching back that was driving her to quarrel with him over their old disagreement, she changed the subject slightly. 'I wonder if that woman has returned safely, that Alise Finbok. She gave me such comfort and heart on the day she said she would go with them. She spoke so confidently and learnedly about Kelsingra.'

Malta turned to look at her husband. His eyes were a lambent blue within his hood's shadows. He spoke reluctantly. 'I've heard rumours that she was actually fleeing her husband and running off with his servant. There was some talk that her husband had disowned her, but that her father and the servant's family were seeking news of them, even offering a reward for any word.'

Malta felt a pang of deep dismay. She pushed it aside. 'I don't care about any of that. She spoke like someone one well versed in ancient things. The way she described the city, it was as if she had already walked there. She might have been fleeing her husband; she would not be the first wife to do so. But I think she was also bound toward something. So. Let's go out into the rain and down to the Council Hall. We'll learn no more about the expedition standing here.'

'Take my arm, then. The walkways may be slippery. I know better than to try to talk you out of this, but at least I shall beg you to be cautious.'

'I won't fall.' She took his arm nonetheless, and was glad of it when he opened the door. A wind curled into the room, full of damp and chill. 'If it's blowing like this under the trees, what is it like out on the river?' she wondered aloud.

'Worse,' Reyn replied succinctly as he closed the flimsy door behind them. 'And no, you won't fall, because I won't let you. But be cautious in more than that. Please, do not let the Council excite or upset you.'

'If anyone becomes excited or upset, I'll wager it will be them,' Malta replied sanguinely.

It was early afternoon, but it was winter and perpetually dim this far under the canopy of the great trees. Reyn held her arm tightly as they ventured along the narrow path from their tree branch to the main branch. When it joined a wider way on a thicker tree limb, she felt him relax. He was native to the Rain Wilds and their tree-built communities. She had come here when she was almost grown, and felt she had adapted to it well. Usually she moved confidently even on the narrowest paths and when crossing the swaying bridges that connected the neighbourhoods of the tree cities. But in these last few months, the burgeoning child in her belly had unbalanced her normally slight body. She held Reyn's arm firmly, unabashedly claiming his aid and protection. They'd suffered four miscarriages since they were wed; she would take no foolish misstep out of pride now!

The tree-house city, typical of all Rain Wild settlements, spread out in every direction around her. Above her in the higher branches dangled the smaller, flimsier houses of the poor; deep in the shadowy depths below her where the tree limbs were thick and sturdy, she looked down on mansions, warehouses, and the sturdy walls and windows of the Traders' Hall. Yellow lamplight lit those windows from within.

The Cassarick Rain Wild Traders' Hall was the newest

Trader hall to be built, and there was still some grumbling among the Rain Wilders about their independent stance from Trehaug. For years, there had been only one Rain Wild Trader hall, and that had been the one in Trehaug. The Rain Wild Traders and the Bingtown Traders had been two halves of a whole, united by a shared history of hardship. With the opening of the new Trader Hall in Cassarick, younger sons and lesser Trader families had come suddenly into more power than they'd ever had before. The politics were still settling. Greed and the need to be decisive had put a sharper edge on their Traders' Council. Malta did not entirely trust them to hold to the old Trader standards of equality and the absolute enforcement of signed agreements.

She saw that she and Reyn were not the only folk bound for the hall, and by this Malta judged that the word had spread of the *Tarman*'s arrival. Other Rain Wilders were emerging from their homes and onto the walkways that led to the Council Hall. Robed Traders hastened down the winding staircases that necklaced the immense tree trunks. The tidings that would await them there would affect everyone. Still, she did not hurry to get a good seat. She was Malta Khuprus, not only an Elderling but wife to Reyn Khuprus, second son of a powerful Rain Wild Trader family. His older brother Bendir might control the family vote, but he relied on the information Reyn brought him in deciding how to cast that vote. Neither she nor Reyn could claim an official seat at the Council table but she would be heard. On that, she was resolved.

Wind gusted against them, flapping her cloak and tearing leaves from the surrounding trees. Sturdy railings of woven vines edged the path they travelled. Beyond their safety, she saw only thick branches, dense greenery, and small houses dancing in the wind as they dangled from the trees' great branches like peculiar fruit. The unseen marshy ground was a long fall below them. She gripped Reyn's arm and let him lead.

Leftrin had deliberately taken his time. He'd gone to the bird-handlers first, and there sent off the messages that had been entrusted to him before he'd left Kelsingra. It had cost him more than he'd expected. Some sort of bird sickness had put message service at a premium. Some of the birds would have a short flight. Several of the keepers had chosen to send messages back to Trehaug to let their families know they were safe. There had been two death notices to send as well. Greft's and Warken's families needed to know what had become of their sons. Greft had been a trial to the captain, but his death was still a tragedy and his family deserved to be first to know of it. Lastly, he had posted Sedric's and Alise's missives to their families in Bingtown. All the way downriver to Cassarick he'd agonized over the wisdom of sending those. He'd urged all of them to be circumspect in what they told people about Kelsingra and how they had arrived there, but he had not read any of the messages. By the time this day was over, people in Cassarick would know as much as he intended to tell them, and message birds would be flying in all directions. Best to see that the messages from his friends had a chance of reaching their families first.

By the time he reached the ship's supply store, he'd acquired several followers. Two small boys tagged at his heels, loudly announcing to anyone they encountered that this was Captain Leftrin, back from his expedition. This led to hand-shakes and questions that he courteously refused to answer. One young man, probably a gossip-monger, had trailed him for some way, peppering him with a score of questions, only to be frustrated by Leftrin's insistence that he would report first to the Council. One other, a man wearing a long, hooded grey cape, had hung back and not spoken to him at all but followed at a more than discreet distance. Once Leftrin was aware of him, he took care to remain so. The man was a stranger, and in the brief glimpses the captain had had of him, he did not move with the easy familiarity of the tree-top born. He was no Rain Wilder. Dread uncoiled in Leftrin's chest as he speculated about just who the man might serve.

At the ship's supply, Leftrin ordered the preserved foods and basic necessities that would restock his ship's larder. Oil, flour, sugar, coffee, salt, ship's biscuit . . . Bellin's list seemed endless. He also bought every sheet of paper and bottle of ink that the store possessed, as well as a stock of new quills. He smiled as he did so, imagining Alise's pleasure at this trove. He asked that all the supplies be sent immediately down to the *Tarman*. He'd traded there for years, ever since the store had opened, and it did not take much to persuade the owner to accept his signature in lieu of coin. 'Council pays me, I pay you within the hour,' Leftrin promised the nodding man, and that was that.

By the time he left the store, his legs ached. Walking the deck of his ship and even hiking the meadows around Kelsingra did not prepare a man for the many vertical climbs of a Rain Wild city. He took a lift down to the Council Hall level, paying the tender with his last coin as the man's basket passed his own in transit. As he drew near to the Council door, he recalled that the last time he'd come here, Alise Finbok had been on his arm. It had been in the early days of their acquaintance, when his infatuation with her was dizzyingly new. He thought of her shiny little boots and her lacy skirts and smiled a bit sadly. Her finery had dazzled him as much as her ladylike ways. Well, her lace had gone to tatters and her boots were scuffed and worn now, but the gracious lady inside them prevailed as if wrought from iron. He suddenly missed her with a pang more powerful than hunger or fear. He shook his head at himself. Was he a mooning adolescent, to be so thoroughly engrossed with her? He smiled. Perhaps he was. The sensations she woke in him were wilder and sweeter than any other experience in his life. And once he was paid, he anticipated buying little luxuries and dainties to take back to her. The thought put a wider smile on his face.

When he pushed open the door to the Traders' Hall, he was greeted with light and the murmur of voices and warmth. Braziers burned in scattered locations throughout the room, contributing heat and the sweet smell of burning jalawood. Light came from another source, the tethered globes that floated within the hall. Elderling artefacts unearthed from the buried ruins at the foot of Cassarick now illuminated the meeting place of the humans in a flagrant display of wealth. For a moment, he imagined the surge of greed that would be stirred if he spoke on an Elderling city that stood intact and virtually untouched. His eyes went to the tapestry of Kelsingra that hung on the wall behind the Council dais. Alise had once used that tapestry to prove to them that their destination had existed. And when he told the Council that its gleaming walls still sparkled in the sunlight? His smile tightened.

Tiers of benches surrounded an elevated dais. Several dozen people had claimed seats; it was not exactly a packed gallery, but it was a lot of people to have gathered spontaneously for an unannounced meeting, and more were arriving behind him. All of the seats at the Council table on the dais were already occupied except for one. Selden Vestrit's seat was empty, as it had been the last time he'd been here.

But Malta the Elderling had taken her place at one end of the front row of audience seats. Her husband Reyn Khuprus sat beside her. All around the Elderlings, seats had been left empty. Leftrin wondered if it were out of respect or avoidance. Reyn and Malta were not dressed glamorously, but their simple clothing was well-tailored to them, and in colours that glorified their scaling. Reyn wore a long jacket of dark blue buttoned with gleaming silver buttons over grey trousers and soft black boots. Malta wore a choker of flame jewels that gleamed yellow against the delicate scaling of her throat. Her soft white over-tunic was long, to her knees, and her brown-gold trousers were cut full and loose, and by that he judged that she still carried her child. Good. Gossip said she'd had several miscarriages, and some had begun to doubt that the couple would ever produce a child. But she could not be far from birth now. Her husband beside her had a protective air. He looked at them, and realized that they showed him what his keeper youths would become. Full Elderlings.

As he entered the chamber, both of them looked directly at him. He fought an impulse to straighten his ragged shirt. Instead, he stiffened his spine and returned their gazes. It had been a hard trip; let them look at him and see what his expedition had cost. Then he nodded to them gravely and received their answering nods. He did not approach them. Not yet. Alise's message for Malta was safe in his bag. He would give it to her privately.

Leftrin's gaze roamed the chamber briefly, confirming that the fellow who had been following him had ghosted into the Traders' Hall behind him. He did not look at him directly; he didn't need to, for the man was no stranger to Leftrin. It was the Chalcedean 'merchant', Sinad Arich. He kept his wet cloak and hood drawn close about him as if he were still cold, but Leftrin recognized his eyes. The man had threatened him with blackmail once before over his liveship, forcing Leftrin to give him passage up the river. How he regretted it now. He should have followed his first impulse and killed the man and dropped him overboard. It chilled Leftrin to know the Chalcedean merchant was still in the Rain Wilds. It meant he had not given up on his mission.

Why was he here tonight? Leftrin was virtually certain that Arich had been involved in planting that traitor in the expedition, but he was also convinced that the man could not have acted alone. The Council had hired Jess Torkef and sent him to Leftrin as a hunter to provide for the dragons. Possibly he was hoping that Jess had returned on the *Tarman*, bringing parts of slaughtered dragons with him. A grim smile twisted Leftrin's mouth. He was going to be disappointed. And desperate enough to try something else. Arich had no real choice. His monarch, the Duke of Chalced, held his family hostage; unless the merchant could provide him with dragon parts for the cures the Duke supposed would heal him, their lives would be forfeit. Arich had deceived, threatened or bribed someone on the Council to put a traitor on the *Tarman*. Someone, or perhaps several someones.

Leftrin descended the steps slowly until he stood before the Council table. He cleared his throat but there was really no need to draw their attention. All the Council members had straightened in their chairs and were staring at him. Silence spread behind him: he heard the small sounds of people rushing to take seats, shushing one another as they did so. He raised his voice. 'Captain Leftrin of the liveship *Tarman* requests permission to address the Council.'

'The Council is pleased to see you have safely returned to us, Captain Leftrin. We cede you the floor.' This husky pronouncement came from Trader Polsk. Her brush of grey hair had been groomed back from her face but was slowly resuming its usual unruly stance.

'And I am pleased to see you in good health, Trader Polsk. I return to announce that our expedition was successful. The dragons are safely settled. I am pleased to report that every dragon survived the move. I am saddened to say that two of our keepers lost their lives. One of the hunters assigned to our expedition died also. The rest of our party was alive and well when I left them.' He used his right hand to scratch his left shoulder, contriving to turn toward the doors as he did so. Grey-cloaked Arich was just slipping out. Well. That was interesting and very unexpected. Had he already heard enough? He longed to follow the Chalcedean, but it was impossible right now. He turned back to the Council. All eyes were focused on him.

'I bear written authorizations from the dragon keepers and the hunters Carson and Davvie to collect the second half of their wages, as was agreed would be paid upon the successful completion of their task. I also request that the rest of the contract money for the liveship *Tarman* and his crew be paid in full this day.' He opened his shoulder satchel as he spoke. The authorizations were all on a single sheet of Alise's precious paper, rolled and tied with a string. He pulled the string free, extracted the keepers' contracts and stepped forward to set them on the Council table.

Trader Polsk and several of the other council members had been nodding. She ran her eyes over the papers, and then slid them down the table. As the papers moved from member to member, they kept nodding. But when they reached the last member of the Council, and Leftrin did not resume speaking, the agreeable bobs slowed and then stopped. Trader Polsk glanced at her committee members and then fixed him with a gaze. 'And the rest of your report, Captain Leftrin?'

'Report?' He raised one eyebrow at her.

'Well, of course. What did you find? Where did you leave the dragons and their keepers? Did you indeed locate Kelsingra? How far from here, and what are the river conditions along the way? What are the salvage possibilities? We've many questions that need answering.'

He was silent for a moment, framing his reply carefully. No sense in angering them too soon. How best to approach this? Directly.

'I'd prefer to settle this contract before we move on to casual conversation. Perhaps we can discuss my sharing the expedition's findings after we've received our pay, Trader Polsk.' And perhaps not, he thought to himself.

She straightened in her seat. 'That seems highly unusual, Captain.'

He shook his head slowly. 'Not at all. I prefer to finish with one contract before negotiating another.'

Her voice was acerbic. 'I am sure the Council agrees with me that hearing your report is an important part of "finishing" this contract. I do not believe we have discussed the possibility of another contract.'

Alise had helped him prepare for just this moment. He opened the shoulder bag again and extracted his copy of their original contract. He unrolled it and feigned reading through it, his brow wrinkled as if puzzled. Then he looked at Trader Polsk over the document. He made his voice almost apologetic. 'Nothing in our contract specified that a report was due to the Council on our return.'

There. As if on cue, a man at the end of the table drew a sheaf of papers toward him and began to leaf through them. Leftrin tried to save him the trouble. 'If you read the contract, Trader Polsk, you'll find that my crew and I, and the keepers and the hunters you hired, have all fulfilled each designated task as negotiated. The dragons were removed from the area. The creatures were fed and tended on the journey. We found an appropriate area for their resettlement, and there they are settled.' He cleared his throat. 'We've fulfilled our end of the bargain. Now it's your turn. The final payments are due.' He shrugged his heavy shoulders. 'That's all.'

'It can scarcely be all!' This came not from Trader Polsk but from a younger man seated at the far end of the table. When he turned his face, the light of the hanging globes danced along a fine line of orange scaling on his brows. 'This is no sort of a report at all! How can we be sure of a thing you've said? Where is the hunter Jess Torkef who was to accompany your expedition and represent the Councils' best interest? He was to take notes and make charts as the expedition advanced. Why hasn't he accompanied you here today?'

Exactly the question Leftrin had been waiting to hear. 'Jess Torkef is dead.' Leftrin delivered the news without regret but took close interest in the expressions it startled from the various Council members. As Alise had told him to expect, a woman Trader in a dark-green robe looked stricken; she attempted to exchange a look with the orange-scaled fellow but he was staring at Leftrin in horror. He paled as Leftrin added, 'I cannot be responsible for anything that Torkef agreed to; his contract is voided by his death.' He paused only a moment before revealing, 'One distressing thing I will disclose. Jess Torkef died trying to kill a dragon. He intended to butcher her and sell the parts of her body. To the Chalcedeans.'

He heard a gasp from Malta, but did not turn to look at her. He needed to watch the reaction of the Council members. When no one spoke, he pointed out the obvious. 'Either Jess Torkef was a traitor to this council that hired him, or the "best interests" of the Council were different from what I was led to believe, and did not coincide with those of the dragons and their keepers.' He looked at each council member in turn. The Trader in green gripped the edge of the council table before her. Horrified fury was building on Trader Polsk's face. Leftrin spoke to their silence. 'Until I know for certain which supposition is true, I'll be withholding any sort of a report to this council. And I'll remind the Council that while my contract stipulated I would keep a log of our journey and make note of any extraordinary discoveries, there was nothing in the contract that said that information had to be shared with the Council on my return. Only that I must gather it.'

Alise had pointed out that detail to him on their last night together in Kelsingra. She'd shaken her head over the sloppy wording of the document. 'You are right, my dear. The Cassarick Traders' Council was in such a hurry to see us out of town that they truly were not thinking of anything more than being rid of the dragons and their keepers. Some, obviously, dreamed of another Elderling city to plunder, but they dared not write of it too clearly, for they feared others might wake to the possibility. They did not want to share.

'And some, perhaps, were imagining that the dragons would be rendered into very rare trade goods long before anyone found a place to settle them. Nothing in this contract dictates that we must share our discoveries with them. But I'll wager that when you return, if you speak of what we've found, they'll try to find a way to take it away from us.'

They'd been sitting together in the small shepherd's hut they had claimed as their own. A fire burned on the hearth, its red flames waking echoing red lights in Alise's curling hair. They'd raided blankets and other furnishings from his stateroom on Tarman to try to make their new lodgings as comfortable as they could, and Tarman had been surprisingly tolerant of his absence. Alise had relished their new found privacy even if it was much less comfortable than living aboard the ship. Leftrin had cobbled together a roped bedstead for them, as well as a crude table and a bench for seating. But it was still a rough and bare retreat, and outside, the days of winter were growing colder and wetter. They'd been sitting side by side on the floor, close to the firelight, going over the pages of the contract they'd signed with the Cassarick Traders' Council. Alise had leafed through it carefully, chalking notes to herself onto the hearth stones with the burned end of a stick. He'd been content to sit and savour watching her. He'd known then that soon he'd have to leave her, and while he didn't expect it would be for long, he still dreaded any time apart from her.

When she had finally looked up from her study of the documents, her fingertips were black with soot and there was a stripe of it down her nose. He smiled. It made her look like a little striped ginger cat. She'd frowned at him in return, and then tapped the contract with a businesslike finger. 'There's nothing here for us to fear. Nothing that we agreed and signed, and I looked over Warken's keeper contract earlier. None of the keepers signed anything away; their contracts were all about how they must care for the dragons or forfeit their pay. There is no mention of them having to share anything they might find. Even your contract only stipulates that you are to *keep* a log; it doesn't say that your notes on exploring the waterways will belong to the Council, or give them rights to anything we discovered. Including Kelsingra. No. They were in such a rush to be rid of the dragons that that was all they focused on. They wrote in penalties for you if you returned with the dragons and keepers, and they stipulated how much money they'd have to pay each keeper "with his or her dragon(s) safely settled and content". But nowhere did they provide for what they would ask of us if we were successful in finding Kelsingra. It's odd. That omission didn't seem so obvious or so dark when I was first reading it and signing it. But now it's as plain as the ink on the page; they didn't expect the keepers or the dragons to survive, and they never really expected us to find Kelsingra. At least, the official Council didn't. I still think there were some who imagined riches to be discovered, and at least two Council members who were dismayed when I said I would come along and speak for the best interest of the dragons.'

'Well, there was one barge captain who was so thrilled at the thought that he didn't notice if anyone else was opposing it.'

She'd pushed away his fingers that were curling her wayward hair into spirals, but her rejection was reluctant. 'My love, we need to finish this tonight. I had only one piece of good paper left. I used half to write what I needed to tell Malta the Elderling. Do not let anyone else see it. I had to write in such tiny letters, I hope her eyesight is good! The other half sheet I used to make a document that authorizes you to collect the keepers' pay for them. They've all signed. And so, on this scrap of hide, we will write out what we must try to bargain for, and what we are willing to concede in return.' Her voice faltered a bit and she cast her eyes down.

He had lifted her chin with his two fingers. 'Never fear. I will not barter Kelsingra away. Little enough have we found on this side of the river that would interest the Traders, but I know your fears: that once they see the city, they will strip it to the paving stones.'

She nodded grimly. 'As was done to the first Elderling cities that were discovered. So many mysteries would probably have been solved if all the pieces had been left in one place. Now the artefacts of Cassarick and Trehaug are scattered all over the world, in the hands of rich families and crafty merchants. But Kelsingra, the real Kelsingra on the other side of the river, gives us a new chance to discover who the Elderlings were, to understand and perhaps master the magic they used so freely . . .'

'I know.' He interrupted her gently. 'I know, my dear. I

know what it means to you, even if some of the youngsters do not understand. I'll protect it for you.'

The buzz of confused conversation in the Council chamber drew his mind back to the present. The din did not die down but increased as the onlookers conversed with their neighbours and voices were raised to be heard over the rising hubbub. Trader Polsk stood and shouted for order; no one paid attention. Then, abruptly, the room was plunged into dimness. The suspended globes of light winked out and only the red glow of the hearth fires lit the place. Every voice was stilled in shock.

Malta Khuprus's words rang out in the darkness. 'It is time for silence. Time for us to listen to Captain Leftrin rather than asking each other questions we cannot answer. Let us be orderly and hear him out as Traders should. The man speaks of a contract fulfilled, a just debt to be paid, and a possible threat to not only the dragons, but a threat to all Rain Wilders as well. A Chalcedean plot carried out in the midst of the Rain Wilds? Let us hear him out.'

'Agreed!' shouted Trader Polsk when Malta paused, and a chorus of affirming voices answered hers. Whatever restorative magic Malta worked on the floating Elderling globes was successful. They brightened slowly to a warm glow that filled the chamber with a pleasant rosy light. Malta had left her seat in the darkness and now stood at the end of the Council table. Her pregnancy was obvious when she stood: her ripening belly interrupted the long, lean lines of her body. Leftrin felt she deliberately called attention to herself. A pregnant woman was not a rare sight in the Rain Wilds, but neither was it a common one. He knew that more than one person looked on her fecundity with envy. She let them.

'Captain Leftrin.' Trader Polsk's tone demanded that he

focus on the business at hand. 'You've made a serious accusation. Have you evidence to offer?'

He took a breath. 'Not as would satisfy the Council. I can repeat the words of the Keeper Greft, and tell you what Jess Torkef admitted to Sedric Meldar of Bingtown before he died. Torkef plainly said he had come in the hopes of killing dragons and selling off their parts, and tried to persuade Sedric to join him in those plans. Keeper Greft was equally plain in telling us that Jess Torkef had tried to recruit him. I suggest that whoever hired the man and put him aboard my ship may have known that hunting meat to keep the dragons well fed was not the task closest to his heart. Before my barge even left, I received a threatening note, unsigned, but one that directed me to do all I could to aid him.'

'Do you have this note?' Polsk immediately demanded.

'No. It was destroyed.'

'How exactly were you threatened, Captain?' This from the young, orange-scaled Trader at the Council table. A small smile played across his face.

'I'm afraid I don't recall your name, Trader,' Leftrin observed.

'Trader Candral.' Trader Polsk seized control of the discussion. 'Please do not destroy the order of this Council by speaking out of turn. Do you have a question you wish to ask Captain Leftrin?'

Trader Candral was not pleased to be rebuked. Or perhaps he did not like being named to Leftrin. In either case, he leaned back in his chair and replied insolently, 'I did have a question, and I've asked it. How was our captain threatened? And if the threat arrived before he sailed, why didn't he report it before his departure?'

Trader Polsk narrowed her eyes but nodded permission to Leftrin to speak. He kept his eyes on her face as he replied.

'It was blackmail. The note threatened to reveal certain pieces of personal information. I didn't report it because I felt I could handle it, and the Council was already urging a more than speedy departure for us. Immediate, if I recall correctly.'

'The dragons were dangerous! They had to go!' This from a man in a heavy canvas jacket and trousers, standing to be heard. 'Me and my boy, we ended up running for our lives, right into the excavations, and that little green dragon followed us, knocking out the supports as it came. It wanted our supper, even though it was just bread and cheese in a sack. It ate it sack and all, and might have eaten my boy next, except that we ran while it was eating! I'm here to say, if the dragons are gone, then good riddance. And if there's any talk of them being brought back, then me and the other diggers will put our shovels down.' He crossed his heavy arms on his chest and scowled fiercely all around.

'No more outbursts!' Trader Polsk spoke severely to the man who had shouted out his tale. He sat down with an exasperated grunt, but the people around him were nodding in agreement.

'They'd have killed somebody if they hadn't been lured away. They were always a poor bargain,' he added, not as loudly, but still getting a glare from the Council leader.

Leftrin took advantage of the prevailing mood of the audience. 'Today, good Council and Trader folk, I'm just here to get our rightful pay. The dragons are settled; I'll never bring them back. So give us our pay, mine and my crew's, and the keepers' and the hunters'. I've their authorizations with me, all signed with permission for me to get their coin. Some want part sent to their families, one wants all to go her family and the rest have authorized me to pick up their full pay.'

'Prove it!' Trader Candral abruptly demanded, and the Trader in green nodded in emphatic agreement.

Leftrin looked at him for a moment in silence. Then he again unslung the leather bag on his shoulder and opened it slowly. As he removed the rolled paper, he observed quietly, 'Some men would be insulted by how that request was made. Another man might demand satisfaction of a pup that so insulted his honour. But,' he stepped forward to set the documents on the table and looked directly at Trader Candral. 'I think I'll consider the source.' He did not wait for the man's response but went on as if his reaction were of no consequence, setting the paper before Trader Polsk. 'Every signature is there, for every hunter and keeper and crewman, and Alise and Sedric as well. Except Warken's. We lost him to the river. I brought his contract back with me. I think his pay ought to go to his family. He spoke kindly of them. Greft didn't say much about his folks and I don't know if he had any. You can keep his coin, if that's what you think fair. As for Jess Torkef's wages, do whatever you want with them. It's dirty money and personally, I wouldn't touch it.'

Candral was pressed back in his chair. 'If all those keepers survived, why aren't any of them here? How do we know they aren't all dead, and you just come back to claim their wages?'

Leftrin's face reddened at the foul accusation. He took a deep breath.

'Trader Candral, you speak with no authority from the Council. Captain Leftrin!' Trader Polsk spoke sharply. 'Please step back from the table. The Council will look over the documents. We've never had any cause to complain of our dealings with you in the past. And we will want to discuss your suggestion that there were improprieties in how Hunter Torkef was hired.' He shot Candral a speculative look.

Leftrin didn't move. He shifted his stare from Trader

Candral to Trader Polsk. 'I'll ignore the insult. This time. But when the Council is looking for improprieties, it might consider that liars are often suspicious of honest men. I'll even answer the question. The keepers chose to remain with their dragons. Two keepers died, and I suppose if I were the sort of man who'd profit from the dead, I would have told you that everyone was alive and well and then taken their wages as well. And now I'll step back, just as soon as I've received the pay for myself, my ship and my crew. As agreed upon and signed by the entire Council.'

'I don't think any of us would have an issue with that,' Polsk warned Candral, who opened his mouth to speak, and then shut it again. Trader Polsk motioned to a page for ink and paper. But the woman on Polsk's left abruptly asked, 'What of the Bingtown Trader, what of Alise Finbok? Where is she? And the man who accompanied her, Sedric Meldar? Surely *they* didn't choose to stay with dragons?'

'Trader Sverdin, those questions should be presented to the Council, to be asked in an appropriate way!' Trader Polsk's rebuke was unmistakable. Her cheeks were red and she ran her hand through her hair in exasperation, standing it up in a grey brush.

Leftrin didn't look at her. He stared at Trader Sverdin directly. 'Alise Kincarron chose to stay with the dragons. She gave me letters to send to her family. They've already been dispatched. As for Sedric, well, seeing as how he didn't sign anything with the Council, it's scarcely your business what's become of him. But I left him alive and well, and I expect he's still that way.'

Trader Sverdin was undaunted. She leaned back in her chair and lifted her pointed chin as she spoke to Trader Polsk. 'We have no evidence that any of the keepers survived. We don't truly know what became of the dragons. I think we should withhold payment on our contract with this man until he can prove he has fulfilled its terms.'

'That would seem to be the most intelligent route,' Trader Candral swiftly agreed.

Leftrin looked at each Council member in turn, letting his gaze linger. Candral busied himself looking at his nails while Trader Sverdin flushed red and rolled a small scroll back and forth on the table. Trader Polsk looked embarrassed.

'Captain Leftrin, I have confidence in the services you have provided and in your honesty. But with two members of the Council dissenting, I cannot release your funds until we have clear evidence that you fulfilled your contract.'

Leftrin was silent, refusing to let his anger show in his face. Negotiations were best done coldly. Was it safe to leave his papers with the Council? He met Polsk's apologetic gaze. 'I'm entrusting these documents specifically to you, Trader Polsk. They should not leave your possession. Examine the signatures and the dates on the requests the keepers have added. Do what you think is proper with the monies owed to Greft and Warken. I don't think you owe Jess a penny; he didn't live up to his contract at all and plotted to kill both dragons and keepers. I suggest you look hard at who selected him. If you read my contract, you'll see that you clearly owe me my money. You know where I'm tied up. When you choose to send my pay, send it there. And if you don't choose to send me my pay, then you'll wait a long time to hear any more details about where the dragons are and what we discovered.'

He turned away from the Council and pretended to notice Malta Khuprus for the first time. He bowed to her. 'Elderling lady, I have a letter for you from Alise Kincarron. And a small token from the city of Kelsingra.'

'You found it? You found the Elderling city?' This in a

shout from a Council member who had not spoken before, a jowly man with curling dark hair.

Leftrin glanced at him and then at the rest of the Council. 'We did. But before you ask me for details, perhaps you and the rest of the Council should decide if you can believe what I say. I don't want to waste your time or mine if you think I'm just spinning sailor yarns.'

He turned back to the Elderlings. Reyn was at Malta's side, not touching her but clearly supporting her. Her face was alight with joy though her mouth was set in a firm line. He offered her a small scroll and a little cloth bag. She accepted it with long, elegant hands. The scarlet scaling on them looked like gloves of the finest reptilian leather. Malta opened the bag slowly and removed from it the hearth tile. She smiled as she looked at it. Then she lifted it high to display it, for only a moment, before returning it to the bag.

Leftrin spoke to her through the uproar of voices that followed her gesture. 'If you have questions, I'll be happy to speak to you. I'm tied up to the Cassarick docks. You can't miss us.'

Malta inclined her head and said nothing. Reyn answered for them. 'This Council has shamed us. I hope you know that we have full faith you have accomplished your goal. I'm certain we will come to see you as soon as we possibly can. But for now, my wife is weary and needs to go home to rest.'

'At your convenience,' Leftrin agreed. 'I think it would be best if I clear out of here quick.'

'Captain Leftrin! Captain Leftrin, you cannot simply leave!' This from the curly-haired Trader.

'Actually, I can,' he replied. He turned his back on them all and strode out of the room. Behind him, the roar of conversation rose to a din.

Day the 26th of the Change Moon
Year the 7th of the Independent Alliance of Traders

Detozi, Keeper of the Birds, Trehaug
Bird Log, Loft 4

3 female swift birds dead this morning. Eggs gone cold in 2 nests. Salvaged 2 eggs from one nest and put under young female in Loft 6. Noted in breeding log. Moved all birds from Loft 4 to emptied and cleansed Loft 7. Loft 4 to be dismantled and burned as this is the third time infestation has recurred there.

CHAPTER TEN

Kidnapped

'I'll be fine,' she had insisted. 'Go after Leftrin. Find out everything that happened. The scroll he gave us barely brushes the surface of what has befallen them. I'm so tired I can scarcely stand, but I won't be able to rest until I know everything.'

Reyn had smiled worriedly as he looked down into her upturned face. The wet wind blew between them. 'How can you be fine if you can scarcely stand? Darling, I'd best see you home first. Then I'll find the *Tarman* and talk to the captain. I'll beg him to come home with me and speak to you there.'

'Please, don't be silly over me! I'm not some frail little creature. I'll get back to our room just fine on my own. But you should go now before everyone else thinks of the same thing. This tiny note from Alise only taunts me. There are dozens of things I must know. Please,' she had added when he continued to frown at her in disapproval. They had lingered in the doorway of the Traders' Concourse where Malta had done her best to pick sense out of Alise's cramped writing on the scrap of paper Leftrin had given them. In the flickering light of the windblown lantern's flame, she had scarcely been able to read any of it. She could not stand the suspense and had begged Reyn to take her to speak to the captain immediately. But now, halfway down the walk that led to a lift, she was too weary to go on. Her plan was that she would go back to their rented rooms, and Reyn would persuade Captain Leftrin to come there to talk to her.

Reyn had sighed. 'Very well. As usual, Malta, you'll get your own way! Don't wait up for me. Go to bed and rest until I get there with Leftrin. I promise that as soon as I come in, I'll wake you and then you can badger him with questions for as long as you like.'

'You had better,' she had warned him. 'Don't you stay to have a drink or two, or take him somewhere else to talk because you think I've fallen asleep! I'll know if you do, Reyn Khuprus, and then woe betide you!'

'I will,' he had promised again, smiling at her threats, and reached out to pull her hood up more snugly around her face. And then he had left her, just as she had commanded him.

'Not some frail little creature,' she reminded herself now. When the spasm passed, she stood breathing for a few moments. Around her, the threatened storm had arrived. Darkness seemed to fall with the sheets of rain. She had been so sure she could find her way back to their rented rooms. Now dead twigs and bits of moss showered down with the rain and wet leaves rode the wind. In the distances around her, she saw the lights of treetop homes bob and sway in the onslaught of the wind. If she had been in Bingtown, she could have fixed her eyes on a light and simply made her way toward it. But in a town like Cassarick, things were not so easy. The walkways made a spiderweb through the trees: there was never a straight path anywhere. A nearby light might bring her to the back of a home that faced a different branch, with a sheer drop to the forest floor between her and it.

She looked back the way she had come, wondering how she had managed to take a wrong turning. To do so forced her to turn her face to the wind; she squinted against the driving rain, but saw nothing familiar. Was there a man standing at the far end of the last bridge? The wind gusted more rain into her face, but the figure did not budge. No. Probably just an oddly shaped post. She turned her face away from it and looked at the dancing, taunting lights. She was cold, her clothing soaked through. And her nagging back pain had become something else now. When the next terrible contraction of muscle rippled through her body, she could not deny what it was. The baby was trying to be born. Here. On a tree branch in the rain. Of course.

She clung to the railing, digging her nails into the tough and twisted wood, trying to think of anything except the terrible squeezing of her body. Focusing on her clenching hands, she gritted her teeth silently until the pain passed. Then she hunched over the railing, gulping air. Pride be damned. If their child was born here, on this walkway during this storm, what chance would he have? Would she let their baby die because she didn't want to call out her need to strangers? She drew her breath and forced out a shout. 'Help me! Please, anyone, help me!'

The wind and the endless rustling of the leaves swept away her words. 'Please!' she cried again, the words crushed out of her as another tearing cramp swept through her. She clutched the railing and set a hand to the top of her belly. She wasn't imagining it. The child was lower than he had been; he was moving down inside her. She waited, caught her breath again, and shouted again. But the storm was building, not abating. No one else seemed to be out on the walkways tonight. She bared her teeth in an almost-smile. Who could blame them?

Blinking rain off her lashes, she lifted her head. There were fewer lights than there had been. People went to bed early in winter. Well, this path had to lead somewhere, to a house or a shop or a trunk walk. All she had to do was follow it. She glanced back the way she had come, hoping to see someone, anyone. Somewhere, back there, she'd taken a wrong path. She should go back. The wind gusted, twigs and leaves flew into her face, and she turned her back on it. It didn't matter. She'd go where the wind was pushing her, and bang on the first door she came to until they let her in. No one would turn away a woman in labour. She gripped the railing with both hands and edged doggedly along it. It would all turn out all right. It had to.

Reyn hurried down the walkway in pursuit of Captain Leftrin. He muttered angrily to himself as he slipped, recovered and hurried on. He had taken too long arguing with Malta. Even now, he longed to turn back and see her safely home before he went down to the *Tarman*. She hadn't insisted on going with him, and that was a frightening clue to how tired she was. He gave a futile glance over his shoulder, but in the rising wind that shook debris and water from the trees, he could scarcely see the bridge he had just crossed, let alone spot Malta on her lonely way back to their rooms. He lifted both hands to dash rain from his face and then forced himself to a run. The sooner he spoke to the captain, the sooner he could get back to his wife.

The walkways swayed in the growing wind. He moved swiftly, travelling with the easy familiarity of the Rain Wild born, but worried again for Malta. She had adapted well to her new home in the trees, but the weight of the child had made her balance more uncertain in the last few weeks. She would be fine, he told himself sternly as he reached a trunk. There was a huddle of folk waiting for the lift. Impatiently, he moved to the inside of the platform and began a hasty descent down the long winding stairway that wrapped the tree's immense trunk.

He was winded and soaked through long before he reached the leather way on the ground at the foot of the pillar tree. He saw no one else in the area. The storm and the approaching night had driven everyone else inside. He hoped that it had discouraged all those who had been hurrying after Captain Leftrin as he left. He didn't want to compete for the man's attention. He had to persuade Leftrin to come back with him for a private audience and the chance to go over the long list of questions that Malta had scribbled down during the meeting. He knew his wife's temperament well enough that to know that she would not let Leftrin leave until he had answered every one of them!

Reyn hurried through darkness, his way unevenly lit by lanterns along the platform road. The river was up; the floating docks had risen on their stout tethers until the pilings that anchored them were scarcely taller than Reyn was. The moored boats shifted and complained about the wind and rushing water as they rubbed and bumped against the dock and tugged at their lines. The *Tarman* was long and wide; he would be tied to the outside moorage. Most of the lamps that were supposed to illuminate the docks at night had surrendered to the wind and rain. Reyn had to go more slowly as he made his way along the dock and then onto the moorage gangways.

Luck favoured him. He arrived in time to see someone holding a hooded lantern as Captain Leftrin clambered from the dock onto his ship's deck. 'Captain Leftrin! Please, wait! You know me. I'm Reyn Khuprus. I need to talk to you.' The wind snatched at his words, but Leftrin paused and glanced over his shoulder, then lifted his voice to shout, 'Come along, then, and welcome aboard! Let's get out of this storm.'

Reyn was only too willing to follow him. He clambered over the liveship's railing and followed the captain across the deck. The ship's galley was warm and snug. A long table dominated the room with benches to either side of it. At the end of the room, a fat iron stove pulsed heat out into the small room. String bags of onions and tubers hung from the rafters, adding their own aroma to a room that smelled of men working in close quarters. Hanging lanterns burned yellow, and the smell of a savoury stew bubbled out with the steam from a great covered pot on the stove. The woman who had held the lantern for Leftrin took Reyn's cloak and found it a hook where it dripped alongside the captain's.

'Hot tea!' Leftrin proclaimed and despite Malta's parting threat, Reyn nodded in appreciation. Reyn was glad to see it was already brewed and waiting in a fat brown pot on the galley table. A mug was quickly set out for the captain, and one for Reyn joined it as the captain poured. Through an open door, Reyn could see the interior of the deckhouse. It was lined with tiered bunks. On one, a big, well-muscled man was scratching his chest and yawning. A smaller fellow lithed himself past the yawner and angled in through the door like a cat to slide into a seat at the table. He gave Reyn a curious glance but then fixed his attention on the captain. Without any ado, he began his report.

'Council didn't send us any coin, sir. But the one store delivered everything you ordered on credit. And we got most of the other supplies you told us to get the same way; the merchants here know us well, and know that if they won't advance what we need now, when we do have funds, we won't be coming back to them.'

'Well done, Hennesey, and enough for now. We have a guest.'

Reyn knew that Leftrin was shutting down the crew's

chatter, effectively cutting him off from any knowledge they might want to share until Leftrin had evaluated him and what he wanted. He employed his own gambit. He glanced at Hennesey, obviously the mate, and then back at Leftrin as he said, 'The Khuprus lines of credit are as good here in Cassarick as they are in Trehaug, cousin. I am sure that our family would be happy to flex a bit of influence since the Council here is not treating you fairly.'

Leftrin watched him for a long moment. 'Surprised you remember me as a cousin.'

Reyn widened his eyes. 'Oh, come, there weren't that many of us annoying the men working on the wizardwood back in those days. You were good at the shaping. I recall there was some talk that your mother might persuade your father to let you follow that trade instead of taking over the *Tarman*.'

'Only talk. My heart was always with the ship; I actually feared that I'd wind up working wizardwood! And where would I be now if I had, I wonder? Whereas you, I recall, were always fascinated with the uncut logs. Always slipping away to go exploring.'

'I was. And always in trouble because of it.'

'It was feared you'd developed too much of a bond with the city. That you would drown yourself in it . . .'

'As my father did,' Reyn filled in quietly.

The silence in the galley grew charged. The woman had picked up the tea pot to refill it. She stood still, just holding it and watching him. There was something here, and he'd best get to the bottom of it quickly. Speaking plainly now might buy him plain talk in return. Reyn nodded as if to himself. 'But I didn't drown. Because, for me, it wasn't the stone and the memories it held. It was the dragon Tintaglia, trapped and aware in her wizardwood log. She drew me and held me and eventually I served her. As I still do, in many ways. The dragon is what brings me here tonight. I must know, Captain. What became of the dragons and their keepers?'

Leftrin had seated himself near the stove. Now he lifted his mug of tea and took a cautious sip. Over the rim of the mug, he regarded Reyn thoughtfully. Reyn wondered how he saw him. To the Liveship captain, was he a freak, a man too deeply touched and changed by the Rain Wilds? Or did he see him as an Elderling, one of the mystical and revered creatures who had first built the hidden ancient cities of the Rain Wilds? Or a shirt-tail cousin, vaguely remembered from what now seemed a distant childhood? Reyn sat straight now and let Leftrin stare at his scaled face and think what he would. He waited.

A rangy orange cat with white socks suddenly floated up from the deck and landed on the table. He walked the length of it, undeterred by Hennesey's shooing hand, to meet Reyn's gaze with gleaming green eyes. He bumped his striped head against Reyn's folded hands on the table-top, demanding homage. Reyn lifted a hand to pet the creature, and found his fur surprisingly soft.

As if the man's welcome of the cat's attention had decided something for him, Leftrin spoke. 'Where's Malta? I know Alise would want her to know everything. That's why she wrote her that letter, and sent her that bit of tile.'

'Her pregnancy weighs heavily on her now. I sent her home to rest. She only went because I promised I'd come here and beg you to return to our rooms with me. She will give me no peace until she gets answers to her questions.' Reyn took from his pocket the small scroll of scribbled questions that was covered in Malta's tiny but looping handwriting. He squinted at it ruefully. 'All of them,' he said, as much to himself as to Captain Leftrin, and was surprised when the man let loose a guffaw of laughter.

'Women and their scribbling,' he commiserated. 'Do they never get enough of finding things out, and then writing them down? Wasn't Alise's letter enough for her?'

Reyn smiled and suddenly relaxed. He picked up his mug of steaming tea and warmed his hands around it. 'Malta has always had endless curiosity. She tried to read the note you gave her, but the writing was tiny and the light outside the concourse very bad. The questions she wrote here are just the ones that occurred to her as you were speaking to the Council. As for me, I had no chance even to look at Alise's missive before Malta dispatched me here, to beg you to come and talk with her.'

Leftrin shifted in his seat and looked down at his hot tea. 'Would tomorrow do?' he asked reluctantly. 'I've been up since before dawn, and I'm soaked and chilled to the bone. And I need to get my crew's report on the errands I sent them on.'

Reyn sat very still, trying to read the man. He had to bring him back to Malta tonight: if he didn't, she would immediately start making plans on how soon she could get down to the boat and speak to him herself. Ever since the *Tarman* expedition had left Cassarick to herd the dragons up river, Malta had been anxious about it. She had always been clever with sifting through gossip to find out things that were going to happen or might happen. In Trehaug, she could tell him which ships were going to arrive and what cargoes they were bringing days before they reached the city. And she had been certain that there was something else going on when the Cassarick Traders' Council practically drove the dragons and their keepers out of town.

'It wasn't an expedition to seek haven for them,' she had told him, more than once. 'And it wasn't just an exile, though I believe there are several on the Council who were happy to be consigning them to just that. The dragons were expensive, and messy, and dangerous. And they were in the way of the ongoing excavation. But there was something more beneath the surface, Reyn, something sinister. Something nasty that involves a lot of money and possibly our dear, dear friends the Chalcedeans.'

'What did you hear to make you think that?' he had asked her.

'Just bits of things. A rumour that one of the hunters for the expedition would do anything for money, that possibly he had murdered someone a few years ago to help someone else get an inheritance. And that perhaps someone now on the Council knew that, and was either instrumental in getting that hunter on the ship, or that the hunter used what he knew about the Council member to get the job on the ship. Oh, just gossip, Reyn, in little bits and pieces. And uneasy feelings about all of it. Selden has been gone far too long, with no real word from him. I know there was that last letter, but it didn't seem right to me. And why, oh, why has Tintaglia not returned to see what became of the other dragons? Could she be that heartless about her kindred? That once she found a mate and the possibility of having her own offspring, she would abandon the others? Or has something terrible befallen her? Has the Duke sent hunters after her and her mate?'

'Don't think the worst, dear. Selden's a young man now, well able to take care of himself. For all we know, he may be with Tintaglia right now. As to why she hasn't returned, well, maybe Tintaglia thought the young dragons would not need her. Maybe she thought we'd do better at keeping our promise to care for them.' He'd meant the words to be comforting, but after he'd said them, he heard how sad they sounded. Why she was so fixated on the dragons, he was not sure. Tintaglia had saved both their lives and brought them together, that was true. But only after the dragon had repeatedly endangered and tormented them. Did they really owe the blue dragon anything? Sometimes, he would have been very content to simply settle with Malta, to leave behind the exultation and exaltation of being an 'Elderling' and be just another Rain Wild couple expecting their first child.

Leftrin cleared his throat and Reyn started. He saw the weariness on the man's face and felt churlish to be asking such a favour. But it was for Malta, and he had promised he would try. 'Please,' he said, and for a moment the word hung alone in the silence.

Someone coughed deliberately. Reyn turned his head to find a young woman looking at the captain. By her rough clothes she was a deckhand, and by the tracing of her features, she was somehow related to Leftrin. And thus, in all likelihood, some sort of cousin to Reyn as well. She didn't flinch before her captain's stare. 'I could go in your place, if you're too tired,' she offered. 'I don't know everything you do, but I'll wager I could answer enough of the Elderling lady's questions to content her.'

'Oh, would you?' Reyn asked, relieved at such a solution. But before she could respond, Leftrin gave a weary groan.

'I'll come. Let me find something dry to put on. Though doubtless I'll be just as wet when I get there.'

'May I still come?' his deckhand asked hopefully.

Leftrin glanced at Reyn. 'Would your lady welcome two visitors so late at night?'

'I'm sure she would,' Reyn replied gratefully. He smiled at the girl, who grinned back mischievously.

'I'll get my oilskin,' she announced happily and darted from the room.

Malta had crossed the last quarter of the bridge on her hands and knees. The rising wind had set it to swaying dangerously and the guard ropes were slick. Once she reached the trunk platform that secured the end of the bridge, she crawled to the leeward side of the trunk and huddled there. She wanted to scream and she longed to collapse weeping and had neither the breath to do the one nor the luxury of time to do the other. 'The baby is coming soon,' she told herself, as if speaking the words aloud would make her feel less alone. She drew her cloak tighter around herself and leaned against the tree as another pang moved through her. She was shaking with cold, not fear. There was nothing to fear. Women had babies all the time, and many of them delivered their own children alone. It was a perfectly normal and natural part of being a woman. She was fine. 'I'm not scared. I'm just cold.' She clenched her teeth against the sob that tried to force its way out. 'I can do this. I have to do this and so I can do this.'

She pushed away the thought that what was normal and natural for another woman might not be so for her. The Elderling changes that had beset her body had had consequences that she had never foreseen. Weeping was uncomfortable now; it enflamed her eyes. She had heard tales of other women who had been heavily touched by the Rain Wilds, women who had died trying to push out a child. But surely that would not happen to her. Her changes had been caused by the dragon Tintaglia, not by chance exposure to the Rain Wilds. Surely her body would be equal to this task.

She lifted her eyes and looked around hopelessly. Night had come and most of the Rain Wilders had extinguished their lights and gone to bed. Some lights still shone, but in the blowing wind and darkness, she could not discern a path to any of them. Her hands were cold. She hitched up the loose white tunic she wore under her cloak. Her fingers fumbled at the fastening of her trousers as she tried to loosen them. 'No dignity,' she complained to the wind. The loose trousers fell around her ankles and she managed to step free of them. She bundled them close to her and then stuffed them inside her tunic to keep them dry. If her baby was born right here, they would be what she would wrap him in.

Another contraction passed through her and this time she was sure she felt the baby move down with the press of her muscles. When at last her own body stopped squeezing her, she drew a deep breath and made one final effort. 'Help me! Please! Someone help me!'

Then she gave a startled shriek as a figure detached itself from the shadows and stepped toward her. In the dim light from a distant lantern, she saw it was a man in a long cloak. She had not heard anyone approach. How long had he been there, watching her? She decided she didn't care. 'Please, please help me get to shelter. I'm about to . . . I'm having a baby.'

The man crouched down beside her. She could see nothing of his face inside his deep hood. 'You are the Elderling woman, the dragon woman, yes?'

He had an accent. Chalcedean? Possibly. Then he was probably one of the freed slaves who had come to the Rain Wilds during the war. Most of them had been from Jamaillia, but a few had been Chalcedeans. 'Yes. Yes, I'm Malta, the Elderling. If you help me, you will be richly rewarded by my family.'

'Come, then. Come.' With no regard for her travails, the man seized her upper arm and tried to haul her to her feet. She groaned and nearly fell and then managed to stand upright.

'Wait. I can't . . .'

'You come, then, come with me. There's a safe place, not far from here. Come.'

It seemed horrid of him to expect her to walk, let alone tug her along by her arm, but he was the only help available. It didn't matter if he were stupid or just thoughtless; he would help her get to shelter, and once there, perhaps she could ask him to run and get a woman to help her. She tried to lean on him, but he stepped away from her, keeping hold of her arm and tugging her along. Was it distaste for her, or his unwillingness to touch a woman in labour? Let it go. She followed him awkwardly, back across the swaying bridge she had just crossed, around a trunk and then off across an even thinner bridge. 'Where are we going?' she gasped.

'To an inn. Come. Come now.' He dragged at her forearm insistently.

She jerked her arm free of him and sank to her knees as another pain took her. He stood over her, saying nothing. When she could speak, she gasped, 'There aren't any inns in Cassarick. Not . . .'

'Brothel, inn. A place to stay. I have a room, you will be safe, you make the baby there. Better than out in the rain.'

That was true. But despite the desperation of her situation, she liked this man less and less by the minute. A brothel. Well, at least there would be women there, and probably women experienced in dealing with her plight. She let him take her arm again and staggered to her feet. 'How far?'

'Two bridges,' he said, and she nodded. Two bridges. Two more than she could possibly manage.

She drew her breath and firmed her jaw. 'Lead me there.'

Leftrin was not a man to move quickly, Reyn had decided. Especially when he was feeling inconvenienced. Or possibly just exhausted. He had drunk his tea and then disappeared to change into dry clothing. When he finally emerged from his stateroom, he looked more ragged than when he had gone in. Reyn was beginning to understand exactly how much the expedition had endured. And while it stirred his sympathy for the man and his crew, he did not release him from his word. Leftrin's niece and deckhand, Skelly, was already cloaked and booted and obviously ready for a late-night adventure on shore. But Leftrin drank yet another cup of tea and borrowed a knit hat and a waterproof from one of his crew before he finally stood and announced that he was ready to leave.

Reyn had hurried them from the docks and to the lift, where he rang the bell-pull half a dozen times before there was any indication that the tender was on his way down. The man scowled at him, obviously displeased to be called out on such a stormy night, until Reyn gave him a handful of coins that was as much bribe as payment and made him promise that when Leftrin and Skelly wanted to return, they would be able to find him awake when they knocked on the door.

Reyn had never liked lifts. He'd always rather do the climb than endure the sickening lurch and sway and the unpredictable hitches and halts along the way. He clenched his teeth and hoped the man was good at minding his line and pulleys. Neither Leftrin nor Skelly said much. Leftrin was huddled in his borrowed waterproof, while Skelly grinned and peered out at the night as if fascinated by every detail. Suddenly, Reyn was glad she had come along. He suspected that Malta would get more out of interrogating the girl than quizzing the reticent captain.

Once the lift halted, he'd been eager to unlatch the safety net. 'Along here,' he'd told them as they trooped out of the lift basket after him. 'I'm sorry it's so dark. There's little to rent in Cassarick; the town is too young yet to offer the sort of inns and taverns that Trehaug has. We've had to take whatever temporary lodging we could get for this visit. Mind the guide-ropes. They're set lower than they should be. Across that bridge, a loop or two up the trunk steps, one more bridge, and we'll be there. And I do thank you for coming. Very sincerely.'

As they finally drew near to the rented cottage and Reyn saw the darkened windows, he scowled to himself. If Malta had decided she was too weary for this and gone to bed, he'd be embarrassed to have dragged these two so far through the storm. But the scowl was more for the worry he felt. If Malta had given up on them and gone to sleep, it meant that she was far wearier than she had indicated when they'd left the concourse.

He pushed the flimsy door open and ventured into the darkened room. 'Malta?' he said quietly into the darkness. 'Malta, I've brought Captain Leftrin for you . . .'

His words tapered off as he felt the emptiness of the chambers. He could not have explained it to anyone. He simply knew that she was not there and had not been there since he had left. He stepped to the table and ran his fingertips lightly across a jidzin centrepiece there. The Elderling metal responded to his touch by bursting into life, giving off a ghost light, bluish but penetrating. He lifted it and it lit the room. Malta was not there. Cold flowed through him. He heard himself speak in a deceptively calm voice.

'Something's wrong. She isn't here, and it doesn't look as if she's been here.'

The hearth for the small chambers was not much more than a clay platter. He found a few embers still burning and coaxed them back to life, and lit the lamp again. The stronger light only confirmed what he already knew. She had not come back from the meeting. Everything was exactly as they had left it when they hurried out of the door.

Leftrin and Skelly stood in the open door. He had no time to spend on courtesies. 'I'm sorry. I have to go look for her. She was tired when I left her, but she promised she'd come straight back here. She . . . her back was hurting her. The baby . . . she is so heavy . . .'

The girl spoke. 'We'll go with you. Where did you last see her?'

'Right outside the Traders' Concourse.'

'Then that is where we'll begin.'

He'd brought her to his room. A labour pain had taken her just as they'd reached the threshold of the brothel. She'd doubled over at the door, wanting only to crouch down and be still until it passed. Instead, he had seized her by the arm and dragged her through a small empty sitting room and into a very untidy bedchamber. It smelled of male sweat and old food. A chair was buried under a burden of discarded clothing. The bedding on the narrow bed was rucked up on a stained mattress. There was a chipped platter on the floor near the door. Ants clustered on the crust of bread on it and explored the overturned flagon and sticky cutlery next to it. The only light came from a nearly extinct fire on a pottery hearth. Several baskets huddled near the door held his personal possessions. She caught sight of a boot and a sock stiffened with damp. Then he pushed her again.

Malta staggered, caught herself on the side of a low table and sank down beside it. 'Get a woman,' she told him fiercely. 'Someone who knows about child birth. NOW!'

He stared at her. Then, 'You'll be safe here. I'll be right back,' he said, and left.

When he shut the door, the room was plunged into dimness. Not far away, a woman laughed and a man gave a shout of drunken surprise.

Malta sank to the floor, panting. Just as she caught her breath, another cramp seized her. She curled around her clenched belly and a low moan escaped her. 'It will be all right.' She was not sure if she begged that of Sa or pleaded with the child inside her.

Two more contractions seized her and passed before she heard the door open. Every time one passed, she promised herself she would stagger out the door and look for help as soon as she caught her breath. Each time, a new wave of pain seized her before she could. She could not guess how much time had passed. The pains made everything an endless now. 'Help me,' she gasped, and looked up to see that the useless fool had brought another man with him. She stared up at him. 'A midwife,' she hissed. 'I need a midwife.'

They ignored her. The man who had brought her crossed the small room, stepping around her, almost over her. He took up a cheap yellow candle in its holder, lit it from the hearth, and used it to light several more around the room. Then he stood back and gestured at her, well pleased. 'You see, Begasti? I am right, am I not?'

'It's her,' the other man said. He stooped to peer at her, his breath thick with harsh spices. He was more richly dressed than the man who had dragged her here, and his words more heavily accented with Chalcedean. 'But . . . what is wrong with her? Why have you brought her here? There will be trouble, Arich! Many of these Rain Wilders revere her.'

'And as many despise her! They say she and her husband are too full of themselves, that family, power and beauty have made her think herself truly a queen.' He laughed. 'She does not look so queenly now!'

The words barely registered with Malta's awareness. She was being torn open; she was sure of it. She managed a breath and commanded them, 'Go find a woman to help me!'

The one named Begasti shook his head. 'Such a fuss to make over birthing. Do you think we should gag her? I have heard some women scream when they birth. It is bad enough that you and I are both here, in the same room. It's dangerous. We shouldn't be seen together; we should not want to draw attention to ourselves.'

The other one shrugged. 'This is a noisy place at night, even without the storm. There are shrieks, shouting, and yes even screams. No one will come to investigate.'

Malta was panting and trying to think. This was so wrong. They were not going to help her, they were not listening to her at all. Why had the man pretended to be helpful, why had he brought her here?

Another contraction snatched her attention away from them. She could not think while she was in its grip. And when it passed, she knew she had only a few moments to try to gather her thoughts, try to think of something. Something, there was something she knew, something that was obvious, but her mind would not focus. Their Chalcedean accents were too strong, and neither man had facial tattoos. If they had come here as part of the immigrant wave of freed slaves, then they should have borne the facial tattoos that marked such refugees. Then, as the pain clamped down on her again and the two men idly watched her struggle against it, the pieces of the puzzle tumbled into place for her. Such an obvious answer: these were the spies, the ones that Captain Leftrin had referred to. Chalced's dirty fingers had reached into the Rain Wilds, to corrupt and tempt with money. These were the ones behind Jess the hunter and his plot to slaughter dragons for profit. Of course.

And she was helpless and in their power. To what end? What would they want with a woman in labour?

One of the men asked her question of the other.

'Why did you take her, Arich? She is too well known and her appearance too unusual for you to take home as a slave. And we are not in a position to negotiate for a hostage payment! We agreed we would be invisible here, that we would get what we needed as quickly as we could and then leave this god-forsaken place!'

Arich was grinning now. Malta thrashed and tried not to groan as her child fought to be born. Birth was among the most intimate moments in a woman's life, and here she was, helpless on the filthy floor of a brothel, bereft of husband and midwife, sneered at by a couple of Chalcedean spies. Concealed by her skirts, she could feel her child was struggling to emerge, so close to being born and in such a terrible place. She wanted desperately to crawl away from the men, to seek the shelter of at least a corner of the room. She panted, trying to be silent, trying to conceal from them that her child was arriving now. Their voices pushed into her awareness.

'Begasti, you look but you don't see. She is scaled, just as you said, like a dragon. And the child that will come out will likely be just as heavily scaled. She was lost on the bridges tonight, begging for my help. No one knows I have her here, and no one except you and I will ever know what became of her. Scaled flesh is scaled flesh, my friend. And who is to say what a dragon torn from the egg looks like? Take off her head and hands and feet, remove anything on the baby that looks human and what do we have? Exactly what the Duke has said we must bring him! The flesh of a dragon, for his physicians to render into the cures that he requires!'

'But . . . but . . . this is no dragon! They will make the medicines and they will not work! We will be executed if anyone discovers the deception.'

'No one will discover it, because no one will know of it except you and me! We will go home, we will deliver our goods and our families will be released to us. And we will have at least a chance to escape while the physicians are fighting over who will make the elixirs that will prolong the

Duke's life. Do you think our families are faring well while we are here, struggling to find a way to slaughter dragons when we do not even know where they are? No. You know the Duke! For every tiny pang of pain he feels, he will find a way to take vengeance on our heirs. He is a desperate, dying old man who refuses to believe that his time has come. He will do any wretched or evil thing he must do to prolong his own life.'

Her baby, her newborn child, lay between her legs now. He or she was warm and wet with fluids. And still, terribly still and silent. Malta remained motionless, breathing shallowly. The men were shouting at one another and she did not care. She had to be still and betray nothing, not that her child was here and vulnerable, not that he might be stillborn. She knew that she must somehow save both of them; no one else would come to their aid. Her long loose tunic draped her knees, concealing her child. So she must wait, in stillness, while she wondered if her child lived, until the afterbirth emerged from her body. Once she was uncoupled from the child, then she must find both the strength and a strategy to attack these men and rescue her baby from them. Her baby was so quiet; not a mewl, not a wail. Was he all right? She could not look at him even; not yet. She lay, suddenly shivering with cold after her long exertion, and their words once more intruded into her awareness.

'You speak treason!' Begasti was aghast, looking wildly about as if some witness might leap from the walls to condemn him. 'You would risk the lives of my family with this crazy scheme!'

'Not a risk, old fool! Our only chance. The dragons are gone, far out of our reach now! Do you think the Duke will care that we did as best we could? Do you think he will forgive a failure? No! All will pay with pain and death. He has left us only one route. We deceive him, and possibly we and our heirs escape. If we do not, well, what we will suffer then will be no worse than what we would suffer if we went home now, with nothing! It is our only choice. Luck has put her in our hands! We cannot lose our only chance.'

Abruptly, they were both looking at her. She curled forward over her aching belly and gave a long drawn-out yowl. 'Get a midwife!' she panted. 'Go. Go now! Bring a woman here to help me, or I will die!' She thrashed and felt the small warmth of her baby's body against her thighs. Warm, he was warm. He must be alive! But why so still and silent? She dared not look at him, not while these men were watching her. If they knew he was already here, they would snatch him from her. And kill him, if he were not already dead.

Begasti shrugged. 'We need something to preserve the flesh and something to transport it. Vinegar, I think, and salt. Pickling will preserve it and perhaps make it look more convincing. I think a little keg would serve our purposes best, something that hides what is inside.'

'Tomorrow, I will . . .'

Begasti shook his head. 'No. Not tomorrow. We need to be done with this tonight, and take ship tomorrow morning. Can you imagine that no one has missed her? By tomorrow, the search will be intense. We must do this thing, dispose of whatever is left and be gone.'

'Be reasonable! Where will I find such things at this hour? All shops were closed hours ago!'

Begasti gave him a flat and ugly look. He turned his back on Arich and began to dig in one of the baskets near the door. 'And you will wait until the shops are open and go in to make your little purchase, and then come back here for what must be done? Don't be a fool. Go and get what we need, however you must. Then pay a visit to our dear friend

Trader Candral. Tell him he is to arrange transport for you, on a swift ship bound downriver, one with an enclosed cabin we can share. Do not tell him I am leaving with you. Let him think that I remain here in Cassarick and that the threat still dangles over him. By the time he realizes we are both gone, it will be too late for him to betray us.'

Arich shook his head angrily. 'And while I am doing all these dangerous things, what will you be doing?'

Through slitted eyes, Malta saw Begasti tilt his head toward her. 'Preparing the shipment,' he said flatly, and Arich had the small decency to pale.

'I am gone,' Arich announced and reached for the door.

'You have the stomach of a rabbit,' Begasti announced disdainfully. 'See that you do your part and quickly. We have many tasks to do before the sun rises.'

Child and afterbirth were now clear of her body and still the baby had not made a sound. Malta tented her knees protectively over him and moaned and panted wildly as if still in the throes of labour. The men ignored her as Arich angrily arranged his hooded cloak and then left. Her scrabbling fingers had gradually drawn the hem of her tunic from under her motionless child so that when she got to her feet she would not tumble him to the floor. She tried not to think of her precious newborn, still birth-wet, lying on the filthy floor of a brothel. Rolling her head to one side, she moaned, and gauged the distance to the dirty knife that rested by the plate and spilled flagon.

She'd waited too long. 'Time to be quieter,' Begasti said. The coldness of his words snapped her gaze up. He loomed over her, a loop of fine line in his hands. A bootlace? She met his eyes and saw in them both determination and disgust for what he had to do.

Malta lifted her feet from the floor and shot them out at

him, catching him in the midriff. He oofed out air and staggered back. She rolled away from her baby, crying out with the effort, grabbed the knife with one hand and the sticky flagon with the other. The Chalcedean was already back on his feet and coming at her. She swung the flagon in a wide arc and it cracked against his jaw. She followed it with a wild thrust of the knife.

It was not a weapon for killing, only a short-bladed kitchen blade for cutting cooked meat and not a very sharp one at that. It skittered on his vest, not penetrating. She set her body weight behind it and just as he grabbed her wrist, cursing her, the skating tip of her blade found his unprotected throat and sank in. She joggled the knife back and forth wildly, horrified at how it felt as the greasy warm blood hit her fingers and yet wishing nothing more than to cut his head completely off.

He flailed at her, his curses suddenly gurgled threats. One of his desperate blows caught the side of her head and sent her crashing into the wall. His hands found the knife she'd left stuck in his neck and pulled it out. It clattered to the floor. Blood followed it, leaping out in pulsing gouts.

Malta screamed in horror and staggered back. The next instant, she sprang forward to catch her babe and snatch him to safety as Begasti staggered in a circle in the room. The Chalcedean crashed to his knees, both his hands at his throat, trying to hold in the blood that sprayed out between his thick fingers. He stared up at her, his eyes and mouth wide open. He grunted at her, blood coming out with the sound, spilling from his lips and over his bearded chin. Slowly he toppled over on his side. His hands still clutched his throat and his legs kicked. She retreated from him, her baby clutched to her chest, the umbilical cord spilling over her wrists to the connected and dangling afterbirth.

She looked down, finally, for the first time, at her child. A son. She had a son. But as she regarded him, a low cry of dismay escaped her.

Her dream of someone handing her a chubby infant wrapped in a clean swaddling cloth had come to this. Birthed in a brothel. Dirt from the floor clung to his wet cheek. He was thin. He stirred faintly in her arms. His tiny hands were bony, not chubby, and the nails were greenish. He was already scaled, on his skull and down the back of his neck to the nape. Reyn's eyes but deep blue looked up at her. His mouth was open but she was not certain at first that he breathed. 'Oh, baby!' she cried out in a low voice that was both apology and fear. Her knees folded and she sank to the floor, the child on her lap. 'I don't know how to do this. I don't know what I'm doing,' she sobbed.

The knife was on the floor near her knee, but it was covered in the Chalcedean's blood. She could not bear to touch it, let alone cut the birth cord with it. She remembered her trousers, still shoved into the front of her tunic, and pulled them out. She set her child on them, and bundled the legs around him, wrapping the cord and the afterbirth with him. 'It's all wrong, so wrong,' she apologized to him. 'It wasn't supposed to be like this, baby. I'm so sorry!'

He gave a sudden thin wail as if to agree that this was not how life should treat him. It was a terrible sound, lonely and weak, but Malta laughed aloud that he could make even such a noise as this. She could not recall that she had taken off her cloak, but there it was, on the floor where she had laboured, wet with two kinds of blood. Her beautiful Elderling cloak. It would have to do.

Begasti gave a low, drawn-out moan that sent her staggering away from him until she cowered by the wall. Then he was still. No time. No time to think about anything. The other man would come back and he must not find her here. It was hard to get her cloak around her and fastened without setting the child down, but she would not let him be out of her arms. She opened the door and tottered out into the small common room she had passed through earlier. Night was deep and the room empty. She heard no sounds from the whores or their customers. She was exhausted and every muscle in the centre of her body felt overused. Blood was trickling slowly down her legs. How far could she get like this?

Bang on the doors of the brothel chambers? Demand help? No. She could trust no one that would knowingly shelter Chalcedeans in the Rain Wilds. Even if they were sympathetic to a woman in such a desperate situation, when Arich returned, they would likely give way, out of fear or in response to bribery.

She crossed the room and carried her newborn son out into the storm and the night.

Day the 26th of the Change Moon
Year the 7th of the Independent Alliance of Traders

Dear Detozi and Erek

How peculiar to send you this post by boat instead of bird, but the Guild has grounded almost all birds until the contagion can be contained. Those that can fly are reserved for the most urgent messages. I have heard a rumour that they have ordered more birds from Jamaillia, but even if they arrive it will take months to establish breeding pairs and imprint on them that they are to home here rather than return to Jamaillia. Nor do I think that the quality of birds we import can match what we have been breeding here, thanks to the programme that Erek began. I am heartsick at the loss of birds, not just as breeding stock but as small flighted friends. I have only two pairs of swift birds left in the cotes assigned to my management. I have isolated them as pairs and allow no other keeper to bring feed or water in or to clean their cote. As soon as they hatch the eggs they are setting and the youngsters fledge out, I will remove them and hand-feed them in the hopes of preserving as many swift birds as I can from the contagion. I hope you have been able to preserve some of this stock, as I wish to be very cautious of breeding them.

They tell me this letter will travel rapidly on their so called 'impervious ship'. I have to laugh. They do not know the meaning of swift transit! Nothing will ever replace our birds.

By the time you receive this, I imagine the wedding will be over. How I wish I could have been there!

Reyall

CHAPTER ELEVEN

Flight

How could life go from being so right to being so wrong, so very quickly? The dragon had flown, she had hunted and killed, and then slept so deeply, slept with a full belly for the first time in days. She had wakened, chilled after her sleep and already thinking of hunting and killing again. Sintara had stood and stretched and felt, for the first time in this life, that she was not only a queen dragon, but a true Lord of the Three Realms of earth, sea and sky.

She had snuffed carefully all about her kill site to be sure she had not missed a single morsel. She hadn't. Striding to the steepest edge of the stony ridge, she had looked down. It was a long drop. Doubt tried to uncurl inside her but she crushed it. She had flown to get here, and she would fly to get back. Back? Why would she go back, she wondered suddenly? Back to the other dragons in their pitiful earthbound huddle? Back to an inadequate shelter and a keeper who could barely sustain her most basic needs? No. There was no reason for her to go back to any of that. She could fly now, and she could kill for herself. It was time to leave this cold place and fly to the heat-soaked sands she had dreamed of ever since she had emerged from her cocoon. Time to live as a dragon.

She had launched, springing out wildly from the ridge. With powerful beats of her wings, she had risen to where she could catch the currents of air that flowed with the river far below her. She caught the wind, her wings cupped wide and she let it lift her higher and higher. The altitude and the freedom intoxicated her. Drawing a breath, she trumpeted a wild challenge to the gathering evening. *Sintara!* she roared, and took pleasure in the fact that she heard no reply.

She circled wide over the river, tasting and smelling all the information that the wind carried to her. The first stars were starting to show in the darkening sky; the sight of them sobered her.

Dragons were creatures of light and day. They did not, by choice, fly at night. She needed to find a place to land, somewhere that offered her shelter against the night's cold and the threat of rain. And, she realized, she should choose a place that offered an excellent launching spot. Taking flight from the ridge had been far easier than trying to lift herself from the riverside.

She had banked, intending to circle widely. But with the coming of evening, the day had cooled and the winds had risen. A current of air caught her and sent her out in a much wider spiral. Relentlessly, it had swept her out over the depth of the rushing river.

No panic, she told herself sternly. She could fly. Being over the river did not mean she was in any danger. She had pushed away her memories of battling for her life against a flash flood. She had survived and beaten the river. No fears now. She beat her wings and rose. It was not raining, and for that she was grateful, but the clear skies had brought cold with them. As the sun sank, the day was chilling and she had suddenly felt the full weariness of her long day. This was her first day of flight, and bereft of the excitement of her first launch, she suddenly felt how tired she was. Not just her wings but also her spine ached from her labours. She was suddenly aware of the effort of holding her hind legs in flight alignment with her body. Her joints ached. And then she noticed how far she was from either shore.

She turned again in another circle, and again felt the cheating wind pull her out, away from the shore and toward the river's centre. She scanned her horizons, seeking for a place to land, any elevated piece of terrain. The river spread wide below her, either shore a daunting distance away. As she circled yet again, determination flared in her. She fixed her gaze on Kelsingra, and beat her wings, making straight for the city.

Almost straight. She had not allowed for her weaker wing, or for her weariness. The wind pushed her, she tipped and lost altitude before she could correct. The moving air over the river seemed to suck at her now, trying to pull her ever lower. She fought it but could not maintain her course. Then, as if fate had decided to offer her a small measure of mercy, something tall loomed up from the river. It was a darker shape against the dimming landscape and she could make no sense of it. What was it? Once, some ancestor told her, there had been a bridge there, but . . . And then she realized what it was. The jutting mass was what remained of the bridge approach. It reached partially out into the river and it would do for a landing place. She fixed her gaze on it and willed herself there.

But she was tired. No matter how strongly she beat her wings, she sank lower and lower. And her shorter wing turned her, despite her best efforts to compensate. Just short of her destination, a sudden gust of wind slammed into her. It tipped her and she did not have sufficient altitude to correct her attitude. Sintara fought to rise into the air again, but the tip of one wing brushed the river and the moving water snatched it. She cartwheeled around her wingtip and slammed into the river. The surface slapped her and then, as if suddenly admitting it was liquid, it welcomed her in. The dragon sank into the cold and the wet and the darkness. Down she went, felt her claws touch the rocky bottom of the river for a single instant, and then was dragged along by the current. She fought to close her wings, to streamline her body so she could resist the water's relentless drag. Her nostrils reflexively closed the instant the water touched them. Her eyes had remained open but she saw only darkness. Kicking, clawing, lashing her tail, she fought the water.

Her head broke clear and she had a brief view of the bank. It was not far away, but it was steep and tall. The river claimed her again, resisting her effort to fight her way to the surface. She kicked steadily, trying to swim against the swift current.

Sintara! Thymara's cry of anguish echoed only in her mind. Water drowned the dragon's hearing. Somewhere, the girl was racing through the streets of Kelsingra, heading toward the river and her dragon. To do what? Save her from drowning? Ridiculous human! Yet despite her disdain for the girl's foolishness, the act warmed her ego. She lashed her tail and was pleased when it helped push her toward the shore. Her front claws touched gravel. She snatched and scrabbled at it, and after an eternity, her hind feet found purchase, too. Another eternity passed before she fought her way to the river's edge, and it took even longer for her to claw her way up the steep and rocky bank.

Sintara dragged herself out of the water's reach and collapsed, cold and exhausted. She felt sluggish with the cold, two of her claws were torn bloody and every muscle in her body throbbed.

But she was alive. And in Kelsingra. She had flown, hunted,

and killed. She was a dragon again. She lifted her head, and snorted water from her nostrils. When she could, she drew a deep breath and trumpeted: 'Thymara! I am here. Come to me!'

Malta clasped her bundled baby to her chest as she fled. Few lights showed in Cassarick this late at night. Rain was falling again, the narrow trunkways here were slick, and terror and exhaustion had taken their tolls on her. She could feel blood trickling down her thighs and though she knew that bleeding after birth was not unusual, every terrible tale she had heard of new mothers bleeding to death came to torment her. If she died now, if she collapsed in the dark and rain, her baby would die with her. He did not seem strong; he did not cry loudly but only wailed weakly, protesting that his life must begin in such a rough way.

She put distance between herself and the brothel and the man she had killed. She stared all about in the dark as she went, wondering where Arich had gone and if he was even now returning. If she encountered him, he would not drag her back to that place. He'd kill her and her child and then take her body back. She could not hope to fight him; she had no weapon, she was exhausted and encumbered with her tiny son.

Down, she suddenly decided. She was completely lost but one thing that was always true was that down led to the river and the docks. And the *Tarman*. Perhaps Reyn was still there, trying to persuade Leftrin to come to their rented room. It did not seem likely. She could not decide how much time had passed since they had parted, but surely it had been hours. Perhaps even now, Reyn was looking for her, alarmed not to find her in their room. Well, she did not know the way back to her rooms, but she did know that down led to the river.

At the next bridge she crossed, she chose the larger way and on reaching the trunk, followed the rough, steep stairway that spiralled down around it. The city seemed deserted, friendly house lights extinguished for the night. When the stairway stopped on a broad landing, she crossed on the largest bridge attached to it, and again followed a thickening branch-way until she reached a trunk with another spiralling stair. And down she went.

The baby, so distressingly small when she had first beheld him, had become a burden to her weary arms. She was thirsty and shaking with cold. The man's blood was still sticky on her hands, on the hands that held her baby, and the memories of it kept blossoming into her mind. It was not regret but the horror of the act that assailed her.

When her feet found packed earth at the end of a stairway, it startled her. She was on the ground. The smell of the river welcomed her as she turned toward it. The trees thinned enough to allow her to see the flickering of the torches that always burned on the river docks. The path at her feet was submerged in shadow, but as long as she stumbled toward the lights, she would reach the dock. And the *Tarman*. The old liveship suddenly seemed the only safe place in the world, the only place where she knew she would be believed if she told her outlandish story of kidnappers who wanted to cut her up and sell her scaled flesh as false dragon meat. Almost she felt the ship calling to her.

The ground grew softer as she approached the river, and then she was wading through mud. She stumbled suddenly and went to her knees, catching herself on one hand. The other clutched her babe to her breast. Her cry was equal parts pain and joy, for her hand had slapped onto the hard wood of a walkway. Knees burning with fresh scrapes, she crawled onto it, staggered to her feet, and followed the path. It led to the docks. All the tears that she had forced herself to hold back poured down her cheeks. She staggered, passing small open boats tied up for the night, and larger cargo vessels with darkened windows. When she saw a wizardwood barge with the cabin lights ablaze in it, she knew she had reached safety.

'TARMAN!' She shouted in a shuddering voice. 'Captain Leftrin! Tarman, help me!'

She reached for the railing of the liveship and tried to drag herself aboard. But the ship was riding high on the water. Clinging to his railing with one bloodied hand, she fought to find the strength to pull herself and her child to safety. 'Help me!' she cried out again, her voice weakening. 'Please. Tarman, help me, help my baby!'

A voice queried another inside the ship's cabin. Had they heard her? No door opened, no voice answered her.

'Please, help me,' she begged hopelessly. Then a surge of awareness from the vessel washed warmly through her. Daughter of a Trader family and familiar with the way of liveships, she knew what it was. And knew also that it was a touch that was usually reserved for kin. It was welcome, and carried strength with it.

I will help you. He is a child of my family. Give the baby to me.

The thought pulsed through her, as clear as if the words had been spoken aloud. 'Please,' she said, 'Take him.' Her bundled child became an offering of trust and kinship as she slid him over the railing and onto Tarman's deck. She held tight to the bundled cloth and lowered him gently to Tarman's deck. Her baby was out of her sight now, and out of her reach, and yet for the first time since she had birthed him, she felt he was also out of danger. The ship's strength flowed through her. She drew a deeper breath.

'Help me! Please, help me!'

The ship's awareness seemed to echo her cry, a demand that the crew must obey. And from the deck, from a baby she could not see, a sudden angry crying rose, far stronger than any she had yet heard from him.

'It's a baby!' a woman's voice suddenly cried out. 'A baby, a newborn, on Tarman's deck!'

'Help me!' Malta cried again, and suddenly a very large man leapt down from the deck to land on the dock beside her.

'I got you,' he said, his voice deep and his words simple. 'Don't you be afraid, lady. Big Eider's got you now.'

Thymara ran through the darkening streets of the city. Rapskal had left her, with a cry of 'Heeby's here! I'll get her to help us.' He had run off into the darkness while she had set off on a different course through the city, following not a memory of how they had come but the pull of her heart.

Anger fuelled her. She was furious with the dragon for putting herself in danger. The anger was much easier to feel than her underlying fear. It was not just her terror that Sintara was drowning but her general fear of the city and its ghostly denizens. Some of the streets she ran through were dark and deserted. But then she would turn a corner and suddenly be confronted with torchlight and merry-makers, a city in the midst of some sort of holiday. She had shrieked the first time, and then recognized them for what they were. Ghosts and phantoms, Elderling memories stored in the stone of the buildings she passed. Despite her knowledge she ran jaggedly through them, dodging vendors' carts and amorous couples and small boys selling skewers of smoked and spicy meats. Their huckstering cries filled her ears and the smells taunted her with memories of the delicious titbits they offered. Hunger assailed her and as the running dried her mouth, thirst as well.

Her experience with the memory stone had opened her to these ghosts. She no longer needed to touch anything to stir them to wakefulness. All she had to do was pass one of the black stone walls, and the memories of the city flooded out and engulfed her. She entered a plaza dominated by a recently erected wooden dais. There were musicians up there, playing horns of shining silver and striking immense drums and cymbals. She put her hands over her ears but could not block the ghost music. She crossed the plaza at a run, giving a small shriek as she inadvertently dashed right through a young man bearing a platter full of foaming mugs over his head.

'Sintara!' she shouted wildly as she reached the edge of the plaza. She halted, looking wildly about her. There, she saw a dark and empty street fronted by silent buildings. One street away, a pale-faced street performer dressed in white and silver was juggling objects the size of apples that sparkled like jewels. She tossed one high and it burst in a sudden shower of sparks and scintillant dust and the crowd oohed and shrieked. Thymara was breathing hard and realized her legs were shaking. She pulled her cloak tighter over her wings. She had lost her bearings and had no idea where she was in the city. Worse, her awareness of the dragon had faded. Was she drowning? Dead?

Here. Come here.

Thymara did not hesitate. Down the darkened street she went, picking her way over uneven cobbles and fallen masonry. Then, after one more turn, she suddenly smelled and saw the river, gleaming silver under the moonlight. And there, on the broken pavement at the very brink of the river, sprawled her beloved dragon. As she ran toward her, she suddenly shared how cold and weary Sintara was. And also how . . . proud? The dragon was pleased with herself?

'I thought you were drowning?'

'I was.' Sintara heaved herself to her feet. Her wings she held half open and dripping still. Water sheened off her scales to make mirrors for the starlight on the broken paving stones. Sintara snorted, and sneezed suddenly, surprising them both. 'I flew,' she said, and the force of the thought behind the words eclipsed her dip in the river. 'I flew, I hunted, I killed. I am SINTARA!'

She roared the last word and Thymara felt it as sound, wind and thought. The dragon's elation lifted her own spirits. For one moment, all fear and anger was gone, replaced by mutual triumph.

'You are indeed,' the girl affirmed with a grin.

'Build a fire,' the dragon commanded her. 'I need to warm myself.'

Thymara glanced about hopelessly. 'There is nothing here that will burn. The driftwood that does wash up is wet. This city is all cold stone. Most of the wood left is rotted to splinters and dust.' As her words dashed the dragon's hopes of warmth, the girl shared again just how cold Sintara was. Colder than she'd ever been, and hearing the slowing thumps of her heart as her body reacted to that cold.

'Can you walk? We can at least get you inside of a building. It might be a little warmer there.'

'I can walk,' the dragon asserted, but not strongly. She lifted her head. 'I almost, no, I can, I do remember this place. The bridge is gone. And the river has eaten more than two streets and half of a third. There used to be warehouses along here. And docks for the smaller boats. And up the hill from them were the Grand Promenade, and then the Plaza of Dreams. And past that, two streets past that, there was the . . .'

'The Square of the Dragons.' Thymara spoke the name quietly into the gap left by Sintara's pause. She did not know where the knowledge came from, not clearly. Ancestral memory. Was this what Rapskal had been trying to explain to her? That once she had dreamed deeply enough with the stones, she could remember the city for herself?

'And a grooming hall fronted it. I remember it well.'

Sintara stepped up her pace and Thymara hurried to keep up with her. The dragon lurched as she walked. 'Are you injured?' the girl demanded.

'Some cracked claws on my right front foot. They are painful but they will heal. Once, the grooming hall was where a dragon might go for such an injury. Elderlings would cut away the cracked claw and bind the nail with linen and then varnish to protect it until it grew again. They stitched gashes from mating battles, too. And removed parasites and scale lice and such.'

'Would that they were there now to help you,' Thymara said softly.

The dragon did not seem to hear her. 'And there were soaking pools, some just of hot water and others with a layer of oil on top. Oh, to soak in steaming water again. And then emerge to wallow in a sand basin, and then to have servants groom the sand away and leave my scales gleaming . . .'

'There is nothing like that left intact,' Thymara said quietly. 'But at least we can get out of the wind there.'

The dragon soldiered on, walking silently now, and Thymara matched her pace. They turned a corner into a street brightly lit with memories, but if Sintara was aware of them, she made no sign. She strode through the night bazaar of incense and freshly cooked meats and breads and Thymara followed her.

The reality of the dragon made the ghosts seem paler in comparison. Their gaiety seemed frail and false, an echo of a past that had never lasted into a future. Whatever they celebrated, they did so with futility. Their world had not lasted, and their windblown laughter seemed to mock them.

'Here,' Sintara said, and turned to mount a long flight of shallow stairs.

Thymara ascended beside her in silence. Then, when they were within two steps of the top, the entire frame of the doorway suddenly burst into golden light. A welcome of music and fragrance swelled out as the remnants of the doors creaked back on their hinges. Thymara thought it a part of the stone's illusion but the dragon halted, and looked about in wonder.

'It remembers!' she said suddenly. 'The city remembers me. Kelsingra remembers the dragons!' She lifted her head high and suddenly bugled a clear call. The sound echoed in the chamber before her, and in response, light flooded it.

Thymara was transfixed by wonder. It was light, real light, not a memory of bygone times, and as she watched in awe, the second and then the third storey of the buildings lit and golden light flowed like beacons from the windows. As if they were twigs catching a flame, the buildings to either side suddenly responded as well. Light flooded and filled the Square of the Dragons. Thymara turned to look back on it. The statues that edged the square flushed with colour, and for the first time she realized that the coloured tiles that had seemed random when she walked over them were actually a mosaic of a great black dragon.

In the distance, Thymara heard a dragon trumpet. Heeby, it would be Heeby in flight with Rapskal on her back, looking for them. Well, they would definitely know where Sintara was, she decided. No need to wait outside in the wind. She followed her dragon into the welcoming chamber.

Wonder upon wonder. The mosaics on the walls, a vista of rolling plains, glowed with light and warmth. Thymara stared all around at a room that had obviously been built to host not a single dragon, but a score of them. The ceiling soared overhead, a permanently blue sky with a dazzling yellow sun in the centre. The pillars that supported the distant ceiling were textured like the trunks of trees. The floor beneath their feet was dusty but it, too, gave off warmth that Thymara could feel through the broken soles of her boots. The fragrance grew stronger as they progressed into the room, but pleasantly so. In the far corner, a human-sized staircase led upwards to other chambers. The music beckoned, a sound like water over a pebbly stream bed, luring them into the next room.

'Sweet Sa,' she exclaimed as she entered. The air of the room was warming and the humidity was increasing. A row of a dozen immense troughs interrupted the floor of the chamber, each with a slanting ramp leading down into it. And one was filling slowly with steaming water . . .

Sintara did not hesitate but walked straight down into the rising water and arranged herself with her chin propped on a stone pillar set at precisely the correct height to cradle her head above the water that already lapped around her knees. She gave an immense sigh. 'Warm,' she said, and sank into it and closed her eyes.

Thymara watched, caught between wonder and envy as the water filled the basin until it lapped over the dragon's back. 'Sintara?' she queried cautiously but the dragon gave no indication of being aware of her. She desperately wanted to ask permission to join the dragon. In all her life, she had never seen such a quantity of clean, heated water. In her home in Trehaug, they had had a bath hammock, a tightly woven 'tub' that in the summer was filled with rainwater and warmed by the sun. But she had never seen or even imagined anything like this bath for a dragon. There seemed to be plenty of room in it, and as she studied it, she noticed that a set of human-sized steps led down into it from the far corner. Oh.

Now she 'remembered' it: there had been a force of Elderlings who had lived on the premises and provided scrubbing and grooming services to dragons that required it. Once, there would have been a stock of brushes and oils and other grooming tools in the collapsed wooden cupboards along the wall.

Thymara looked down at her well-worn clothing. Well, more dirty than just well worn, she admitted. When one was reduced to little more than one set of clothes, washing them and having them dry before they were required again was a bit difficult, especially in winter. But in this large warm room, they would probably dry quickly. The temptation was suddenly too much to resist.

She walked swiftly to the steps, set her boots to one side and dropped her cloak beside them. Her 'stockings' were no more than rags to wrap her feet. She removed them carefully. They were much better than nothing. She pulled her long tunic off carefully, working her wings through the opening cut in the back. The tunic joined her trousers in a pile. She sat on the edge of the warm tiles and put her feet into the water.

And swiftly snatched them back. The water was hot, far hotter than any she'd ever bathed in. She looked at the comatose dragon. Sintara seemed to be enjoying it. Thymara ventured her foot into the water again. Yes, hot, surprisingly hot, but not unbearably so. She eased her feet down one step and slowly entered the water. It took time but eventually she was immersed up to her chin. She opened her wings and felt the heat of the water touch them. And ease them. Thymara had always accepted that they ached slightly, all the time, as her hands and feet ached when they were cold. The cessation of that constant pain was a blessing. She leaned back then, wetting her hair, and then reaching up to loosen it in the water. It felt so good. She ducked her head under and rubbed her face, and then repeated it until her skin squeaked under her fingers. Clean. Clean was such a miracle of simple pleasure. She rubbed her hands together, digging the dirt out from under her nails. Then she leaned back with only her face out of the water. Paradise.

The hot water was rapidly sucking all ambition out of her. She just wanted to rest her head on the edge of the pool and relax in the warmth. It had been so long since she had felt completely warm. She forced herself to think about putting on filthy clothes over her clean body in the morning; that roused her to activity. She pulled her garments in, soaking them and then pummelling them in the hot water. A brown cloud of dirt tinged the clean water around them and she glanced fearfully toward Sintara. She had not known her clothes were that dirty! Would the dragon be offended? But Sintara seemed beyond feeling anything, so Thymara hastily finished her laundering. She squeezed as much water as she could out of the clothes, wiped an area of the heated floor clean of dust with her foot wraps, washed them out again and then spread all her clothes out flat on the warm tiles. She had just finished arranging them and was slipping back into the hot water when she heard a sound. Her heart skipped a beat before she decided it was the intrusion of memory into her mind.

She was halfway back into the hot water when Rapskal exclaimed happily, 'You're naked!'

Thymara leapt out of the water with a splash and snatched up her tunic, turning her back on him to pull it over her head. It got caught on her wings and she struggled with it endlessly before she was covered. 'What are you doing here?' she demanded over her shoulder, realizing how ridiculous a question it was even as she asked it.

'Looking for you and Sintara! To help you, remember? You said she was drowning, but she doesn't look too worried right now. How did you do all this? Seems like half the city is lit up! I bet they're boiling with curiosity across the river! And look at all the water. Where's it coming from? Heeby! Heeby, wait, darling, what are you doing? How did you do that?'

For the red dragon had proceeded to enter a bath trough. The hot, scented water had already begun to flow into it. Heeby was settling into it with a happy wriggle when Rapskal shouted, 'Hey, wait for me!' and began to strip.

'You can't do that in front of me!' Thymara exclaimed, offended, but he only turned and grinned at her.

'You did it first. And I'm cold to the bone.' He dropped his clothes to the floor and jumped directly into the water. 'Oh, yowtch, that's hot! How do you stand it?' He'd lifted himself on the side and was staring at her over the edge.

'Go in slowly,' she suggested, and turned away from him.

Sintara had opened her eyes and was regarding them all with annoyance. Rapskal stayed as he was, letting the slowly rising water come up on him. He moved to the end of the dragon bath to be closer to Thymara and hung on the edge of it, cheeks red and dark hair dripping.

'So, hey, Sintara. Hey, big girl? Look over here at me, princess! How'd you do it? How did you light up the city? Heeby and I been here before, lots of times. It never lit up or made a bath for us. At least, not until now.'

Sintara swivelled her head on her chin rest to regard them. Thymara was shocked at how he had addressed her dragon, but sensed too that Sintara did not mind being called 'princess'. Perhaps he could not tell how much his words had pleased the dragon, but Thymara could. She, Sintara, had wakened the city when Heeby had not. Perhaps that was why she deigned to answer him.

'Perhaps the city was awaiting the return of a real dragon. I simply told the city what I wanted. It's how Kelsingra works. All the Elderling cities worked this way. These cities were built for the convenience of dragons. To lure us to come and spend time among the Elderlings. If they did not please us, why would we have bothered?' Her eyes spun in lazy pleasure and slowly she lidded them, leaving them all to think about that.

'Look at your wings!' Thymara exclaimed suddenly and walked over to gaze down on her dragon.

'One is weaker. It will grow.' Sintara sounded annoyed to be reminded of the flaw.

'They are growing now. Like the dragons all grew when they stayed the one night on the warm place on our journey here. They are . . . extraordinary! The webbing, the veins . . . I don't know what to call it, but it is thicker already and the colours are richer. I can almost see them grow like vines overtaking a tree. All your colours are brighter, everywhere, but your wings are incredible! If one is weaker, I cannot see it.'

'The weakness was very small. Probably apparent only to me.'

Sintara stood suddenly and opened her wings. She flexed them once, showering the room with droplets of water. 'Yes. They are stronger!' The dragon sounded very pleased. She sank down into the water again and this time she left her wings half-opened as if to soak them better. 'This was what I needed.'

'I wonder if it is what all the dragons need?' Thymara ventured. She had glanced over at Heeby. Rapskal's scarlet dragon was smaller and rounder than Sintara and always had been. Her legs had always seemed stumpy to Thymara, and her tail shorter than it should have been. Sintara's body was lizard-like while Heeby had always seemed square as a toad to Thymara. But now, as the little dragon stretched and lolled in the steaming water, her transformation was almost as stunning as Sintara's. The web of veins in her red wings gleamed gold and shining black. It did not seem possible that her tail and legs had grown, but already she looked longer and more proportionate. Thymara spoke softly. 'Is Heeby changing, too?'

'Oh, yes,' Rapskal seemed blasé about it. 'Remember, we found one of those get-warm places when we were separated from the rest of you. She spent a lot of time in it. I think that's why she got to fly before anyone else. Dragons like heat. Makes them grow.' He suddenly grabbed the edge of the pool and levered himself half out of it. 'They're not the only things that grow in hot water!'

'You're so rude! Cover yourself!'

Rapskal glanced down, snickered, but obediently picked up his shirt and draped it around his waist, clutching it one-handed at his hip. 'That's not what I'm talking about. Your wings, Thymara! If you think Sintara's wings changed in the hot water, well, you should see your own. Open them up, butterfly girl. Let's see them all the way.'

Water was streaming down his chest and bare legs. Scales delineated the muscles of his chest and belly but he seemed to have grown a lot of black hair as well. It was shocking to see him this way, but worse was that her memories of coupling with him shot suddenly through her, filling her body with a different sort of warmth. *No. Not him*, she reminded herself sternly. *I didn't couple with him. I've never mated with anyone!* Yet the thought could not negate her knowledge of it, nor cool the lust in her belly. She backed away from him, only a step, but he halted where he stood and his grin grew wider.

'I won't touch you,' he promised. 'I just want to see your wings.'

She turned, her face burning.

'Open them up, then,' he complained, and she did. Water droplets had been trapped in their folds and slid down when she opened them. They tickled and she shivered. Rapskal laughed. 'That's amazing. The colours flickered. Oh, Thymara. So beautiful. I wish you could see them for yourself. You would never feel shy of them again, never cover them again. Move them, just a little, would you?'

She was tantalizingly aware of him standing behind her. She distracted herself by fanning her wings slightly and was startled at what she felt. Strength. And increased size, as if they had only been waiting to unfold. She fanned them again. Flight. Was it possible now? She stifled the thought. Sintara had told her she would never fly. Why did she torment herself?

Rapskal had come closer. She felt his breath on her back, sensed his closeness. 'Please,' he said quietly. 'I know I said I wouldn't touch, but can I please just touch your wings?'

Her wings. What was the harm? 'Very well,' she said quietly.

'Open them wide, please.'

She spread them, and felt him take hold of the ribbed end of one. It was oddly like holding his hand; the sensation was rather like her fingers. He spoke softly. 'I wish you could see this. This line here is all gold.' He traced a line with his finger, and she shivered at the touch. 'And behind it is a blue like the sky right before it gives way to night. Here, there is white that gleams almost silver.' He stretched her wing wider and very lightly drew his finger from her shoulder to the very tip. She shivered again, but with heat, not chill.

An odd thought intruded. He was using both hands.

She snapped her wings shut and spun around. His shirt was on the floor. 'Oops.' He grinned.

'Not funny!' she objected.

His grin grew wider and as she turned away, she could not

keep an answering smile from her face. It *was* funny. Rude, but funny. So very Rapskal. But it also made her uncomfortable. She walked away from him.

'Where are you going?'

She didn't know. 'Upstairs. I want to see what else is here.'

'Wait for me!'

'You should stay with the dragons.'

'No reason to. They're both asleep.'

'At least put on your trousers.'

He laughed again but she refused to look at him. She didn't wait but returned to the first chamber they had entered and walked over to the stairs. It was cooler in this room compared to the bathing chamber and goosebumps popped up on her back under her damp tunic. She was still hungry. She pushed that thought from her mind. Nothing she could do about it tonight.

The stairs wound around a pillar and led to an upper chamber that was sized to humans and not as elaborately decorated. There was a main room with a scatter of collapsed and unidentifiable furniture remains in it. The ceiling glowed softly, illuminating the room evenly. A single window looked out over the Square of the Dragons. Thymara lost a few moments staring out of it. Rapskal was right. Whatever Sintara had done to light this building had spread. The windows of the adjacent buildings gleamed with light, and throughout the city, other random structures seemed to have wakened. Some were outlined with lights even though their windows were dark. Had the Elderlings used light to decorate as some cities used paint or carving? Random buildings had awakened in the distance, even as far back as the cliffs at the edge of the city. Lights burned as if there were people there. It was a sight both cheering and unnerving.

'I told you so. This city isn't dead. It's waiting for us, for dragons and Elderlings, to wake it and bring it back to life.' He had come up the stairs quietly and stood behind her.

'Maybe,' she conceded and turned to follow Rapskal as he explored. He came to a tall door. It was wood, but it had been decorated with panels of metal with shapes beaten into it. Perhaps that was why it had survived. He opened it and wondered aloud, 'Where does this go?'

Thymara followed him as he entered a wide corridor. More doors, similar to the one he had just opened, lined the walls. 'Are they locked?' Rapskal wondered and pushed on one. It swung open silently and he hesitated on the threshold.

'What's in there?' she asked, hurrying to join him.

'Someone's room,' he said, but still he did not enter.

Thymara stood on tiptoe to peer over his shoulder. Someone's room indeed. So many of the houses she had seen were empty, as if the inhabitants had packed and left, while others held only splinters and shards of furniture. This was different. There was a desk and a chair, of dark wood, but coated with something very shiny and inset with colours. She had once seen a very small and expensive box from Trehaug that was finished like that. A tall shelf in the corner matched the desk and on the shelves there were containers of glass and pottery, most of them blue, but a few orange and silver ones for contrast.

'Look. A bed made of stone. Who would want a bed made of stone?' Rapskal walked boldly into the room and Thymara followed shyly. She felt like an intruder here, as if the narrow door in the opposite wall might open at any time and the room's inhabitant emerge to demand what they were doing here. She moved to the shelf and found a comb and a brush, seemingly made of glass. The bristles of the brush were stiff when she poked at them.

'I'm taking this!' she heard herself say and was shocked at

the greed in her voice. But she had not had a proper hairbrush since hers had been lost months ago. A flat object on the desk looked rather like a book, but when she opened it, it unfolded into three hinged mirror panels. She looked at herself and then could not look away. Was that her? Had Sintara changed her so much?

Gone was the girl who had been 'marked by the Rain Wilds'. An Elderling, narrow of face, her features traced in fine blue scales, looked out at her. Her wet hair, sleek and black, revealed fine blue scaling in the parting. She lifted her hand to touch her face, to prove the reflection was her own, and was struck by the deep cobalt of her claws, and the tracery of silver, like a vine, that now ran from each fingertip up the back of her hands to her elbows. She was sure it had not been there before the bath.

She was still staring when Rapskal interrupted her. 'You're going to like what's in here even better. Girl clothes. Elderling stuff, like that gown Alise has. Pretty stuff. Silver and blue and green, your colours. And slippers of the same stuff, only heavier.'

'Let me see!' she demanded.

He turned from the set of shelves behind the narrow door, holding up a shimmering garment of green and blue. Thymara's heart leapt.

Rapskal was grinning at her. 'There's a lot of them in here. You could share. If they fit anyone.'

She pushed past him, her fingers running over the stacked folds. Silver like the running river, green that was greener than Fente. Blue like Sintara. She was breathless with excitement.

'Hey. Look over your shoulder,' Rapskal commanded her.

She did, and found he was holding the unfolded mirror up for her. 'How do you like your wings?' he demanded, and then fell silent at the stunned look on her face. Tears welled up in her eyes and she felt her lips trembling. She couldn't speak.

'You don't like them?' he demanded, shocked.

She was even more shocked. 'Rapskal. I'm beautiful.'

'Well, I've been telling you that!' Now he sounded disgusted that she had doubted him. He wandered back to the desk and set the mirror on it. He glanced at her, and then away, as if suddenly uncomfortable with her. Instead he went to the stone bed. 'Weird', he said, and sat down on it. Then he gasped and sprang up. 'It grabbed me!' he exclaimed.

They both stared at the fading impression of his bottom on the bed. As they watched, it returned to a smooth, blank surface. Cautiously he set his hand to it and pushed down. His hand sank slightly into it. 'Looks like stone, but it gets soft when you push on it. And it's warm.' He sat down and then lay back on it. 'Oh, sweet Sa! I've never slept on anything like this. Come feel it.'

She pressed it first with a hand, then gingerly sat down. It obligingly shaped itself to her.

'Lie down. You have to feel this,' he told her, moving back to make room for her. She did, and for a moment rested on her back, looking up at the gently glowing ceiling. She sighed suddenly. 'It makes room for my wings. It has been so long since I've been able to lie flat on my back. And it's warm.'

'Let's sleep here.'

She rolled her head to look at him. His face was very close, his breath brushing her lips. The warm water of the dragon bath had brought out his colours as well, she thought. Gleaming scarlet Rapskal. He was beautiful. And so was she. It was the first time in her life that she had felt beautiful. His eyes were on his face, and she could suddenly believe what she saw in them. It was heady to know she was attractive, to see that mirrored in his eyes. Intoxicating like nothing else she had ever felt. She tried her smile on him. His eyes widened and she heard him swallow.

She met his mouth and accepted his deep kiss. It was both familiar and strange. He shifted closer. 'I just want you,' he said softly. 'I've wanted you since I first saw you, even when I was too stupid to know what I wanted. Just you, Thymara. Please.'

She didn't answer with words, didn't even let herself think about an answer. She opened her mouth to his kiss and did not flinch from his exploring hands. She took his weight and the Elderling bed cradled them both and returned their warmth. A moment came when she expected pain but there was only sweet pleasure. *I was ready*, she thought to herself, and then thought no more about anything.

'I just want to leave here.'

Water was still running down his face and he had scarcely caught his breath from running back to the ship. Reyn had been the first to reach the *Tarman*; he supposed it was luck that Hennesey had found him first and told him that Malta and the baby were safe aboard the liveship. The mate had told Reyn to get to her, that he would find Captain Leftrin and Skelly. His sister Tillamon was out there, too, hurrying along with Skelly, looking in all the places that Malta might have gone to ask for help. He looked at his wife, wrapped in a rough ship's blanket, standing by the galley stove and blinked rain from his lashes, trying to comprehend what was going on. At last, he found a question. 'Where's the baby? Hennesey said you had the baby.'

Malta stared at him, and if it were possible, her face went paler. It made the scaling stand out more sharply. She looked as if she were carved of ivory and embellished with jewels. 'On the foredeck,' she said quietly. 'Tarman needed him to be there. So he could help him. I was so hungry and thirsty that I came to the galley. I wanted to bring the baby with me, but the ship said no. He needs to be where he is.' She paused, biting her lip. Then she added hoarsely, 'But Tarman says that there is only so much he can do, that if we want him to live, we need to find a dragon that will help him. And Reyn, I killed someone tonight, a Chalcedean.' She said the words and then met his gaze, and his disbelief that she could do such a thing was mirrored in her eyes. Her forehead furrowed as she added, 'I think he was the spy that was trying to have the dragons killed and the parts sent back to Chalced for medicine. But there's another one and he's still out there. Reyn, he was going to kill me and the baby and chop us up and take our body parts back to Chalced. To try to pass our flesh off as dragon flesh. To make medicine to cure the Duke of Chalced.'

He stared at her. 'Sit down, dear. Drink your tea. None of what you just said makes any sense. But before you try to talk about it, I want to see our child.'

'Of course. Bellin is with him. I only left him for a moment, to clean myself and have something hot to eat.' She looked down at her scrubbed hands, and then up at him. 'I wouldn't abandon him. You know that.'

'I never thought you would. Darling, you are not making sense. I don't think you're all right, but before we talk about that, I'm going to see our baby. You rest and I'll be right back.'

'No, I'm coming with you. This way.' She lifted her mug from the table and walked slowly.

He followed her numbly, back out into the rain and along the side of the deckhouse, moving forward through wind and dark. Tarman was not like any other liveship that Reyn had been aboard. He had no figurehead, no mouth with which to speak. Nonetheless, Reyn could sense his presence plainly, even before he had stepped aboard the wizardwood ship. Awareness permeated the liveship. There was a dim glow from the foredeck, where a canvas shelter had been rigged. Reyn ducked under the hanging flap and saw a large woman sitting beside a hooded lantern, and a very small baby on the wooden deck beside her. He stared wordlessly.

Malta clutched his arm tightly and held him. 'I know,' she said breathlessly. 'He doesn't look as we thought he would. He's Marked, I know. Just as the midwife warned me. Just as everyone feared he would be. But he's alive, Reyn, and he's ours . . .' Her voice broke on the final words she uttered. 'You disappointed, aren't you?'

'I'm amazed.' He sank slowly to his knees and put out a shaking hand. He glanced up at her over his shoulder. 'Can I touch him? Can I pick him up?'

'Touch him,' Malta urged him, sinking down beside him. The large woman was moving out of their way, slowly and carefully. She ducked out from under the canvas shelter, leaving them alone. She hadn't spoken a word. He set his hand to his son's chest. His hand spanned it. The baby moved, turning his face toward Reyn, looking at him with deep blue eyes.

'But don't pick him up,' Malta warned him.

'I won't drop him!' He had to smile at her worry.

'That's not it,' she said quietly. 'He needs to stay close to Tarman. Tarman's helping him breathe. And helping his heart beat.'

'What?' Reyn felt as if his own breath faltered, as if his own heart paused in his chest. 'Why? What is wrong?'

Her slender hand joined his on their son's chest, closing the circle that the three now made. 'Reyn. Our son is Touched by the Rain Wilds. Heavily Touched. That is what it means, why so many women set their children away from them, before their hearts are too bonded. He fights to live. His body has been changed. He is not human and he is not Elderling. He falls between, and things are not right inside him. Or so Tarman says. He says that he can keep our baby alive, but that for him to change as he must change to survive, it will take a dragon. There is something special that a dragon can do, similar to how Tintaglia changed us. Something that will make his body work for him.'

There was a heavy tread on the deck behind him and the flap of the canvas was lifted abruptly. 'My ship speaks to you?' Leftrin demanded. He sounded affronted.

Malta looked up at him without rising. 'It was necessary,' she said. 'I did not know what my baby needed. He had to tell me.'

'Well, it might be good if someone tells me exactly what's going on onboard my own vessel!'

'And I could do that, sir.' It was the woman, Bellin, ducking under the canvas to join them. It was becoming crowded in the makeshift shelter. She seemed to sense Reyn's need to be alone with his wife and child, or perhaps she wanted her own privacy to speak with the captain. 'Let's go back to the deck-house and I'll tell you why the baby is here. Has Skelly come back?'

'I ran into her as I was trying to wake a lift-tender. Hennesey found them and sent her to let me know. He's bringing Tillamon. Reyn's sister. She was helping us search for Malta.'

'All's well then. Come. I'll put on more coffee and tell you as much as I know.'

Leftrin teetered on the edge of the decision for a moment. Perhaps the plea in Reyn's eyes decided him. 'I'll do that,' he said abruptly, and ducked out under the canvas.

The moment he left, Malta eased herself down beside her baby, curling herself around him. Without hesitation, Reyn mirrored her, so that their son was framed by the arcs of their bodies. He put his head close to Malta's, breathed the scent of her hair and the sweet knowledge that she and their child were safe with him. 'Tell me,' he requested softly. 'Tell me everything that happened after I left you.'

Day the 26th of the Change Moon
Year the 7th of the Independent Alliance of Traders

From Kim, Keeper of the Birds, Cassarick to Trader Finbok

You will be the first in all Bingtown to receive these tidings. Captain Leftrin and the liveship Tarman *have returned from their journey up the river. In a meeting at the Traders' Hall tonight, he revealed that the expedition has rediscovered Kelsingra, but he has so far refused to say much more than that. He challenges the right of the Cassarick Traders' Council to see his charts and notes, claiming that such knowledge belongs to him and to the dragon keepers who went with him. He asserts that a careful reading of the contracts will prove this is so.*

The gossip is that perhaps he has killed all the others and will claim Kelsingra as his alone. Captain Leftrin asserts that almost the entire expedition has survived and is well and in a place where the dragons are comfortably settled. Of your son's wife, he says that she chose to stay where she was. He also makes accusations against one of the hunters who travelled with him, saying he was a treacherous spy for Chalced and saying also that perhaps there is corruption in the Cassarick Traders' Council, for they were the ones to hire the man.

Do you now see the value of private birds? This information will reach you days before others know what is happening here. I trust you also see the value of having a friend among the Bird Keepers and that my payment will reflect that gratitude.

Kim

CHAPTER TWELVE

Illumination

'Who could that be at this time of night?' Carson wondered aloud as he rolled from the bed.

'And what sort of trouble?' Sedric muttered. He'd just been on the verge of falling asleep. He watched Carson drag on his trousers and then walk the short distance to the door. He pulled the blankets closer to try to make up for the warmth the big man had taken with him.

'Tats?' he heard Carson ask in consternation, and the boy's muttered response.

'Can I come in? Please?' The boy spoke his request more clearly and Carson stepped back from the door to let him enter. He shut the door behind him, and then crossed the fire and tossed a log onto it. Sparks flew up and a few flames woke.

'Well, sit down,' Carson suggested to Tats, and took his own suggestion, taking a seat on one of the benches he'd built. Tats shook rain from his hair and then took his place on the other one. 'Is something wrong? Sick dragon?' Carson asked when Tats didn't speak.

'Nothing like that,' Tats admitted in a low voice. He glanced at the fire and then away into the darkness. 'Thymara and Rapskal didn't come back from the city. They flew off on Heeby in early afternoon. He said he wanted to show her something there. I thought they'd be back before night. Everyone knows Heeby doesn't like flying in the dark. But it's been dark for hours and there's no sign of them.'

Carson was quiet for a short time, watching the tongues of flame lick up the side of the log and then begin to devour it. 'And you're worried that something bad happened?'

Tats took a deep breath and then sighed it out. 'Not exactly. My dragon, Fente, she got all excited for a bit and said that Sintara was in the water. Drowning, maybe. Fente didn't seem exactly heartbroken about it. So I went to Mercor, because he's, well, more steady. Less jealous and vindictive than my Fente. And more likely to talk straight about things. He put up his head and acted like he was listening and then said, no, as far as he could tell, she was fine. That she had been in the water and distressed but seemed fine now and he thought she was in Kelsingra. Well, we all know she can't fly, so I went looking for Sintara. She's gone.' He looked down at his hands. 'I think maybe Sintara *is* on the other side of the river. In the city. And that Rapskal, Heeby and Thymara are there, too.'

Sedric sat up, cloaking the blankets around him. The boy sounded miserable.

Carson spoke judiciously. 'I've seen tracks in the meadow first thing in the morning. At least one of the dragons has been trying to fly. Makes sense that it was Sintara, and that she finally made it over there. That might be why Thymara stayed. But with weather this nasty, maybe it was raining too hard and they decided to wait it out there. They're probably fine, Tats. If something had happened to Thymara, Rapskal would have been frantic and come back here. And if something bad had happened to Rapskal, Heeby would be trumpeting up a storm. And if Heeby and both of them were in trouble, then I think all the dragons would know. Sintara would certainly know if Thymara was injured or in danger. And despite how difficult she can be, I think she'd spread the word if we needed to worry.'

Tats looked down at his feet. 'I guess I know that,' he said softly.

'So,' the big man's voice was considering. 'Sintara made it across the river. That's quite a flight.' He turned to smile at Sedric. 'I wish I knew what had finally motivated her. I'd try it on Spit.' He turned his grin back on Tats, but got no response from him.

Silence again, save for the scatter of rain outside and the soft crackling of the awakened hearth fire. Tats shifted on his bench. 'I guess I'm not worried that they're hurt. I'm worried that they're together.' He hunched his shoulders more tightly, as if that would ward off his pain.

Sedric watched him in sudden understanding. He knew the pangs of jealousy when he saw them.

The bench creaked as Carson shifted his weight. He was in profile to Sedric and the light of the fire lit the consternation on his face. 'Well. Nothing you can do about it if they are, son. Things like that happen.'

'I know that.' Tats had locked his hands together. He trapped them between his knees, rocked slightly and then suddenly said, 'I made a mess of things with her. I thought everything was going well and then suddenly it wasn't. She was so angry that I'd slept with Jerd. And I didn't get it, because when Jerd and I were together, Thymara didn't even seem interested in me. She was just being my friend, like always. So why was she so angry about it? Well. Now I guess I understand it better.'

Carson leaned down and used a piece of kindling to poke

the log deeper into the hearth. 'It's a hard way to learn, but I think that's how most of us learn about jealousy. It seems like a stupid way for anyone to feel, until someone makes you feel it.'

'Yes,' Tats was animated now, and perhaps angry. 'And I can't stand thinking about them together, and I can't stop thinking about it. How can she do that to me? I mean, couldn't she have told me about it, warned me, or given me a chance to do better before she chose him, or, or something?'

Carson glanced over at Sedric and then back at the boy. 'Sometimes things aren't all that planned. They just happen. And, well, you're talking as if her being with him, *if* she is with him, is something that she's doing to you. Now, I'm not trying to hurt your feelings, but chances are that you didn't figure at all in her decision. When you decided to be with Jerd, did you stop to wonder what Thymara would think of it? Or Rapskal or Warken? Or anyone?'

A bemused smile twisted Tats' mouth. 'When I "decided" to be with Jerd. Hah.' Despite his misery, the memory lit his face with a smile. 'I don't remember deciding anything that night. Or thinking at all.'

'Well, perhaps for Thymara . . .'

The smile faded abruptly from his face. 'But she's a girl. Girls do think about those things. Don't they?'

An incredulous smile spread slowly across Carson's face. 'You came here tonight to ask me for advice about women?' He turned and looked pointedly at Sedric. 'Are you sure you knocked on the right door?'

Tats looked uncomfortable. 'Well, who else can I talk to? The other keepers would just make fun of me. Unless I talked to Jerd, and that would go places I don't want to go. Or Sylve, and then I just might as well talk straight to Thymara because anything I said to Sylve would get right back to her.

So I came here. You, both of you seem happy. Like you got it right. And I thought, of everyone that's here now, you seemed the best to talk to. You're older. And it can't be that different, can it? People being jealous, people being in love.' The last word came awkwardly to Tats and he didn't look at Carson as he said it.

Sedric found himself glancing away from Carson, as if he dared not read what might be on his face. For a time, the hunter didn't speak. Then he said quietly, 'Happy comes and goes, Tats. Loving someone isn't that crazy infatuation that you feel at first. That passes. Well, not passes, but it calms down, and then sometimes, when you least expect it, you get a glimpse of the person and it all comes back again, in a big rush. But even that's not what you're looking for. What you're looking for is the feeling that no matter what, being with that person is always going to be better than being without that person. Good times or bad. That having that person around makes whatever you're going through better, or at least more tolerable.'

'Yes. That's it, exactly. That's what I feel about her.'

Sedric looked up at Carson. The hunter was slowly shaking his head. 'Sorry, Tats, but I don't believe it.'

The boy shot to his feet. 'I'm not lying!'

'I know you aren't. You believe what you're saying. Now, don't get angry. I'm going to tell you the same thing I told Davvie not long ago. Don't take offence, but you just aren't old enough to know what you're talking about. You want Thymara, and I'm sure you like being around her. And I'm sure it's making you crazy tonight that she's with Rapskal instead of you. But what I see is a young man with a very limited selection of partners and a very small experience of . . .'

'You don't understand!' Tats cried and spun toward the door. He snatched it open and then paused to pull his hood up.

Carson didn't try to stop him. 'I do understand, Tats. I've

been where you stand. Some day, you'll be where I am right now, saying these same words to a youngster. And he probably won't—'

'What is that? Look! Is it a fire? Is the city on fire?' Tats had halted in the doorway, staring out and across the hillside and river and into the distance.

In two steps, Carson was at his side, peering over his shoulder. 'I don't know. I've never seen light like that. It's coming from windows, but it's so white!'

A rumbling began, so deep that Sedric more felt than heard it. He rose, clutching the blanket around his nakedness and joined them at the door. In the distance, in the night, he could see the city as he never had before. It was not a distant huddle of structures, but an irregular pattern of rectangular lights scattered over the far shore and into the distance, right up to what he surmised were the foothills. As he watched, more lights kindled, spreading downriver, and his breath caught in his throat as he suddenly realized that he was looking at a city much larger than he had imagined. It easily rivalled Bingtown for size.

'Sweet Sa!' Carson breathed, and at the moment the rumbling Sedric had felt became a full-voiced trumpeting from a dozen dragon throats.

'What is it?' he demanded of everyone and no one, and felt Relpda echo his query. His dragon had wakened to the lights and trumpeting. For a moment, he sensed only her disorientation, and then he felt her thought, both joyous and anguished. *The city awakens and welcomes us. It is time we went home.*

But we cannot get there.

Alise awakened to dragons trumpeting in the night. She put her feet over the side of the bed and winced as they hit the cold floor. She slept in the Elderling gown that Leftrin had given her, as much as to feel it as his touch as for the unfailing warmth it gave her. She hurried to the door of the hut that seemed so much larger and emptier without the captain, and opened the door to rain and darkness.

No. Not complete darkness. Stars had blossomed across the river. She stared, rubbed her eyes, and then looked again. Not stars. Not fires. Windows lit with the sort of light that could come only from Elderling magic. Something had happened over there, something had been triggered. She stared in awe and frustration. 'I should have been there when this happened. Who did this, and how?'

But she knew. Rapskal had been impulsive since she first met him, reminding her of a mischievous boy from the very start of the expedition. She knew that he had continued to visit the city in Leftrin's absence and strongly suspected that he had ignored the captain's warnings about immersing himself in the memory stone dreams. Now he had discovered something, and had done something to waken that reaction in the city. If it was like other Elderling magic she had witnessed it would last for a time and then, as abruptly as it had begun, it would fail and be gone, never to be seen again.

And here she was, on the wrong side of the river.

Tears pricked her eyes. She shook her face angrily, denying them. No time to weep. Instead, it was time to stare, to try to mark in her memory which of the distant buildings had lit and which had remained dark. It all had to be recorded. If this was as much as she could witness of this last great display of Elderling magic, then witness it she would, and make a record for any who came after her to study the ancient ruins.

'I think the first thing is to rig a better shelter for the Elderling and her child,' Hennesey suggested. He was sitting at the galley table. He glanced at the veiled woman beside him as if awaiting her confirmation. She remained silent and still.

Leftrin nodded numbly. He was exhausted but there was no time to rest now. His ears buzzed with weariness and he shook his head, trying to clear his thoughts. 'Is there any coffee left?'

'A little,' Bellin replied. She took the pot from the iron stove and brought it to the galley table. She poured more for him, and when Reyn nudged his mug to the middle of the table, she refilled his as well. Leftrin looked at the Elderling who sat across from him, so weary and so anxious. He wanted Leftrin's help. He needed him and his ship, for the sake of his child. But from the story that Reyn had told, helping him could involve him in thwarting the Chalcedean spies. And he feared he knew at least one of those spies by name. If he openly defied him, what might Arich do? Betray that not only had Leftrin made illegal use of wizardwood to supplement his ship's life, but that he had been the one to smuggle Sinad Arich up the Rain Wild River? He saw the guilt in the eyes of his crew. They'd done something wicked to protect their ship's secret. At the time, they'd accepted their captain's word that they had had no choice. When Arich had vanished from the ship when it docked, none of them had questioned him about it. But they all felt it now. Their wickedness had come right back at them. The very thing they'd done to try to protect themselves was what would damn them further. No one would excuse him on the grounds that he'd done it to protect his secret. Either of those crimes was scandalous. If both became known, he could not think of a Rain Wild faction that would not be furious with them. Alise among them. He wondered if Reyn or Tillamon felt their nervousness.

Skelly spoke hesitantly. 'Malta the Elderling didn't do anything wrong! They were going to kill her and her baby.

Why can't we just go to the Council? Shouldn't we warn them, shouldn't we tell someone so they go hunt down that other fellow?'

He gave Skelly a warning look. Time for her to be quiet. 'The Council is corrupt.' Leftrin felt the certainty of that now. Someone was turning a blind eye to Chalcedeans in Cassarick. It was not that big a town. If they were moving about as Malta had said they were, coming and going, buying supplies, one of them living in a brothel, then people knew. And someone was shielding them, either for money or because they were being threatened.

'The whole Council?' Reyn sounded horrified.

'Possibly. Maybe not. But we don't know, and if we go to the wrong person, we may be running our heads into the snare.'

'And there's no time,' Bellin observed heavily. 'If there are Chalcedeans crawling all through this town and they're not getting rid of them, they're welcome to them. The ship spoke to all of us, plainer than he ever has. He can keep that baby alive for now, but the sooner we get the child to a dragon, the better.'

Leftrin swallowed his mouthful of coffee. 'It bothers me that a newborn baby needs a dragon.' He knew how the dragons had changed their keepers, giving each a few drops of blood or a scale to eat. But that was keeper business, and perhaps the secret was not his to reveal. Still, it was easier to talk about that puzzle than dwell on what it might mean to have the Council in league with Chalcedeans. How far had the Cassarick Traders fallen? Trafficking with Chalcedeans was forbidden. He'd known that when he'd felt forced to bring Arich up the river. Trafficking in dragon parts was worse; it was the breaking of a signed contract, an offence to the very core of Trader culture. That idea spoke of changes to Rain Wild society that seemed almost impossible to consider. Easier to ponder why a baby needed a dragon to live than to wonder what could persuade a man to betray his own people for money.

Reyn was the one who attempted to answer his question. 'I don't understand it completely myself, Captain.' He sighed. 'Malta and I know that we changed, and her brother Selden changed, after exposure to the dragon Tintaglia. We've had years to think and talk about it. We think that being around dragons and the things of dragons, such as the artefacts from the Elderling cities, are what change people – even babies in the womb, if the mothers have been exposed. But with us, Tintaglia guided our changes, and intensified them. So instead of deforming or killing us, the changes gave us grace and beauty. And possibly an extended life span, though that we can't know as yet.'

He sighed again, more heavily. 'It was, we thought, a blessing. Until now. I had assumed that our baby would inherit the same benefits we had received. Malta was more worried about the changes than I was. But her fears were justified. Our baby is born Changed, and the changes are not for the better. Malta said that he was greyish and not even crying at first. She says that since she brought him to the ship, Tarman has helped him. And we know that a liveship's wood comes from a dragon's cocoon, so perhaps Tarman can adjust some of our child's Changes. But Malta says the ship has told her he cannot remedy all that is wrong with our baby. That it will take a dragon's intervention to put his Changes on a path that will at the least, let him live to be an adult and perhaps transform him into an Elderling.' Reyn stopped speaking and simply looked at Leftrin.

Earlier in the day, he had seemed to Leftrin so grand and elevated, an Elderling of old, scion of a wealthy Trader family, dressed in his fine clothes and carrying himself as a man of importance. Now he looked dazed with misfortune, and very young. Very human.

The silence held in the galley. The sense of waiting was broken when Reyn made his request. 'Please. Can you take us to Kelsingra and the dragons? As soon as possible?'

It was his decision. He was the captain of the *Tarman*, and no one else could tell him what to do. The running of a ship was never a democracy. But as he lifted his sandy eyes and looked at his crew members crowded into the galley, their thoughts were plain. If he gave the word, Bellin and Swarge would cast off the lines this instant, and Skelly would help them. Hennesey was watching him, waiting for his words, leaving the decision up to him. Big Eider stood by, waiting as he always waited for his next order. He wore a clean new shirt: he'd been to see his mother, then. Grigsby, the ship's ginger cat, floated up and settled on top of the galley table, and then walked over to bump his head confidently against the Elderling's folded hands. Reyn absently petted the cat, and Grigsby gave off his rattling purr.

'You don't want to tell the Council anything? Not about the Chalcedeans, not about what Malta had to do?'

'I'm sure they'll know soon enough, if they don't already.' Reyn's voice was grim. 'As soon as he's found dead, someone will be reporting back to the Council about it.'

'That could be enlightening to watch. See who flinches, see who knows more than he should.'

'It could be dangerous, too.' Reyn made a sound that was not a short laugh but something darker. 'And I don't really care any more. Their dirty politics don't matter to me. My son does. Malta does.'

Leftrin nodded curtly to that. 'I see your point. But we came back here for several reasons. The keepers and Alise wanted their families to know they were alive. I wanted to report that I'd fulfilled my contract. But the main reason was to get our pay and resupply the vessel. And we're still held up on that. We need that money. The merchants let me use credit today, and sent down enough to take care of my crew here. But that's a drop in the bucket of what we need. We have what amounts to a small colony up the river there, with little to nothing in the way of supplies and winter right on top of us. Things are harsh up there. Food is what we can hunt; shelter is what we can contrive. The city isn't ours yet, and even if it was, it's a stark place. If we don't get the money, if we don't stay here long enough to load with ship with what we need, chances are some of us may not make it through the winter.'

Reyn was watching him intently, his face solemn. 'Money is not a problem. Let them keep their blood money.' He dismissed that concern with a disgusted flip of his hand, and added, 'The Khuprus credit is good. I'll stock your barge with all it can hold and count it a small payment for what I'm asking. My son's life is what matters to me. I understand, I think, what we are going into. We will face harsh and dangerous conditions. But if we stay here, my son dies.' His shoulders rose and fell in a tiny shrug. 'So we go with you, if you'll take us.'

The quiet in the room was pent breath, all waiting for the captain to speak. He thought of Alise, of what she would expect of him, and how she would react when he told her the tale. Make her proud.

We share blood with this child. His mother already gave him to me. And I will take him to the dragons.

It was seldom that his ship spoke to him in such a direct fashion. He looked at the others, wondering if they had heard Tarman as clearly, but they were all watching him. Alise had once asked him if liveships had the same sort of glamour as the dragons did. He had told her they did not, but now he wondered. But only for a moment. The impulse felt so much like his own that he spoke the words aloud.

'Family is family. And blood is thicker than water, even the water of the Rain Wild River. We'll try for a departure tomorrow afternoon.' As Reyn's eyes lit with relief and joy, Leftrin cautioned him, 'A lot is going to depend on your being able to muster the credit to outfit the ship. And we'll have to take what they have here, and what can be brought here quickly from Trehaug, and be glad of it.' He shook his head, knowing there were things he could not obtain that quickly. 'Damn,' he said, more to himself than Reyn. 'I wanted to try to arrange for some stock. Animals. A few sheep, a couple of goats, some chickens.'

Reyn looked at him as if he were mad. 'What for? Fresh meat on the trip upriver?'

Leftrin shook his head, thinking of all that he hadn't shared with the Council, all the things that no one knew yet. 'To raise. To start flocks with. There's land there, Reyn Khuprus. Meadows. Deep grass on dry ground. Hills and mountains in the distance. If we can get what we need, we'll prosper.'

Reyn looked sceptical. 'You'd have to order seed and livestock from Bingtown, and chances are you wouldn't get them until spring.'

Leftrin nodded impatiently. 'I knew that. But the sooner I order them, the sooner they come. I'll make time to do it somehow. I'll send a bird off to a fellow I know there, one who knows I pay my debts. He might arrange it for me.' He was doubtful. No one wanted to traffic in live animals unless they could deliver them quickly and get away before they dropped dead.

'No.' Reyn shook his head decisively. 'You forget that my

wife's family has a liveship, too. I'll send a message to Trell and Althea. They'll get you what you want and bring it when we say you want it. You name the date, and they'll have it in Trehaug waiting for you. My word on it. Part of our passage inland.'

A slow smile crept over Leftrin's face. 'Young man, I like the way you do business. The deal's done then, and if a handshake is good enough for you, it suffices for me.'

'Of course.'

Reyn spoke as he leaned across the table to grip hands with Leftrin. 'I'll set the wheels in motion tonight. I'll wake the storekeepers and have goods moving down here when dawn breaks.'

Leftrin did not release his grip on the other man's hand. 'Not so fast. I'm thinking we don't want to call too much attention to our departure. And that maybe it would be better if there were no connections made between you and your lady and my ship. Someone's already tried to kill her and your child, and she took blood in return. We know there's one more Chalcedean in the city, maybe more and someone must be helping them. We don't want them to know or even suspect where you two are. You two stay aboard and hidden. You disappear.'

'Three.' The woman at the corner of the galley table had been sitting so quietly that Leftrin had almost forgotten she was there. She was veiled, not unusual in the Rain Wilds, but not so common in Cassarick as it was in Trehaug. Now she lifted her veil and revealed her Touched features, a signal of trust and acceptance. 'I'm going with you. My name is Tillamon Khuprus. I'm Reyn's sister.'

'Tillamon,' Leftrin acknowledged her with an abbreviated bow.

'Going with us?' Reyn was astounded. 'But . . . Tillamon, you need to think about this. Mother will be worried sick if we all disappear. I had thought I would send you back with word of all that has happened. And that perhaps you could be the one to accompany Captain Leftrin with a letter of credit from the Khuprus family, to be sure it was honoured at the . . .' His words died away slowly. She had begun shaking her head and with every phrase he uttered, the motion only become more emphatic.

'No, Reyn. I'm not going back to Trehaug. I hadn't planned to, anyway. I'd thought that I'd find more freedom here in Cassarick. But I was wrong. Not even in the Rain Wilds can I avoid the stares and the comments from strangers. I know that mother thought she was doing good when she invited the Tattooed to come here and live among us and become part of our community. But they've brought outside intolerance with them! We're told to care nothing that they were slaves, many of them criminals and all of them marked as chattel. But they feel free to mock me and stare at me and make me a stranger in my own land.'

'Not all of them are like that,' Reyn pointed out wearily.

Tillamon rounded on him. 'You know something, Reyn? I don't care. I don't care what percentage of them are good people. I don't care how many of them were unjustly enslaved, or how much anguish some of them feel over their tattooed faces. What I care about is that I had a life before they came here. And now I don't feel like I do any more. So I'm leaving. I'm going to Kelsingra, where there are no outsiders. I'll help you in any way I can tomorrow; I'll hire a small boat to make a very quick round trip to Trehaug, or I'll send messages by bird. I'll back up the family letter of credit with the merchants to see that we get what we need. I'll say I'm the one investing in a new expedition and that my contract with Captain Leftrin is confidential. However I can help, I will. But you won't leave me here in Cassarick. I'm going to Kelsingra.'

'Have things really become that bad in Trehaug?' Hennesey asked quietly.

'Not all—' Reyn began, but 'Yes!' His sister cut him off with a word. She met Hennesey's gaze squarely as if challenging him to meet her eyes. 'If you are only lightly marked, little is said. But those of us who are heavily Changed hear the comments and feel the shunning. As if we were dirty or contagious! As if we were disgusting. I can't live like that. Not any longer.' She swung her gaze to Captain Leftrin. 'You said you have a small colony up there? Well, if you want to gain new citizens for it, you will have no trouble at all populating it if you let it be known that Kelsingra will be a city where those Changed by the Rain Wilds can live in peace.'

'More than peace,' Hennesey observed. He grinned and looked directly at her. 'When you see the keepers, you'll know what I mean. Their Changes are just as far along as any Elderling's. That's what they say they are becoming. More Elderlings.' He pushed his sleeve up to reveal the extent of the scaling on his arms. 'Not just the keepers. All of us Changed more as we spent time among the dragons.'

'More Elderlings?' Reyn looked stunned.

'An Elderling colony? A place where to be Changed is normal?' Tillamon's eyes lit with hope.

Leftrin looked around the galley. Abruptly, he was exhausted. 'I'm going to bed,' he announced. 'I need my sleep. And I suggest that you all get some rest while you can. If you can't sleep,' and here he glanced at Reyn and Tillamon, 'then I suggest you get done what paperwork we might need to buy our supplies or send messages to family. Hennesey, give some thought to what you'll need to rig a better shelter on the foredeck. Skelly, show Reyn and Tillamon to the little deck cabins we made for Alise and Sedric. They're mostly empty now. They can use them for our trip upriver.' He yawned suddenly, surprising himself. His last order was for Swarge.

'Set a watch on our deck and on the dock. I don't want any visitors taking us by surprise.'

As Leftrin walked toward his cabin, he wondered what he had got himself into. And if there was even a chance of his own involvement with Arich remaining unknown.

Cold woke Alise before dawn. She got up and built up the fire and then sat close to it rather than go back to her empty bed. Empty bed. Now there was an idea. In all her years of marriage to Hest, she'd never missed him in her bed, save for that one fateful wedding night that he had largely failed to attend. But Leftrin, whom she had loved for less than a year, him she missed. His absence made her bed empty even when she was in it. She missed the warmth of his bulky body, she missed his gentle breathing. If ever she woke in the night and touched him, he always responded by awakening enough to gather her into his arms and hold her close.

And sometimes closer. She recalled that part with lust and her body responded with a pang more poignant than any hunger pain she had ever felt. She wanted that back, as soon as possible. Sex with Hest had never been good; with Leftrin, it had never been bad.

She pulled the blankets tighter around her shoulders and huddled closer to the fire. Then she gave in and rose, to go to her makeshift drying rack. Her Elderling gown was there, just as lovely as when Leftrin had first given it to her. She had washed it last night, not because it showed any dirt, but because it was something she did every week. Now as she poked her head out of the neck hole, it slid down and over her body, contouring to it and enveloping her in comfort. Very quickly it trapped the warmth of her body and returned it to her. She sighed with relief, and momentarily grumbled to herself that it did not cover her feet as well. *Ingrate*, she chided herself. She was fortunate to have such a wonderful garment. She tried not to wear it when doing heavy or dirty work. Even though it had never torn despite all she had put it through, she did not want to take risks with it.

There was smoked fish for breakfast. Again. She was so tired of it. She fantasized about toast and eggs, a bit of jam and a pot of real tea. Such simple things to long for! Leftrin would do the best he could with bringing back supplies, but there was no predicting when he would return. He had assured her that the trip downriver would go much more swiftly than the one upriver had been since the ship now knew the way to Kelsingra. But she did not discount all that Tarman might experience on his journey and refused to count the days. Every morning she wondered if this would be the day her captain returned, and every morning she resolved to busy herself and not think about the event until it happened.

Well, today that would not be a challenge! She filled a pot with water, to brew a tea made from local herbs. It was palatable, and a hot drink in the morning was welcome, but it wasn't 'tea' as she desired it. A small slab of smoked fish accompanied it. There was the benefit, she supposed, that there was no lingering over meals any more. There wasn't enough of a meal to linger over!

Breakfast finished, she splashed her face and hands, wrapped her feet and put her holey boots on, then slung her worn cloak around her shoulders before stepping outside. The night storm had blown and rained itself out. Thin sunshine sparkled on the wet grasses of the hillside. She looked over and beyond it, across the wide river to the distant city.

She could not tell, at this distance, if lights still burned in any of the windows. The coming of night would tell her that. But she suspected the phenomenon would be shortlived. The

Elderling magic seemed to have lingered for many decades, but most often it exhausted itself with a final brief display of wonder. It galled her that it had happened when she was not there to witness it personally. She had already written down her experience of what she had seen. With great regret, she had entered it completely out of chronological order, for she had had to resort to writing on the back of a sketch of an Elderling tapestry, one that she had created when she still resided in Bingtown. Faced with an extreme lack of paper for her documentation, she had recently begun to look through her earlier transcriptions to see which ones had wide margins or blank spaces at the bottom. She hated doing it but last night she had become resigned to it. She could not suspend her exploration of the city until Leftrin returned.

She already burned with impatience to return to her work. As soon as Heeby brought Rapskal back, she intended to confront him and demand a full accounting of his activities. She hoped he had done no lasting damage to the fragile remains, but in her heart, she was braced to hear of foolishness and destruction. She feared Leftrin was right. The boy was soaking himself in memories from the stone; if he kept it up, he'd soon be a dreamy-eyed shadow of himself, completely lost to this world and today. He'd lose his life in sharing the dream life of Elderlings who had lived centuries ago.

As if her dreams had summoned the dragon, she saw the scarlet dragon in flight over the river. For a moment, her anger faded and she stood transfixed by the sight. Wisps of fog wreathed and then revealed the creature. Heeby seemed to fly more strongly than ever: hunting for herself seemed to agree with her. Then, as the dragon banked and turned back to the far shore, another dot of motion in the sky caught her eye.

Alise peered, rubbed her eyes with both fists, and then

peered again. Was it a blue bird over the river? No. Her eyes were not tricking her. Something else was flying over the city. As it banked, wings wide, the distant silhouette became a blue dragon in flight, and unmistakably Sintara!

Shock at the dragon's newfound ability vied with awe at her beauty. She gleamed like sapphires set in silver in the sunlight. 'Oh, Queen of the sky, blue, blue and beyond blue,' Alise breathed.

And felt, with a tingle of pleasure, the distant dragon's acknowledgement of her heartfelt praise.

Day the 27th of the Change Moon
Year the 7th of the Independent Alliance of Traders

From Detozi, Keeper of the Birds, Trehaug to Reyall, Acting Keeper of the Birds, Bingtown

I have won the permission of the Master Keeper here to send you this pigeon with this news. Erek and I have devised a smudge that kills the red lice inside the coops. Begin with a good quantity of cedar boughs, the fresher the better, chopped into small bits. Add to that bitter wort vine; if you do not have it there, let us know, for the trees here are now heavy with it and it is no effort to send you a good supply. Bind the mixture with any oil, until a handful of it squeezed together will hold its shape. Use a good charcoal at the base and be sure there is enough to burn through the night.

The birds must be removed before the smudge fire is made in a pot and left in the coop to smoulder all night. Then the coop must be swept, and all nesting materials removed. We have been washing the walls down with lye water as well, but I think it is the smudge that did the work, for we have found such a quantity of the red lice dead on the floors of the coop in the morning, far more than we could imagine had been hiding in the cracks of the wood.

I am sure I need not tell you that all birds returned to the cleaned coop must be absolutely free of red lice or nits, or you will still have dying birds and the smudging to do all over again.

We are receiving reports of non-guild messenger birds seen flying. The pressure for us to break the quarantine has been intense, but the Master Keeper here intends to keep us caged until a full day has passed with no more dead birds. I myself would make it three days.

A small bit of news. The Tarman *has returned, but neither the Meldar son nor that runaway wife was on board. The captain claims they wished to remain in the city they found upriver. So the gossip goes, but it is not enough information to claim the reward money, I am sure! Some suspect the captain of foul play. Others froth that he will not tell them all, and make noisy plans to follow him when next he goes up river. They will need far more than good luck to succeed at that!*

Remember, the smudge must burn all night for it to work. I look forward to our birds flying again!

And tomorrow I must set aside all my concerns as a Bird Keeper and take on the worries of a bride!

Detozi

CHAPTER THIRTEEN

Second Thoughts

Thymara awoke with Rapskal's arm and one leg thrown across her body. He awakened at the same moment and tried to embrace her. 'No,' she said, not harshly, and moved apart from him. He made a wry face but let her go. Trepidation had chilled her ardour. Was it guilt for breaking her father's rules for her, or fear of pregnancy? Grey dawn had invaded the room and in its light, everything seemed to take on a different perspective. She could recall only too clearly what she had done last night; what she could not fathom was why she had done it. She remembered how she had felt, beautiful and desirable, and oddly powerful because of that. But how could that have overridden every scrap of her common sense?

The room was comfortably warm, even in her bare skin, but she didn't feel comfortable parading around naked. Her worn tunic looked less appealing than it ever had. Feeling like a spy and a thief, she made her way to the closet and selected one of the folded Elderling robes. It was silver and blue when she shook it out, shimmering between the two colours. She slipped it over her head and thrust her arms out of the sleeves. It had been made for someone larger than she was, and that was good in at least one aspect. There was plenty of room for her folded wings. She turned back the cuffs of the sleeves and then hiked up the length. Looking hopefully in the closet, she found sashes or scarves on a row of hooks. She took one and belted up the robe so that she could walk. When she rolled her shoulders the fabric adjusted easily to the bulk of her wings.

'There are shoes, too,' Rapskal reminded her.

Thymara looked over her shoulder. He was propped up on one elbow, unabashedly watching her dress. She looked away from the admiration in his eyes. A blush warmed her face. Embarrassment, or pride that he would like looking at her? She could not say. Stooping down, she found the footwear. She chose a blue pair and pulled them on over her feet, wondering if they would fit. The scaly fabric adjusted, finding her heel and taking the shape of her foot. When she smoothed them around her ankles and lower calves, they hugged her legs and stayed in place. Clothing that fit her changing body, clean warm clothing. Such a simple thing, and so miraculous.

'Choose one for me,' Rapskal suggested.

'A woman's robe?'

He shrugged his bare shoulders. 'In my time in the dream stone, I saw Elderling workers all wearing these sorts of robes. Men and women. Some of the robes were shorter, with trousers underneath. My clothes are in rags, and I really don't care who wore those robes last.'

The folded garments were stacked on the shelves. Her fingers travelled down the pile until she found one that was gold and brown. 'Try this,' she suggested as she drew it out.

'Not red?' he asked, and she shook her head.

'Very well,' he said and embarrassed her by standing up and walking toward her. She tried to pull her eyes away from his dangling genitals and could not until she heard his pleased chuckle.

'Cover yourself,' she suggested sternly, tossing the garment to him.

'You're sure that's what you want?'

'Yes,' she replied emphatically, and wondered if she spoke truth. The sight of him had stirred her to warmth. She was torn between crushing her reaction and allowing herself to indulge it. She watched him draw the gown over his head and shrug his shoulders into it. The Elderling garments were sleek and long, designed to be ankle length. The skirt of the robe was loose enough to accommodate a full stride, but the top clung nicely to his shoulders and chest. Once donned, there was nothing feminine about the garment on Rapskal. He chose a bright red sash to tie it, and green footwear. The colours rioted gloriously and she found herself smiling. It was so Rapskal of him to deck himself out so. He hastened to admire himself in the mirror, and then turned to her saying, 'It feels so good to be dressed so finely, doesn't it? If only we had something to eat right now, I'd say there wasn't a thing in the world left for me to wish for.'

The moment he mentioned being hungry, Thymara's appetite awoke with a roar. She had nothing left in her bag; she had thought they would only be in the city for an afternoon. 'Do you have any food?' she asked hopefully.

'Not a scrap!' he replied cheerfully. 'Shall we explore a bit more before we go back?' He cocked his head and his eyes went distant. 'Heeby woke up early. She's already gone to hunt. So she may kill and sleep before she comes back for us. Unless Sintara would carry us back?'

'Not a chance,' she admitted. She knew that without asking. She tried to copy what he had done, reaching out to her dragon, but felt only her presence, with no awareness of where she was or what she was doing. Well, that was Sintara. If she wanted Thymara to know anything about her, she'd tell her. For her trouble, she sensed the dragon's agreement. That was all.

Rapskal shrugged at her. 'Well, no dragon to ride, no food to eat . . . We may as well finish exploring here. Come on.' He held out a hand to her and without thinking, she took it. His hand was warm and dry in hers, the fine scales sleek under her thumb. He showed no sign of sharing her distraction at their touch. Instead, he led her out of the room and into the corridor.

The first door they tried was locked and did not yield to Rapskal's thumping and kicking at it. In a hallway of a dozen doors, they found only two others that were open. Both were similar to the one where they had slept. In one, only the large furniture items remained, as if the owner had packed possessions and left. In the other, the wardrobe held a similar supply of robes, shoes and in that room, leggings. Thymara decided it had belonged to a male Elderling, but as she helped herself to a set of leggings she found she didn't care.

The clothing was pushed helter-skelter onto the shelves, and every horizontal surface in the room was littered with small items. A handful of peculiar stones were stamped with images of flowers and trees.

Rapskal came over to glance at them, shrugged and said, 'Money is my guess. Useless. But look. He's left me a comb, and some funny little brushes. Two necklaces, wait, no, one is broken. This is just some old string, all rotted away. Empty little pots, perhaps for salve or ink or something. Whatever was in there has dried away to dust. Here's a nice little knife, but the sheath is all rotted. What are these?'

'No idea.' The objects were made of metal, hinged together, and had catches to add more links. 'A belt?'

Rapskal hefted the heavy metal items. 'Not one I'd wear! Maybe something for a dragon.'

'Maybe,' Thymara agreed dubiously. Her stomach growled loudly. 'I need food,' she observed and heard the irritability in her voice.

'Me, too. Let's take the stuff we found and walk down to the river. Maybe we can find some edible plants to chew on or a fish or something.'

'Not likely,' she replied, but had no better plan.

She felt like a thief as she used an Elderling gown for a sack and bundled the rest of their loot into it. She paused to pull on the leggings, and Rapskal chose a pair and did the same. All of the others would be glad of any new garments, and she suspected that they'd be especially pleased with items as bright and sturdy as these. Dutifully, she gathered up her worn out clothing and stuffed them in as well. All the keepers had learned not to throw anything away. Their resources were so few that any item that could be reused in any way was valued.

The dragon baths were empty of both dragons and water. The room remained warm and gently lit. It was a comfortable place. Thymara dreaded going back outside. But there was no help for it. They shouldered their burdens and walked out into the wintry day. The sky was clear and blue, the air cold on her face. The rest of her stayed warm. Light blessed them, and for a time they walked in silence. The Elderling shoes were like nothing she had ever worn. She looked down at them, wondering if she should have tried to put her old boots on over them. Her feet were warm and it was almost as if she were walking barefoot. She hoped she wouldn't ruin them.

'It's so good to have warm clothes,' Rapskal observed. Then he added pensively, 'City feels different, doesn't it? Awake.'

'It does,' she agreed and said no more because she could not precisely say what had changed. If she had not been so hungry, she would have wanted to do more exploring. But all she could think of right now was food and their best opportunity for that was along the river's edge.

'Things will be different for you now that Sintara can fly,' Rapskal offered.

She glanced at him in surprise, and then followed his gaze. Blue wings in the distance over the foothills behind the city. Her dragon. In flight and hunting. She was silent, considering it, but Rapskal was not.

'She'll be able to feed herself now, and that will get her growing, too. Heeby grew so much so fast when she could finally hunt all she wanted and eat all she wanted. And I think it was all the exercise, too. And now that they both know how to get to that hot water, well! She's not going to be the same dragon at all. And you're going to have a lot more time to do whatever you want to do.'

She tried to fit that idea into her mind. 'It won't be so different,' she suggested. 'I'll still hunt to help feed the other dragons and the keepers.'

'But Sintara's not going to need you as much,' he pointed out. She glanced at him: how could such a casual observation seem so cruel?

'Probably,' she agreed morosely. Suddenly, it seemed an opportunity lost. The dragon had needed her, and Thymara had had months in which to win her over. Instead they had quarrelled and chafed, ignored and snubbed and then insulted one another. And now Sintara had, in the space of one night, finally mastered flight and no longer needed her. They had never bonded, dragon and keeper, as some of the others had. And now they never would.

'Up! There goes Heeby. She's diving on something. So she'll kill it, eat it and probably sleep for a bit before she comes back for us.'

Thymara watched the distant red silhouette dive, looked over her shoulder for Sintara's blue wings and saw nothing. So perhaps she had already killed and was eating. And she didn't even have enough of a bond with her dragon to know.

They'd reached the riverside now. It could be a hazardous

place. In its latest incarnation, the river had swung in close to the city, eating away at the old docks. Downstream, streets and buildings were undercut and eroding into the water. There were no shallows, and Thymara was leery of standing too close to the edge, for she could not tell what was sound and what was undercut. She followed Rapskal and he led the way with comfortable familiarity. They reached a place where old pilings jutted out of the water. Here, the stone edge of the city had already collapsed into the icy water, creating a steep and rocky shore. 'Wait here,' Rapskal instructed her, and she hunkered down to watch him. He clambered down and then moved carefully from outcropping to outcropping, sometimes pausing to gather something from the water's edge into a sling of his sash. He glanced back at her once. 'See if you can find some driftwood and build a fire,' he suggested.

She rose with a groan, doubting she'd have any luck. But by the time he came skipping back to shore, she'd piled up one decent log, and an armload of twigs and branches. Rapskal had his fire-starting materials in his pouch around his neck and was only too happy to demonstrate his expertise. While he got the fire going, she poked through his catch. He'd gathered freshwater limpets and streamers of water weed and some bivalves she didn't recognize. 'Are you sure we can eat these?' she asked.

He shrugged. 'I've eaten them before. I'm still alive.'

They steamed them on the heated paving stones right beside the fire, and ate them as they opened. They were not delicious, but they were edible and that was all she required at this point. It was not a large meal, but it took the edge off her hunger. Afterwards, they sat side by side next to the fire and watched the river. The Elderling gown kept her comfortably warm and the sun sparkling on the water dazzled her eyes. Without quite meaning to, she was leaning up against

Rapskal's shoulder when he asked her, 'What are you thinking about so quietly?'

And then the words popped out of her mouth. 'What if I'm pregnant?'

He spoke confidently. 'Girls don't get pregnant the first time. Everyone knows that.'

'Girls DO get pregnant the first time, and only boys say that stupid thing about how it can't happen the first time. Besides, what about the second, third and fourth time last night?'

Despite the seriousness of her question, a smile threatened her face.

'Well.' He appeared to consider her words carefully. 'If you are pregnant, than a fifth and a sixth time would do no harm. And if you aren't, well, then you probably aren't ripe right now, and a fifth and a sixth time wouldn't get you with child.' He turned toward her, his eyes both merry and inviting.

She shook her head at him. How could he be so tempting and so annoying in the very same instant? 'You can talk like that and make jokes about it,' she told him sourly. 'You don't have to wonder if something you did in a few minutes last night will change the entire course of your life. Change your whole world.'

When had he put his arm around her? He gathered her in tenderly, tucking her head under his chin. 'No,' he said, in a voice more serious than she had ever heard him use. 'I don't have to wonder. I know that my whole world changed last night.' He pressed a kiss onto the top of her brow.

'I feel so useless.' Reyn sat down cross-legged on the deck beside Malta. Despite the darkness of his words and tone, he was smiling at her, captivated by the sight of his beautiful wife nursing his son.

She looked at him. 'At least you can move about freely.'

'It's safest for both of you if you stay here. And Leftrin doesn't want me coming and going from the boat any more than is absolutely necessary. And he wants you and the baby to remain invisible.' He'd said the words before and he didn't doubt that he'd say them again before they managed to depart. Logic did not always have a great deal of influence on Malta, especially when it did not agree with her preferences. 'The other Chalcedean may very well be looking for you. And even if he isn't, the word is out that a man was murdered in a bagnio last night. They are looking for his killer.'

'Do the reports say that he was a Chalcedean and here illegally?'

Reyn gave a small sigh. 'I've done my best to feign great lack of interest in the tidings. Instead, I've been doing all I can to help Leftrin beg, borrow and almost steal every sort of supply we can load on this ship. Tillamon insisted that we had to send a bird to my mother, to let her know what has happened so she will not worry about us. As if such tidings could make her not worry! We have begged her to do nothing until we are safely underway, but I do not know if she will listen to that advice.'

'Did you get extra messenger birds for us to take with us?'

'Oh, as if that were easy! Good messenger birds are highly prized and valuable. And the Guild is very fussy about who flies birds. I still managed to strike a bargain with the bird keeper here. He told me he cannot sell Guild birds, but he had some of his own that he said he was actually raising for meat. Evidently they grow very large and are not as swift on the wing. They looked like sad creatures to me, but he says they are just in a moult stage and will be very handsome when their new feathers grow. He sold me a few, and said no matter where we release them, they will fly back here to him. He gave me message capsules also, and the scrolls that go in them, but swore me to absolute secrecy about all of it. So. When we arrive in Kelsingra, we can at least tell my mother that we are there and she can pass the news on to Keffria and Ronica. And that, my dear, was the very best I could do about that.'

Malta nodded, then gave all her attention to their baby. He had fallen asleep at her breast. She wrapped him and set him in a little wooden biscuit box, well cushioned with a rough ship's blanket. As she covered herself, she said, 'I had packed a supply of things for him when we came here, just in case he arrived early. Can you . . .'

'Tillamon is taking care of all that. She has gone back to our rooms and will repack as much as she can into a couple of cargo boxes, and then have them carried down to the boat.'

'Why is everything taking so long? I will not know a moment's peace until we get him to a dragon that can help him.'

'He looks much better to me already. The ship is doing all he can.'

'I know.' She set her hand to the wooden deck and hoped Tarman could sense her gratitude and would not take her words amiss. 'But I can feel what he is doing and it frightens me. Reyn, he reminds our baby to breathe. He listens to his heart beating.' She reached over and set her hand on her baby's chest, as if to be certain for herself.

Reyn was silent, and then asked the question that he must. 'And if Tarman did not remind him?'

'I think he would just stop,' Malta said.

Reyn slid across the deck to gather her into his arms. 'It won't be long now,' he told her and prayed he was not lying. 'As soon as we are loaded, we'll depart. Captain Leftrin promised us this.'

He sat still, listening to the busy sounds of freight coming aboard the ship. There was a bed in the tiny box-like cabin that Leftrin had provided for him, and part of him longed to be there. But the baby needed to stay here on the foredeck where Tarman's wizardwood was thickest in order to remain in contact with the liveship. Malta, he reminded himself, had been here all night. 'Would you like to go to the cabin and sleep for a bit? I'll stay here with our son.'

She shook her head. 'Maybe once we are out on the water and I know we are on our way, maybe then I can relax. But not yet.' Then she smiled. 'Our son. How strange and wonderful it sounds to say it aloud. But he needs a name of his own, Reyn.' She looked down at the sleeping infant. 'Something strong. A tough name to carry him through.'

'Ephron,' Reyn suggested promptly.

Malta's eyes widened. 'Name him after my grandfather?'

'I always heard good things about him. And for a second name?'

'Bendir,' she suggested.

'My brother's name? My elder brother, who has spent his entire life bossing me around, sitting on me when we were children, even mocking me for falling in love with you!'

'I like Bendir,' she admitted, grinning, and for the sake of that smile, so unexpected on her weary face, he nodded. 'Ephron Bendir Khuprus. A large name for a small boy.'

'He will be Phron until he grows into it. It was what my grandfather was called as a boy.'

'Phron Khuprus, then,' Reyn said, and touched the sleeping child's pate. 'You have a big name to live up to, little one.'

Malta covered her husband's hand with her own and smiled at her son's small face. Then she gave a brief, choked laugh.

'What's funny?' Reyn demanded.

'I was remembering Selden when he was a baby. He was

the only one in the family younger than me, so he was the only baby I really knew.'

'Did you love him from the moment you saw him?'

Her smile grew wider as she shook her head. 'No. Not at all. My mother was horrified the day I carried him into the kitchen and showed her that he would fit exactly in a baking dish.'

'NO!'

'Yes. I did it. At least, so I've been told repeatedly. I don't remember it myself. I do remember when Wintrow was sent off to be a priest. Because I asked if Selden couldn't go with him.'

Reyn shook his head. 'A bit jealous, were you?'

'More than a bit,' Malta admitted. Her smile faded a bit. 'And now I would give anything to know where my little brother is. Or to at least know that he is safe.'

Reyn put his arm around her and pulled her closer. He kissed her forehead. 'Selden is tough. He's been through a lot. He was just a little boy when we watched Tintaglia hatch. Any other child would have been terrified and weeping at our dilemma. Selden just kept on trying to work out how we could get out of it. And now he's a man. He can take care of himself, dear. I have a lot of faith in Selden.'

Lantern light woke him. Selden half-opened his eyes. They were gummy and the figure before him was a blur. He pulled one hand from under the coarse blanket to rub at his eyes. They stung. He coughed abruptly, and then coughed more. He leaned as far from his bedding as he could before spitting out the mouthful of phlegm. The person watching him made a disgusted sound.

Selden spoke hoarsely. 'You don't like what you see, go away. Or treat me decently so I have a chance to get better.'

'Told you he could talk.'

'That doesn't mean he's really human,' said another voice, and Selden realized there were two of them staring at him. Young voices. He pulled his legs tighter under his bedding, and the chain around his ankle rattled on the deck as he did so. The blanket had stuck to the oozing wound on his shoulder, the one that had won him this trip aboard a ship.

'I'm human,' he asserted hoarsely. 'I'm human and I'm really sick.'

'He's a dragon man. See that scaling. So I was right and you owe me the bet.'

'Do not! He says he's human.'

'Boys!' Selden spoke sharply, trying to bring their attention back to him. 'I'm sick. I need help. Hot food or at least something hot to drink. Another blanket. A chance to get up on deck and get some—'

'I'm getting out of here,' one of the boys announced. 'We're going to be in trouble if anyone finds out we were down here talking to that thing.'

'Please, don't go!' Selden cried, but one of the boys had fled already, his bare feet pattering away into the darkness of the hold. Another coughing fit took Selden. He curled around the stabbing pain in his lungs. When it finally calmed and he wiped the tears away, he was surprised to see that one of the youngsters was still standing there. He rubbed his eyes, but the brightness of the lantern and the stickiness of the discharge made the boy's form a blur still. 'What's your name?' he asked.

The boy cocked his head, his pale hair falling in a ragged sheaf across his eyes. 'Uh . . . not telling you. You could be a demon. That's what the other fellows said. You should never tell a demon your name.'

'I'm not a demon,' Selden said wearily. 'I'm a human. Just

like you. Look. Can you help me at all? Can you at least tell me where we are, where I'm being taken?'

'You're on the *Windgirl*. And we're making for Chalced. The city Chalced what's the capital of Chalced. That's where you get off. Your new owner paid a lot for us to head straight there, no stops on the way.'

'I'm not a slave. I don't have an owner. I don't believe in slavery.'

The boy made a sceptical noise. 'But there you are, chained to a deck staple. Seems like what you believe doesn't matter much.' He paused and thought about this for a moment, perhaps considering his own plight. Then, 'Hey. Hey. If you're a human, how come you look like you do? How come you got all those scales?'

Selden pulled his blanket in closer. He'd taken the cleanest straw from the floor and scraped it into a heap before he lay down on it and put the blanket over himself. For a time, it had cushioned his aching body from the rough timbers of the deck. But it had packed down and shifted under him in his restless sleep. He could feel the cold, splintery deck below him. A blanket over him was small use when the cold planks under him sucked away the warmth of his own blood. He needed the boy's help. He spoke quietly. 'A dragon made me her friend. Her name is Tintaglia. She changed me, as you see. To make me special to her.'

'If you got a dragon for a friend, how come you got taken to be a slave? Why didn't your dragon save you?'

The boy had come a few steps closer. By his worn clothing and shaggy hair, Selden judged him to be on the lowest rung of sailorhood. Probably a street boy, taken on in the last port, to see if he could be hammered into use as a deckhand.

'The dragon sent me out. She feared she was the last of her kind, for the other dragons she had seen hatch were weak and sickly things. So I set out from Bingtown with a group of people I thought were my friends. Tintaglia asked me to travel afar and ask for news of other dragons. And for a time, that's what I did. I went to a lot of places. Things went well, and people listened to me and my tales of my dragon. But I didn't hear of any other dragons. Then my supply of money began to run low. And my friends proved to be false.'

He saw that the boy was hanging on the tale. He paused. 'Bring me something hot to drink, and I'll tell you the whole story,' he offered. Not that he wanted to remember it himself. They'd drugged him in a tavern, probably something dropped into his ale. He'd awakened in a wagon with a canvas tossed over him, his wrists bound behind his back. A few days later, he'd been put on display, as the 'Dragon Man'. How many months ago had that been? A year? More than a year? For a time, he'd tried to keep a tally of his days. He'd lost count of them during his first bout of fever and realized the uselessness of it since.

The boy shifted restlessly and glanced away into the darkness. 'I'll get a beating if anyone finds out I was down here looking at you. I bring you anything, I'll get a double beating. Besides, I couldn't even get a hot drink for myself, let alone take it out of the galley. Me and the other deck boys, we aren't allowed in the galley to eat.' The boy scratched his dirty cheek. He turned away from Selden. 'Sorry,' he added, almost as an afterthought. The lantern swung and cast stretched shadows as he walked away.

'Please,' Selden said, and then 'PLEASE!' he shouted. At his cry, the boy took flight, the lantern jogging wildly as he ran. The darkness around him deepened and then was absolute again. The boy was gone. With him went all hope. He wouldn't be back. The threat of a beating was stronger than the lure of a tale. 'I should have said I was a demon,' he muttered to himself. 'I should have threatened to curse him if he didn't bring me a blanket and hot food.'

Curses and threats. That was what worked in the world.

Nothing was going well for Leftrin. People were too curious, asking him too many questions at every turn. Merchants wanted to know why he was using the Khuprus line of credit so freely. He'd replied that they were advancing into a partnership, one he could not yet divulge. He didn't even want to say that much, but he needed it to be plausible for Reyn and his sister to have signed off on such massive purchases of supplies. Tillamon was bearing the brunt of the gossip-seekers, and coping well with it. She put her veil to its maximum use, ignoring people as she chose. The Khuprus interest in the mysterious 'expedition' had fuelled no less than three other offers of financial backing from young Traders. Leftrin had feigned great reluctance as he turned them down, saying that Tillamon had specified that their arrangement was to be both exclusive and private. He regretted that now, for it seemed to have ignited curiosity to a feverish pitch. Two Traders had come in hastily from Trehaug and urgently requested meetings with him. He had scheduled them for a date three days hence, knowing full well he planned to be gone by then.

Worse were the messages from the Council. They had begun to arrive as soon as the winter light filtered down and proclaimed day on the Rain Wild River. The first one had suggested a meeting to discuss 'unclear' language in the original contract and the 'clear and true intent' of the contract as 'revealed by its general purpose'. He knew what that meant. Given a chance, they'd reinterpret the contract to their great benefit and try to frighten him into complying. They wanted his charts of the river, and they wanted to know what he had found up there. They'd get neither from him.

As the day crept by and he continued to load the ship, more queries and demands were piling up. Why was he in such a hurry for these goods? In some cases, he'd paid double to have goods ordered by other customers diverted to his ship. It was exciting animosity as well as curiosity. His own relatives were pestering him with queries, especially his brother. Why hadn't he come to visit? Why hadn't Skelly come to spend time with her parents? She should visit her fiancé, too. She was getting close to an age at which Leftrin would have to give her up as a deckhand for a time so that she could be married, and then, after a year or so, she and her new husband would be expected to move aboard Tarman and begin to learn its routines, so that when Skelly inherited the liveship, her husband would be competent enough to help her run it. He hadn't replied to that one. A letter was no way to tell his brother that once Alise could free herself from Hest, he intended to marry her, and possibly get his own heir. Even less did he want to tell his brother and his sister-in-law that their daughter was currently very infatuated with a dragon keeper who was rapidly turning into an Elderling, and that she had spoken of her hopes that her fiancé would break off their marriage agreement when he learned that she was no longer the first heir to the ship, because then she would be free to marry Alum. When he asked her, of course.

Just thinking of that whole tangle made Leftrin's head ache. And freight was coming aboard too fast, making Hennessey and Swarge quarrelsome about the best way to stow it. When consecutive notices arrived from the Council commanding that he come to meet with them, and then one forbidding him from departing without the Council's consent as he 'may have in his possession documents and charts that are the rightful possessions of the Cassarick Traders' Council,' he once again set his teeth and dismissed the courier with no reply. When yet another letter arrived for him, this one from the Trehaug Council, asserting that he had no right to turn any documents over to the Cassarick Council until a representative from Trehaug was there to be sure that their interests would be fairly considered, he tipped the courier heavily, tossed the missive over the side, and went to Hennesey.

'Is that load there on the dock all we have coming?'

Hennesey all but snarled at being interrupted at his tasks, but pulled a rolled manifest from a leather tube at his belt and unfurled it. He ran his eyes down it quickly. 'The crates that Tillamon Khuprus sent down were just loaded, and she came aboard herself right after them. Looks to me like two merchants haven't delivered yet. No, one, here comes the shipment from Lowson now, and I'm glad to see it. Lamp oil should be in that one, and six folds of heavy canvas, not to mention spare oars.'

'What else is still to be delivered?'

'Oh, it's a mix, from Contority's River Supplies.'

'Anything we can't live without?'

Hennesey raised an eyebrow and then scanned the manifest more closely. 'Well, Bellin won't be pleased to leave anything behind. Let's see. More tea. We have some, but Bellin said we needed more. Fish hooks. More blankets. Two bows and several dozen arrows. More tobacco and coffee. No one would be happy to leave without those. And—'

'If they get here before you've finished loading the stuff from Lowson, then go ahead and take it aboard. If it isn't here, forget it. We managed this long and we'll have to manage for the rest of winter. As soon as that dock is empty of cargo, we're leaving.'

'Might be too late to do that quietly.'

Leftrin turned his head to follow Hennesey's gaze. In many ways, Cassarick was still a young and raw settlement, and their constabulary reflected that. Becoming a city guard was regarded as a temporary career, one taken up because there was no more profitable work available or because one lacked the skills or reputation to gain better employment. The guards moving unevenly down the docks reflected this. There were five of them, identifiable by their green trousers and tunics. Two looked very young and seemed excited. One of the men was a greybeard with a bouncing belly and a pike in his hand. None of them looked happy about their current assignment, or particularly familiar with the moving docks and the traffic on them.

'Get it loaded, and be ready to cast off at my word. Tarman, old friend, you be ready to help if we need it.'

Behind the guards came Trader Polsk and another council member. Polsk carried a document case. She was puffing as she hurried along. Leftrin didn't leave his deck, but moved aft as far as he could to meet the oncoming delegation. They would probably stop to look up at him and talk, buying his crew a few more precious moments to get cargo aboard. As he passed Skelly, he asked in a low voice, 'All crew and passengers aboard?'

'Except for Big Eider. But he's right on the dock there, helping to load, and can jump for the deck in an instant.'

'Good. Be ready. Warn our passengers.'

'Sir.' She pattered away down the deck.

Leftrin put a smile that he didn't feel on his face and sauntered aft, his thumbs tucked into his belt. As he had hoped, the guards skittered to a halt at the sight of him and formed up in a rough semi-circle to look up at him. He looked down at them, not speaking, his expression one of mild curiosity. When Trader Polsk hustled to join them, he transferred his gaze to her but did not speak, leaving the burden of setting the tone of this confrontation to her.

She was out of breath and her words came out without much force. 'Captain Leftrin, you have not responded to the missives that the Traders' Council has sent you.'

He raised one eyebrow in puzzlement at her charge. 'Well, no, I suppose I haven't. But I've been rather busy today, and thought I'd best make sure of my schedule before trying to arrange a meeting time with the Council. Seems like everyone is after a piece of my time.' He cocked his head and appeared to make a mental reckoning. 'Would an evening meeting six days hence work for the Council?' He leaned his forearms on the railing and looked down on them as he spoke. All reasonableness and affability.

Polsk looked down the dock to where the loading was proceeding. 'You appear to be making preparations for departure!'

He glanced in the direction of her interest. 'Just loading our supplies, Trader Polsk. Loading a ship takes time, you know; cargo has to be inventoried, and the ship has to be ballasted to adjust. It's not a thing to rush. A river man learns to make the best use of every free minute, you know. And between you and me, it's a wise captain who keeps his crew occupied at all times. Otherwise you can't know what sort of mischief they'll be getting into. Tavern brawls, public drunkenness, and whatnot. You know how sailors are.' He grinned at her conspiratorially and saw a shadow of uncertainty pass over her face. Had she been sent down here on a wild rumour? Had the Council overreacted and made her look foolish?

'Well, Captain Leftrin, perhaps it seems suspicious on our part, but we wanted to be sure that you knew our business with you was not completed. We don't want you to leave until we have received a full report of the expedition's findings from you.'

'Well, Trader Polsk, as the Council has refused to pay me

my wages, I'm certainly not regarding our business as concluded! I do hope the Council wasn't thinking they could insult me and then just send me and my crew on our way with no recompense for risking life and limb out there on the river! Fair is fair, you know, and we got a right to expect our pay! Now, I'm willing to give the Council a day or three to consider the situation, but if that evening meeting is convenient to all involved, well, I'll expect my coin to be on the table. There are two sides to every contract. The Council should be ready to fulfil its share.'

He saw her relax the set of her shoulders. This was bargaining, something every Trader understood. 'Fair is fair indeed, Captain Leftrin, and no one knows that better than the Traders' Council of Cassarick! We will be happy to discuss the settlement of your wages just as soon as you have delivered to us all that we expected from the completion of your last voyage. And I will state plainly that we expect to be allowed to view and copy your log books, as well as duplicate the river charts that you have undoubtedly created. You will remember that we hired a hunter for you, one Jess Torkef. He was to hunt meat for the expedition, but he was also to record events and keep charts for the Council. We are saddened to hear of his demise, and shocked to hear your accusations that he was a traitor, but we also know that we have the right to demand those documents and his other personal effects be turned over to us.'

Leftrin darted a sideways glance down the dock. The last of the freight was swinging aboard. Big Eider would soon follow it. 'Well, I can't say as I share your sadness at his "demise". And I wouldn't know what private arrangements you might have made with him about notes and charts, though I'll plainly say I believe he had other "private arrangements" that had more to do with slaughtering dragons for profit and maybe striking up a deal with Chalced. In any case, he's dead and gone, and the wave that went over my boat carried off everything that wasn't tied down. So, I'm afraid that even if I were obligated to satisfy his contract on his behalf, which of course I'm not, I couldn't do it. I would suggest you take a real close look at whoever recommended that man to you. Jess Torkef was a traitor, and whoever put him on board my ship did so with evil intentions.'

He heard the thud of Eider landing on the deck. Leftrin turned his head and smiled at Skelly, who had appeared at his elbow. 'Cast off,' he said in a conversational voice, and then turned back to look at the delegation on the dock. 'You might want to stand back,' he suggested affably. 'We need to reposition the barge for further loading. Won't take but a minute.'

'He's leaving!' the council member at her side hissed, and then, to the guard he shouted, 'Don't let them untie! Hold onto their mooring lines, don't let them get away.'

'Abandon the lines if you have to,' Leftrin suggested without worry. The forward lines were already snaking aboard and Swarge was at the tiller-sweep. The guardsman with the pike had stepped up to guard the aft line. Big Eider shrugged, shaking his head at the waste, and stooped down to unfasten the moorage line from Tarman's cleat. He tossed it overboard and Tarman floated free. 'To your poles!' Swarge sang out, and the crew moved as if they had one mind.

'Tarman?' Leftrin pleaded quietly, and the liveship responded with an unseen but powerful kick of his hidden hind legs. Leftrin was glad he was holding on to the railing. Big Eider gave a whoop of surprise and staggered sideways as the barge surged forward. The cries of amazement from the watching guardsmen were both satisfying and alarming. Leftrin took pride in his modified liveship's abilities, but also usually took care to keep Tarman's differences secret. Ever since the true origin of wizardwood had been acknowledged, any usage of it by humans had not only been frowned upon but forbidden by Tintaglia. That the dragons he had escorted up the river accepted Tarman was something that he had attributed to Mercor's tolerance. He never wished to have it become common knowledge. 'Enough, ship,' he suggested quietly, and though Tarman continued to paddle, he did so discreetly, only enough to make it appear that his crew was exceptionally rather than supernaturally talented.

'We've got followers, Captain,' Hennesey called to him.

Leftrin turned to see, and uttered a curse. The mate was right. Either the Council had not believed their city guard was sufficient to the task, or several small boat owners had decided that following the *Tarman* might lead them to a real prize. The way rumours spread in any Trader city, Leftrin was not surprised that lesser traders might have heard that the *Tarman* expedition had found Kelsingra but refused to disclose the location. Doubtless they thought to follow him tenaciously until he betrayed his destination. And he was just as confident that they would fail. He grinned. 'Keep your distance from them but there's no need to—'

He had not time to finish his words. Tarman took matters into his own keeping. This time it was not his feet, but a strategic lash of his hidden tail that roiled the river's surface and set the smaller boats to rocking wildly in his wake. For just an instant, his tail was visible as it moved just beneath the grey river water. Then the liveship shot forward as the smaller vessels struggled to avoid being swamped by the waves he had stirred. Some did not succeed at that and Leftrin winced in sympathy. There'd be some scalded sailors when they scrambled out of the water.

The surge of speed nearly knocked Tarman's crew off their feet. He arrowed upriver, and the cries of amazement from all witnesses made Leftrin wince. There'd be little denying it now; some would work it out all too quickly. Just as well that he and Tarman did not expect to return to any of the Rain Wild cities before late spring. Perhaps by then, rumour and speculation would have died down.

But as Tarman moved steadily against the current, the remnants of the flotilla of small boats still attempted to follow in his wake. Hennesey came to consult with him. 'Think they'll try to board us?'

Leftrin shook his head. 'It's all they can do to keep pace with us now. And when darkness falls, they'll be blinded. They'll have to tie up for the night. We won't.'

'You think Tarman can find his way up the river in the dark?'

Leftrin grinned at him. 'I have no doubt of it.'

'And so we're away on another adventure,' Malta said. Her voice shook. She cleared her throat, pretending that it had been something else, but Reyn put his arm around her.

'Perhaps we are, my dear. But this time, we are together. All three of us.'

Tillamon made a small sound as she lifted the canvas flap and angled under it to join them. 'Four, if you'll count me,' she said. She was smiling widely and there was a light in her eyes that Malta could not understand.

'You're not frightened?' she asked her sister-in-law. 'We've no idea of where we are going or how far. Captain Leftrin says there will be hardship and cold in the days to come. We're leaving our home behind for Sa knows how long. But you're smiling?'

Tillamon laughed out loud and tossed back her veil. When was the last time anyone had seen that smile? It made the row of dangling growths along her jaw line jiggle. 'Of course I'm frightened! And I've no idea what we are heading into.

But Malta, I'm alive! I'm moving out into the world, on my own. And from what Reyn told me, I'm headed toward a city and a little colony of people where I'll no longer have to wear a veil or hear muttered remarks as I pass. Leaving my home behind? Perhaps I'm leaving my mother, but I think she'll understand. And I feel as if I'm headed toward my home rather than leaving it behind.'

She settled herself on the deck beside Ephron's box-bed and smiled down on the waking baby tenderly as he stirred. 'May I hold him?' she asked eagerly.

The sun was hastening toward the hill line as Heeby carried them back across the river. The wind was pushing clouds to fill up the evening sky and the damp breeze swished past Thymara's face, but only her cheeks burned with cold. Even her feet and calves, clad in the scaly Elderling shoes, remained warm. And the fabric of her footwear seemed to help her cling more tightly to Heeby's sleek sides. She held tight to the sides of Rapskal's Elderling garment, their backpack of looted artefacts sandwiched between them. She bowed her head against the wind's rough kiss, putting her brow against Rapskal's back. She thrust her fear down and focused her eyes and her thoughts on the comforts that they were bringing to their fellows. She doubted that every keeper would find a gown or tunic or trousers to fit, but enough would benefit that their worn clothing could be shared out generously to the ones who could not find Elderling garb to cover them. Tonight, everyone would be a bit more comfortable, thanks to her and Rapskal.

As if he could read her mind, Rapskal called over his shoulder, 'You know that Alise isn't going to like this. She's going to say that we should have left everything exactly as it was, for her to record before we moved it. She may even try to make us put it all back where it was.'

'I'll talk to her,' Thymara promised him confidently. Despite the differences in their ages, she and Alise were friends. She had felt awkward around the older woman at first, but Alise's admiration for her hunting and fishing skills had won her over. Thymara was not sure how she would react to the pristine Elderling goods that they were bringing back now. She did not think Alise would agree that sharing them out to the keepers would be the best use of them. But she herself wore an Elderling garments from the ruins of Trehaug. Surely she would not be hypocritical enough to forbid the same comfort to the keepers.

'They're waiting for us!' Rapskal spoke loudly over the wind. 'Look!'

She lifted her head and peered down through squinting eyes. Yes, keepers were gathering on the riverbank, and even a few of the dragons were strolling down. Golden Mercor was already there. His head was lifted and he peered up at them. 'They must have been worried about us!' she called to Rapskal.

'Silly of them. We can take care of ourselves,' he declared grandly. She felt a rippling of unease to hear him set them apart from the others. He seemed to think that something had changed, something important. Had it? Did he take last night as some sort of declaration from her that she had chosen him? Had she?

No, she answered herself emphatically. She had mated with him, but that was all. It had been an impulsive thing she had done, not a commitment to him. Not a long term decision.

As they circled the gathered keepers and Heeby trumpeted triumphantly as she began a long glide to the ground, Thymara wondered if he understood that as clearly as she did.

Tats stared up at the circling red dragon. The rain and wind tried to blind him, but he squinted his eyes and decided he had not been deceived. Something had changed about Heeby. Her wings seemed more proportional, her flying more sure. And she glittered and gleamed even in the low light of the overcast day. As they came closer, he could discern the two riders on her back. Relief vied with jealousy. Thymara was safe, but she was with Rapskal. Then a stray ray of sunlight struck them and the riders glittered as brilliantly as the dragon they bestrode.

'What is that they're wearing?' he wondered aloud.

'Where is Sintara? Why isn't she returning with them?' Alise had joined him and the other watchers, and answered his query with one of her own.

'Sintara hunts.' This statement came from Mercor. The golden dragon and his keeper Sylve looked up at the sky. 'She has found her wings and her strength. Now that she can hunt for herself, she will not depend on Thymara so much.'

'Which means Thymara can help feed the rest of us,' blue-black Kalo commented sternly.

'You have a keeper, and your keeper is a hunter. You should have no need for extra attention.' Sestican angled himself into the group. He was not as large as Kalo, but often seemed intent on provoking the larger male. Tats broke in before Kalo could respond, 'We keepers all do the best we can to provide meat for all of you.'

'And yet, we are always hungry.' Kalo's gaze did not leave the scarlet dragon. Heeby was closer now, circling lower before landing. Her landings were always exciting. Tats suspected they were more the product of trial and error than any clear ancestral memory of how a dragon should land. And this time was no exception. She looped low, flying into the wind to slow herself. She had chosen a long strip of open riverbank and everyone well knew to stay out of her way. She opened her wings wide and leaned back. Her legs had been tucked so neatly against her body and in line with her tail; now she suddenly splayed them out. Her hind feet touched the ground, she ran a few staggering steps and then dropped down on her front feet and slid to a halt, her tail lashing for purchase. Rapskal took it all with aplomb but Thymara clutched tight to him, her face hidden on his back. The moment that they were still, she began her slide down Heeby's shoulder.

With all his heart, Tats wanted to dash forward and catch her in his arms. But he did not. He was not sure that she would have welcomed such an action.

'They're wearing Elderling garb!' The words burst from Alise in wonder mingled with horror. As Rapskal slid down to join Thymara, Tats heard cries of wonder and a scattering of laughter from the other keepers. The bright colours were ludicrous on a man; that was Tats's first scornful reaction. But then as Rapskal made a showy bow to all of them, they suddenly seemed not only appropriate to his tall and slender form, but elegant. They were clothes fit for an Elderling, as colourful as Rapskal himself had become. And had he become more scarlet since last Tats had seen him?

He transferred his gaze to Thymara and knew that his initial impression was correct. Overnight, she had changed, and it was not just the gown she wore. The bluish tone of the scaling on her face was now indigo traced with silver. She was looking around the circle of welcome, and when her gaze came to Tats, their eyes met. And he knew. She looked away from him.

There was a roaring in his ears and a minute trembling ran through him. He felt that he swayed in the wind like a tree about to crash to the earth. He knew, and yet it did not seem possible that it could be true. She had given herself to Rapskal. All the years they had known one another, the accumulated closeness of friendship and his desperate courtship of her in the last few months, it had all meant nothing to her. She had chosen Rapskal over him. He tried to veer his thoughts away from imagining their bodies tangled together. He did not want to wonder if she had kissed Rapskal first, did not want to imagine that they had been flung together in passion or worse, come together in slow and delicious delays.

Heeby moved off, ignoring the gathered keepers and the other dragons to go down to the river and drink, but Tats stood where he was, staring and numb, unmoving, as the other keepers swept forward to engulf the pair in questions.

'What happened in the city last night?'

'Was it a fire in the streets? We saw lights everywhere!'

'Where is Sintara? Can she truly fly now?'

'Why didn't Sintara return?'

'Where did you get those clothes?'

The questions rained down on them, and Rapskal and Thymara were both talking at once. He watched Thymara open a bundle she had carried between them and began to pull out tunics and gowns and trousers and shoes. No one seemed to notice that the rain was getting harder and the wind was rising. Thymara was handing out the garments as swiftly as she could shake them out, and keepers were exclaiming in excitement and joy. All was exhilaration until Alise suddenly lifted her voice and shouted, 'STOP! Stop tugging them about and handling them so roughly! Put them down, this instant!' The excited gabble died away and all eyes turned to the Bingtown woman as she abruptly advanced on the huddle of keepers. There were bright red spots of anger on her cheeks and her voice shook with fury as she asked, 'Thymara and Rapskal, what were you thinking to take things from the city? I must know exactly where you found them, and we have to measure them and . . .'

'Alise. Please.' Thymara's voice was lower pitched and

almost calm. 'I know what the city means to you. I know you want to know its every secret, and that you think we must not disturb so much as the dust on the floors until you have written about it. I understand that—'

'You can't possibly understand.' Alise's voice was strained as she controlled herself. 'You're half a child still, with no experience of the world save the forest you grew up in. If you'd lived in Bingtown, if you had seen the stream of Elderling treasures and artefacts that passed through the market, to be scattered and lost in the wide world . . . Wondrous things, treated as novelties to be enjoyed only by the very wealthy and collectors. Half the time, the people who ended up owning those things cared nothing for where they came from, only that they could astonish others with a new possession.'

Thymara stood silent against the onslaught of words. Her face remained impervious. Tats saw that rattle Alise, heard a small shaking in her voice as she spoke on in the silence.

'I've studied the Elderlings for years, working with the scattered bits that the ravagers and scavengers left for the scholars to try to interpret. Time after time, I've been frustrated with a few pages from a manuscript, a section of a long tapestry that obviously celebrated an important event, or a few tools that, if I had known where they were found, I might discover their purpose. We have a chance, and I fear it will be a very brief chance, before the hordes will descend on Kelsingra and reduce it to stripped stone and rubble. Will you start to destroy it before they even get here? Care you nothing for your heritage?'

A silence followed her words. Tats felt empty. *This is a day for things to break*, he thought to himself. *My heart. The fellowship of the folk who had come here together. We all move apart from one another today.*

Alise spoke to the keepers from a shared history, one in

which his people barely mattered. He had no Rain Wild ancestry to claim. That he was becoming as scaled as the rest of them and taking on the attributes of an Elderling body was due to the affection of his dragon. Her words reminded him that he'd come to this expedition as an outsider, the sole keeper who had not been Marked heavily by the Rain Wilds. He felt he had no right to speak, and then a new pang smote him as he wondered if that was why Thymara had chosen Rapskal over him. Was that shared background more important to her than their years of companionship?

'No one will destroy Kelsingra,' Rapskal said suddenly. He had been so silent that Tats had thought he was hiding from Alise's disapproval by pushing Thymara to the fore. But now, when he spoke, he sounded so certain that even Alise was silenced by his words. 'We won't let them,' he added. 'Because it *is* our heritage. Kelsingra is an Elderling city. Yes. But it isn't a dead thing to be studied. Leaving the city as it is now would be as big a neglect as tearing it apart to try to discover its secrets. Alise, you only have to be open to the city to know that it does not want to keep secrets from you. Everything you want to know, it is willing to tell you. It wants to share itself with you. The city is alive and waiting for us to return to it. The presence of the dragons woke it. I do not know what Sintara did that Heeby had not done before; perhaps she recalls more of the city and how it is supposed to function than my Heeby does. Perhaps she recalled for the city what it needed to know to awaken. I cannot say for sure. But the city did awaken and it waits for us.

'Let me tell you what we found there, Thymara and I. I want you to know every bit of it. Write it all down, if you will, even though there is no need. I want you all to know what we know now! And we know so much more than cold stone walls and broken tools can tell you! There is a building that was a bath house for dragons. Inside, the rooms are warm, and the beds are soft. We found clothing that seems to shape itself to our forms. Thymara and I may be hungry, but we are clean and warm right now, something I haven't been for weeks. And when our dragons soaked in the hot water, they grew again, just as they did when they found the get-warm spot in the river on the way here. This morning, when Sintara awoke, she took flight and went off to hunt. She hunts for her own meat now, as a dragon should, and she flies, as a dragon should.'

It was not only the keepers drawing close in rapt silence to hear Rapskal. The eager listening of the dragons was almost palpable.

Rapskal tried to make his voice gentler and did not completely succeed. 'Alise, instead of trying to preserve a dead city, we must think of how to get the other dragons and all the keepers over to the other side of the river. We need to be there, if we are to become full Elderlings. And we need you to be there. Once we are settled there, you may study our living city as much as you wish. But you must not try to keep from us the things that we need to become Elderlings. What you should document and record is how we came to the city and woke it and brought it back to life. That should be your task now.'

It was hard for Tats to focus on the words and take the sense of them in. It was not that the concepts were difficult; jealousy and envy roared in his ears. *He is my friend*, he reminded himself. But it did little to calm his emotions. Rapskal stood before all of them, Thymara at his side, dressed like a king and with a man's calm bearing as he unfolded the future for them all. His words were bold. It was not just how Thymara looked at him, nor how Alise plainly gave deep consideration to what he had told them. If Sa himself had put a mantle of leadership on Rapskal's shoulders, it could not be clearer. Rapskal had seen their future, and meant to guide them to it. Everything that Tats had ever hoped to possess or to be, Rapskal had and was. He had come so far, hoping to finally feel that he belonged. But the place that he had hoped to occupy had been claimed by someone else.

He felt Fente as a light touch on his thoughts. His green queen, among the smallest of the dragons, sent him consolation and her irritation with him. *While you belong to me, you belong here,* she assured him. *Stop worrying about finding a mate. You will have years of your life to do that, decades, a long time by human reckoning. What I see is that both Heeby and Sintara have reached the city and that they can now fly and hunt, while I go hungry still. How will you get me to the city, so that I can bathe and grow and fly? That should be the thought that fills your mind above all others.*

A wave of calm flowed through him. It was tinged with pleasure and excitement that his dragon deigned to speak with him. Intellectually, he knew it was glamour. Emotionally, he was glad to turn away from his aching pride and toward the purpose the dragon offered him. He did have a place in the world, and he was of value. Fente told him so. Let his human cares fall away. He had a dragon to tend.

Alise was still considering Rapskal's words. The others awaited her response. Tats stepped into that gap, lifting his voice to speak for the dragons. 'As keepers, we have an immediate task as well. We need to get the dragons to the city. That is plain. Some of our dragons are capable of short flights. Achieving flight that will let them cross the river must now be our primary task.'

Mercor snorted. It was not a loud noise, but all turned toward the golden drake. 'Keepers cannot teach a dragon to fly. Dragons must recall what we once knew. But Tats is right.

It must be our sole focus, from dawn to dusk. Some of us have been trying. Others have been content to complain and sulk. Know now that those of us who master flight will leave you behind here, without regrets. Begin today. Become dragons or die here.'

The quiet that followed his words was sombre. Of the dragons who had congregated, none spoke. When a short time had elapsed, Alise lifted her voice. 'I've made a decision about the city,' she began.

'It does not matter what you have decided.' Mercor's tone was gentle, almost kindly for a dragon. It was also relentless. 'The decision is not yours. Rapskal has almost grasped the truth of it. The city lives and it awaits us. But it is not an Elderling city. They built it, and they lived alongside us. But Kelsingra was created for dragons. As soon as we can cross, Alise, we will revive the city. You are welcome to come with us. There have always been scribes, human and Elderling, who recorded our lives and thoughts. We have always elevated our poets and singers and those who celebrated our lives. You have a place among us. And honour.'

He swung his head, studying the keepers. 'Dress as befits those who serve dragons. And go forth to the hunt today, all of you. Much meat will be needed, and giving strength to your dragon is now your primary goal. We will fly. When we cross to Kelsingra, you will all go with us, and the city will be ours again.'

Day the 2nd of the Fish Moon
Year the 7th of the Independent Alliance of Traders

From Detozi, Keeper of the Birds, Trehaug to Reyall, Acting Keeper of the Birds, Bingtown

Reyall, I am happy to once more have birds cleared to fly to you, and to tell you that all our news is good for a change. Since Erek and I have smudged our coops, we have not lost a single bird to the red lice. I have said little of how poorly Erek was initially received here by the other Keepers and the Trehaug Master of the Birds. Now I am delighted to say that all have expressed awe at his wisdom in solving this crisis and are treating him as befits his skill and knowledge of birds. I am so proud of your uncle.

For that, of course, is my other good news. Despite many worries and the mishaps that plague any occasion, Erek and I are now wed. Our ceremony was held at the highest platform in the canopy, blessed by sun and a light wind fragrant with blossom and dancing butterflies. We would both have been content to speak our promise with considerably less formality, but as your grand-parents had never expected me to wed, I think they felt a need to flaunt this wedding! And the beauty of that ceremony will be mine to keep for the rest of our lives.

And now comes the time when I must consider well what to pack up to take with me to Bingtown. And even harder, I must choose what to leave here, and bid farewell to my own birds. I caution you to have your uncle's cotes and coops in perfect condition for when we arrive! All he can speak of is seeing his birds again. I dread the veils I must don for the journey to Bingtown, and it is hard for me to think of walking veiled in his city by the sea. But, of course, being with Erek is well worth these sacrifices.

Detozi

CHAPTER FOURTEEN

Shopping

'I really don't see what you think I can do about it. Or why I should do anything at all.'

Hest spoke the words knowing the reaction it would get from his father. The man had been determined to be unpleasant to him since the day he was born. Some time in his teens, he had realized that he might as well enjoy provoking him, as Trader Finbok was going to behave like a pompous fool to him no matter how well he spoke him. And after his recent scare, it felt good to be defiant without flinching. So he said the words and then quite deliberately leaned back in his chair as if perfectly relaxed.

His father's flushed face went a darker red and his left eyelid twitched. He rattled in a breath through his red-veined nose. His features were more the product of his early years spent on the deck of a ship making trading trips to the north countries than his current fondness for dark wines. Not that he wasn't drinking today. And an excellent vintage, too. While Hest waited for him to cobble a rebuke together, he sipped from his own glass. Yes. A very nice bouquet. Was that a touch of cherry? He held it to the winter afternoon light that was streaming in the windows. A lovely colour. But the hand that held it was still bandaged, and the sight of it snatched away his pleasure in the wine. The cuts on his nose and chest had been fine and shallow; they had closed quickly and were easily concealed. But his hand was a daily reminder to him of the man who had terrorized and humiliated him. He set his teeth and then became aware his father was speaking.

'As to what you can do, you can go and fetch your wife home! As to why you should do it, for the sake of your family name. For your marriage. For the sake of getting an heir for your line. And to put an end to the gossip about all of it.'

'Gossip?' Hest lifted one sculpted eyebrow. 'Is there gossip? I've heard nothing in my circles. My friends regard Alise's abandonment of me as old news. Sad and dreary but totally unworthy of gossip. All the excitement about it was over with months ago. By the time I returned from my trading trip to Jamaillia, well, the situation had settled. She was gone. I did my best with the woman, but she ran off. With my secretary. There was a bit of drama when it was presumed they'd been drowned in that flood, but now that we've heard that they are alive and fine, well, what more was there to say? She has left me, and quite frankly, her absence is a relief. I'm glad to let her go.'

Hest corrected the fall of lace from one of his cuffs. The shirt was a new one, in the latest style from Jamaillia City. He enjoyed how the lace held its shape in a half-cup around his elegant hands even as he was privately annoyed with its scratchiness. Sometimes there was a price to pay for appearances. Rather like the price he'd had to pay to hire the ruffian who assured him he could track down and do away with the Chalcedean. The fellow he'd hired had an impeccable reputation for foul play. It had been rather exciting to meet him clandestinely in a filthy waterfront tavern. Garrod was a man a few years old than Hest, with ears so studded with tiny glittering earrings that they reminded him of abalone shells. 'One for each man finished,' he'd told Hest.

'And soon you'll add another,' Hest had replied, sliding the packet of money across the table. Garrod had nodded, his teeth white, his eyes confident. The perfect man for the job. At another time, Hest might have found him attractive in quite a different way. He smiled at the memory as he lifted his eyes to his father's furious gaze.

Trader Finbok leaned forward and set his glass down on the table at his elbow. 'Are you truly that stupid?' he demanded in disgust. 'Just "let her go"? Walk away from the biggest opportunity that fate has ever tumbled into your lap?' He rose with a grunt to pace the room.

It was a large room with good light in the winter. Hest looked forward to calling it his own one day. Of course, when he inherited it, he'd brighten it with colour and style. The curtains were the same unimaginative brown ones that had hung at the windows for the last decade. Good quality to have lasted so long, of course, but there was a great deal to be said for keeping up with the times, if one were to appear truly prosperous. And among the Bingtown Traders, to appear prosperous, even in difficult times, was the key to *being* prosperous. No one wanted to trade with a man who was down on his luck. If you bought from him, you probably got the shoddy goods that were all he afford. And Sa forbid that you try to sell to such a man; he would do nothing but whine about the cost rather than trying to negotiate honestly and sharply. Yes, new draperies were the first thing that he'd do when this room was his.

'Are you even listening?' his father barked, and then went off in a coughing fit.

'I beg your pardon, Father. The garden view distracted me. But I'm attending now. You were saying?'

'I will not repeat myself,' his father replied haughtily, and then immediately broke his word. 'If you cannot see what you are throwing away, my words will not sway you. But perhaps my actions will. So let us be plain, son and heir. If you wish to retain both those titles, go to the Rain Wilds, find your wife, discover what made her unhappy with you, and *change* it. Do it with as little public noise as possible. If you act quickly, if you can bring her home a satisfied woman, perhaps it is not too late for the family to claim our rightful share of whatever it is they've found.'

'What?' Despite himself, Hest felt a sudden shock of both astonishment and interest.

His father gave an exasperated sigh. 'Your reputation as a shrewd trader is vastly exaggerated. I've known that for years. But can you truly have overlooked the fact that, with or without your consent, Alise signed on as a member of the *Tarman* expedition? That expedition has, according to rumour, discovered riches beyond imagining far up the Rain Wild River. Not just Elderling habitations and whatever artefacts and treasure they contain, but vast tracts of arable land. So the rumours fly. All know the liveship *Tarman* and Captain Leftrin returned briefly to Cassarick. What I have heard is that he quarrelled with the Council and refused to give up his charts of the river. He accused them of putting a spy on his ship, and even insinuated that some of them were in league with Chalcedeans who were more interested in slaughtering the dragons than keeping our bargain with Tintaglia.'

'Chalcedeans.' The word was lead as it dropped from his tongue and a wave of dread engulfed him.

'Well, it was ridiculous! The notion that any Trader would conspire with Chalcedeans, let alone back out on an honourable contract! So the Council righteously refused to pay him. Nonetheless, the very next day, he outfitted his ship extensively, drawing on a credit line from the Khuprus family. I don't need to remind you that the Khuprus family controlled the lion's share of wizardwood from Trehaug for years. With that trade taken from them, Jani Khuprus has probably been looking for a new investment for her family. She's no fool. My suspicion is that they have struck a deal of their own with this Leftrin, and are making a grab for a fresh find.

'In addition, it has come to my attention that Captain Leftrin sent birds to Bingtown, to put in orders for livestock! Breeding animals. Sheep, goats and chickens. And seed grain, and other seeds. Vine stock, and two dozen young fruit trees. Put that together with certain hints dropped by crew members, and you have arable land. It's very possible they've made the most substantial discovery since Trehaug was first uncovered.'

Hest was numbed into silence. He knew his father had spies, people who were prone to reading their masters' messages, people in Trehaug and Cassarick who would send off a bird at the merest rumour of a good bargain. But this was beyond any rumour of wealth that his father had ever gambled on.

'Well. I see by your open mouth that you are finally listening to me! So let me put the rest of it together for you: Alise, as a member of that expedition, has a rightful share to what they've discovered. Because the *Tarman* expedition is claiming ownership of not just knowledge of the route, but the discovery itself. The Trehaug and Cassarick councils are disputing it, saying that as they hired the ship and hunters, whatever was discovered is theirs. The *Tarman* expedition captain and the keepers who went off with the dragons are disputing that, of course . . . Look at you, gaping like a fish! You've paid no attention to any of this, have you? All you cared was that your wife was gone and you and your bachelor friends could sprawl and drink and carouse as you pleased in her home!'

That nettled Hest. Bad enough that his father had considered that angle thoroughly and it had not even occurred to him, without the further insult of his father's mockery of his surprise. '*Her* home? It happens to be my home, and surely I am free to do as I wish there and entertain whom and how I please.'

'Certainly you've done plenty of that over the years,' his father complained. 'I know the sort of entertaining you indulge in. And I suspect that it may be why your wife prefers the company of your secretary over yours.'

Hest commanded his face to stillness. A sip of wine to gain time to recover his aplomb. *Do not allow the conversation to go in that direction. Do not confirm, do not deny, do not confront.*

'I'm not sure, truthfully, that Sedric was the object of her attention or even that he has anything to do with her absence. True, his failure to return home with or without her is decidedly odd and very unlike Sedric. But she did not "run off with him" as some imply, for I was the one who chose that he would accompany her. He was not at all pleased with the idea of a Rain Wild journey.' Another sip of wine and then he rose and strolled casually to the window. 'We've had too much rain this year. I fear the roses will suffer from the sodden ground, and the quick cycle of thaws and freezes.'

He waited until he heard his father draw breath to speak and then quickly interrupted him. 'You know that I've been back in Bingtown less than twelve days from my last trading trip. The first three days were spent disposing of the trade items I'd bought and then in catching up on my sleep and recovering from my travels. I've not had much time to do more than that. And I told you of the dreadful accident to my hand; it's been very painful and I haven't been able to tend to business as I usually do. So perhaps you should give me the full benefit of what you've heard about the so-called *Tarman* expedition. The messenger birds you sent were helpful, but one can scarcely get full information from a tiny roll of paper.'

His ruse worked, as it almost always did. Cede his father a bit of authority, stroke his vanity with the thought that he was the expert in a situation, and he immediately calmed. Hest returned to his chair and sat in it, leaning forward expectantly, hoping he would be able to sort the facts he needed from his father's tendency to over-explain. His expectation that his father would first begin by criticizing him was well-founded.

'Well, why you let Alise go off to the Rain Wilds alone, I will never understand, but that I suppose is where we must begin.'

Hest dared to interrupt. 'I could not prevent her, Father. It was in the terms of our marriage contract, that if and when she wished to do so, I'd permit her to travel to the Rain Wilds to continue her study of the Elderlings and dragons. At the time I thought it was just an eccentricity of hers, a leftover dream from her lonely life as an unwed woman. I thought she'd forget such ambitions once she was married with a household of her own to manage. And for years, she did. But when she insisted last spring that she would go, I could not refuse her. Nor could I cancel my trading trip to the Spice Islands. So I did what I thought best, and put her in the care of Sedric Meldar. He's been my right hand man for years now, and had been a childhood friend of Alise. They've always got along well. I trusted Sedric to be the sensible one of the pair. I thought she'd make the journey, discover how uncomfortable and provincial Trehaug is, and immediately come back to Bingtown. Truthfully, Father, I expected them to be home long before I returned to Bingtown.'

'If you are finished,' his father said severely when Hest paused for breath, 'I'll continue what I was trying to tell you.'

Hest hated his father's paternalism, his assumption that he was far shrewder and much wiser than his son would ever be. But in this instance, he had information that Hest had not yet acquired. *Keep silent. Nod.*

'Alise and Sedric were in Cassarick when the *Tarman* expedition was forming up. Now, as I read the contracts, for I've been able to get copies of them, the Rain Wild Traders' Councils at both Cassarick and Trehaug hired a dozen or so heavily Changed youngsters to accompany the dragons as keepers and tenders. They also hired two hunters, and chartered the barge *Tarman*, the oldest liveship that exists by the way, to accompany the expedition and provide support for them. The councils paid for the supplies that were loaded onto the ship. Keepers, hunters and the ship owner were given half their pay as an advance, with the rest to be collectible when they returned to Cassarick after settling the dragons elsewhere.' His father laughed, a brief, dismissive sound. 'I'll wager they never expected to have to pay out much of that second half!'

'How did Alise get involved? That's what I don't understand.' Hest spoke earnestly, hoping to nudge his father beyond the obvious.

'I'll get to that. What is important for us to see here is that the contract does not mention Kelsingra by name, nor is there any specific language about searching for an Elderling city. It says only that the keepers are to find a place that is safe for the dragons to settle. And that if the dragons die before they do so, the Council will regard the contract as fulfilled. Not voided, mind you. Fulfilled.'

'And that is significant because?'

Trader Finbok's eyes, always heavy-lidded, narrowed even

more as he looked at his son with disgust. 'I should think it would be obvious. If the contract stated only that the purpose of the expedition was to resettle the dragons, then the keepers and the hunters and the ship's crew have fulfilled their contract. Once the councils pay them, their mutual obligations are finished. Neither council has any claim on anything else that may have been found, such as arable land or a deserted city, or information that the expedition gathered, such as charts of the waterways.

'Now,' and his father held up a restraining hand when Hest tried to speak, 'the councils are attempting to introduce the idea that since the existence of Kelsingra was verbally discussed at the negotiation session, and that the lone dissenting vote, that of Malta Khuprus, was swayed by the arguments of one Alise Kincarron Finbok, then it was implied to all parties that the rediscovery of Kelsingra was part of the expedition's mission and therefore the councils have a claim to the captain's charts, the city, and all it holds.'

'That does seem reasonable to me,' Hest interjected.

His father glared at him. 'No, stupid. We wish the judgment to fall in the other direction. We must say that Alise was hired solely as an expert on dragons, to help in caring for them on the journey. We want it to be decided that the contract was only for the resettlement of the dragons. Because if it is decided that way, then Alise has as much a right to a share of the city and whatever it holds as any other keeper, hunter, or sailor on the ship. Now I don't know the exact number of people in the expedition, or if those youngsters will be counted as having a valid claim. But I estimate that fewer than thirty people set out on that day. Therefore, Alise might own as much as one thirtieth of Kelsingra and all it contains. AND . . .' Again the forbidding hand was raised as Hest sought to inject a question. 'AND, as Sedric was obviously in your employ at the time, paid by you and doing your bidding, it is only right that whatever interest he has in the city is actually your interest, as you were his employer at the time. Still are his employer, and therefore have the right to the fruits of all his labours while you pay his salary. Which means that the Finbok Traders may very well control two-thirtieths or one fifteenth of the wealth of an Elderling city. A substantial fortune if Kelsingra is anything like Trehaug or even Cassarick.'

Hest's mind was racing. Despite his acuity as a Trader, he'd never considered the matter in that light. He'd been too infuriated over the humiliation that Alise and Sedric had heaped on him. One fifteenth of a newly-discovered Elderling city, under his control to exploit? The thought took his breath away, even as another idea soured his belly and made his heart hammer. He obviously had a piece of information his father did not. When he'd heard that Alise had apparently abandoned him and run off with Sedric, he suspected the first part was true and that the second part was gossip. Nonetheless, he had entrusted her to Sedric's management. That his paramour 'secretary' had not shepherded his wife back home to him was both Sedric's failure and his insult to Hest.

Hest had sent a messenger bird of his own, one that announced he would not be responsible for any debts they incurred on their expedition and that he would not allow his credit to be used to advance them any funds. Did that mean he had severed Sedric as an employee? Could Sedric then claim a share of the city in his own right?

A few moments ago, he had not even considered that he might have a claim to Kelsingra. Now, to think that it might be only half as large as it could have been, due to a moment of temper on his part, made him blanch. His father would be furious with him. But only if he found out about it. If he got to Sedric first, he was sure he could bring him back to heel and restore him to his previously doting status. He had been infatuated with Hest since he was a youngster. An assurance that Hest would not turn him out was probably all that was needed to have him dangling after him again.

As for Alise . . . well, a marriage contract was, first and foremost, a contract. What she 'felt' about the situation mattered not at all. She was bound by her word and signature as a Bingtown Trader's daughter. He would hold her to it. That was all. She could come willingly, and he'd put her back in his home, with her scrolls and books and papers. Or she could fight him, and come back to find herself little better than a servant. He'd done her a great social favour by marrying her. Her family would have to be fools not to urge her to return to her proper place. And that would be the lever he could use against her: if she fought him at all, he could threaten her family's dignity and fortune. Then she would do as she was bid.

'Are you listening?' his father demanded abruptly.

'Of course I am!' Hest lied indignantly.

'Well, then, which ship and which departure date do you prefer? News of this new city has increased interest in the Rain Wilds to a fever pitch. Everyone with a cousin in Trehaug or Cassarick will be trying to book passage, to see if there is a way to make some money from this. If you want a berth on one of the ships going up the river, you'd best buy your passage today.'

'Have your man do it for me, would you? With Sedric off gallivanting, I'm afraid I've had to do all my own secretarial work—'

'Go to the docks. Book yourself a passage.' His father spoke in an adamant voice tinged with all the disgust of a man who did things for himself and found it inconceivable that his son would delegate those tasks to underlings.

Hest kept his expression bland. Once, years ago, he'd tried to explain to his father that he was a man of some importance in Bingtown, a Trader with a substantial fortune and ships of his own and that men like that did not go tramping off to arrange their own travel or choose their own ham from some merchant's smoking rack. The argument that followed had been long and tedious as his father had asserted that that was how he had risen to importance and he would not consign the detail of his life to someone else. Hest was braced for just such a lecture again when his mother made her entrance into his father's study.

His mother never just walked into a room. Sealia Finbok entered like a ship in full sail. Her luxuriant black hair was pinned up and topped with a flower arrangement that Hest privately thought more suitable to a table than a woman's head. She had always been buxom and age had only increased her abundance. She wore, as she almost always did, a garment modelled on an old-fashioned robe in their Trader's colour, a rich purple. He suspected that she thought it reminded everyone she might encounter of their status. Also it was less confining than a more modern gown would have been. The simplicity of her attire was negated by the costly fabric she had chosen for it. She advanced, arms already gaping wide to engulf him.

'My poor dear boy! How can he expect you to manage anything when your heart must be aching so! Who would have thought it of Alise? She seemed such a mouse of a woman, so content to simply stay in her own home. I am convinced that when the full tale is told, there will be much more to the story. No woman in her right mind would ever forsake you! What other man could compare to you! And Sedric has been your friend for so long; however could he betray you so? My dear, dear boy! No. Something has befallen them in that foul place, some sort of dark Rain Wild magic.'

She moved and gestured as she spoke, almost dancing as if she were still the graceful dark-haired woman that smiled sweetly from her wedding portrait on the wall behind his father's desk. His father was smiling at her, as he always did when she swept into his study, but a slight narrowing of his eyes indicated that, also as always, he did not approve of her melodramatic sympathy for Hest.

Hest did. It had always played to his favour. Three sons had died before him, carried away by the Blood Plague, leaving him to step into the role of eldest son and heir. There had always been speculation that the Blood Plague came from the Rain Wilds, either as a curse or as an infection caused by handling of Elderling artefacts. His mother believed that and had never forgiven the Rain Wilds for the deaths of her three little sons. Sealia was perfectly ready to blame it now for the collapse of her son's marriage and the defection of his 'best friend'. And he was perfectly willing to let her. He fixed her with a soulful gaze and saw her brim with sympathy. 'Would it were so, Mother.' He spoke softly. 'But I fear that someone else has claimed her heart.'

'Then claim it back!' she exhorted him, her voice rising in the challenge. 'Go to her. Show yourself side by side with him. Remind her of all you have done for her, the beautiful home, her own little study, the priceless scrolls, and the evenings you have had to spend alone while she fussed and stared at them. She owes you her loyalty. Remind her of the oaths of your marriage contract.' His mother's voice deepened and slowed as she added, 'And remind her of the costs, both social and financial, of breaking those oaths.'

His father steamed out a breath through his nostrils. 'My dear, do you not fear that Alise may in her turn remind Hest of all the weeks she has spent alone while he was off on his trading voyages? All the evenings when he has chosen to entertain his friends at places other than his home. And the lack of a babe to cherish . . .'

'How dare you place that blame on our son?' His mother sprang to his defence before Hest could say a word. 'It may well be that she is the barren one! And if she is, well, then perhaps he is the one who is doubly wronged! And if she has been faithless in the hopes of proving that the fault is in him, then let her bring the little bastard up on her own! The Finbok family is not so destitute of honour that we must put up with that sort of thing. Her running off has give Hest ample reason to set her aside if he chooses; surely such a long absence violates her marriage contract. And it isn't as if Bingtown is lacking in lovely, eligible, well-brought-up young ladies who would be delighted to have him as a spouse. Why, when we announced he would wed, all I heard from every quarter were cries of dismay! Every one of my dearest friends had a young woman in mind who they had hoped to present to Hest! If I'd only known that he had decided he was ready to settle down, I could have presented him with a dozen, no a score of eligible women! And of better houses and fortunes, I might add!'

She crossed her arms on her chest as if she had just proven something. And perhaps she had. Hest had not stopped to consider that a runaway wife might offer his mother a chance not only to saddle him with another inconvenient spouse but one that might not be as easily dominated as the missing Alise. Having rid himself of one wife, he had no desire to acquire another. In truth, he had no desire at all to regain Alise . . . unless, of course, she came with a fifteenth of an unlooted Elderling city attached.

His father looked both weary and stubborn, his mother

determined. It was a familiar stance for both of them. When, as a youngster, he'd broken or lost a toy, his father had always expected him to deal with it, while his mother's strategy had always been to replace it quickly with something more expensive or interesting. He thought of that applied to a wife and felt a wave of dread. Time to stop her, time to divert her. If his father challenged her will on this she'd never give in!

'I chose Alise,' he said heavily as his mother opened her lips to speak. 'I chose her, Mother, and I married her. I signed a contract. And perhaps my father is right. I might be wisest to first make peace with the wife I chose before shopping around for a new one. I have spent many nights away from her, in my ambition to improve our fortune. I meant it to be for her benefit, but perhaps she did not understand that and felt neglected. And while our efforts to have a child have not proven fruitful yet, well, I am not so hard-hearted a man as to blame that on her. Perhaps, as you have said, she is barren. But is she to be blamed for that? Poor thing. Perhaps she feels shame on that account, and that is what has led her to flee our home. First, I shall take Father's advice and see if I cannot win her back. Later, if that does not avail me, later, when my heart has healed, then we can think of other courses.'

His mother melted. 'Hest, Hest, you were ever the tender-hearted one.' A smile of gentle resignation claimed her face.

His father leaned back in his chair and crossed his arms on his chest. Dour amusement dominated his features. With the wisdom of years of managing his wife, he held his silence.

Sealia Finbok clasped her ringed fingers together and tilted her head at him. 'Well, even if I do not think she is worthy of this effort, I cannot deny the nobility of your intention. And I will defer my own judgment, and put all my efforts to furthering yours. Now, you wait here. I just need to change into something more appropriate for the day, and have Bates tell the stableman to harness up and be ready. We are going to the market, my dear. And not just to find gifts suitable to wooing back your wayward bride. Oh, no. We are going to deck you in such fine feathers as she has never seen. Let her see you with fresh eyes; let her see that you have made an effort to gain her attention again. She will be unable to resist you! No, no, don't roll your eyes and look at your father. In this, you must trust me, darling. I am a woman, and I know what will sway her woman's heart! And if it costs a pretty penny, then so be it. Your dear, loyal heart deserves no less than that.'

She brought her clasped hands up under her plump little chin, shook her head in merry denial of his supposed protests and then swept from the study, already calling for her serving-man Bates.

Trader Finbok heaved himself from his chair, crossed the room and shut the door firmly behind her. 'And a partial share of an unexplored Elderling city may well be worth the nuisance of putting up with a wayward woman. That I understand. But the matter of an heir, Hest, is one that we cannot ignore much longer. It pains me to bring it up yet again, but . . .'

'But until I have brought Alise back to Bingtown and into my bed again, there is absolutely no sense in our discussing it. I know of no man who could impregnate his wife at such a distance, regardless of his eagerness to do so. Not even *your* son is that well-hung.'

Hest had gauged it exactly. Despite his father's exasperation, the crude jest brought a smile to his face. Trader Finbok shook his head and let the matter drop. 'You need to hear the rest of what I've learned about the *Tarman*. The ship is a liveship, and as I've told you, one of the first ones built, if not *the* first one. Never quickened is what everyone believed, as it was built as a barge, with no figurehead. But when the *Tarman* decided to depart Cassarick without giving the councils an opportunity to challenge Leftrin's interpretation of the contract, there was an attempt to restrain the ship by force. The crew of the *Tarman* fought back, throwing a number of people into the river with no regard for their safety. Then, as the ship moved off, and smaller boats followed in hopes of tracking them back to their find, there was a strange disturbance on the river. Rumour says it was as if the barge itself had legs, or a tail, and struck out at the craft following it, causing many of them to capsize. Others followed at a distance of course. But when night fell and all was dark, the *Tarman* quenched all lanterns and continued up the river, as if the ship itself were choosing the course. Most of those who followed quickly lost sight of the barge, and by morning it was well away of them. Some gave pursuit, including one of those new vessels, but so far there is no word of any of them sighting *Tarman* again. So it seems likely to me that here we have Elderling magic at work. It's more evidence they've found something.'

'And whatever it is, one fifteenth of it belongs to me.'

'To your family, Hest. Through your wife. She is key to all this. So go book your passage. Make it part of your shopping trip with your mother. And do your best not to beggar the family this afternoon. Until you bring Alise back, the prospect of owning a share of Kelsingra is only a dream.'

'I'll give priority to booking passage to Trehaug for Redding and me.'

He was halfway to the door when his father spoke quietly but severely. 'Book passage for yourself, son. Not for Redding. When a man goes after his runaway wife, he goes alone. He doesn't take a secretary. Or assistant. Or however you are referring to Redding these days.'

Hest didn't pause. There were times when he suspected that his father knew much more than he let on. This was such a moment, but if his father only suspected, he would not give himself away. 'As you suggest,' he replied in an off-hand tone.

He left his father's study and shut the door firmly behind him. Then he paused to straighten the lace of his cuffs, thinking of a certain wine-red fabric that he had seen at the tailor's only a day ago, and wondered if he could persuade his mother that a jacket of that fine stuff might win him Alise's heart. Then the lace of the cuff snagged on his bandage, and a too-familiar welling of anger and fear engulfed him. For an instant, he literally choked on the sensation.

Glancing around, he realized he was looking for Sedric, and hissed out a breath in disgust with himself. That vicious Chalcedean had brought his former companion back to mind, just when Hest had succeeded in banishing him from his thoughts. It would have been a comfort, a great comfort, to have Sedric at his side, he thought, and then amended that to, *Sedric as he once was*. Not the Sedric who had argued and defied him, to the point of provoking his temper and making Hest send him off on that stupid voyage. The tractable and doting Sedric, the Sedric that was always at his disposal, competent, calm, clever even. Something very like a twinge of regret passed through Hest, and he very nearly blamed himself for how Sedric had changed. He had pushed him too far.

Then he shook his head and a smile of remembered pleasure twisted his mouth. Sedric had enjoyed being pushed; Hest had, perhaps, erred in how far he had pushed the man, but Sedric had been a party to it. Not Hest's fault. Everything had an end, and they had simply found theirs. Hest could have accepted it with equanimity if only the man had not run off with his wife, caused a scandal and perhaps endangered his claim to one-fifteenth of an undiscovered, unlooted Elderling city.

'Shall we go?' his mother proposed.

He turned to look at her. He had not expected her to be ready so promptly. How swiftly she had changed into more stylish dress suggested that she was extremely bored and pleased for the excuse for an outing. And a bored Mother was often a generous Mother. Clearly there would be a luncheon involved in this outing, perhaps at one of the better places in Bingtown. He would encourage her to treat herself well, and flatter her in her purchases. He knew that he could expect full reciprocation from her in that regard. He smiled. 'Yes. Let's.'

Bates had operated with his usual efficiency. The smaller family carriage with his mother's favourite team of white horses was at the front door. Hest handed her up into the upholstered interior and then followed her in. They did not have far to go, and the weather was not so terrible, but his mother enjoyed being seen descending from her carriage into the busy market. The coachman would wait for them, letting all know that Trader Finbok's wife was at the market.

As soon as the carriage was in motion, Hest cleared his throat. 'Father suggested that we first book my passage to the Rain Wilds, before we do anything else.'

She frowned. He had known that such a stop would not please her. It would take them down to the docks, and she would have a long boring wait as he exchanged pleasantries, found out which liveships were going up the Rain Wild River, and when, and then decided which to take passage on. Not all carried passengers. Most of their valuable cargo space was devoted to the goods they carried. Upriver went all the necessities of life that the Rain Wilders could not create or harvest for themselves. And that was almost everything.

Downriver came the rare and the unusual, the magical artefacts of the ancient Elderling cities that the Rain Wild Traders had been plundering for generations. The long-buried cities were difficult to mine, and dangerous, but the value of the goods that came out of them was what had created Bingtown's reputation as a town where 'if a man could imagine it, he could buy it in Bingtown'. Was Trehaug almost mined out? There had been rumours that the supply of wonders would soon come to an end. The discovery of more buried ruins at Cassarick had been heralded as a renewal of the fountain of Elderling goods, but Hest knew what few cared to talk about: Cassarick had been a much smaller city and did not seem to have withstood the ravages of time and damp as Trehaug had. Which made the theoretical discovery of Kelsingra all the more tempting.

'No. That's foolish.'

He had almost forgotten what had begun the conversation in his wandering thoughts. 'Foolish?' he asked.

'How can you book passage when you don't know when your new wardrobe will be ready? Or when you will find the perfect gifts to turn her silly head back to you? No, Hest, we will visit the Great Market first and lay all the groundwork for your renewed courtship. Later, when we know when the tailors will be finished, then you can go on your own to book your passage. That is a much more practical plan.'

'As you wish, Mother. I only hope Father agrees with you.' He sounded appropriately dubious about crossing his father.

'Oh, let me worry about that. I'll ask him if it would have been better for you to buy a ticket and then not be able to sail on that date. He rushes into things too much, your father does. He always has. And he does not listen to me at all. If he had, he would know that there are swifter ways to travel up the Rain Wild River now. There are these new boats,

Jamaillian made, and their hulls are specially treated to withstand the river's acid. And they are not big sailing ships like our liveships, but narrow river craft, shallow draught, designed to be swift when rowed against a current yet have room for cargoes and passengers. What is it they're calling them . . . impervious. Because of the hulls. Your father thinks them a bad idea; he says that our Bingtown liveships must keep a monopoly on trade on the river if Bingtown is to survive. Luckily there are other Traders who are more forward looking. And you shall be among them, when you book passage up the river on one.

'So. That's settled. Now. Here's our day. We'll do a bit of shopping, and then stop for a cup of tea. There's a new place that I've heard is marvellous. Teas from beyond the Pirate Isles! They grind their spices right at your table, and pour the boiling water right into little pots, just the right size to hold two cups of tea. Trader Morno told me all about it, and I simply must see it for myself. Then we can visit your tailor.'

'As you wish,' he complied contentedly. The prospect of being among the first to try the new transport was appealing. And he had no wish to book passage until he had conferred with his own rumour-mongers. His first question of them would be: Why had his father heard these things before he had?

Because Sedric hadn't been there to bid him pay attention, and prattle endlessly at breakfast about what he thought was most important for Hest to know. With a scowl, he banished that thought.

The Great Market of Bingtown had been built, not on a square, but on an immense circular plaza. It had changed a great deal since the Chalcedeans had made a very enthusiastic effort to invade and destroy the city all on one night. Hest liked some of the improvements. The tall, old-fashioned warehouses on the waterfront had blocked the view of the sea.

Many of those had burned in the attack, and the Council had seen fit to decree that the newer warehouses be built with a lower profile. Now the Great Market had a wonderful view of the harbour. Many of the shops and businesses that had been destroyed or damaged in the battle had rebuilt since then, and the last few years of recovering prosperity had meant that the Great Market now had a fresh new look.

Hest had been born in Bingtown. As he stepped out of the carriage and looked around the market prior to helping his mother down the steps, he reflected that in his childhood and youth, he had taken the town for granted. It was only when he was a young man and old enough to travel that foreign cities had shown him the superiority of his home.

'This way,' his mother announced decisively, and he was content to follow her through the thronged marketplace. He smiled. Bingtown was a place where the entire world came to trade, for only in Bingtown could one find the magical and wondrous artefacts of the Elderlings. Merchants who came to Bingtown to trade knew to bring their very best trading items if they wished to acquire Elderling magical items. As a result, the stocks in the stores of Bingtown were varied and rich, and the Bingtown Traders enjoyed a lifestyle that was unrivalled in the known world. That suited Hest admirably.

He enjoyed travel and the exotic pleasures that foreign cities might offer, but he had always been glad to return to Bingtown and its comforts. It was by far the most civilized city, for here trade was of the utmost importance, and a bargain was a bargain, for ever more. He was born of one of the old Trader families and expected to inherit his family's wealth and their vote on the Traders' Council. The best goods of the world made their way to his door, and he had the fortune to buy what he chose, hampered only by his father's tight-fisted ways. But his father would not live for ever. One day he would own it all, and the wealth would be at his disposal. He would inherit it all . . . as long as he provided an heir to satisfy his father's concern that there be yet another Finbok after Hest.

'Did you say something?' His mother looked over his shoulder at him. She had paused at one of the tiny market stalls that crowded the alleys between the proper shops.

'Just a slight cough.' He smiled at her and then, with an effort, kept the expression on his face. Just past her shoulder, his Chalcedean assailant mingled with the crowd. He was not looking their way; he appeared to be considering the purchase of some freshly-fried fish, but the man's profile was unmistakable. Also unmistakable was that the fellow was alive and apparently well. And he should have been neither. Hest had hired the best to deal with him, and paid him well. Annoyance at being cheated of his money was a distant second to the rising fear in his heart.

He took his mother's arm firmly. 'What about that tea shop?' he asked her, and tugged at her as he had not since he was a child. 'Please, let's visit it first, and then ramble through the stores.'

'Oh, you are such a boy, still!' She turned to smile at him, obviously delighted at his demand. 'We'll go then. Come. The tea shop I want to try is this way, right near the intersection of Prime with Rain Wild Street.'

Hest quickened his pace. He longed to look back, to see if the man had seen him and was following. But he didn't dare. That glance back might be just the motion that would call the assassin's attention to him. His smile was getting stiff. 'You know, I haven't been on Rain Wild Street in a while. Let's shop there a bit, before we have our tea.'

'Well, aren't you a weathervane today? But we can begin on Rain Wild Street, if you wish,' she agreed easily.

He wanted only to leave the Great Market and put some distance between himself and the Chalcedean. It had come to him suddenly that the warren of small and elegant shops that lined Rain Wild Street was the ideal place for them to disappear. They entered Rain Wild Street and as he let his mother slow to a saunter to consider the various shops and wares, he glanced back the way they had come. No sign of the man. Excellent. But he'd still have words for his so-called assassin. The man had promised him a quick quiet job. He'd want a bit of his money back for that failure. It was a good thing Hest himself had a keen eye and was quick thinking enough to get himself out of danger.

His nemesis evaded, he let the magical merchandise of the Rain Wild Street shops distract him. This was the street that Bingtown's fame was founded upon. Here was where one came to buy goods from the Rain Wilds: perfume gems with their eternal fragrances, wind-chimes that played endless, never-repeating, melodies, objects made of gleaming jidzin and hundreds of other magical items. Here, too, one might find the one-of-a-kind discoveries, often at one-of-a-kind prices. Containers that heated or chilled whatever was put into them. A statue that awoke as a babe every day, aged through the day and 'died' at night as an old man, only to be reborn with the dawn. Summer tapestries that smelled of flowers and brought warmth to the room when hung. Items that existed nowhere else in the world and were impossible to duplicate.

And scrolls and books, of course. He'd lost count of how many he'd had to pay for when Alise had found them here. That damned woman and her obsession with dragons and Elderlings! Look at all the trouble she had caused him. But, if she truly had made a claim on the new city, well, perhaps she would have been worth all the nuisance she had put him through.

Hest and his mother wandered the street of shops, exchanging comments on the merchandise. His mother bought a ring that changed with the phases of the moon, and a scarf that had a cool side and a warm side. Hest quailed at the prices she paid, but did nothing to dissuade her. Eventually, they found her tea shop, and enjoyed an excellent repast together. The tea was as good as she had said it would be, and Hest arranged that a supply of several varieties be delivered to his home. Refreshed, they began to shop in earnest. They visited several tailor shops and Hest allowed his mother to make all decisions about what was purchased for him. In each case, the tailor knew from past experience to wait to hear from Hest as to changed fabrics, colours and cuts. He was most particular about his clothes, and as he did not often spend much time in his mother's company, she never expected to see him wearing the clothing she had selected.

They visited a new cheese market she had heard of, and this time both of them made purchases to be sent to their homes. His mother then insisted that they go shopping for 'gifts for that fickle woman you married' and demonstrated her disdain of Alise in her choice of gaudy scarves, cheap, sparkly jewellery and hats more suited for a dowager than a woman of Alise's years. Again, Hest gave way to her in all things. He had no intention of taking the trove of trinkets with him. Alise did not deserve any gifts. He would go to the Rain Wilds, assert his rights to her, and be damned to anyone or anything that stood in his way. He had an absolutely legal claim to her. She was his wife, and he intended to assert the marriage contract that they had both signed. He'd put an end to her foolish declaration of freedom, and reclaim his right to share in whatever claim she'd made to the city. That was all there was to it.

* * *

'Don't grind your teeth, dear. It's a most unsettling noise,' his mother observed.

'I suppose I'm just a bit weary. Shall we go home, then?'

She had her carriage drop him at his own door. He went in to discover that some of his purchases had already been delivered. He sent the tea and the cheese off to the kitchens, with a message that he wished a pot of hot tea prepared for him immediately. He went to his study, composed a list of the various changes for each tailor, and called one of his servants to deliver those. Annoying to do all these small organizational tasks himself, but Redding was hopeless at them and Ched would have stood at attention, asking questions about each detail. Not like Sedric who had often known his mind before Hest knew it himself. Stupid Ched.

A tap at the door was Ched with the tray of tea and some sweet biscuits. 'And I should like to remind you, sir, that the healer will be dropping by later today to see how your hand is.'

'Fine. Leave me.'

The brief winter day was ending, and the rain that had threatened all afternoon began to fall. He poured himself a cup of the new tea and took it to the window to look out on the garden. Draggled, brown and depressing: he pulled a cord and the curtains fell. He sought his favourite chair by the fire and sipped the tea. The flavour was good, but not as excellent as it had been in the market. There was an undertone to it, a sweetness that was not altogether pleasant. He sipped more, and then shook his head. The idiot cook had spoiled it, added honey or something. He lifted the lid on the pot and smelled it: yes, there was something else there. Suddenly, he had a foul taste in the back of his throat.

He was scowling when there was yet another rap on the door.

'Enter!' he cried, and when he saw it was Ched, he ordered immediately, 'And take this back to the kitchen and let the cook know that the cost of the tea he has spoiled will be taken out of his wages. Have him brew it again, in a clean pot, and add nothing but the tea I purchased.'

'Of course, sir.' Ched bowed and set a small parcel on the edge of the desk as he took up the tray. 'This just arrived for you, and the courier said he was told it was most urgent that you open it immediately. Something about it spoiling. Oh. And here's a package from the tea vendor as well.'

Ched was already moving toward the door. Hest scowled. The new package was probably the rest of the cheese he had ordered. He should make him take it directly to the kitchen. And more tea? Had they doubled his order by mistake? His stomach gave an unhappy rumble as the door closed behind Ched.

Hest picked up the small unmarked package that Ched had said was so urgent. Far too tiny to be cheese; crumpled paper was wrapped carelessly about something small and tied with string. As he fought with the knots on the string, he glanced at the additional tea. It was wrapped nicely in a lovely blue paper and the wax seal bore the merchant's stamp. Not at all like the earlier package of tea . . .

An ear tumbled out of its wrappings. Hest gave a cry of mingled horror and disgust and stepped back from his desk. Then a terrible fascination pulled him in for a closer look. It was bare of earrings, but the multiple piercings remained. Only one man this ear could have belonged to. Reflexively, he dropped the crumpled paper in his hand. Spidery writing marred the inside of it, he saw. He forced himself to flatten it and read the missive there.

You'd best find your slave and my merchandise. Don't think your ears or your life are any safer than your hireling's were.

Did you enjoy your tea? At any time, I can kill you. Take this as a foreshadowing of what will become of you if you continue to defy me.

A terrible cramping tore at his belly and he fell to his knees, retching. The room spun. 'Poisoned,' he gasped. 'Poisoned.'

But there was no one to hear.

Day the 7th of the Fish Moon
Year the 7th of the Independent Alliance of Traders

From Erek, Trehaug to Reyall, Acting Keeper of the Birds, Bingtown

A private note to you, nephew. How strange to call you that!

The Master of the Birds here seems to have finally recognized that perhaps I know a thing or two about the care and feeding of pigeons. Yesterday, he offered to allow my Keeper rating to be transferred here to Trehaug. I am quietly thinking of accepting his offer. Although Detozi puts on a brave face about it, I know she has been dreading the move to Bingtown. And I will admit I find this birdhouse city far more charming and interesting than I expected to!

But if I accept this position here, then we must recognize that it will leave my spot on Bingtown empty. And I have the right to nominate a journeyman who should step up to care for my birds.

That would be you, of course.

Send me a private message to let me know what you think of this. If you accept the post, you would be expected to stay there in Bingtown indefinitely.

Remember, none of this is settled yet, so not a word to anyone. And think well before you let your answer fly to me.

Your uncle, Erek

CHAPTER FIFTEEN

Strange Bedfellows

'I'm here and ready to listen.' Leftrin folded his scarred hands on top of the galley's scarred table top. He tried to remember if Bellin had ever before asked to speak to him privately. He didn't think so. He tried to be calm but feared what she might tell him. Was she ill? Was Swarge ailing and trying to keep it to himself? Both were sturdy folk. The thought that one of them might be threatened alarmed him, not just for his friends but for his ship. The crew of a liveship tended to stay aboard for a lifetime. Losing any one of his crew would unsettle Tarman badly. Leftrin tried not to jump to the worst conclusion, but when Bellin quietly latched both the doors to the galley and brought mugs of coffee to the table, dread roiled in his belly.

'I've got two things to tell you,' she said without preamble. 'Neither is any of my business, and maybe one of them isn't your business, either. But what happens on Tarman's deck affects all of us, and as a member of the crew, I feel I've a right to speak out. Maybe a duty to speak out.'

Fear lurched through his bones. 'Is someone sick?' he demanded.

'Ha!' The laugh burst out of her. For an instant, she grinned and she kept her smile as she said, 'Some call it that, and as I've felt it myself, I won't disagree. Seen you catch that sickness, too, not so long ago.'

'Bellin,' he warned her and she dropped her smile.

'Captain, Hennesey is in love. With Tillamon Khuprus, a woman far, far above him. Thought you needed to know that, as captain. I don't know what Reyn Khuprus might think of his sister dallying with a common riverman. We're a tight crew here, and even in the hard times, we've all pulled together. So when trouble tries to come on board, well, I think we all need to shove him off before he sets foot on the deck.'

Leftrin stared at her, and then transferred his gaze to the black surface of his coffee. He tried to think. This was the last piece of news he'd ever expected to receive. Hennesey in love? That was bad enough. Hennesey sniffing after a woman, a passenger on his ship, was even worse. Especially a well-born woman of a house that had just financed their resupply.

He took a breath and spoke heavily. 'I'll take care of it.' It was his task and he knew it. He just wished he knew how to approach it, what tack to take. First, he'd sound Hennesey out, he supposed. If it was just his pecker leading the way, that would be one thing, something that Leftrin wouldn't hesitate to crush. But if Hennesey was losing his heart . . . He thought of how Alise had made him feel, and recalled too how sternly Sedric had spoken to him, forbidding him from loving her. It hadn't stopped him.

'There's something else to consider, Captain. She likes him back. Really likes him. I saw her sitting with Skelly on the deck late last evening. They both looked of an age in that light and when I came up to join them, they sounded of an age. Talking about boys.' Bellin shook her head and smiled fondly. Then, with a sigh she added, 'And that brings me to my second thing we got to talk about. Skelly.'

Leftrin made as if to speak but Bellin held up a hand. 'Captain, you promised to hear me out. I know she's your family. She's my family, too. It doesn't look like Swarge and me will ever get a baby of our own. That girl, she's in both our hearts. And we've been talking about her of a night, more than once, and we don't see this going anywhere good for her. We know what she hopes. She wants that Trehaug family to break her engagement now that maybe she won't be your heir. But if that happens, and she flies off to that Alum boy, well, that's not going to end good. To put it plainly, he's an Elderling now, and she isn't. He isn't going to come aboard and learn this ship and work it. He has to stay with his dragon. And she might think she could walk off Tarman's decks and be happy ashore, but she won't. For a month or two, she might. But in the long run—'

'I know,' Leftrin cut in abruptly. He lifted weary eyes. 'Do you think I haven't thought of all that, Bellin? I have. I was hoping she'd have a chance to see her fiancé when we were in Cassarick, that perhaps that spark might kindle. She's young. It may be that what she feels for Alum is just an infatuation. We'll see. But that, too, I'll take care of.'

She tipped her head and appeared to be on the cusp of saying something more. Then she gave him a curt nod. 'I know you will, Cap. You take good care of all of us, and Tarman, too. I don't envy you right now. But I know you'll do whatever has to be done. Or said.'

Bellin got up heavily, drank the last of her coffee and hung her mug on the rack. She unlatched the door to the crew quarters, and then the one to the deck, and left him there. The wind banged the door shut behind her.

Leftrin sat for a time longer, his mug cradled in his hands. He heard a woman's voice out on the deck. Tillamon. He leaned to look out of the small window and saw her smiling.

She was unveiled and her hair was free to the wind. Today there was a break in the rain and sun actually shone on the decks. 'But how do you know where it's deep enough for him and where it's too deep?' she was demanding of someone.

'Well, you just look at the river's face, and you know.' Hennesey. With a lilt in his voice that Leftrin had never heard before. 'When you've been doing this as long as I have, you can tell just by looking.'

Leftrin stepped to where he could see Hennesey's face. Yes. There were some times when you could tell the depth of something just by looking. 'Oh, Hennesey,' he said under his breath. 'Best I tell you to talk to Reyn. Better you ask permission to court now than later.'

He wondered what the Elderling would say to his first mate.

A knock sounded at the cabin door. Hest sighed and rolled over on the narrow bed. 'What is it?' he snapped.

'It's just me!' Redding replied cheerily. The door opened and he entered, walking carefully, a tea tray in his hands. He caught the door with his heel and tried to flip it shut, stumbled, and barely managed to land the tray on the small table as he caught his balance. Remaining slightly hunched, he braced his hands on the table. 'We're nearing Trehaug, and I still haven't got my sea legs,' he announced with a wan smile.

'We're on a river, man. The ship scarcely rocks at all. It's not as if we're contending with waves.' Hest rolled onto his back to stare at the low ceiling. These new ships might be impervious to the river's acid, but the shipwright had given far too little thought to passenger comfort, despite being Jamaillian. The captain had explained to him that they were intended for the swift transport of freight, but even so! It vexed him to know that the captain and the first and second mates on the *New Glory* had more luxurious accommodations than he did. Doubtless they cared not at all how he suffered. There wasn't even a common area for sharing meals or a friendly game of chance. He and Redding had been forced to take their meals in their tiny room. For entertainment, one could stroll a bit on the deck, and that was it. Much of the ship was off limits to passengers. They'd have to change that if they wished to build a brisk passenger trade in the future!

'No. I mean, yes, you're right. I'm just not accustomed to the floor moving at all.' Redding waited for a response and when Hest gave none, he smiled too brightly and said, 'Well, I suppose this will be our final meal on this part of our adventure. We should dock before nightfall. I'm quite looking forward to seeing Trehaug. I hope the weather clears a bit, and we finally get a chance to socialize. This is my first visit to the Rain Wilds, you know.'

'Don't anticipate great things and you won't be disappointed,' Hest observed sourly. He swung his long legs off the bed and stood up carefully. 'Don't expect the weather to clear. It's rained for days and I expect it will continue to rain. As for touring Trehaug – hah! Rain Wild cities are scarcely worthy of the name. There are a few buildings of substance on the big low branches and then residences that are strung about in the trees like random fruit, so there are few of the conveniences of civilization. They look down on the folk of the Six Duchies and the other northern countries, but in truth, the Rain Wilders are just as backward and provincial. The only reason to come here is to buy Elderling artefacts and magical goods. It's the only thing that keeps these cities alive.'

Hest wandered over to the small table and perched on a chair. As soon as he was seated, Redding plopped into his own chair and took up his napkin. Plainly he was famished, as he was at every meal. He licked his lips and gave an anticipatory wriggle as he eyed the covered dishes. The man wallowed in his pleasures with no pretence of disciplining his appetites. His blatant greed and venality had initially intrigued Hest after years of Sedric's careful manners and public restraint, but of late, Redding's obsequiousness and unsubtle pleas for gifts and bribes had begun to chafe. The man had absolutely no shame. As a result, he was actually more difficult to manipulate than Sedric had been. Implied threats of pain seemed to motivate him best. But even that amusement was beginning to pall. The man had proven a poor replacement for Sedric. Bringing him along had been merely a matter of realizing that there was no one else available at such short notice and knowing how much it would irritate his father when he saw Redding's passage billed to his account.

Hest poured himself some tea and lifted the lid on a dish. He shook his head. Why did they even bother to cover the food? It wasn't hot, and it was exactly the same thing they had offered him every day of his journey. A loaf of brown bread sweetened with molasses had been sliced and buttered. The other dish on the tray held slices of smoked ham, a wedge of indifferent cheese and half a dozen little sausages. He didn't uncover the third dish. It would be boiled potatoes. He was so bored with the food he could scarcely bring himself to put it on his plate, but Redding seemed to have no such problem. He served himself quickly, as if fearful that Hest would eat more than his share, and then immediately filled his mouth. Hest sipped his tea. Warm, but not hot. And useless to complain about it.

Well, they would dock in a few hours and he would find a decent lodging in Trehaug. One more day to be finished with all of this horrid mess that Sedric had left him. In Trehaug, he'd have a good meal and a proper sleep, and then finally he'd take on his unwelcome errand from the nameless Chalcedean assassin. His gut tightened whenever he thought of the man. The pain, the ignominy, the humiliation . . .

The poison had dropped Hest. Ched had not come, despite his feeble cries for help. But someone else had. The Chalcedean had entered the room as if he owned it and stood over Hest with a smile. 'I've come to watch you die,' he'd said, and pulled one of Hest's armchairs around to where he might sit in it and watch Hest squirm on the floor. After that, he had said not a word. He'd watched Hest vomit until it seemed there was not a drop of bile or even moisture left in his body. He'd witnessed Hest begging for help until he could no longer form words.

Only then had he stood and produced, from his waistcoat pocket, a tiny glass flask with a bluish liquid in the bottom. 'It's not too late,' the Chalcedean had told him. He swirled the pale liquid in the tiny flask. 'Not quite. But nearly. I could bring you back from the brink. If I thought you'd stop being stupid. Which I don't. Think hard, Bingtown Trader. What could you do, right now, that might make me think I should save you?'

Hest was curled around his belly. Fiery knives were trapped inside it and trying to slash their way out. He had soiled himself and ruined the rug; he stank and he was dying and it hurt. He could think of nothing he could do, though he would have been willing to do anything to stop the pain he was enduring.

The Chalcedean nudged him with his boot. 'I know you, Trader. Such a fine fellow, such a fancy fellow. I know the people you visit, and I know how you amuse yourself. I do not understand why you find it amusing, but that doesn't really matter, does it? You like to think yourself the master, don't you?' He'd stooped down then, seized the hair on top of Hest's head and twisted it to force Hest to look up at him. 'It arouses you, doesn't it?' the Chalcedean had asked him knowingly. 'To think you are in charge. To make others grovel before you take your pleasure from them. But now I am showing you an important thing, aren't I?'

The Chalcedean had crouched down even lower to put his face close to Hest's. He was smiling as he whispered, 'You aren't the master. You pretend. The people that you play with, they are pretending, too, my little friend. They, like me, know that you are not really the master. I am the master. You are just a dog, like them. A shit-sniffing, boot-licking dog.'

He had released his grip on Hest's hair, let his head thump back onto the soiled rug, then had walked three paces away and suggested softly, 'Why don't you show me that you know what you are, Trader Hest?'

Hest hated recalling what came after that. Despite the stabbing pain in his belly, despite his shrieking pride, he had wanted to live. He had dragged himself through his own vomit to where the assassin stood, smiling slightly. He had licked the man's boot. Not once or twice, but like a dog, lapping at it over and over until the Chalcedean had stepped away. He had pulled an embroidered cloth from Hest's lamp stand and used it to wipe Hest's spittle from his boot before tossing it disdainfully aside.

'You may live,' he pronounced at last, and threw the little vial to Hest. But as it fell, the stopper came free. The precious liquid spattered out as the vial struck the rug and rolled away. With feeble twitching hands, Hest had grasped at it, spilling still more, so that when he finally held it to his parched lips, only drops remained. He sucked at them, and when the Chalcedean laughed aloud, he knew he had been cheated. But he would not be cheated, he would not die! He scrabbled onto his belly, he sucked at the drops that had fallen to the rug while the Chalcedean laughed even louder. He tasted dirt and the fibre of the carpet and only the barest trace of moisture. He had rolled away from it, feeling grit and filth on his lips. Tears had begun in his eyes.

As they slid down his cheeks, the Chalcedean had spoken. 'Water. Water with a touch of dye in it. That's all my "antidote" was. You aren't dying. You never were dying. You will suffer for a few more hours. You will feel ill for a day after that, but you will go out anyway, to book your passage to Trehaug on a ship called *New Glory*. It's not a liveship; it's a new sort of ship, out of Jamaillia. That is the one you will choose. You will hear from me one more time before you depart. There will be messages for you to deliver. And when I return you will remember that you are not only stupid, but my dog, and that I am your master.'

He'd walked over to Hest and set his boot on his belly. The pressure was an agony, and Hest had nodded numbly. Helpless fury had seethed inside him, but he had nodded.

And he had obeyed.

The nasty trophies in the pretty boxes were well wrapped in Redding's luggage. Hest didn't want to take the chance of any smell permeating his clothes. Redding had no idea of the contents.

The Chalcedean had kept his word. In the dark of night, he had materialized in Hest's bedchamber and forced him to kneel while memorizing a list of contact names in Trehaug and Cassarick. When Hest had attempted to write the information down, the Chalcedean had threatened to carve the names into his thighs so he could consult them there without risk of dropping an incriminating list. Hest had chosen to memorize the names.

When he had tried to ask questions, to discover more of his task, the Chalcedean had slapped him. Hard. 'A dog does not need to know his master's mind. He sits. He fetches. He brings to his master's feet the bloody, dead game. And that is as much as he needs to know. He will be told what he is to do when he is to do it.'

The lack of knowledge ate at Hest like a canker. Who were the men he must contact and what would they demand of him in return? Only one name was familiar. Begasti Cored. Sedric's Chalcedean trader. He clung to that bit of knowledge with every speck of anger in his heart. The Chalcedean trader would lead him to Sedric.

He looked forward to that. He looked forward to humiliating Sedric as he had been humbled, to threatening him as he had been threatened. Whenever he thought of it, his heart beat faster and the muscles in his belly tightened. There was, he decided, only one way to purge himself of the terror and humiliation that the Chalcedean had forced on him.

He would pass them on to Sedric.

Hest had no doubt that once he found Sedric, he would discover Alise as well. With or without dragon parts, he intended to herd them both back to Bingtown, reinstall Alise as his lawful and dutiful wife and then formalize his family claim to a substantial percentage of the newly found Elderling city. It was the only part of his mission that he actually anticipated with pleasure.

Bringing Alise home was the only mission that Redding knew about; Hest had not confided to him that once Sedric had been made tractable, he would probably displace Redding. Several times on the journey up the river, Hest had toyed with the idea of abandoning Redding to his own devices in Trehaug or Cassarick. It would give him a great deal of satisfaction to leave the greedy little man penniless in a strange city, and make for a wonderful tale for his inner circle when he returned to Bingtown. Unlike Sedric, Redding had not found much favour with Hest's intimates. They'd be glad to see him gone. As would Hest. Except for a few small things. As Hest watched him patting his pursed lips with his napkin, he felt a minor stirring of interest. Sedric was classically handsome, but Redding was far more imaginative in some ways.

The little man became aware of Hest's gaze. A smile bowed his lips and he licked them thoughtfully. 'Before *that*,' he said coyly, 'I've something else that may interest you. Something I learned on the deck.'

Hest leaned forward on the table, intrigued. 'On the deck? Redding, have you found a new playmate for us?'

Redding chortled. 'My dear fellow, restrain yourself. I'm speaking of gossip, not a new bed-game! I went out on the deck to get a bit of air, and there were two fellows out there already, chatting and smoking. I hadn't seen either one of them before, so I held back a bit, and yes, I eavesdropped a bit. One of them was speaking of his cousin in Chalced. He was saying that his cousin had seen two dragons in the sky. A large blue one and an even larger black one. And I thought to myself, this is most likely Tintaglia and her mate.' He paused and wriggled his eyebrows at Hest, waiting to hear how clever he was.

Hest had no time for such niceties. 'Over Chalced?'

'So I would assume,' Redding replied merrily. 'So I thought to myself, if Tintaglia returns to Trehaug and asks what has become of the hatched dragons, well! That could lead to some very interesting times for the Rain Wilders, couldn't it?'

'Indeed.'

What *would* it mean? The fury of a dragon unleashed on a tree-top city? Perhaps. While he was *in* the city? Hest's focus changed suddenly. He had seen the aftermath of a dragon's fury, had seen stone furrowed from the acid spray of venom, seen men's bodies reduced to liquefied flesh inside pitted armour. At that time, Tintaglia had been incensed with the Chalcedean fleet and invaders. But if she turned on Trehaug, there was nowhere to flee, no structure sturdy enough to provide shelter.

'Redding. How long ago with Tintaglia seen? And in which direction was she flying?'

And might the Duke of Chalced find a way to get his dragon parts closer to home?

'Oh, well!' Redding shook his head in mock-dismay. 'So much you want me to glean from an overheard sentence or two. I tried to get a bit more out of them. I bid them good-day and said, "I couldn't help but overhear that your cousin had seen a dragon." And before I could ask anything more, they turned and went back into their cabin. So rude! But I think we've little to fear. Think how long it would take for the news to travel to reach this fellow; much slower than a dragon could fly. So, I'm sure if she were coming directly here, she'd be here by now. If she's coming at all.'

'All the speculation I'd heard was that she was dead. It's been so long since either dragon was seen, and she seemed to have simply abandoned the younger dragons.'

'So the rumours of her death were wrong, weren't they?' Redding speared one of the little sausages. 'At least, if this fellow's cousin was telling the truth. Dear Hest, it was only a snippet of gossip. Don't let it trouble you when there are other, more urgent matters to consider.' Redding smiled at him and with the tip of his tongue licked the sausage suggestively.

'How many more days to Kelsingra?'

Reyn's question was urgent. But it had been urgent the first time he had asked it, and every time since, and Leftrin was becoming weary of trying to answer it. He forced himself to keep his voice reasonable. 'I can't give you a specific answer. I've told you that. We're travelling against the current now. It's hard work, especially with all the rain we've had. It swells the river, puts more debris in the water and makes it harder for us to stay to the shallows where the current is calmer.'

'But Tarman . . .' Reyn began stubbornly.

Leftrin cut him off. 'Is a liveship. With some special abilities. That doesn't mean that travelling upriver in winter is effortless, or that we can push on day and night. When the rains are relentless and the water rises, it's harder for us to move upriver. So I can't tell you when we're going to get there.'

'And the boats that are following us?'

Leftrin gave a small shrug. 'Nothing I can do about them, friend. The river doesn't belong to me. All river-men are free to go where they will.'

'But if they follow us to Kelsingra?'

'Then they do. What would you have me do, Reyn? Attack them?'

'No! But we can travel by night and they cannot. Cannot we outdistance them that way?'

'Tarman is strong but even he must rest sometimes.' Leftrin spoke plainly now, more plainly than he liked. 'Someone is paying those men well to track us. They were upriver and waiting. I suspect that when we were first sighted coming back down the river, someone let a bird fly. Those little boats were lying in wait for us, and even though it's hazardous for them to travel by night, they can, especially for the kind of money they are being offered. All we can hope is that they weary before we reach Kelsingra. But even if they lose sight of us, there will remain signs that some could follow. Every time we tie up for the night, we leave traces of our presence, and on our first passage when we had the dragons with us, we left lots of evidence of where we stopped. Most of it was obscured by the flood. But not all. If they are as desperate to find us as we are to get your son to the dragons, then follow us they will. Unless you think we have time to play games with them, lead them astray or whatever.'

'No.' Reyn answered quickly as Leftrin had known he would. 'We have no time for delays. But after what Malta told us, I fear for what their intentions are. Someone was willing to kill her and our baby just to pass their flesh off as dragon meat. If they are that desperate, who knows what else they are capable of doing?' He looked back at the small boats. 'We may not have the time or the inclination to attack them. But that may be their purpose in following us.'

'Well.' Leftrin walked to the railing and looked back the way they had come. An arm's length away from him, Swarge was on the tiller, studiously ignoring his captain's conversation as he guided Tarman with slow sweeps. Past Swarge, Leftrin glimpsed three small boats, all keeping a distance from the Tarman and each other as they rounded the last bend of the river. The men in them were paddling diligently. Leftrin felt a bit sorry for them. Their vessels were little more than open boats, vulnerable to the elements, offering no comfort or safety for the men who manned them. They could move more swiftly than his ponderous barge, and even when Tarman had pressed on all night, the spy boats had caught up with them before noon of the next day.

'They handle their craft like experienced river-men. Maybe they don't have anything to do with Chalcedeans and slaughtering dragons for meat and blood. Maybe they're just paid by some other Traders who think they can make a quick grab for whatever we've found before the Council sends out its own expedition.'

Reyn turned to him. For an instant, he looked startled, then the look faded. 'Yes. Of course. It's more likely they are seeking treasure than hunting my wife and child. The Council will smell profit and send out its own ship as soon as it can. And it's very possible that those who follow are employed by other Traders. The rumour that Kelsingra had been uncovered swept through the city like a fire.'

'Uncovered,' Leftrin said with amusement. 'They're expecting a city to dig out of the mud. They think they'll be excavating. Wait until they see it. They won't be able to grasp it. Nor will they be able to get to it, unless they risk their lives to do so. Even if they are able to follow us all the way there, they'll be short or out of provisions before we get there. And if they are bold enough to cross the river to the city side, they'll find much to fill their eyes but nothing to fill their bellies. So let them exhaust themselves following us. Either they'll give up and turn back, or tough it out, and have to turn to us for help once they arrive.'

While he had being speaking, a fine rain had begun to fall. He turned to Reyn with a grin. 'I don't see the need to deal with them until I have to. Especially when the Rain Wilds just may solve them for me.'

Reyn followed Leftrin's gaze but he didn't smile. Instead, he pointed. 'What's that? I haven't seen that vessel before.'

Leftrin peered through the thickening rain. The falling drops mottled the river's face with rings and made a shushing sound. It also acted as a curtain between him and the vessel that had just rounded the bend behind them. He peered at it in disbelief. It was a larger craft, narrow and low-roofed. The hull was black, the house bright blue with gold trim. Banks of oars rose and fell in unison. It looked to be shallow draught and to be making better speed than the smaller boats. As he watched, it passed the last boat and moved up on the second one. 'Can't be!' he exclaimed.

'What is it?' Reyn leaned over the side to stare back.

'It's that damn impervious ship.' Swarge answered his question. 'She was tied up to the dock when we got to Cassarick.'

'We've heard the rumours for months now.' Reyn agreed grimly. 'None of the liveship families like it. A Jamaillian has developed a new coating for boats, one that he claimed will withstand the acids of the Rain Wild River. He offered to send several of the new ships up the river, to prove that their hulls were impervious and to demonstrate the sort of speed they could make with cargo or passengers. A consortium of Bingtown Traders were said to be interested investors, but there were darker rumours that the Jamaillian didn't care who he sold to as long as they could meet his price. I'd heard one was due to visit Trehaug, but I didn't pay much attention. Too much else on my mind.' He looked at Swarge for confirmation. 'She was tied up at Cassarick when we were there?'

The tillerman shrugged a big shoulder. 'When we first arrived. Then she left for Trehaug, and I thought she'd go all the way back to Bingtown. Looks like someone sent a bird and hired her to follow us.'

Leftrin eyed the boat with dismay. She had good lines for a river barge, and her crew appeared strong and disciplined. 'And there might be more of them?'

'Almost certainly. There are some, even among the Traders, who say that liveships have strangled trade on the river. The Bingtown and Rain Wild councils gave permission for the impervious boats to make the attempt. The owners are aggressive, and they will be hungry to find a way to pay back their investment. If they were in Trehaug when we left . . .'

'There would have been plenty of folk willing to hire them to try to follow us.'

'There would have been plenty of money, too.' Reyn added sourly.

Leftrin stared aft, thinking of all such ships would mean, not just to Kelsingra, but to trade on the river and its settlements if river traffic became heavier and more affordable. He wondered if the Traders who were backing the venture knew that they would be ending a way of life.

As he watched the blue ship began to close the gap between

them. 'They'll keep pace with us easily. Our only hope to lose them will be to travel more by night.' He shook his head and glanced at his tillerman. Swarge nodded grimly.

'And you think we can lose them?' Reyn sounded anxious.

'I think we can try. Maybe put more distance between us. We can at least hope to reach Kelsingra before they do rather than at the same time.' Leftrin replied grimly.

Reyn nodded. The downpour suddenly became a deluge, the rain hissing like quenched iron as it struck the water. It curtained their pursuers from sight. Reyn spoke quietly. 'You know that eventually, they will come, Captain. In large enough numbers that they'll get what they came for. You know that.'

'I know they'll come.' Leftrin spoke quietly. He turned to meet Reyn's eyes and a wolfish smile came over his face. 'But they think all they'll face is a band of half-grown kids and some crippled dragons. But when they reach Kelsingra, what they'll get may not be at all what they were expecting.'

Five bodies lay on the floor of the Stone Way Chamber. The Duke of Chalced looked down on them with annoyance. It had been an exhausting morning. Each man had insisted on his right to tell his story to the fullest before judgment fell upon him. Each had endeavoured to spin out his life's thread a bit longer. What fools they were. They had failed and they knew it, and they knew they would die for it. They had only come back to report in the foolish hope that perhaps their families would be spared.

They would not. What good would it do to keep the seed of failed men alive, to let them inherit their fathers' lands and possessions? They would only breed more weaklings to disappoint in the future. Better to cleanse the ranks of his nobles and soldiers of weakness before it could spread through them and undermine the ancestral might of Chalced. His chancellor was looking at him, waiting. The Duke looked once more at the sprawling dismembered bodies. 'Clean the room. And clean their houses,' he gave the order.

The Chancellor bowed deeply, turned and relayed the command. At the rear of the hall, six commanders turned to their chosen squads of men. Sixty spears thumped the floor in unison, the heavy wooden doors swung open, and the troops departed. Once the soldiers had exited, a very different squad entered. Crawling on their bellies, dragging their sacks, a ragged swarm of death-men scrabbled into the chamber and advanced on the bodies. No one looked at them. They were disgusting, born to wallow in filth and carrion, forever beneath notice of real men but they had their place in Chalcedean society. They would carry off the body parts, scouring the floor with their rags before they departed. Whatever valuable items remained on the bodies became their possessions, as did the clothing of the dead and the meat from their bones. There would be little that was worth anything. These men had all known they were going to die; doubtless they had rid themselves of anything of value before they came, selling off rings and armbands to pay for one final visit to the whores, one final meal in the bazaar.

The smell of the spilled blood was thick and unpleasant and the scuttling of the supine men disgusting. He looked at his chancellor. 'I wish to be in the Sheltered Garden. Chilled wine should await me there.'

'Of course, my lord. I am certain that you will find it is so. Let us go.' The Chancellor turned and signalled the bearers to approach the throne with the palanquin. The Duke studied their careful pace; they were allowing time for his order to precede him, so that when he arrived in the Sheltered Garden, chilled wine and a freshly blanketed and cushioned divan would await him. There were days when the pain and the shortness of breath made him so foul-tempered that he would deliberately order the men to move more quickly. Then he would lash out at them for jostling him, and when he arrived at the garden before it had been prepared for his every whim, he could berate the Chancellor and send all the servants off for punishment. Yes. There were times when the pain prompted him to such pettiness.

But not today.

They transferred him gently from his throne to the palanquin. He gritted his teeth against a moan. So little flesh remained to cushion his bones. His joints ground against one another when he moved his limbs. Sores afflicted his body from his long periods of stillness, growing deep over the jut of bone. In his pole-chair, he sat curled and hunched, a humped caterpillar of a man. When the curtains closed around him, he was glad to be able to grimace privately and try to shift away from the worst of his bedsores.

Trouble was brewing. He smelled it and tasted it. He was no fool. He saw how the eyes of the men shifted, how they conferred silently with one another before obeying his commands. Chalced was slipping from his grip. Once he had been a powerful warrior, a man mighty of body as well as lineage. Once he had been like a crouching tiger, ready to leap from his throne and slash to ribbons any who doubted his authority. Those days were gone. He could no longer cow men with his physical presence.

But he was not a fool. And never had been one. He had never thought that his physical strength alone would let him hold his power. If he had been a fool, he would not have survived for so many years among the shifting dunes of political power in Chalced. As a young man, he had been ruthless in acquiring power and keeping it. His dearth of living sons demonstrated that. He had no illusions about the men who surrounded him or the greedy heirs anxious to supplant him. Others would be just as ruthless as he had been in securing their share of the spoils once he died. And some would not wait for it to happen naturally.

The pole-chair swayed as the bearers paced through the hallways of his palace. He counted his friends and his enemies and knew that some he counted belonged on both lists. His dear, loyal chancellor was one. And his loving, viperous vixen of a daughter was another. Thrice he had married Chassim off, hoping to be rid of her. Her first husband had left her a widow at fourteen. Barely three weeks after the sumptuous wedding, the man had slipped coming out of his bath and broken his neck. Or so all surmised at the time. There had been no witnesses to the accident. And his young widow, sallow-faced and hollow-eyed, had seemed appropriately mournful when his family had returned her to her father's home.

Her next husband had been a much younger man, scarcely thirty years older than his bride. He had lasted six months, succumbing to a stomach ailment that gave him debilitating cramps and bloody bowels. Again, the girl had been returned to the palace, and he had seen her silent and seething at her fate.

Her most recent spouse had died three years ago. The worthy old man had publicly slapped her over some lapse of manners. He had died before the day was out, subsiding in a frothy fit at the feast table among his warriors. Again, Chassim had been returned to him. This time, he had asked her directly. 'Daughter, do you mourn your husband?'

To which she had replied, 'I mourn how suddenly and swiftly death found him.'

The Duke had made space for her among his own women and she had made her own choice never to emerge from those chambers and their secluded gardens and baths. He knew of her life mostly from his concubines. She tended the herb gardens assiduously, read avariciously, mostly history and healing lore, wrote poetry, and practised for an hour every day with her bow. She had expressed an ardent desire to never wed again.

Her wish had been granted, not by her father's inclination, but by the reluctance of any noble male to make an offer for her. As the eldest of his legitimate daughters, she commanded a high bride-price despite her widowhood and advancing years. But he doubted the cost was what made suitors quail. Any woman thrice widowed might be suspected of witchery, even if no one dared broach such an accusation.

The Duke kept his own counsel on the matter. But he would not suffer her to come near him when he visited the women's quarters, not that she had ever seemed so inclined. Nor did he eat anything that might have passed through her hands. There was no sense in taking chances. But now, as his chair swayed to the measured pacing of his bearers, he forced himself to consider her as an option.

By the oldest law of Chalced, a favoured daughter might inherit, if a father so wished. He did not. But by those same old laws, if he died with no heir son, his eldest daughter and her husband could rule until her first son came of age. If unwed, the daughter could rule until she found a worthy mate. He did not think Chassim would look very hard, if she were to inherit. In any case, her succession depended on his own death, something he was determined to avoid.

He did not think he could blame her for his prolonged illness. He had been far too careful for that. The greatest caution of all, of course, prescribed that he kill her. But a duchy with no heir at all was more prone to civil unrest than a duchy with an inappropriate one. How many of his nobles, he wondered, hoped that he would live simply to avoid the possibility of Duchess Chassim coming to power over them?

Besides, it was the worst sort of bad luck to kill a witch, even more so if she was his daughter.

He had closed his eyes to the swaying of his palanquin. He opened them now as his bearers' pace slowed. The curtains remained closed as his pole-chair was lowered onto a set of rests. He listened to the soft scuff of their boots as his bearers departed. But what he did not hear was what alarmed him: no play of waters in a multitude of fountains, no chirping of caged songbirds. He smelled no waft of flowers. The sound of his own heartbeat began to fill his ears. With bony fingers, he groped inside one of his cushions to find the sheathed dagger it concealed. He pulled it out and silently bared it. It weighed heavy in his hand. He wondered if he would have the strength to wield it effectively. He did not wish to die with an unbloodied blade in his hand.

'Most gracious Duke.'

It was Chancellor Ellick's voice. Of course. He would be the traitor. His most intimate and trusted advisor was the man in the best position to murder him and seize the reins of power. The Duke was only surprised that he had not acted years ago, when he had first fallen ill. He did not respond to the man's voice. Let him believe his lord had dozed off. Let him come close enough to open the curtains and meet his blade.

As if he could see through the curtains to the heart of the Duke's intent, the Chancellor spoke again. 'My lord, this is not treachery. I have but stolen this moment to speak to you privately. I approach to open your curtains. Please, do not slay me.'

'Flattery.' The Duke spoke the word flatly, but held the dagger in both hands before his chest. If he glimpsed treachery, he would do his best to plunge it into the man's heart.

But the Chancellor was on his knees and empty-handed as he carefully drew the cloaking curtains back. The Duke surveyed him as he knelt, neck bent and bare, before the parted curtains. If he had wished to do so, he could have planted his dagger in that vulnerable neck. He did not.

'Why privately?' he demanded. 'You have always had my ear. Why here and now?' He looked suspiciously about the Chancellor's own comfortable chambers.

'You do, indeed, my gracious one, always grant me your ear. But where you listen, others listen as well. And I would warn you of treachery, and have only you hear my warning.'

'Treachery?' The word was dry on his tongue. The pounding of his heart was becoming painful. Too many threats in too short a time; courage alone could not sustain a weakened body. He looked down at the man still kneeling before him. 'Get up, Ellik. I need water. Please.'

The Chancellor lifted his eyes and then his head. 'Of course.' Without ceremony, he stood and walked across the chamber. It was a man's room, hung with weaponry and tapestries that recalled famous battles. The work-scarred table in the centre of the room held a large ledger, a pot of ink and a scatter of pens. The Duke had not been in the Chancellor's study for years, but it had changed little in that time. Beyond the table was a cupboard. Ellik took a bottle of wine and glasses from it. 'This will do you better than water,' he informed the Duke. With adroit efficiency, he pulled the cork and filled the glasses. As he returned, he walked as a warrior would and presented the glass without formality.

The Duke took it in withered hands, and drained off the wine. He felt welcome warmth course through his body. Without asking, Ellik refilled the glass from the bottle he still held. Then he sat down cross-legged on the floor by the pole-chair as easily as if he were a young man settling down by a campfire. 'Hello,' he said, as if they were old two friends come together in a chance meeting. And perhaps they were. Ellik watched the Duke steadily until he spoke.

'You know why it's necessary. The bowing, the formality, the harsh order. It's not to demean you, Ellik. It's to enforce discipline and maintain distance.'

'So they only think of you as the Duke,' Ellik said.

'Yes.'

'Because if they thought of you as a man among them, you are not the man they would choose to follow now.'

The Duke hesitated. 'Yes,' he admitted finally. 'A harsh evaluation, but an accurate one.'

'And it works,' Ellik conceded. 'For most of them. For those young enough not to question the order. It works not so well for your old comrades who warriored beside you in the early days when you were coming to power.'

'But not many of them are left,' the Duke pointed out.

'That is true, but a few of us remain.'

The Duke nodded gravely.

'And a few of us remain loyal to the man you were, as well as to the present Duke of Chalced. And so I have come to warn you of treachery, though the nature of the warning may cost me my life.'

'And so I listen to you, Ellik, man to man, warrior to warrior, knowing what you risk to serve me. Be brief. What treachery threatens me?'

Ellik tossed his wine back, considered a moment longer and then replied, 'Your daughter Chassim. She wants your throne.'

'Chassim?' The Duke shook his weary head, annoyed that the man had discomforted him just for this. 'She is discontented, widowed thrice, a woman unfulfilled. I have known this for years. I have no fear that she has any ambitions of her own.'

'You should.' Ellik spoke brusquely. 'Have you read her poetry?'

'Her poetry?' Now he felt insulted. 'No. Girlish yearning for a handsome man to grovel before her charms, I suppose, or musings on a hummingbird hovering by a flower. Ponderings on love and daisies, all done in blue brushstrokes and ornamented with posies and ivy. I haven't time for such things.'

'No. Her poetry is more like a trumpet call to arms. A rallying of women to rise up in Chalced, to help her inherit your throne so that she can lift other women to the status they once held. It's fiery stuff, my lord, more fit to a fanatic in the market than a woman living a quiet, cloistered life.'

For some time, the Duke regarded the other man in silence. But his chancellor's face remained grave. He was in earnest.

'Women rising up . . . nonsense! You know this how? When would you have had cause to encounter my daughter's poems?'

'In my wife's chambers. Two days ago.'

The Duke waited.

'I entered without warning, in mid-morning, an unusual time for me to call on her. She quickly tried to conceal a handful of scrolls she had been reading. So, of course, I wrested one from her to know what secret a woman sought to keep from her husband.' He scowled. 'The scroll was tatter-edged, well worn from being passed hand to hand, with many additions on the bottom and back of it. To the casual eye, it was a girlish poem just as you have described, ornamented with flowers and butterflies. But only for the first two verses. Then the words became scholarly and martial, citing historical references to times when the women of Chalced's noble houses ruled alongside the men and governed their own affairs and properties and chose their own husbands. The little vines and flowers framed nothing less than a call to revolution.

'I rebuked her sternly for reading such treason, but she was unrepentant. And fearless, in that way of a fit that sometimes seizes dried-up old women. She mocked me, asking me what I feared. Did I dare deny that such a past existed? That my own family's fortune had been founded by a woman, not a man?

'I slapped her for her insolence. She stood up and invoked some northern goddess, some Eda, praying her to withhold earth's blessings from me. So I struck her again for daring to curse me.'

Ellik paused. Sweat beaded his brow and for a time he was caught in the memory. His fingers tugged at his lips and he shook his head in denial. 'Can any man ever know a woman's mind? I had to beat her, my lord, as I've not had to for years, and still she held out longer than many a young soldier I've chastised. But in the end, I had the rest of her cache of scrolls, and the source of them, and then the author's name. Your daughter, my lord, as is plain from what she proposes.'

The Duke sat in silence, hoping nothing of what he thought showed on his face. But Ellik was merciless.

'It is not just your daughter. The other women of your household are involved. Chassim writes the words, but your women make copies and ornament the scrolls and tie them with little bindings of lace and ribbons, and scent them with perfume. And out they go, to the markets and the laundries and the weavers' halls, the banyas and the gaming parlours, like a pretty spreading poison.'

The Duke was silent. He was astonished. And he was not. Truly, Chassim was his daughter. A thorny pride in her sprouted in him. If only she had been male, he might have found good use for her. As it was, 'I will have her killed.' A poor solution, but his only choice. He wondered how many of his women he would have to eliminate. He folded his lips. Well, he had little use for them now as it was, and when he was cured, he would want fresh women anyway. They could all go. He shifted uncomfortably, ready to be on his way to the Sheltered Garden. He wanted to rest.

'No,' Ellik dared to say. 'Do not fall into her trap. I read all the scrolls that my wife possessed, and every one makes mention that she expects to die at your hands. She says it will prove how much you fear and hate her and all women. She claims that you hate her so much that you gave her over to a monster to tear open when she was barely a woman.'

'Hate her?' The Duke was incredulous. 'Would I waste my time? I barely know her. Old Karax was a coarse old man; all knew that. But he was my strongest ally at the time. That was what her wedding was about. Securing the alliance.' Hate her? As if he would have emotions about a girl-child, let alone consider her in a matter of political manoeuvring. Truly, she attached far too much importance to herself.

'Nonetheless,' Ellik asserted. 'My lord, if you kill her, you will trigger an uprising in the female populace. Her followers have promised poisonings, infanticides, arson, abortions and yes, outright violence. The scrolls I read were well handled and such were the pledges appended to them by the various women who had read them. Women of all stations have read these things, and added their vows to avenge her if she dies on their behalf. I think they inflame one another, competing to outdo one another in their vows of loyalty and ruthlessness should she be "murdered" by you.'

'This is intolerable!' The Duke shouted the words and then went off into a fit of coughing. Ellik poured him more wine and steadied the glass to his lips that he might drink. The glass chattered against his teeth and he spilled wine down his chest. Intolerable, indeed, all of it. He seized the glass and waved Ellik off. He managed a sip, coughed, and then calmed his breathing until he could take a long draught. When he could speak, he asked Ellik, 'What other remedy is there for a treacherous witch like Chassim?'

'Give her to me,' Ellik suggested softly.

'So *you* can kill her?'

Ellik smiled. 'Not immediately. I will wed her.'

'But you are already married.'

'My wife is dying.' Ellik's expression did not change as he shared his news. 'I will soon be a widow, free to wed again. For my many years of faithful service, you will reward me with your daughter. It is appropriate. Cruel fate has widowed both of us.' He drank from his own glass.

'She is dangerous. I think she killed at least one of her previous husbands.' The Duke admitted this reluctantly as he considered Ellik's solution.

'She killed all three,' Ellik replied. 'I know it, and I know how she did it, thanks to my wife's confession. Thus, I know how to pull the viper's fangs and she is small danger to me.'

'Why do you want her?'

'I will wed her, isolate her, and impregnate her. She will continue to write her scrolls of poetry and they will leak out gradually from her new home. But they will prattle of her wedded bliss, the joys of an experienced lover, and the sweet anticipation of a babe to fill her arms. Her fangs will be drawn, her poison diluted to tea. And news of an heir will calm your nobles.'

The Duke was undeceived. 'And you will reign after me.'

Ellik nodded and pointed out, 'I would in any case.' His gaze met the Duke's steadily as he added, 'This will simply make it clear to all that such is your wish, and any other plan would be opposed by both of us.'

The Duke closed his eyes, carefully delineating all the possibilities. In the end, it came down to one thing. He opened his eyes. 'The sooner I die, the sooner you come to power.'

Again Ellik was unflinching. 'That is also true. But coming to power "sooner" is not always the best way. Nor what I wish, old comrade.' He tipped his head slightly and smiled as he asked, 'What reassurance are you asking of me? Consider what I have done. I have warned you of a threat, and protected you by warning you also not to take the most obvious solution to it. For years, as your health has waned, I have served you. Were I disloyal, I would have proved it years ago. Loyalty, however, is harder to prove.'

The Duke wheezed out a cough and leaned back on his cushions. 'Because loyalty can change,' he pointed out when he could draw a breath. 'It must be proven every day.' He considered for a time. 'If I give you my daughter, I have dealt you a powerful card.'

'And if you do not, a viper remains in your house, poised to strike.'

The Duke capitulated suddenly. 'I will let it be known I have promised her to you. And I will put her in isolation that she may meditate upon becoming your bride.'

Ellik waited for a short time. Then he asked, 'And?'

The Duke smiled coldly. 'And when you bring me dragon's blood as her bride-price, then she will be yours. And my blessing on your marriage.'

'And declare me your heir.'

Ellik was pushing. The Duke did not like it, but he considered it carefully. Ellik had been a youngster when he came under the Duke's tutelage. He had made the man as much or perhaps more than any son he had created with his seed. And when he was dead, would he care who reigned after him?

'And I will designate you my heir. With preference given to any child that you might get on my daughter.'

'Done. And done soon.' Ellik smiled. 'You should command your servants to prepare the wedding feast.'

The Duke cocked his head at him. 'What is it you know that I do not?'

Ellik's smile widened. 'I've bought a prisoner, my lord. He is being shipped to me as we speak. He is not a dragon. But in his veins runs the blood of a dragon. And you shall have his blood.'

The Duke stared at him sceptically. Ellik dared to smile. 'A proof of my loyalty,' he said quietly. 'Offered with no conditions attached.' He rose as gracefully as a maiden and returned to the wine cupboard. This time he returned with a small paper packet tied with string. He squatted before the Duke and pulled the string from its knot. As he unfolded the oiled paper, a once-familiar smell rose to the Duke's nostrils.

'Jerky?' he asked, torn between incredulity and offence. 'You offer me jerky? A foot soldier's rations?'

'The only way to preserve it for the journey was to salt and smoke it.' Ellik held the opened paper like a blown blossom in the palm of his hand. In the centre of it was a small square of blue scaled flesh, smoked to a dark red. 'The meat of an Elderling. Not a dragon. I could not obtain that for you . . . yet. But I offer you what I am told is the smoked meat of a creature that is part dragon. In the hopes that it may restore you to health.'

The Duke looked at it silently for a time.

Ellik spoke softly. 'Command me to eat it, and I will. It is not poisoned.'

The thought had been in his mind. He thought of commanding his chancellor to divide it and eat his portion first. But it was not a large piece of meat, and his infirmities were many. If he ate it and it poisoned him, he would die. But if he commanded Ellik to eat half of it first, and then discovered that it had the efficacious power he hoped for, there might not be enough left to do him any good. He reached for the meat, his bony fingers trembling like the feelers of an ant. He lifted it up and sniffed it. Ellik's gaze was steady on him.

He put the smoked flesh in his mouth. The flavour of the smoke and salt, the texture of the dried meat carried him back to his days as a young warrior. He closed his eyes. He had not been the Duke then. He had been Rolenbled the swordsman, the fourth son of the Duke of Chalced. With his sword he had proven himself to the enemies of Chalced and to his father. And when his elder brothers had risen against his father, plotting to kill him and divide the rule of Chalced among themselves, he had denounced them to his father, and stood at his side as the Duke slew his other sons. In blood he had risen, on proven loyalty.

He opened his eyes. The room seemed brighter than it had. He looked down at the crumpled paper clutched in his hand. Only paper, not the hilt of a sword. A trifling ability, being able to crumple paper into a wad with one hand. Also one that he had not had for some time. He took a deeper breath and sat a little straighter. Ellik was regarding him with a smile.

'Bring me your dragon man, and you will have my daughter.'

Ellik took a deep breath and abruptly bowed low, touching his forehead to the floor.

The Duke nodded to himself. The man was as good as a son to him. And like a son, if his loyalty proved false, he could kill him. His smile deepened.

EPILOGUE

Homeward Bound

IceFyre liked hunting the rough hills that bordered the desert. He was adept at following the contours of the land in flight. He glided close to the ground, sometimes barely skimming the pungent grey-green brush that cloaked the rocky foothills. When his black wings moved, it was in deceptively lazy, powerful down-strokes. He was as silent as the shadow that floated over the uneven terrain below him.

His was an excellent hunting technique. The two dragons had been here since spring and the large game animals which had once had no fear of the sky had learned to keep a wary watch overhead now. IceFyre's tactic carried him soundlessly over low rises. He fell on creatures basking in noon sunlight in the sheltered canyons before they knew he was there.

It did not work as well for Tintaglia. She was smaller, and still practising the sort of flight skills that IceFyre had mastered hundreds of years ago. Even before he had been trapped in ice for an extended hibernation, he had been an old dragon. Now he was ancient beyond belief, the sole surviving creature that could recall the time of the Elderlings and the civilization the two races had built together. He recalled, too, the cataclysmic eruptions and the wild disorder that had ended those days. Humans and Elderlings had died or fled. He'd seen the scattered fragments of the dragon population dwindle and die off.

To Tintaglia's frustration, the black dragon spoke little of those days. She herself had only shadowy memories of her serpent self creating a case before her metamorphosis into dragon. But she recalled too well how she had stirred to awareness inside her cocoon, trapped in a buried city, denied the sunlight she needed to hatch. Elderlings had put her there, she suspected. They had dragged her case and others of her generation into a solarium to shelter them from falling ash. That rescue attempt had become her doom when falling ash buried the city. She had no idea how long she had been imprisoned in her case in lonely darkness. When the humans had first discovered the room where she and her fellows were trapped, their only thought had been to salvage the dragon cases as 'wizardwood' for the building of ships that would be impervious to the Rain Wild River's acid floods. It was not until first Reyn and then Selden had come to her that she had been freed to light and life.

Selden. She missed her little singer. How he could flatter and praise, his clear voice as pleasing as his tickling words that glorified her. But she had sent him away, impressing on him that he should travel in search of tidings of other dragon populations. At the time, she had been hopeful that the late hatch of elderly serpents could yield viable dragons. She had not been willing to believe that all dragons everywhere had died out. So she had sent Selden off, and he had gone with a willing heart, to do not just her bidding but to seek allies for Bingtown in their neverending war with Chalced.

In the years since then, her time with IceFyre had cured her of any optimism. They were the only true dragons left in the world, and thus he was her mate, no matter how unsuitable she found him. She wondered again what had become of Selden. Was he dead, or just beyond the reach of her thoughts? Not that it really mattered. Humans, even humans transformed by dragons into Elderlings, did not live all that long. It was scarcely worth the effort to befriend them.

She caught a whiff of the antelope as IceFyre dived on them. They were a small herd, only five or six beasts, dozing in the trapped warmth of the winter sun. As IceFyre fell on them, they scattered. He crushed two beneath his outstretched talons, leaving Tintaglia to pursue the others.

It was harder than it should have been. The festering arrow just under her left wing made every flap of her wings a torment. The narrow arroyos of the rocky hillside offered the game beasts shelter in spaces too narrow for a dragon to navigate. But one foolish creature broke free of the others and fled uphill and onto the ridgeline. She pursued him and in a frantic dive knocked him to the earth before he could reach the next gully. Her front talons tore him as she seized him and clutched her to the keel of her chest. He struggled briefly, spattering her with his warm blood before going limp in her clutches. She did not delay but tore into the warm meat. It was her first kill of the day and she was famished.

The antelope was not a large creature, and it was winter lean. Soon, there was nothing left of it, not a skull or the hooves; only sticky blood on the rocky earth. It did not fill her but nonetheless she felt herself sinking into somnolence as soon as she had finished eating.

Tintaglia stretched out and closed her eyes. Then she shifted and tried a different position. It was worse. It was not the stony ground that discomforted her, but the broken shaft and the arrow head and the infection that surrounded it. She lifted her wing and craned her neck to sniff at it, then snorted. Bad.

Rotting meat smell. The claws on her forepaws were too large to be of any use; clawing at it only made it hurt more. And the end of the broken arrow shaft was no longer even visible. She feared that instead of being pushed out of her body by the infection, the missile was actually digging in deeper.

IceFyre landed nearby in a rush of dust from the braking beat of his wings. *We should hunt more.*

I want to sleep.

He lifted his head and snuffed the air. *That arrow festers. You should pull it out.*

I've tried. I can't.

He leaned closer, snuffing at her injury, and she allowed it, but not graciously. *Of old, sometimes humans used poisoned weapons against us. They would dip the heads of their lances in filth before they tried to stab us. They knew that they could seldom kill us outright, but that a lingering infection might kill a dragon.*

She flinched away from his scrutiny, and immediately craned her neck to inspect the wound. *Do you think this arrow was poisoned?*

Impossible to tell. He seemed very calm about it. *Do you wish to hunt again?*

What did they do, the dragons with poisoned injuries?

They died. Some of them. Sometimes they went to the Elderling healers for aid. Little human hands can sometimes be useful in cleaning a wound. The silver water could cure many ills. I am going hunting. Are you coming?

Do you think I should go back to the Rain Wilds and try to find my Elderlings? Malta and Reyn?

The black dragon looked at her for a time. Whatever thoughts he had, he was not sharing with her. When he spoke, it was only to say, *I do not think I could trust a human again. Even an Elderling.*

I might trust them. If I had to. Malta and Reyn have both served me before; they would serve me again, I think.

Again, he was quiet. Then he said, *The silver well of Kelsingra. It was a rare and wondrous thing, and to drink from it brought dragons great strength. Sometimes it was used for healing. You could go there, to Kelsingra.*

I've been to Kelsingra. The well is no more. The city was empty and dead, with dust blowing through the streets. And when I went to the well, the windlass had fallen to ruin. Even if there had been Elderlings there at that moment, they could not have drawn the silver for me. She did not speak of how angry it had made her; of how she had trampled and broken what remained of the windlass and shoved it down the fruitless well.

Kelsingra. IceFyre spoke the word regretfully. *It was a place of wonder, once. If, as you say, it is abandoned and empty, then that is a loss. I recall it as a place of poets chanting my praises as Elderlings worked scented oil into my scale-beds. There were baths there. And sunning spots. Fat herds of all sorts of meat creatures; bullocks and sheep and swine. They made many memorials to us, statues and mosaics.*

He held his thoughts still and Tintaglia's mind wandered. She had her ancestors' memories of Kelsingra, but they were faded and scentless. Her own perceptions of the abandoned city overlay them and dimmed them even more.

I go to hunt! IceFyre announced abruptly. *I hunger still.*

I am going to rest. She recognized suddenly a determination that had been forming in her for some days. *And then I am going back to the Rain Wilds.*

Perhaps later we will go there. The feel of his thought was dismissive of her idea. *Perhaps another time, I will go to see Kelsingra for myself. When I decide the time is right to go.* He turned away from her and leapt into the air. The wind of his battering wings rushed past her, stirring her injury to a dull ache.

Wearily she settled herself for sleep. It was difficult to find a position that did not irritate her wound. It was getting worse; she could smell it and the spreading poison from the infection was a throbbing deep in her muscles. It was not healing and she could do nothing to better it. The longer she waited, the weaker she would be. But IceFyre cared nothing for that.

And abruptly she knew that when she awoke, she would not wait for him to return or for his decision. She needed the services of her Elderlings, Reyn with his strong hands and Malta's clever little mind. It was time to go home.

Back to the Rain Wilds.